DEMON STONES

By
Michael Drakich

Amazon Edition

Copyright © Michael Drakich
ISBN-13: 9780987770646

First Edition Traanu Enterprises, July, 2014

Cover Mary Drakich
Editor Kate Richards
Artwork Ted Kruzsely

NORTHERN REACHES

PIAX RIVER

LIA

ROK

PIAXIA

THE GREAT SEA

KARSARGI LANDS

XIA RIVER

FEL

JAG

ZON

VISK

MORICA

SECHLAND

EAGLE RIDGE

SECHWISK

MORENCE

STORBURG

FERMIA

GATWAY

QUEENSLAND

BRAXBOROUGH

THE GREAT SEA

N
W   E
S

CHAPTER 1

Garlin eyed the small meadow. From the plow, the few trees and bushes near the rill separating his family's land from their neighbors called to him. The shade they cast offered a welcome diversion from his current toil. He extended his arm to get an exact count of the number of hands left in the day. A glance up at the beating sun allowed a rivulet of sweat to divert into his eyes, stinging them. He wiped at them with the back of his hand to little avail as the dirt on them only exacerbated the problem. "Damn it!"

His grandfather, working the plow with him, gave him a slap to the back of his head. "Silence, Gar. You'll not curse when I'm about. Keep a civil tongue in your head."

He rubbed where he had been punished. "Sorry, Pap. It's just this blasted heat. It's baked the ground so hard, even the oxen are laboring. The dust is choking us all. What about taking a break down by the stream and getting a little shade for a while?"

His grandfather glanced toward the swale then back to him. "It's too early in the day for us to be doing nothing. We need to finish turning this field before the sun goes down. Your sister's behind us looking to get the seed in, and my old bones tell me it will rain tonight."

"Aw, the whole field? I was hoping to go into town later."

"You can see your friends tomorrow. Getting this done is more important. The rain won't wait for you. Your friends can. You don't hear your sister complaining."

Scouting the area, he spotted his little sister, some twenty paces behind them. "Come on, Darlee. Get a move on!"

Although only two years younger than him, she was diminutive when compared to his large frame. He could see her struggling with the big seed bag draped over her shoulder.

1

"I'm going as fast as I can. There's two of you and only one of me."

"Yeah, but, with each furrow, your load lightens, while mine gets harder."

Another rap to his head from his grandfather returned his attention forward. "Ow! What was that one for?"

"Less talk, more work. You can argue with your sister when you get home."

He gave one last glance at Darlee, who stuck her tongue out at him then returned to the task of guiding the plow and urging the ox forward. *This is going to be a long day.*

He stayed at the task for the rest of the afternoon and managed to get the ox into its pen before darkness fell.

As he entered the house, the smell of dinner set his mouth watering. His mother had already set the table and everyone else had settled in to eat. His father pointed at the empty chair. "Come on, Gar. Sit. We're all waiting for you."

It irked him to be pointed out as the reason supper was delayed. After all, he'd just finished berthing the animal for the night. But he knew better than say his mind in front of everyone. The raps he'd received from his grandfather that afternoon would be considered love taps compared to punishment from his father. "Yes, sir."

He took his place between his father and his sister and, like the others, clasped hands with those next to him.

His father took a deep breath. "The gods have once again bestowed their bounty on us and we dine in their honor. All is well for the Murdach family."

He let go of the hands he held and waited as his father helped himself to a generous portion of the food on the table. Beet stew. *Not again!* His mother had explained how it was all they could afford. What about the bounty they were supposed to be enjoying? They lived in a ramshackle house on a farm too small to bring any real profit, so his father held a menial job in town, working for the tanner. Between the sheep and the ox, they ate the bulk of everything they grew.

2

The time came to take his portion. After his father, grandfather, and mother, what remained was enough to sate his own hunger but would leave precious little for Darlee. *Why am I the one who has to share what's left? It isn't fair. I worked hard today, harder than the rest. I deserve more.*

He scooped the stew until his plate was covered, handed the near-empty bowl to his sister, grabbed the last of the bread, and began to eat. Halfway through stuffing in his second mouthful, he saw the backhand swing of his father too late to avoid the blow. It sent him sprawling and his stew with him. He scrambled up and backed away as his father descended on him with another attack. "What I do?"

The next blow sent him reeling to the floor once again. "You know full well what you did. Is it your intention your sister should starve?"

He sat up and put his arms in front of him to ward off any further blows. He didn't expect one, though, as his father returned to his seat.

His father sighed. "Now look what's happened. You've forced me to lose my temper and made a mess while you're at it. Clean it up then go to your room."

Gar bent to the task rather than risk being pummeled once more. The family continued to eat in silence and after wiping up the last of the mess, he made his way up the stairs with the renewed twitter of talking following him. He entered his room and closed the door, putting down the temptation to sob with a strong sniff. The window was open and the night breeze cooling. He stared out at the field where he had labored. Such were his days, when not in school. Tomorrow, he would return to class and escape the drudgery of working round the home but, in the meantime, he could no longer abide staying there that evening. He climbed out the window and headed for the meadow.

It was always a place where he was able to find a certain level of contentment. He reveled in the gentle gurgle of the stream, the soft whisper of the wind through the leaves of the trees, and the long grass to lie in. A large stone poking out of the grasses made a comfortable place to lean and contemplate things. A number of symbols were carved into it that he did not recognize. He often lay there and traced the figures, trying to guess at their meaning. Even when the weather would chill, for some reason, the stone was always warm.

That night was no different from any other visit as he absently ran his finger over the markings. *Why does my father hate me so? I turned sixteen three months ago. That makes me a man. I can go out into the world and find my own place, make my own way. If I left, who would tend the farm? Pap? Not likely. They'd starve without me.*

A silhouette on the hill told him someone was approaching. He watched as the stars illuminated his grandfather trudging toward him.

"I figured I'd find you here."

"Hi, Pap."

His grandfather dropped down beside him and pulled a wedge of bread from inside his shirt. "It's not much, but I couldn't let you go hungry. Take it."

"Thanks." He accepted the bread and took a deep bite.

"You know, you were wrong back there."

He stopped chewing. Pap was always honest with him and not so quick to anger as his father. He'd give it a shot. "Why? Because, like my father, I take more than my fair share?"

His grandfather glared at him for a moment. "Your father is why you have a table and food to put on it. True, he does take a large share, but know that he needs it to maintain his strength. The life of a tanner's helper is not an easy one. There are those worse off than you—those with no roofs over their heads, no beds to sleep and who go hungry more nights than not. Be grateful for what you have."

"Should I really? I go to school and the other kids laugh at my homemade clothes. When my birthday came, I was no longer a child, but a man. After I finish this term, I can no longer go to school but would have to pay for further education. Money I do not have. That will come to an end. My life lies before me at the back end of a plow behind a smelly ox."

4

His grandfather said nothing but gazed around. After a moment, he patted Gar's arm. "I understand. You see no future for yourself beyond this farm. But it is not all as bad as you would make it seem. I was born on this farm. I raised your father and his brothers here. And, back then, we had no oxen. Your father has done well to own such fine beasts. The progression of things takes time. Your children will have more than you. I shall die here, and when I do, it will be not as a happy man but a content one. I did my part."

"That may be fine for you, but I want more in my life than that."

"Like your uncles?"

His lips tightened. Both of his uncles had joined the army. The kingdom of Sechland was one of the poorest of the seven southern kingdoms. It didn't even have direct access to the Great Sea. In the last battle with Morica to the east, both of his uncles were killed. The kingdom was still required to pay for passage on the Lorne River that originated in the hills with many meandering creeks like the one beside him. "No, not like them."

"I thought not. But your moodiness is brought on by this swale. Why do you come here?"

"It's peaceful. I can let my worries go here."

"Too peaceful. Listen, what do you hear?"

He craned his neck in an effort to pick up whatever sounds he could recognize. "The same as always. The water in the rill, the wind in the leaves, nothing more.

"Exactly. There is nothing more. No owl on the hunt or mouse in the grass, not even the chirp of a cricket. The dumb creatures of the world know better than to be here."

The truth of his grandfather's words dawned on him. "You're right. I hear none of those things. I wonder why?"

His grandfather slapped the stone. "Here's why. I've never told you the story because I thought you too young, but maybe now it's time you learned. This…" he patted the stone once more, "is a demon stone. It goes back many a year to before even *I* was a young lad like you."

"A demon stone? Why is it called that?"

5

"In those ancient days, when the Southern Kingdoms were united and our only enemies were the Karsargi to the west, demons were set loose on the land. No one really knows where they came from nor how, but they rampaged throughout the seven realms and Piaxia to the north. It's said some even raided the badlands where the Karsargi hold sway but no one knows for sure. The only thing we did know was they couldn't be killed. Neither blade nor fire harmed them. They were finally vanquished by a great warlock from Piaxia named Bron who entombed them throughout the lands in stones such as this. The tales goes, though beaten, the demons still live, trapped forever within the stones. It's why they're warm to the touch. It's said their blood boils. If you listen closely, you can hear the drumbeat of their demon hearts."

"I've been told how demons came and stole children who were bad, but I thought it was just a tale to scare us." Gar bent and put an ear to the stone. He listened but could not be sure whether it was a heartbeat from inside the stone or the echo of his own in his eardrum. "I don't know if I hear it."

"Huh. Well, no matter. Even if the tale is true, there's no way the beast is getting out of there. It's been that way for as long as I've been around and probably will be, long after I'm gone."

His grandfather rose and extended a hand. "Come, it's getting late and you need to return to your room before anyone notices you're missing. I'll go back in and make enough noise to cover your climb. Don't disappoint me."

Gar grabbed hold and Pap pulled him up. "I suppose you're right. Thank you for the bread. Let's go."

He followed his grandfather back to the house where and true to Pap's word, he stomped inside, grumbling aloud and clomping into the main room, making Gar's ascent unnoticeable. After changing into his nightshirt, Gar slid into bed. He was tired. Sleep sounded like a good idea. He laid his head on his pillow and listened as the noise downstairs ceased and all he could hear was the sound of his own heartbeat.

CHAPTER 2

It was still dark out when Gar and his sister joined their father for a predawn meal of oatmeal before the ride into town. Once his father finished, whether they were done or not, he would rise and head for the door. He and Darlee would help hitch the horse to the wagon and his father would drop them off on his way. When class was over, they would walk home.

His sister sat up front, a spot he used to occupy, although now he preferred to ride in the back where he could stretch out. By the time the wagon left the homestead, the morning sun was peeking over the hills and Gar leaned back to relax in the warming rays.

He liked going to school. Not that his grades were any good. First of all, it freed him from chores round the house. It also gave him a chance to meet up with his friends. Class would end at midday, and he and his pals would take the time to visit the city market. He never had any money to buy anything, but it was still fun to look in all the stalls at the wares people were selling. He would dream of having the actual coin one day to buy some of the finer things available.

Wandering about the market with his sister and his friends, Maurus and Jango, he spotted Lialee, a girl he liked, going to a stall with her brother, a boy he didn't like. *There's that bugger, Wirbon. Because his father is one of the richest men in town, he thinks he can do what he wants.*

A flush filled him. He wanted to see Lialee, but not when her brother was around. Though smaller than Gar, at a year older, he always made fun of him. Wirbon would be buying things he could never afford and waving the stuff in his face. There was nothing he could do without coin. He turned to head in a different direction. "Come on, guys. Let's go see what the traders brought in today."

Jango grabbed his arm. "Wait. I just saw Wirbon go into that stall. I want to see what he's up to."

"Nah, I don't want to. I want to see the traders."

7

"But he's with Lialee. I *know* you like her."

Maurus joined in taunting him. "Yeah, Gar. *Everyone* knows you like her. You're not going to let her brother scare you off, are you?"

They're right. Why do I have to put up with it? "Okay."

He took the lead and marched into the stall to find Wirbon holding up a jeweled wristband in front of Lialee. "Beautiful, isn't it? I bet you'd like to get it for your birthday."

Lialee stroked the wristband as it hung from her brother's fingers. "Really, Wirbon? You'd do that for me?"

Gar rushed up and snatched the band from Wirbon's hand. "He's not getting you anything. If anyone is to get you something, it's me."

Wirbon laughed. "You? You couldn't even buy the box it came in, let alone the band."

"I'll get it. Just you wait and see."

The merchant retrieved the item. "Young man, this band costs seven silver pieces. Do you have that kind of coin? If you do, then I'll hold it for you. Otherwise, I'll have to sell it to whoever does have the money."

Gar thought of the small cache of coins hoarded in his room over the past number of years. Only two silver pieces filled it, the rest coppers. "I'm-I'm sorry. I don't have that kind of money."

The merchant returned the band to the display table. "Then I'm afraid I'll have to find another buyer for it. Good day, young man."

Lialee stepped between Wirbon and him. "Boys, don't argue. My birthday party isn't for a couple of days. Wirbon, Gar is to be one of my guests. Don't be the overprotective brother. I expect all of you to be there. My father is going to throw a big party. I wouldn't want a disagreement between you preventing anyone from attending." She lifted her chin and left the stall.

Gar watched her go then addressed her brother. "I'll find the coins to buy the bracelet—somehow."

Wirbon laughed again. "They don't take cow dung in place of silver." He turned to the stall owner. "I'll be back to get the bracelet. I'm good for it. You know my father."

The merchant nodded. "The band will be yours. I'll put it in safekeeping until then. Be sure to convey my best wishes to your father." He put it in a box, decorated with colored stripes, and removed it from the display area.

Gar couldn't stand it anymore. He fists balled. He swung for Wirbon's face.

Wirbon ducked and stepped backward. "Oh, so you want to fight, do you? Come on then. I'm ready for you."

The merchant grabbed at Gar. "Not in my stall. Take it outside."

Gar shrugged off the stall owner's grip and charged at Wirbon. He leveled another blow at the bugger's chin, but once again Wirbon ducked it and this time delivered a hard punch to the side of Gar's head. Between the blow and his forward momentum, he flew past and crashed into another display loaded with tableware. A shower of broken plates cascaded onto him. Wirbon grinned and Gar had jumped up to launch at the smug face, when the stall owner grabbed him again.

"Enough of this." He pointed at Wirbon. You have your merchandise, please go."

Wirbon sneered at Gar. "Phht! You're no match for me. My father has me taking fighting lessons weekly. I could beat you with my eyes closed. You're just a big oaf."

He dusted off the last remnants of the pottery. "Yeah, I'll show you."

The merchant, holding him by the collar gave him a shake. "You'll be doing nothing except figuring out who's going to pay for all of this." The stall owner glared at Darlee and his two friends. "As for you three, get out of here before I talk to your parents as well."

Maurus and Jango hightailed it out, but Wirbon paused at the entrance. "You're such a farm boy, Gar. Quit trying to pretend you're city folk."

His anger burned inside him. He wanted to chase after Wirbon into the market square, but the merchant still held a firm grip on his collar. He'd proved to Lialee he wanted to be the one to get her the gift. No, he didn't have the money, but he would get it.

The shop owner waved at the merchant in the next stall. "Brandis! Keep an eye on things here for me. I'll be back in a bit." He shoved Gar towards the entrance. "Move. It's time to pay the guard a visit."

The merchant marched him to the army station in the middle of the square and presented him to the guard. "Captain Brusk, this young man started a fight in my stall and damaged some goods. I demand compensation."

The guard inspected him up and down. "What's your name, son?"

"Garlin Murdach."

"Murdach? I knew a couple of the Murdachs who were killed in the last war. I don't think either of them mentioned siring a boy your age."

"They were my uncles. My father works at the tanner's."

"Your uncles, eh? Good lads, both. What a shame to lose them." He turned to the merchant. "I'll take it from here."

"But what about my damages? Who's going to pay for them?"

"What did he break?"

"A dozen or so fine porcelain plates. They were worth a silver each."

Captain Brusk laughed. "A silver? Are you kidding? I've been in your shop. More like a copper." The guard reached into a coin pouch and produced two silvers. "Here, consider yourself compensated. Now leave me be with the boy."

The man grumbled but walked away, leaving Gar with the captain. "Thank you, sir. I'll pay you back."

Brusk tossed him to the ground and planted a foot on his chest. "Listen carefully, Garlin Murdach. I did that out of respect for your uncles. I don't want your coins, but if I ever have to deal with a problem from you again, you won't like me at all. Consider yourself lucky. The next time it's off to the cells. You understand?"

He nodded. "I understand."

Captain Brusk lifted his foot. "Good. Now go home. I don't want to see you round here for the rest of the day."

Gar stood and brushed himself off. "Yes, sir."

As the guard walked away, Darlee came over from where she, Maurus, and Jango had run to. "You okay?"

His cheeks were warm. It was bad enough he'd been bested by Wirbon. Now he had lain face down in the dirt. "Yeah, I'm fine."

She folded her arms and snorted. "Why you waste your time with that phony Lialee is beyond me."

"What do you know? Her family is rich and influential. Think of all the good things that could happen if she and I got together."

"You're an idiot. She's not interested in you. Get it out of your thick skull."

He glared at her. She was always telling him what was what. "I know what I'm doing. Leave me alone."

"Fine with me. Be a stubborn farm boy. See if I care." She headed back the way they'd come.

He made for the town gate and started the long walk home. With each step, he relived the happenings in the market stall. How did that pipsqueak Wirbon get the better of him? Why had he lost his temper? The question bothering him most of all, why couldn't Lialee recognize his affection for her?

Money. He knew that was the root of the problem. Wirbon had it, and he didn't. And he had no way of getting any. *How I hate Wirbon. I wish he were dead.*

He arrived home with plenty of time before supper and decided to visit with his grandfather who was tending the sheep and goats. "Hi, Pap. Mind if I sit with you for a bit?"

"Sure. Sit a spell. What's on your mind?"

"Oh, nothing." He didn't know what to say or where to begin. He wanted to get an opinion but was too afraid to ask.

His grandfather peered at him. "You in some kind of trouble, Gar? You got a mark on your cheek. Have you been fighting?"

His hand flew to the spot where Wirbon had hit him. "Uh, no. No, I haven't been fighting."

Pap shook his head. "It's no use lying to me. I can tell. You'd better tell me what happened."

"It wasn't much of a fight. I just got into an argument with Wirbon, and he hit me."

11

His grandfather stared at him. Gar, starting to feel embarrassed, broke the eye contact and stared at the ground.

"You're still lying. Do you want me to beat it out of you?"

He met Pap's gaze. "I'm sorry. It's just...just...it's just not fair, is all."

"What's not fair?"

"That other guys my age have money and can buy things for girls and I'm always without."

His grandfather chuckled. "Ah, so, this is over a girl. Now I know you're telling the truth. Don't let it worry you, Gar. A woman will come along who'll accept you the way you are. You don't want those who only want you for your money anyway."

"But she's—"

"She's what? Pretty? If all she sees are coins then she isn't pretty at all. Believe me. Forget about her—it'll be for the best. It's almost supper, and I don't think you'd better come in. If your father sees that welt, there'll be hell to pay. I'll tell him you're tending the sheep and bring you out something to eat. By tomorrow, the welt will be gone. Stay here."

His grandfather strode off toward the house, leaving Gar with his thoughts. *He's wrong. He's just saying those things because he never had any money, either. I'll prove them all wrong one day. I'll get lots of money and prove them all wrong.*

He was still burdened with the same problem. He didn't have a clue on how to get any.

When his grandfather returned with a plate of food for him, he thanked him and carried it off to the meadow. Plunking down next to the stone, he ate in solitude. *Pap is right. I can't hear any wildlife.*

When he finished eating, he placed his ear once more on the rock to see if he could hear anything. Yes, there was definitely something there. It wasn't just his blood pumping in his ear.

He strained to listen for a while longer then decided to try and listen lower on the stone. Stretching out, he reposed on his back and placed his head so that his ear rested against the hard surface of the rock. There was no doubt in his mind now. The heartbeat was definitely there.

12

As he lay there, he recalled the events from earlier in the day. How was he ever going to find the silver to buy the bracelet before Wirbon did? He hated Wirbon. If only Wirbon was dead. *With that irksome brother out of the way then I would have Lialee all to myself.*

He relaxed as the rhythmic beat from the stone reverberated in his head. Tired, he decided to close his eyes.

***

Free me.
What?
Free me, and me serve you.
Free you? Who are you?
Me held within stone. Free me, and me be faithful servant.
I don't know how. How do I free you?
Use Key.
A key? I don't have any key.
Not a key, the Key. It is link to great magical power.
Magic? I don't know any magic. Magic is illegal in the seven kingdoms. No one knows any magic.
Me know it. But me cannot do it from inside. You must do it. Me teach you.
What are you doing? My head hurts. It's hurting really bad. Stop it. Stop it.
It stop hurting when you open stone and free me. Open stone now. Imagine it open and it open.
Okay, I'll open it, just stop it from hurting. I'm doing it.
Me...am...free!

Gar bolted upright. It was dark out. He must have fallen asleep. What a terrible dream. Even now, his head hurt terribly. He tried to stand up, but the pain was horrible and he lost his balance and fell. Pushing up to his hands and knees, he shook his head to try to clear it. In the starlight, he could see movement by the stone. He crawled closer. A huge crack had formed, with pieces lying all around. Peeking out from it were long fingers terminating in sharp points.

13

"By the gods." A chill ran through him. *I've got to get out of here.* He forced himself to his feet and, severe headache or not, staggered off in the direction of the house.

CHAPTER 3

Gar's legs wobbled. It took a lot of effort to put one foot in front of the other. The pains in his head were tremendous, like someone pounding on the inside with hammers. What would cause such agony? Never before had he felt such pain. Eyes watering, he reeled left and right. *Home. I've got to get home.*

The light of the farmhouse shone in the distance. He focused on it and urged his legs faster. Each step was a little more bearable than the last.

He tripped and fell on the step to the porch, delighted because he had made it. Once again upright, he grabbed the rail, allowing it to guide him the final few steps. He burst in through the always-unlocked door and slammed it behind him then threw the bar into place and dashed into the main room.

His father rose when he entered.

"You won't believe it. You—"

"*Where* have you been?"

The abruptness of his father's tone caught Gar by surprise and he took a half step back. "I…I was in the meadow. I need to tell—"

"*Where* is the plate your supper was on?"

"I suppose I left it there. Listen, this is really important—"

In one long stride, his father bridged the gap between them and slapped him hard across the head. "Go to your room. You will fetch the plate first thing tomorrow."

"But I'm trying to tell you something. Something imp—"

Another slap sent him crashing to the floor.

"Your room. Now!"

He gathered himself and climbed the stairs. Before he made it to his room, Darlee peeked out of her own.

"What's going on?"

"Darlee, whatever you do, don't go outside. I think there's a monster on the loose out there."

His sister giggled. "A monster? Don't be silly, there are no monsters."

15

He was about to explain when their father's voice boomed up the stairwell, telling him to quit talking. Rather than incur any more of his wrath, Gar obeyed and went into his room.

As he was closing the door, Darlee moved out into the hall. He paused to point at her. "Just do what I say. I'll fill you in tomorrow."

With his door now shut, he made his way to his window. The scattered trees and bushes provided shadows in the star and moonlight, making it difficult to see if anyone—or anything— prowled about.

He sat watching, and after a while, he started to wonder. Maybe it had all been a dream. Maybe he dreamed of the demon escaping from the rock. Maybe his imagination was creating monsters where none existed.

He was just about to give up when a movement caught his attention. *What was that?* He strained to see. Something had skittered from one bush to another.

He stared at the bush until he could stare no more. His head still hurt, from the beating of his father as well as the dream in the swale. Tired, he put on his nightshirt, but before he crawled into bed, he pulled the shutters tight and tied them from inside. *No demon is going to get me.*

He woke once during the night, certain he heard scratching at the shutters. But when he checked, they were still shut tight and the binding in place.

***

Gar woke again in the early morning, nudged by his grandfather.

"Go fetch that platter before you get in any more trouble."

He shrugged into his clothes and stumbled downstairs. When he reached the front door and spotted the security bar still in place, he recalled the evening before. *What if it's still out there? Will it kill me?*

His grandfather, who had followed him down, reached past to lift the bar and put it to the side. "I'll take care of hitching the horse. Now go get that dish before your father comes down." Pap gave him a gentle shove out the door.

The predawn mist gave everything an eerie, ghost-like appearance. He froze on the bottom step, clutching the end of the rail.

His grandfather brushed past him. "Come on, Gar. Get moving. Morning's coming fast."

He did the only thing that, at this point, made any sense to him. He ran.

Once he cleared the trees and bushes and hit the open farmland, the mist was lighter and his vision better. *So far, so good. Nothing's going to catch me by surprise out in the open like this.*

He reached the edge of the swale and looked down into it. The fog blanketed the whole area. He stayed put and tried his hardest to peer into the mist. He couldn't see anything. Not the ground, not the platter, and not the stone.

Knowing the layout by heart, he stepped down the soft hill into the meadow. Making a beeline, he went for the platter. It was exactly where he left it.

Picking it up, he chanced a glance at the demon stone. It was shattered. It wasn't a dream. It had happened. He'd released the demon.

He took a deep breath. *Who knows where that thing got to? It may be just behind those bushes. I've got to get out of here.* Tucking the plate under his arm, he ran for home and the waiting breakfast of oatmeal.

When he entered the house, his father was already eating. Dashing to his own seat, he stuffed the food in. He didn't want to go to school hungry. He finished just when his father rose and headed out to the wagon.

As he clambered into the back, his sister joined him rather than assume her usual perch behind the buckboard. She huddled close, not, he suspected, from cold, but rather to avoid being overheard by their father. "What was that nonsense last night?"

After his early morning trip to the meadow, he didn't know whether to divulge his story or not. *Will she think I'm crazy?* Also,

17

the chance his father might overhear gave him pause as well. "Forget about it. It was nothing."

"Nothing? You were ranting like a madman last night and you promised you'd explain it in the morning. Now give. What happened?"

He wavered on telling her then decided against it once more. "Nothing. It was all my imagination. I must have suffered a bad dream when I fell asleep in the swale."

"What was the dream about?"

Sensing a window of opportunity, he figured he could tell it as just that, a nightmare. "I dreamed the demon in the stone escaped and was loose on the farm."

Darlee snickered. "A demon from the stone? Now I know why you didn't want to talk about it."

"Don't make fun of me. It seemed so real."

"Oh, I promise, *I* won't make fun of you."

"You'd better not." Still, he didn't trust her. It would have to wait. They were nearing the town and he and Darlee would need to walk the last bit. Other kids would be out and about. He didn't want to argue with her in front of an audience.

Classes were boring, and the morning passed too slowly. At last the time came to hang out with his friends. He caught up with Jango outside. "Where's Maurus?"

"He said he'd meet us in the market square."

"Fine. Let's go look for him."

They meandered through the different stalls but saw no sign of his pal. Walking several paces away from them, he spotted Wirbon with a stupid grin on his face. *There he is. He's so smug because he has money. In the open square, I bet it'll be easier to teach him a lesson.*

He was about to advance on Wirbon, when from between two stalls away, Maurus charged at him.

"Help me, Gar! The demon's after me."

Panic filled him as he cast about in an effort to spy the creature. "It is? Where? We've got to get the guard." He started to run toward the guard hut in the center of the square when he heard Maurus and Jango laughing.

18

"Look at him go. He's scared to death!"

He stopped to look back and saw Darlee was now with his friends, doubled up with mirth. Retracing his steps he joined the group. "I was not scared."

Maurus continued to chuckle. "Yeah, you were. You went white as a sheet."

He was both embarrassed and angry at Darlee. Before he could provide another rebuttal, the appearance of Wirbon at Jango's side deflated him even further.

"What scared the farm boy?"

Jango sobered, his gaze swinging back and forth. "Uh, nothing."

Maurus, still snickering, gave Gar a playful shove. "He says he saw a demon."

Jango scowled. "Shut up, Maurus."

Maurus clamped his lips together, but too late.

Wirbon's face lit up with glee. "So, the big lug is scared of children's stories. I always knew he was a coward."

Gar balled his fist and shook it toward Wirbon. "Oh, yeah? How about I show you how afraid I am." He took a step to close the gap when the bright red livery of Captain Brusk heading their way caught his attention. He dropped his fist and took a step back instead.

The guard stepped into their midst. "Is there a problem here?"

Gar met the captain's gaze. "No, sir. I was just on my way home." He grabbed Darlee by the elbow and started for the gate. "Come on, let's go."

She struggled free. "I don't want to go just yet."

"Fine. I'm going. I've got chores waiting anyway. So do you."

He marched away, as Wirbon threw in one last jab at his running from a fight. He knew better than to reply with the captain standing there, so he continued on and soon was on the open road to the farm.

When he arrived home, his grandfather put him to work changing the bedding in the animal stalls. The work took his mind off of his anger at Darlee and Wirbon.

When it was time for supper, he was hungry, and fortunately, there was more than enough for him to take an extra helping. He stuffed as much in as he could then retired to his room. When he got inside he found it was stuffy. The closed shutters had held in the day's heat. He undid the binding and threw them open to let in some fresh air. Resting his elbows on the window ledge, he gazed out toward the darkening yard as the sun dropped below the horizon.

He had not thought of the demon or the stone during the second half of the day. What had happened to the creature? He didn't know what to do, who to tell. He was tired. The afternoon of hard work and a big supper weighed on him. He got undressed, dragged on his nightshirt, and crawled into bed.

***

During the night, Gar awoke. He didn't know why, but tension seized his body. He rolled onto his back in the dark. He glanced out the window and noted the sky was starless. *There must be a blanket of clouds up there.* He scanned the room slowly. In the dark, he could just make out his belongings. Everything was as he'd left it. A creak from beyond the foot of the bed brought a rush of adrenalin through him. He sat up and pushed his way so that his back was to the wall.

The same black spiked fingers he recognized from the night before appeared beyond the end of his bed. The creature crawled up and perched there.

"Master, me am here."

CHAPTER 4

Gar's jaw had fallen open to shout for help when the beast held up a hand. "Please, no cry out, Master. You wake everyone. It make hard me serve you."

He swallowed the words in his throat. *It talks.*

"Yes, Master, me talk. Me read mind, too. Please no afraid. Me good servant."

Gar pulled his knees up to his chest and studied the thing. Surprisingly small, it was barely larger than an infant. It had arms and legs that were far too long for its body and large feet and hands with all the digits ending in sharp spikes. It maintained a hunched position with its arms folded over its knees. Hairless with a leathery, dark grey skin, the demon wore some kind of leather jerkin and pants. The face was bat-like, with pointed ears, and gleaming black eyes. They watched him without blinking.

He swallowed. "What do you want?"

"You not listen? Me serve you. Me excellent helper."

"I don't want you to serve me. I want you to leave me alone."

The creature shuffled a little closer. "Me figure you not understand. Me read mind night last, too. Me go run errand, make happy, you understand." The demon reached into a flap in its outfit and pulled something out. The item was mostly concealed in its fingers as it reached out and held it in front of Gar. "For you, Master."

Should he take it? Or would reaching for it allow the thing to grab him. He half-stretched out his hand, hesitated, then finished his arm extension, palm up. The demon dropped the item into his open palm. He pulled it close to find a small box, decorated with colored stripes. *Could it be?*

The creature smiled at him. Gar pulled the box open. Inside was the bracelet, the one Lialee adored. He pulled it free of the casing to be sure. But how? He had seen Wirbon reserve it.

"Master happy?"

He focused on the demon. "How? How did you get this?"

21

"Me know from mind you want. Me get it. Make Master happy. Master understand. Me servant."

Gar eyed the bracelet once more then put it back in the box. He could give it to Lialee tomorrow. She would like him more. "Uh, I guess I should thank you."

"Master happy then? Master understand?"

"Um, yes, I understand. I-I don't know what to call you. What is your name?"

The demon turned its head away for the first time. "You never be say. It be too hard you word."

"Try me."

The black gaze returned. The creature made a hissing, screeching noise.

Gar tried to copy the sound but gave up after the first couple of syllables. "Hissa—"

The gaze faltered again. "See? Master no say."

The thing actually looks sad. "Listen. You're right. I can't pronounce it, but how about this? At the start it sounds like Hiss. Why don't I just call you Hiss for short? Will that do?"

"Yes. Yes. Hiss be me. Me like." Hiss did a somersault. "Me Hiss!"

Gar was no longer afraid of the comical creature. "Shh! Quiet, Hiss. Like you said, we don't want to wake everyone."

Hiss returned to his hunched position. "Hiss quiet now. What else Hiss do for Master?"

Unbelievable. A few moments ago he had been scared witless at the presence of this little monster. Now, he didn't know what to think. He needed time. "What I want you to do for now is leave the house and go hide somewhere."

Hiss started to move toward the window. "Hiss go hide by stone. Master find Hiss there."

The demon crawled out and Gar tiptoed to the window to watch. The beast was down the side of the wall in no time and scampered across the yard with the speed of a dog. Soon he disappeared among the trees.

Gar climbed back into his bed and picked up the box again. He opened the lid to check once more on the bracelet. *Won't Lialee be surprised?*

***

Gar woke early the next day and hitched the horses to the wagon before his father sat down for the morning meal.

"You're up early today."

"Yes, sir. I've got some plans." Inwardly, he groaned. He shouldn't have said anything.

His father stopped eating his breakfast and narrowed his eyes. "Plans? The only plans you have today are to hoe your mother's vegetable garden."

He needed to backtrack quickly. He hadn't told his father about the party, knowing full well his attendance would be frowned upon. He needed a cover story. He had come up with one but was afraid his father would see through it. At this point, he had no choice. "It's a class trip when lessons are finished. I'll get home as soon as I can to get the garden done."

"A class trip? They didn't do that in my day. Where?"

He hadn't planned for that question. As he rattled his brain for an answer, his sister arrived at the table.

"We're going to the justice hall to see a judicial session held by the king, who's in town. It's to help us understand the laws of the land."

Gar gave a small nod in thanks. Darlee had saved him from another reprimand.

His father dug into his oatmeal again. "Harrumph! I reckon there's some merit in that. Still, it ain't right for the school to take you away from your chores. Make sure you get the hoeing done."

Relief washed through him. "Yes, sir."

His father dropped them at the city gate and Gar gave his sister a playful nudge. "Thanks for bailing me out back there."

Darlee marched toward the school. "If you'd been paying attention, you'd know it was true. The king really is in town. A handful of us *with good grades* get to go."

Gar suffered the slowest morning of classes in his lifetime. He checked on the box in his pocket a thousand times, and a thousand times he feared he lost it and checked again. When school finally ended, he, along with his friends, followed Lialee to her father's home, deeper in the city, and the awaiting party.

Wirbon was not among the partygoers on the street. In fact, he hadn't seen Wirbon all day. He checked for the box in his pocket one more time and smiled. *He's probably too ashamed to show up without the bracelet.*

What would Lialee think when he produced the jeweled band? Would she wonder how he could afford it? Would she think he stole it? What would everyone at the party think? Troubled, he decided he would give it to her privately. This was his chance to prove he wasn't just some farm boy.

When they arrived, he was amazed at the size of the manor. The walled grounds covered an entire city block and sentries were posted at the entrance. Inside, tiled floors, rich tapestries, and gilded sconces adorned the building everywhere.

The dining room held a monstrous table with seating for thirty. It was already laid with fine settings, and a host of breads, sausages, and cheeses were spread across it.

He took the closest seat he could get near the head of the table where Lialee sat. Beside him, his friend Jango was already piling food onto his plate.

"Look at all this food. I won't have to worry about eating again for a week!"

"Jango, you should wait until permission is given before you start eating."

Jango stopped chewing. "Why? In my house, you eat when you can or you don't eat."

He recalled the words of his grandfather of how there were people less fortunate. Could Jango be one of those? He studied his friend from a new perspective. Jango's clothes, unlike the neat homespun garments he wore, were faded and tattered. Gar was a full two hands taller. The thin arms and legs protruding from the spent clothing added to the mental image of someone underfed. He decided to let Jango eat undisturbed.

A richly dressed man seated next to Lialee stood.

"On behalf of my daughter, I wish to thank you all for coming to celebrate her sixteenth birthday. No longer a child, she is now an adult. Let the feast begin."

Doors all round the dining room opened and a number of servants came in carrying plates of steaming hot food to add to the plentiful bounty already there. One giant platter held an entire roast pig. Several others displayed a variety of cooked game birds. Gar had tasted roast pig once long ago but often ate the delicious game birds that Pap snared in the woods near the farm. He decided to emulate Jango and load his plate as full as he could.

When the platters were nearly empty, the servants entered again, this time loaded down with mounds of pastries and cakes. Even though he was full, Gar couldn't resist taking two.

As he bit into the first, Lialee tugged on the arm of her father. "Where's Wirbon?"

For a brief moment, the man scowled but then smiled at her. "I have not seen him all day. When the party is over, I'll find him and give him a good talking to."

She flicked her hair, looked at the ceiling, and let out a heavy sigh. "It's just like him to ruin things." She returned her gaze to her father. "The meal is done. What did you get me?"

The man chuckled. "I guess it's time." He waved to one of the servants. "Bring it in."

The woman left and everyone at the table speculated as to what it might be. The servant returned, trailed by a stable hand who led in a beautiful white horse, already saddled. Lialee's father stood and patted the animal on its neck. "Here it is. What do you think?"

Lialee jumped up and hugged him. "It's gorgeous! Can I take him out for a ride now?"

"I suppose so."

Lialee gave a glance at Gar and the others, smirked, and then followed the stable hand and the animal out the door. Everyone rose and filed along behind.

Once outside, Lialee mounted the beast and rode around the yard several times. After her third lap, her father grabbed hold of the reins.

"I think that's enough for now. You still have guests here."

Lialee stayed mounted. "They can go. I want to ride some more."

Her father did not let go. "Lialee, get down here and be respectful to your guests."

She huffed then slid down from the saddle and joined Gar and the others. "I'm sorry. I got carried away. I was just too excited about my gift. I want to thank you all for coming."

A couple of the others who Gar recognized as ones who were close friends of Lialee handed her gifts. The rest all made for the gate. He waited until there were none left to offer her his. "From me."

Lialee took the box. "What is it, Gar? Something you made?"

"Open it and see."

She lifted the lid and pulled out the bracelet. "Oh, how nice. I think I saw one just like this that Wirbon was going to get for me." She frowned for a moment. Lialee handed the bracelet to the nearest servant. "Put this with my other jewelry, would you?"

"Don't you even want to try it on?"

She turned back to him. "Oh, I will, when I have a matching outfit. Thank you for coming, Gar. And thanks for the gift. I'm sure I'll find a day to wear it."

He didn't know what to say. "Well, okay. I'm glad you liked it. I guess I'd better be going."

"Yes. It's not polite to overstay one's welcome. Good-bye, Gar."

"Uh, good-bye, then." He headed for the gate and the long walk home.

She didn't even try it on.

CHAPTER 5

Darlee spent the afternoon at the back of the town hall with her teacher and three other classmates, watching the proceedings. A steady procession of people came to lay out their grievances or offer rebuttals before King Lowry. His Highness listened to each in turn and then sought counsel from city officials. Once everyone had said their piece, he would render a decision.

A disturbing pattern emerged. When the dispute was between a commoner and one of the elite, the elite always won. *Gar is right about one thing. You have to have money to be anyone in this town.*

How stupid her brother could be. Did he really believe he had a chance to woo Lialee? She showed no interest in him. Why couldn't her brother see that? When it came to understanding girls, Gar was a complete fool.

Her reverie was interrupted by people shouting at the front doors of the hall. Like everyone else, she turned to see what all the commotion was about.

A scowling, very well-dressed man pushed his way past the sentries, followed by a nervous-looking, equally well-appointed woman and an entourage of armed bodyguards. They marched past the waiting appealers straight to the foot of the throne.

"Your Majesty, I beg your pardon for the intrusion, but a most grievous offense has occurred. I have only just discovered my son, Wirbon, has been assassinated—killed—while he slept. He was absent from his sister's birthday celebration and when I went to his room to lecture him, I discovered his mutilated body. I implore his worship to take up immediate arms against Morica to repay this injustice!"

Wirbon, dead? She and her classmates exchanged glances. The gossip would flow when they got back to school the next day.

The king waved away a city official and faced Wirbon's father. "Merchant Trellus, I take it. I've heard of you. You're head of the merchant's guild here in Visk. Word has it you have disobeyed the terms of the treaty and failed to pay for passage of your goods through Morica. Instead, you have conspired with your fellow merchants to smuggle overland to reach the Great Sea. It is understandable that there would be those in Morica who would find your actions undesirable. You create enemies and wish me to fight your battles."

"My liege, is it such a crime to want to avoid such an outrageous tariff? The costs saved are a boon to your citizens in lower prices."

"True, but you forget we were defeated in the last war. To avoid a military incursion onto our soil, we agreed all merchants would pay the duties and ship through Morica. You have put me in a very difficult position."

"My apologies, my king. But killing my child? Is that fair? I ask you."

"You are positive it was agents of Morica who did this?"

"Who else? They have threatened me in the past, which is why I always travel with my bodyguards. The idea that I needed to provide such extra protection to my son seemed ludicrous. The killing of a child in spite because they could not get to me is reprehensible."

The king sighed. "Merchant Trellus, I will take your request under consideration. In the meantime, I wish to investigate this matter a little further to confirm your allegations." He signaled to a soldier standing near. "Captain Brusk, take what troops you need and go with this man. Bring me your report with all due haste."

The captain bowed. "Yes, my king."

Lowry rose from his chair. "Ladies and gentlemen, I beg your forgiveness, but today's proceedings must now come to an end. If circumstances permit, we shall reconvene tomorrow to complete the hearings. I ask all of you to leave the hall."

Darlee flowed with the crowd out into the street. All around her, the people were buzzing about the possibility of another war. She needed to get home as quickly as possible to tell the family the news.

The additional detail about the death of Wirbon was also quite disturbing. Granted, she'd never liked him, always the snooty type, like his sister. Still, he was from her hometown. The idea assassins had infiltrated the city terrified her. Who knew where they would strike next? What happened to Wirbon was terrible, but his father should not have caused this problem in the first place. She didn't know whether to feel sorrow or anger for him.

She found her mother alone in the house, but didn't want to break the news to her first. She knew the automatic answer would be to wait until her father got home. "Where's Gar and Pap?"

Her mother never took her eyes off the clothing she was stitching. "Your grandfather went hunting. I think Gar is out back, hoeing the garden."

She went out the back door to find her brother toiling away at the neat rows of vegetables. "Gar, put down that hoe and come talk with me for a minute. I've got a lot of amazing news to tell you."

Gar paused to meet her gaze. "Father wants this done tonight, or else."

"Fine, I'll come to you." Careful not to step on the plants and mess up Gar's work, she made her way to his side. "Listen, you won't believe what happened at the town hall today."

"It can't be any worse than my day."

Something must have gone wrong at the party. Did they find out about Wirbon there? No, his father said he didn't discover the death until after. "Why? What happened?"

"I got a gift for Lialee and she just ignored it."

"A gift? What did you get her?"

Gar didn't answer but continued his hoeing.

"Gar? I asked you a question. Where did you get the money to pay for it? If you stole the money from Father, he'll beat you within an inch of your life."

Gar straightened up. "I didn't pay for it."

"You stole it?"

"No, I didn't steal it."

"Then how did you get it?"

Gar returned to his hoeing. "I-I found it."

"I don't believe you. Nobody would leave something of any value lying around."

29

Gar straightened. His face reddened and anger darkened his countenance.

"You said you had something to tell me. So go on. Tell me and then leave me alone."

She had forgotten about the news. "Gar, the king might declare war against Morica."

"Why would the king want to declare war? Didn't we get our asses kicked in the last one? We lost two uncles, if you'll remember."

"That's the interesting part. A merchant is demanding it because his son was assassinated last night. And you'll never guess who that was."

Gar sighed. "Darlee, I have no time for idle gossip. Who was it, for the gods' sake?"

"Wirbon."

His brother dropped the hoe. "Wirbon?"

"Wirbon." She waited to see him surprised, but instead, her brother sank to the ground. "What's the matter?"

He shook his head. "Uh, nothing. I'm just picking up the hoe." Gar grabbed the tool, rose, and resumed his work.

She wasn't going to be put off. Something was up. "You never told me. Where did you find that gift?"

Her brother continued his garden tending. "Uh, oh, down by the creek."

"I want you to show me where."

"Later. I'm busy."

She watched him work for a bit then headed inside. "Later, then. Don't forget."

At suppertime, she watched Gar eat, staring down at the plate the whole time. When she told her father of the possibility of war, he brushed it off as none of their concern.

Gar finished his meal, left the table, and rushed out the door. Darlee crammed a last couple of mouthfuls in and went out in pursuit of him.

From the porch, she couldn't spot him anywhere. *Where in the world did he go?*

Perhaps he'd gone down by the creek where he'd found whatever it was he gave to Lialee. *Gar always likes to hang out in the meadow. I'll bet that's where he is.*

She made straight for it and even before she got there, his voice carried to her.

"Hiss! Where are you? Hiss! Show yourself."

When she reached the top of the hill overlooking the swale, she spotted him dashing around, checking behind trees and in the bushes. "What are you doing?"

Gar turned to face her and froze. "Darlee, you shouldn't sneak up on me like that."

She walked right up to him. "I didn't sneak up. You were making such a racket, you wouldn't have heard anything. What are you looking for, and what are you hissing at? Is there a snake somewhere about?"

Her brother glanced around then put his hands on her shoulders. "Listen. Remember a couple of nights ago when I said there was a demon loose?"

"Yes, and the next day you said it was a bad dream."

"Yeah, well the truth is, there is a demon somewhere about. He came out of the stone over there." Gar pointed at the big stone in the middle of the meadow.

Darlee approached the stone. It was broken open, the shattered pieces lying round what remained of the base. "Out of this? How?"

Gar came to stand beside her. "I'm not quite sure. I think I somehow did it."

"Since when can you make a demon out of stone? You know magic is forbidden in the seven kingdoms."

"No! I didn't make it. It was already in there. Pap says this is one of the demon stones."

She recalled hearing the stories as a child. "I thought those were just tales to frighten people."

"So did I. But apparently they're true and one of the demons was trapped in this stone."

"So how did you let it out—and why?"

Gar sighed. "Pap said if you listened carefully, you could hear the demon's heartbeat. When I came down here the other day, I

31

decided to lie on the ground with my ear against the rock and see if I could hear anything. There, very quiet, I could hear the steady, low thumping of the thing's heart. After a while, I guess I fell asleep. What must have happened next is the dream came. It wanted out. My head started to hurt real bad and the demon said for me to wish the stone to open and the pain would go away. So I did. That's when I woke up and saw the creature trying to climb out."

"So you loosed some giant demon on the land. Gar, this is horrible. We need to tell someone right away."

"It's not big. In fact, it's real small, no bigger than a two-year-old. I need to find it."

"Why do you need to find it? Let's get the authorities to do it."

"Because I think it's what killed Wirbon."

She stared at him for a moment, her mind racing without answers. "What makes you say that?"

"Because the gift I gave to Lialee was the bracelet she was eyeing the other day."

The implications struck home. Lialee would hear of Wirbon's death. She would think Gar killed Wirbon for the bracelet and the merchant would confirm he sold the bracelet to Wirbon. They would come for her brother and execute him. "What are you going to do?"

Her brother slumped to sit on the ground. "I don't know. If I could catch Hiss, maybe everything would be alright. But I can't find him."

"Hiss?"

"The name of the demon, or, at least, that's what I call him."

"You…you talked with this thing?"

"Yes, last night. When it came into my room and gave me the bracelet."

She needed time to think. "Okay, you keep looking for this demon. I'm going to go find Pap. He'll know better what to do."

"Aw, don't tell Pap. I don't want to get in trouble with him."

"Would you rather I talk to Father?"

Gar stood up and kicked at the ground. "No."

"I thought not. Now get looking."

32

She started for the house with her brother's call for Hiss fading behind her. *Grandfather is Gar's only chance. I hope he knows what to do.*

CHAPTER 6

Brusk entered the town hall to find the king in discussion with his military commander, Purmin, and the city elders examining the map board of Sechland. "My liege, I've completed my investigation."

King Lowry motioned him to come close. "Tell us of the details, Captain. Is Merchant Trellus exaggerating, or is this something I need to concern myself with?"

He went and stood on the opposite side of the large table. "It's a most gruesome scene. The lad was stabbed multiple times, forty or fifty or so. Some type of conical pointed weapon I'm not familiar with was used. I would think the deed was done after the first few. I can only assume the rest were to send a message."

"How did this happen? The man gave me every impression he was well-guarded."

"That's a bit of a puzzle." He held up a fist and popped up his thumb. "One. Both the gate to the estate and the front doors had two guards posted throughout the night. I interviewed them all and unless a minimum of two were in league together, there was no way anyone entered through the front way."

He opened his fist further to expose his index finger as well. "Two. The top of his estate wall is embedded with shards of broken glass that would shred any man attempting to climb over on his own. It would take a team of men with ladders and more to scale that wall to be able to bring their man out safely once they were finished.

He added his middle finger to the exposed thumb and index. "Three. There are a fair number of ruffians in this town who would kill anyone for the right number of silvers, but I can think of none capable of pulling this off. It smells of an outside job, all right. Trellus just might be telling the truth."

The king turned to Purmin. "It sounds like Morica has forced my hand earlier than I had planned. Are your soldiers in our capital in readiness?"

"We could march within the week."

"Fine. Send out the riders. I want troop levies from all the towns in five days. Have them assemble here." The king placed a marker on the board near the border of Morica. "I will not be a vassal state to them any longer."

Brusk listened for a while as the king and his commander discussed the upcoming incursion. *This is insanity. We were beaten badly last time. What makes them think it won't happen again?* "Begging your pardon, my liege, but doesn't it seem an awful risk to go invading over one killed boy?"

"There have been many more incidents than this one boy. Consider it a cumulative thing that has tipped the wagon."

"Other incidents? I wasn't aware of any."

The king smiled at him, nodding. "Trust me. There are."

There are no others. He's using this one as a pretext for war. He wants to invade. "We don't even know for sure if it was them. Furthermore, we didn't have the manpower to beat them last time. I'm wondering how you intend to do it this time around."

The commander glared at him. "Captain Brusk, know your place!"

The king put a hand on the commander's shoulder. "It's all right. It's a respectable question and one deserving an answer. Normally, I would not surrender to such insolence, but as a veteran of that last war, I can respect your position." He nodded to Purmin. "Show him on the board."

Purmin began placing pieces in Morica. "We know from our spies their troops are spread as so."

Brusk took note of which were representing cavalry and which infantry. Various colors represented the number of troops—one, ten, one hundred, and one thousand. Once he completed the Morica setup, he began to place the Sechland troops. Brusk added up over seven thousand compared to the three thousand for Morica. "There's something I don't understand here. The numbers in Morica sound about right, but from where did we get over seven thousand on our side? I read the reports. At best, we could only field about two thousand and still maintain a skeleton crew to defend the towns. You're not planning on sending them as well, are you?"

"No, instead, we'll be calling for troop levies from each town." The commander pointed at Brusk's hometown. "Visk, for instance, will be required to provide one thousand men."

"One thousand? I've got two hundred and sixty on duty right now, down from the five-hundred-man garrison this town employed before the last war. Where, by the gods, am I going to get another eight hundred?"

"You will press into service every unmarried young man of age who can carry a weapon."

Brusk had been in battle with untested men before. "They'll be slaughtered going up against real troops."

The king nudged the commander aside, moved the pieces from Sechland into Morica, and pulled a number of them off while doing so. "Then they will die with honor for king and country."

"If you lose a whole lot of the young men, the towns will explode."

The king came round the table and put his hands on Brusk's shoulders. "That is why you must be careful in your selection. Choose only the poor, the outcast, and the farmers. Avoid selecting any of the elite or middle class. They will not miss the riffraff should they not return. However many we lose will only be the price we pay to insure our kingdom has its rightful place for years to come. You are best suited to do this job. This is your town. Select well."

What a cold-hearted bastard. "Yes, my liege."

"Good." The king clapped his shoulders and went back to the other side of the table. "We will look forward to you having your men in the field in five days."

Brusk bowed. "As you command." He turned and left the hall. If there was ever a time he hated his job, this was it. *One thousand men. Bah. This is folly. The king must be off his rocker.*

He stopped walking and sighed. He was at an intersection giving him an excellent view of the city in all directions. Behind him lay the market square and the town hall with the merchant's sector even farther back. To his left was the upper town where the

36

well-to-do lived and the pretenders tried to keep up. To his right stood the middle-class quarter where his own home stood and where once his wife and three daughters had been situated. They were gone now, the home empty.

Before him, lay the Ring, a one-block thickness of tenements and broken down houses that ran the entire inner circumference of the city walls.

He recalled hearing that when the walls were originally built, it was all open land between them and the city proper but, over the years, it changed. First, makeshift homes were built against the wall, barely more than hovels. The poor had nowhere else to go. In time, the hodgepodge of decrepit buildings filled the gap. It was occupied by not just the destitute, but by the lowlifes of Visk. *I guess that's where I'll start.*

The orders given to him ran against his better judgment. Despite his misgivings, he would complete his mandate. *After all, I'm a soldier, and I'll do a soldier's duty. Let's just hope that the king is fortunate and this rabble can get him his honor. Because when we lose this one, Sechland will belong to Morica, not Lowry.*

He set his teeth and headed for the fortress near the main gate. He would rustle up a contingent of soldiers to complete a full sweep of the rim over the next two days and fill the troop levee required. *While I'm at it, I might as well empty the jails. A fat lot of good it would do to leave them behind and no one to guard them. Best make soldiers out of them. Better they die for their king than by a hangman's noose. He wants one thousand troops—I'm going to get him one thousand troops.*

CHAPTER 7

Gar stayed and searched the swale past the point when his voice went hoarse from calling out for Hiss to show himself. *The little bugger knows what he did and has run for it, leaving me in deep.*

He was about to give up when his sister arrived with Pap in tow. "Did you find him?"

"Nope. He's scrammed."

His grandfather grabbed Gar by the shoulders. "So what Darlee has told me—is it true? You managed to release the demon?"

Was everyone going to think he released the monster? "No, Pap. It's not like that. I didn't do anything intentionally. It fooled me into doing it while I was sleeping."

His grandfather's arms dropped. "Still, it matters not. Once people learn this thing is free and roaming the countryside, they will blame you, even if you are innocent."

"So what am I to do?"

"Let's figure that out. Who knows about this so far?"

His gaze swept from Pap to Darlee and back to his grandfather. "Just the three of us, for sure."

Darlee nudged him. "There's more than that. Remember I told both Maurus and Jango about it. And don't forget what Lialee might think."

Pap rounded on Darlee. "Why'd you go and do a dumb thing like that?"

"I thought it was all just a bad dream then. That's what Gar told me. I thought it would be fun to tease him about it."

"Okay, they're his friends. Hopefully they'll keep their mouths shut." Pap turned to him. "But what about this Lialee girl? Is she clever enough to put two and two together? Will she come to the same conclusion Darlee did, that the killer of this Wirbon fellah is the one who took the bracelet?"

"I-I don't know. I doubt it. She hardly looked at it—treated it like it was rubbish because it came from me. She might not."

"Hmm, then again, she might. Until this demon is caught, you're going to have to keep low, stay out of sight. Someone like this Lialee seeing you again might spark the knowledge inside her head as to your involvement."

He thought about whether his grandfather's plan would work. Somehow, he didn't think it would. "Okay, I'll do what you say."

"Good. Now the two of you run along and get home. Your father's going to be wondering why you're both out so late. Tell him you were helping me clean a couple of birds and we got a-talking. I'm going to head over to the shed right now and make sure those birds are ready in case he comes to check. Tomorrow, you do like I told you. Go to school and stay low. I'll hunt that creature of yours. Nobody knows the woods around here better than I do."

Gar was tired. The idea of climbing into his bed sounded like a good one. Pap was right about one thing. There was nothing else to do that night. He needed his wits about him in the morning.

***

Master, me here.

Hiss, where were you?

Me hide. Me read mind. Master angry and want give Hiss to bad men. Hiss no want go. Me hide.

You killed Wirbon.

Me do what Master want. Master want boy dead. Me do. Me get thing from boy that Master want. Me give Master. Me only do what Master want. Hiss not do bad. Hiss do good. Hiss good.

I did not want Wirbon dead.

Yes, Master want boy dead. Master think so.

But I-I didn't really want him dead. Because I thought it doesn't mean I wanted it.

Think want, mean want. If no want then why think want?

39

This is confusing. Never mind. From now on I don't want anybody killed—nobody, regardless what I think. Do you understand that?

Hiss understand. Hiss go now.

Wait. Hiss, I need you to tell everyone you killed Wirbon.

Hiss go.

Wait!

Gar woke. It took a moment for him to realize it was not a dream but Hiss in his mind again. He jumped out of bed and checked around the room. There was no sign of the creature. He dashed to the open window where he could just make out the form of Hiss scampering across the yard and disappearing into the mist. *Damn! He's gone again. I hope Pap can catch him.*

He remembered again wishing Wirbon dead. He also recalled how he'd wished he could figure out a way to get the bracelet. Was what Hiss said about only doing what he wanted true? The idea nagged at him.

Too uneasy to get back into bed, he headed downstairs in hopes of finding something to eat besides oatmeal.

Entering the kitchen, it pleased him to find a large heel of bread wrapped in a cloth and still soft. He was taking his third big bite when his mother entered, surprising him. She glanced at him then set to work lighting the stove. "Your father will be down shortly. You'd best be done with that before he gets here."

"Will do." He jammed the rest into his mouth. It marveled him now when he thought about how she had always gone about the house unnoticed. She hardly ever spoke and never admonished him. That was always Father's job. But she wouldn't tell on him, either. He washed down the last of the bread with some water just as the thump on the stairs told him her warning was true.

His father entered the kitchen and stopped to glare at him. "You're up early."

"Couldn't sleep."

"Well, since you're up, you can help me load the wagon. I've a few things to bring into town today."

"Yes, sir." He followed his father out the door.

When they got to the barn, his father pointed out the things he wanted loaded on the wagon and then disappeared out the door. He returned a few moments later with two game birds, still feathered. "These will fetch a good price at the market. Of course, I could get more if they were cleaned but I haven't the time. You told me you and Darlee were helping your grandfather pull off the feathers, yet, here they are. I went straight away and stopped Pap from cleaning them." His father cuffed him hard across his left ear. "What *were* you doing last night? Tell me the truth, as my patience is already thin."

He hates me. I don't know why, but he hates me. I can't tell him the truth. If I did he'd beat me within an inch of my life. "Nothing. I was doing nothing."

He was cuffed again. Gar's eyes clouded as anger welled up in him. His left ear rang with pain. When his father bore down on him to strike a third time, he swung back and landed a fist on his father's jaw. He was surprised to see his father fall onto the ground. The anger drained away. *Oh no! What will he do now?*

His father got up and grabbed the oxen switch hanging behind him. "Hit me, will you? I'll teach you to show some respect."

Gar stared at the switch and made the only decision he could think of. He ran out the door, the sound of curses assailing him from behind.

He slowed when he reached the road to the town as the sun rose. Maybe someone at school would help him figure out what to do.

Glancing behind him, as he neared the city gates, he could make out the family wagon with Darlee riding on her usual seat. He dashed behind some brush and waited until they passed. Darlee looked back as he emerged from his hiding spot. Sadness clouded in her face. *She must have seen me hide.* It made him feel even worse.

At the gate, armed guards stopped him.

"State your name and business."

"Uh, um, I'm Garlin Murdach, on my way to school."

A man seated nearby scanned through some parchments. "Let him pass."

41

Inside, his friend Maurus was waiting for him.

Gar greeted his friend with a nudge and pointed back at the gate. "What was that about?"

"They're on high security. Why weren't you on the wagon with your sister?"

"My father hates me. Where's Jango?"

"I don't know. He usually beats me here. I suppose he'll catch up in a bit."

He didn't want to tell the story just yet. He wanted Jango to hear it as well. Maurus had a habit of teasing him. Jango didn't. In fact, as he thought about it, Jango was his closer friend of the two. "Come on then. Let's head to the school and catch him there."

The school was abuzz with talk of the coming war. It didn't take too long to realize that not only was Jango missing, but so were a few other older kids from his class.

Darlee came over to join up with him and Maurus. "Tell me, Gar. Father wouldn't say what happened."

"I-I hit him."

"You hit him? Why?"

He glared at her. *She never gets the same abuse as me.* "Why? Because he was beating me for nothing. I couldn't just let him do that anymore."

"So what are you going to do when it's time to go home?"

"I don't know. I thought I'd ask for ideas. You're the smart one. Do you have any?" She shook her head. He turned to Maurus. "What about you?"

"No help here. Maybe you should apologize."

He snorted. "You don't know my father. He won't accept that." He looked around over the heads of the others. "Jango still isn't here. Where could he be?"

Darlee put a hand on Gar's forearm. "You haven't heard then. The army rounded up a bunch of the kids and inducted them into the army. Jango was one of them."

He was stunned. "Jango? In the army? I've never seen him in a fight in my life. What does he know about being a soldier?"

Maurus chuckled. "Yeah. I doubt Jango could beat my kid brother, and he's only twelve."

Darlee gave Maurus a scowl then returned her focus to him. "Forget about that. Gar, what are you going to do?"

It was obvious. The solution was right there. "I'm going to go sign up and fight with Jango." He took a step toward the barracks, calling over his shoulder, "Tell Father I won't be back."

Darlee grabbed his arm. "Don't go, Gar. Don't go. I don't want to lose you." She started to cry.

He hugged her then set her gently away from him. "I'll be back. And when I return, I'll be respected, and I'll come for you and take you away from Father and that awful farm."

He clasped Maurus' hand. "Wish me well."

Maurus let his gaze drop toward the ground. "Good luck, Gar. May the gods be with you."

Gar hugged his sister one more time and kissed her on the forehead. "Take care of yourself and Pap."

"Please...stay."

"I can't."

He felt as if a huge weight lifted from his shoulders. He pressed his lips tight in determination and set a brisk pace for the barracks. *I'm doing the right thing.*

CHAPTER 8

Brusk rubbed at his eyes. He hadn't slept all night. At the table in front of him, his junior officer was tabulating the list of new recruits. Too tired to pay attention, he made for the chair on the other side of the desk. Resting his head in the palm of one hand and his elbow on the table, he stifled a yawn with the other. "Whew! I'm beat. One thousand men, he says. One thousand! What are we at now?"

"Five hundred and forty-three, Captain."

"Five hundred and forty-three. Five hundred and forty-stinking-three. That means we got over another four hundred more to go."

"Four hundred and fifty-seven, to be exact."

He scowled at the man. "I *know* the number. The question is, where are we going to get them? We called up all the reserves. We scoured the entire Ring throughout the night and into the morning. I emptied the jail of all of those I could trust. There's no two ways about it. I'm going to have to go to the middle-class areas."

"Perhaps, Captain, we could go back through the Ring, but ignore your order of one per family. We'd fill our quota in no time."

Brusk closed his eyes and moved his hand to his forehead. *The man is insufferable.* He gave a deep sigh and eyeballed the lieutenant across the table. "It's bad enough I'm drumming these people into the forces without their say so. I'll not deprive families of all their men at once. They need the others to feed what's left, poor scum that they are."

"Then perhaps those families with three or more—"

He held his hand in front of the man's face to silence him. The door to the office opened and a familiar strapping youth entered and approached him. "I wish to enlist."

Is the boy daft? "Garlin Murdach, isn't it? Does your family know what you're doing? Isn't it enough the Murdachs have suffered with the loss of your two uncles nigh on four years ago?"

44

Garlin puffed up. "I'm sixteen. I'm a man. I make my own choices. I want to sign up now."

Am I to suffer fools for the rest of my days? He'd started to stand, when the officer tugged his arm.

"He's one less to find. The commander will not be happy if we come up short. At least hear him out."

He slumped back. "Fine. What be your business in coming today? Surely you know we're going to war?"

"Yes, I know. And I remember my uncles and how they were lost. But I come because there is no life left for me here. My father has likely disowned me and I have no home to return to. I intend to make a mark for myself and win back my honor. Allow me the chance to do so."

Brusk shrugged free and stood. "Honor? You think this war will give you honor? The only thing you'll get from it is pain, grief, and, if you're lucky, a quick death. There is no honor in war. Honor is the kind of thing the poets and politicians, who've never held a bloody sword in their hands, talk about. No soldier who has been on the battlefield and seen his friends and his enemies die talks about honor. That kind of talk doesn't exist among soldiers. There is no honor in killing, only duty."

All the time he ranted, Garlin shrunk away. But now, with his speech done, the youth straightened again to meet his gaze. "Then I will perform my duty as a citizen of Sechland. Either way, I'm going."

Tempted to knock some sense into the young man, he lifted his arm then froze. Dried blood crusted around Garlin's reddened left ear. He let his hand fall to his side. "Your father do this to you?"

Garlin reached for his ear and pulled away some of the crusted blood, examined it, and shrugged. "Yes. It's an almost daily occurrence."

For the first time, Brusk doubted whether it was best to send the lad home. "Maybe you deserved it. Maybe you didn't. But this isn't a place for runaways. Have you ever held a sword?"

"No, I'm afraid I haven't."

"Then, what use are you? In your first battle, you'll be the first to die."

"I'm strong. You must have some use for me."

The officer rose and stepped closer and felt across the youth's chest. "He might make a fine pike man. Seems fit enough."

Brusk had thought of that but didn't want to give Garlin anything that might swell his confidence. "Fine. Let's find out whether or not you can handle one. Follow me."

He pulled a large metal-tipped pike, twice the height of the lad, from a rack full of them. "Here, carry this out with you. The new recruits are training in the field outside the gate. If I think you can handle the weapon without getting yourself killed or killing one of your fellow soldiers, you're in. But if you fail, you go home. Understood?"

"I understand."

Brusk led the way to the gate. He waved to the guards then pointed to Garlin as he passed them. "He's with me."

Garlin caught up to walk beside him. "What's with the high security? I thought we were going to go attack them, not the other way around."

"Spies. Morica is sure to have at least a couple of them within the city. We locked down last night after the king gave his orders. Word has hit the street of our recruiting. We can't have anybody heading across the border and giving warning we're coming. Our troops would end up walking right into a trap, and more than enough of them would be slaughtered. Surprise is the single chance this fool campaign has."

He continued on out onto the pitch where his regular troops were putting the new recruits through their paces. A number of targets were set up for longbowmen and those with crossbows. Likewise, there were numerous wood posts for those with swords and axes to practice against. He spotted where the pike men were and directed Garlin to go fall in line.

Despite the need for sleep, he decided to watch for a while, at least until Garlin took his turn with the trainer. After that, he would go get a few hours rest. *I still need to scour up some more troops but maybe, like that lad, I'll get a few volunteers as the day goes*

46

on. We won't need to march until tomorrow, maybe even the day after that, if I push them long.

After a few moments, he was sorry he'd stayed to watch. The number of arrows missing the entire target and the men falling down in their exercises sickened him. A large raven circled overhead, and a couple of the archers took to trying to shoot it out of the sky, without success.

He would be bringing sheep to a butcher.

Shouting from behind him dragged his attention from the field to two men on horses attempting to exit the gate and the guard demanding they get down. "What's all the ruckus about?"

One of the men on horseback met his gaze then urged his horse forward, brushing the guards aside with the animal's bulk. The soldier nearest pulled his sword and swung, but his blade glanced off the rider's saddle bag. "Stop that man!"

When the second tried to follow, he was tackled down from the animal by the guards, but the first kicked his horse into a gallop. Brusk feared the worst—a spy was escaping from town. He glanced around. There was no one on the pitch with a horse. "Quick, archers, bring down that rider!"

A few with bows at the ready let loose their flights with the shots sailing high, wide, or into the ground, but none made contact. *Curses. Not a decent archer among them. We're done, for sure.*

He started to run, too, in hopes of grabbing a bow to take his own shot when a pike sailed through the air, catching the horse in the rump. It made him change direction from seeking a bow to charging the spy. The animal crashed to the ground, throwing the rider.

Brusk was in full stride toward the man and drew his sword when the fellow struggled to his feet and stumbled away. He lunged forward and swiped his blade through the calf muscle of the man's left leg. The runner collapsed, screaming. Brusk kicked the man in the head, knocking him unconscious. A few of his men charged up. "Take this trash to the jail. Get a healer to bind that wound, 'though I doubt he'll ever walk again."

The soldiers picked up the man and carried him off. Brusk returned to where the horse lay panting, the pike sticking out of it.

"I'm sorry, beasty, but you've had it." He struck down with his sword and killed the animal.

After wiping his blade against the horse's carcass, he pulled the pike free. "Who threw this thing?"

Garlin stepped forward and claimed the weapon. "I did."

"Well, Garlin, that was one heck of a toss. It looks like you're in."

"It's Gar. Everyone calls me Gar."

He chuckled. "Gar it is, then. Now get back in line. There's still training to be done."

The raven fluttered down and settled on the dead animal. It gave Brusk a tilt of its head as if waiting for permission.

"Go ahead. Have your fill. Consider it the winnings for the merry chase you gave my archers earlier."

The bird jabbed his beak into the open wound and yanked free a strip of horsemeat.

CHAPTER 9

Darlee spent the morning moping her way through class. She toyed with the idea several times of leaving the school to search out her father in hopes he would do something to extricate Gar from the army. She knew better, though. Her father would do nothing. The idea of racing home in search of Pap also occurred to her, but then she recalled how her grandfather would be out searching for the demon. *What am I going to do?*

When class ended, her way toward the gate was intercepted by Lialee and a couple of other older girls.

"Where is that brother of yours?"

She tried to walk past, but they blocked the way. "What do you care? You don't even like him."

The three girls crowded close. Lialee poked a finger into her chest. "I asked you a question. Where is he?"

Darlee held her ground. "He's gone where a spoiled brat like you won't get to him. Why do you want to know, anyway?"

"He must have stolen that locket from poor Wirbon. I know because I checked with the merchant. My brother bought it, not Gar. If the assassins hadn't killed Wirbon the night before, he would have beaten your brother to a pulp." Lialee poked her harder. "You've got a big mouth, but since neither Gar nor his pals are here to protect you, maybe I'll force the answer out of you."

At least one thing is for sure; the girl is stupid. How would Gar have stolen the locket from their house? It's a fortress. "I'm not telling you anything. You've already made up your mind. Now get out of my way."

"We'll see about that."

Lialee grabbed Darlee's arm and twisted it. It hurt, but no more so than some of the punishments she received back home.

"Let me go!" With her free hand, she landed a punch right on Lialee's nose and jerked free. One of the others came at her, and she kicked that one in the stomach. The girl collapsed to her knees, clutching her midsection. The third helped her friend up. Darlee

49

spun to face Lialee once more, but the girl was mopping with her sleeve trying to stem the flow of blood from her own nose and wipe tears from her eyes.

"If you broke my nose, my father will have you put to death. At the very least, I'll make sure he has you whipped."

Darlee grinned. "The next time, I won't stop with just your nose." She brandished a fist at the girl who promptly turned and ran away. Darlee took a step toward the others. "The same goes for you, too." The pair fled after Lialee.

Darlee watched them disappear into the city. She felt better until she remembered the real problem—Gar. *I've got to go find Pap.*

She raced out the gate and hurried home. Entering the house, she found her mother busy peeling beets. "Where's Pap? Is he back yet?"

Her mother continued cleaning the vegetables. "If he's not in the shed then he's still out hunting for grouse. Your father took the ones Pap caught yesterday to the market."

Darlee hurried out to the shed next to the barn and found her grandfather there. "Did you get him?"

He held a cloth covering half his face. He shook his head. "No, he nearly got me."

He pulled the cloth back to reveal a number of deep gashes on his cheek. Blood still streamed from the cuts. Blood stains marred his shirt and at least half-a-dozen wounds seeped through the shredded fabric. She rushed to him. "Oh, no! What happened?"

He hugged her for a moment then pushed her away. "I don't want to get any blood on you. I'll be all right in a bit. The demon is a dangerous little beast. I trapped it for sure, but when I tried to tie the thing up, it slashed through the bindings with those claws of his. It became a wrestling match. Each time I'd grab his arms, he'd kick at me with the claws on his feet. I'd go to pin his legs and he'd rake me across the face. It's a good thing I didn't lose an eye. Plain and simple, I didn't have enough arms to hold the thing."

"Why didn't you just kill it?"

"I tried. Its hide is tougher than steel. I broke my best knife on it."

"So what did you do?"

"I had no choice but to let it go. In truth, I think it was toying with me. At first I thought it was afraid for its life because it kept calling out *Me no kill—me no kill,* but once I realized I couldn't hurt it, I came to believe it was saying it wouldn't kill me. Still, it cut me up good enough. I'm lucky I wasn't maimed. I'll heal, though. I always heal fast." He looked past her. "Where's Gar?"

Darlee burst into tears. "He's not coming. He signed up with the army this morning."

"The army? What, by the gods, for? I must go get him." Her grandfather started to rise then collapsed back onto his seat.

"It's too late. I heard they are marching tomorrow to meet the king's army near the border with Morica."

"Then there's still tonight. It's not too late, yet." He stood up, but after two steps crumpled onto the dirt floor.

She helped him to rise and guided him back to the chair. *Pap must be hurt worse than he's letting on.* "You're in no condition to walk to town. Father will be home soon. You have to talk to him to do it."

Pap sighed. "Your father's a stubborn man. Set hard in his ways ever since he lost his two brothers to the war. It will be difficult, if not impossible."

"You have to try. It's Gar we're talking about—Gar. I don't want to lose my brother, too."

Her grandfather held out a hand. "Get me to the house. Your mother will patch me up until your father gets home. Let's hope he's in a receptive mood."

She moved under his arm and allowed him to use her as a crutch. Together, they walked a three-legged stagger out of the shed. Darlee's attention was drawn to her left in time to see the demon Gar described scamper away. "Pap, look!"

"I see it. He must have been outside the shed the whole time, keeping an eye on us. It's no matter, now. We have bigger concerns to worry about."

When they entered the house, as Pap predicted, her mother quit her food preparation and attended to his wounds. Pap told an unlikely story of a bear attack. She questioned nothing, merely helped him remove his shirt and stitched the biggest wounds.

Pap looked like a pin cushion with so many holes poked into him. She thanked the gods they were small wounds and most had stopped bleeding. It took the rest of the afternoon for her mother to dress them all. As her grandfather was putting on a clean shirt, the horse and wagon clattered into the yard. Cursing, Father unhitched the horse, a chore usually done by Gar.

When he stomped into the house, clutching the oxen switch, she and her grandfather sat in the common room. Her mother slipped into the kitchen.

"Where's Gar?"

She bowed her head and glanced at her grandfather. *Please, say something, Pap. I can't do this.*

Her grandfather met her gaze, nodded, and then faced her father. "He's not here."

"Where is he? He's got something coming for this morning."

"You might as well put that thing away. He's gone off and joined the army."

Her father purpled, broke the switch over his knee then moved to sit at the table, throwing the chair normally reserved for Gar away. "Where's dinner?"

Pap joined him. "It's coming. Your wife was busy helping me for a bit. Son, what are you going to do about Gar?"

He stared at Pap, noticing his wounds for the first time. "What happened to you?"

"A bear attack. I'm fine. It's nothing a little time won't heal. You haven't answered my question."

Her father hollered through the open door to the kitchen. "Where's my dinner, woman?"

Darlee was feeling very tense. A chill ran through her and she shuddered. *He's ignoring Pap. He doesn't care about Gar.*

The idea of her brother never returning brought tears to her eyes once more. *Gar, please come back to me. Please come home alive.*

CHAPTER 10

With the clanging bell of reveille at sunrise, Gar clambered out of his assigned cot and made his way to the practice field. Captain Brusk and the other senior officers were waiting when he arrived. He stepped into line and waited while the men struggled into place as the last of the morning mist faded away.

Brusk walked up and down, inspecting them. "This morning we will be issuing what armor we can. For most of you, it won't be much—maybe a helmet or a leather jerkin. You all will receive a back kit containing your bedroll, first aid supplies, and food rations. Body armor will only be distributed to a select few. You were issued your weapons already and trials were held. Yesterday you were evaluated. We will be assigning you into teams of—squares—archers, pike men, and swordsmen. Each officer will take his team and instruct them in the basics of inner-city warfare. You are to follow the orders without question. It may mean your life or the life of the man beside you. You will have the morning to practice these drills. At high sun, we will stop to eat, and after that, we break camp and head for the rendezvous site. It's a two-day march, so make sure you pay attention and learn the best you can."

Brusk addressed the officers. "Gentlemen, collect your teams."

The officers singled out soldiers to join them. The one who came for Gar looked hardly older than him, probably somewhere in his mid-twenties.

Gar trotted to the spot on the field where the officer instructed him to go. When he got there, he was happy to see his friend with a crossbow in his hands. "Jango, we're on the same team!"

"Hey, Gar. I saw you throw that pike yesterday. I'm glad you're on our side."

A surly looking fellow standing alongside him sneered at them. "It was luck. He better not be throwing that pike when the real fighting starts. He'll get us all killed. This is all crazy, if you ask me."

53

Gar frowned and examined the man—short, stocky, probably somewhere in his forties. "If you think this is crazy, why did you enlist?"

"I didn't. It was either that or the gallows. I figured better a shot at surviving this thing than no shot at all with the hangman's noose."

The guy's a criminal. "Well, we're in this together. It would be better if we got along. My name's Gar. This here is Jango." He extended his hand.

The man glanced back and forth then clasped Gar's forearm. "Baxus. I suppose you're right. Just don't let me down."

More men kept arriving—young, old, and, like Jango, poorly dressed. He wondered how many were recruited from the Ring. Including the officer, he counted sixty-two in total.

The officer stood before them. "Good morning, gentlemen. My name is Lieutenant Devron Sech. From this point forward, you will be taking your orders from me. We don't have a lot of time so we're going to go straight to setting up our combat square. The basics are simple. We create a box of soldiers consisting of both pike men and swordsmen alternating on the external ring. Inside will be all the archers and crossbow men. Pike men prevent the charge of cavalry through our square and swordsmen will defend the perimeter using both their weapons and their shields. This leaves the central group free to fire on the enemy at will. The front line is dependent on the width of the street. So, if the street is ten men abreast, then so is the front line. That means ten across the back. The rest fill in the sides, so that works out to seven each side. The archers are in the middle. Such a formation will prevent our enemies from encircling us. When I call out a number, it means that's the number at the front line. You will assemble quickly depending on the number I call. Is everything understood?"

Sech? I wonder if he's related to the king? Gar joined in with most of the men who acknowledged it with a "Yes, sir." One man didn't respond.

Devron approached the man. "I didn't hear you." He kneed the man in the groin. As the fellow bent over in pain, he clubbed him across the back of the head, sending him sprawling to the dirt.

Devron pointed down at his victim and scanned the troop. "This is the kind of man who will get you killed. This is war. There is no room for disobedience. You will obey my commands without question and do so smartly. I do not wish to die because someone isn't doing his job." Devron pointed out the two men closest to him. "Pick him up and put him back in line. You two are entrusted to make sure this man is compliant."

Once everyone was back in place, Devron stepped into the middle of the group. "Shall we begin? Ten!"

Gar hustled to find a spot with a swordsman to each side of him. It seemed like a long time before the rest stopped moving.

Devron walked about, banging a few men on the head as he went. "Too slow. Let's try it again. Seven!"

The second time, things developed a lot faster. Devron moved to stand out front. "Better, but still not good enough."

The disorder didn't make sense to Gar. He decided to venture a question. "Lieutenant, why not simply assign each man a specific spot? That way we know exactly where to go."

Devron moved to stand in front of him. "Because you are young and, most likely, foolhardy, I will not punish you this time for speaking out. But make no mistake about it; the next incident will result in a harsh penalty."

He nodded and gulped. "Yes, sir."

"Good. Now I will answer that question in case anyone else wonders about what I am doing. In combat, the man beside you dies. Who is going to fill the spot? In the heat of the battle I will not have the time to assign someone new. To be effective, I will be keeping my commands to one word instructions, nothing more."

They spent the rest of the morning going through different formations. As Captain Brusk promised, a meal was served when the sun reached its zenith. Gar ate as much as he could. He figured it would be the last good one for a long time to come. A fluttering of wings drew his attention to a large, black bird landing near Brusk to eat scraps the captain threw to it.

***

They marched until the sun was less than one hand from the horizon. As they set up camp, Gar could hardly wait to grab a bite and get some rest. Before he could get comfortable, Devron stopped before him. "Our squad has guard duty when the moon is in the first and second hand. You can rest after."

Gar glanced at the horizon. The sun would set soon and their watch would begin. He rose and, like the others, followed the lieutenant toward the camp perimeter.

The lieutenant walked around the camp, stopping every ten paces and pointing into the surrounding woods with the same instructions to each man. "Twenty paces in. Make sure the men to your left and right are visible."

When Gar's turn came, he marched into the trees the required distance. A log on the ground provided him a seat. He checked both ways and spotted Baxus to his left and Jango to his right.

He settled in and waited. As night descended, the forest became quite dark with only the starlight filtering through the leaves. The moon would be cresting the horizon but was blocked from view by the thick foliage.

To his right, his friend sang to himself. *Poor Jango. I'll bet he's scared. We're supposed to stay silent. It must be his way of dealing with the darkness.*

He checked the other way but had trouble making out Baxus in the gloom. It took a while for Gar to spot him sitting against a tree. He wondered if the man was asleep.

A rustle from some distance in front of him brought Gar alert. He stared hard at where he thought the noise came from, but could see nothing. Checking left and right, he noted both of his comrades seemed oblivious to the sound. Returning his focus to where the noise originated, he got off the log, and, holding his pike before him, took a few steps forward. He reached a small opening in the underbrush. Nothing.

He sighed. Probably a mouse, nothing more. About to return to the log, he paused at another small rustle, and Hiss stepped into view.

"Master, me am here."

Gar jumped up and back half a step. "Hiss, you startled me."

"Shh, Master. No make too much noise."

The little monster had found him. It must have followed the army as they marched. What was he going to do? *I guess Pap must have had no luck trying to catch him.* He knelt in hopes of keeping his voice from carrying. "What do you want from me?"

"Hiss serve Master. Master going need Hiss. Master going war. Hiss help."

He'd forgotten the thing could read his mind. "What can you do? You're just little. And you're a demon. No one is going to want you on their side. Go away."

Hiss skittered back and forth. "Master no send Hiss away. Master need Hiss. Master see. Hiss will help."

It was like arguing with his sister. She always won in the end. He reached out and stopped Hiss from moving about. "Look, I'm in the army. I can't be having you by my side. They'll throw me in irons, or worse. I wouldn't even be here if it weren't for you, so don't do me any more favors."

"Hiss know. Hiss hide. When fighting comes, Hiss help."

Gar stood. "Fine. When the fighting starts, if you think you can help, then help. Until then, stay out of my way."

The sound of snapping twigs behind him made Gar spin to see.

The lieutenant stepped into view. "Who are you talking to, Gar?"

He glanced toward Hiss.

Gone.

"Uh, just myself."

"Well, quit it. You're supposed to be on guard duty, keeping an eye out for the enemy, not giving yourself pep talks. As it is, I had to stop that friend of yours from his incessant singing. I could hear it all the way in camp."

"Sorry, sir. I won't do it again."

"See that you don't. It's already close to the third hand of the moon. Someone will be coming to relieve you soon. When he does, get some sleep. You're going to need the rest."

"Yes, sir."

The lieutenant trudged off towards Baxus. Soon he heard a thump and a yelp. He must have guessed right. Baxus had been asleep, and the lieutenant must have kicked him.

He scanned once more for the imp but could find no sign. *Before the fighting does start, I've got to figure out what to do with Hiss. He's going to get me killed.*

CHAPTER 11

They marched for two more days until they met up with a number of other troops gathered in an open valley. Gar never travelled and had no idea where they were.

Baxus, on the other hand, seemed to know every inch of Sechland. He pointed out landmarks all along the way. "This is the south-eastern tip of the kingdom. We're only a half-day's march from Sechwisk. On the other side of the low ridge is Morica. You can just make our guard tower there to the left. It's known as Eagle Ridge. From that vantage point, Lowry's men can see the comings and goings between us and them for leagues."

Gar spotted the structure set on the highest point of land visible. Even from a distance, it looked like a fortress with a high wall of stone round it and a tower in the middle. "How is it that wasn't destroyed in the last war? You would think Morica would have seen to it when they won back then."

Baxus chuckled. "They didn't need to. It's too well defended, so they just marched around it. That's the thing about forts. They can't move, troops can. Sure, Lowry knew of Morica's movements, but there was nothing he could do about it. He was outmanned. It's why he surrendered after losing what troops he sent into Morica in the first place. It was folly on his part to attack a superior force."

"I lost two uncles in that war."

"Well, you might get the chance to avenge them. More than likely, you'll be joining them as another victim to Lowry's insanity."

The lieutenant came to join them and rapped Baxus across the back of the head. "I'll not hear you speak of the king again in such a manner. He may have failed in his last venture, but he attacked with a mere three thousand men. Look about you. Our arrival brings Lowry's forces to seven thousand strong. We have the numbers. It's only the proper deployment of them which matters now."

Gar made note of all the camps set up throughout the valley. Too many for him to count, it seemed like an awful lot of men. He would take Devron's word for it. "So what do we do now?"

The lieutenant pointed out an open spot. "Set up camp. The king's commander will deliver directions to the captains who in turn will inform their lieutenants. When I get word, I will assemble you to hear."

Gar and the others went to work setting up their tents. The supply team came round with hot stew, and he dug in with fervor. He was just finishing when Devron returned from meeting with the captain.

"Gather round everyone. Our assignment has been laid out for us."

Gar rose and crowded in close with the others in his squad.

The lieutenant was down on one knee, marking the ground with a stick and placing some stones down within the markings. "From here it's a one day quick march to Morence, the capital city in Morica. We'll be leaving before first light so there will still be daylight to assault the walls. We have enough catapults to breach them quickly, and it's the street-to-street fighting where *you* will do the damage. Now, pay attention. This is as best as I can show you the layout of the city." He began to point out what each of the scribbles and stones stood for—walls, the major roads, the castle, the armories, and the order in which they would be taken by the forces of Sechland.

Baxus snorted and leaned close to Gar. "Ever the eternal optimist, our kid lieutenant-believes everything old King Lowry says to the end."

"Why do you say that? It looks like they've planned out everything."

"Everything you say? What if something goes wrong? What are the contingency plans?"

"Contingency plans?"

"Yeah, like how do we escape if we're losing?"

The lieutenant finished up and ordered everyone to get some sleep. When he left, Gar and Jango joined Baxus near the makeshift map in the mud. "So what do you think?"

60

Baxus pointed towards the woods marked south of the city. "There's the best way. If things go bad, head for these woods. From there, we can work our way down to the Lorne River and head back home."

***

Everything that could go wrong, went wrong.

Morica had been waiting for them, that much was certain. When Gar and the troops of Sechland arrived in front of the gates, they were set upon by catapult fire from within the walls. While they were busy trying to set up their war machines, a host of cavalry charged and caught them unprepared. His squad barely managed to form their fighting square, while many others were cut to pieces by the horsemen. With so few riders of their own, bolstered only by foot soldiers, it took time to defensively counter the mounted attack, and soon the gates of the city opened and Morica's army poured onto the field.

He had been told Morence was defended by only a thousand men. It looked like a much bigger number when the enemy charged.

Everywhere, men of Sechland began to run away. Shortly, Gar heard a horn sounding Retreat.

A tug on his arm had him checking to his right at Baxus.

"Time to go, Gar."

"Go. I'm not leaving. I'll catch up to you."

Baxus dropped his shield and took off for the forest.

Gar did his best to hold his corner of the square but when the man to his left ran, the next man did as well. Lieutenant Devron tried to single-handedly fill the gap, but men managed to pour past and attack the archers behind. The square disintegrated.

Gar looked around and spotted Jango on the ground, blood pouring from a wound on his shoulder, near his neck. He dropped his pike, shed his kit, scooped up his friend, and took off in the direction Baxus had run. "I've got you, Jango."

As they fled, many of his comrades were slaughtered by the enemy, cut down from behind. Going that way made no sense. He couldn't carry Jango and run from men on horseback. He fled into the woods and continued to run until he could see the field of battle no more.

Exhausted, he lowered Jango to the ground. "I…need…to…catch…my…breath!"

Jango grabbed hold of his arms. "Don't leave me to die here, Gar. I don't want to die." Jango coughed and spat blood onto the ground.

"I'm not leaving you to die. I'm tired. You need to try and walk. Come on. Get up."

He helped Jango stand. Wobbly, but still upright, Jango stumbled farther into the forest. Gar followed, too frightened of dying to think of a better plan. At footsteps behind him, he grabbed Jango's arm to cease his movement. "Shh!"

He knelt and dragged Jango down with him. Peering through the foliage behind him, he could just make out the movements of soldiers searching through the woods. "They're looking for us."

"What do we do? Should we run for it?"

A rustle to his right made him freeze in fear. *So close already?* From between two bushes, Hiss appeared. "Master, come this way. Me save you."

Jango jumped behind him. "What, in the name of the gods, is that?"

"Keep quiet. This is Hiss. He's a demon."

"A demon? You *weren't* kidding about it that day."

Hiss was skittering back and forth. "Master come now before Master found. Come, come quick. This way." Hiss took off south.

Gar rose and followed. "Let's go."

Jango pulled at his elbow. "Are you insane? That's a demon. Why would you follow it?"

Gar nodded toward the searching troops. "We don't have much of a choice."

They stumbled after Hiss for a hundred paces or so until they came to hill with a cave sloping down into the ground. Hiss pointed in. "Go. Hide. Good place. Safe. We get help inside."

He stepped into the gloom and was grabbed and pulled in.

"Hurry, get out of sight." It was Baxus.

62

Relief washed through him. It could have been men from Morica. "You made it. Is there anyone else here?"

"Just me."

He turned to Hiss, who scrambled in after Jango. "Is this the help you were talking about?"

Baxus raised his sword to strike at Hiss. "What's this little monster?"

Gar pulled him back before Baxus could swing. "Leave him be. It's a small demon named Hiss. I freed him some time ago, and he wants only to serve me. He led us here. He said there would be help. I guess you're it."

Hiss moved past them towards the back of the cave. "No, Master. He no help. Me not know he here. Come. Help back here."

He followed Hiss to the back of the cave. Very little light made it that far, but he recognized the markings on the rock wall. They were identical to those on the stone that had entombed Hiss. "What this? Another demon?"

"Yes, Master, yes. Is big demon. Good fighter. You need now."

Gar's thoughts were in a jumble. The last thing he wanted to do was help set another demon loose. "Perhaps the soldiers will pass us by."

Baxus, still by the entry, crouched down to step out and look around. He came back in right away. "There are a lot of them out there, and they're getting closer."

Jango fell to his knees. "I don't want to die!"

Baxus jumped over to him and clasped a hand over his mouth. "Shut up! They'll hear you."

Hiss tugged at Gar. "Master, release demon now. He protect you."

"I don't want to free another demon!"

Baxus let go of Jango and closed on Gar. "I don't know about you, but I don't want to die either. Those troops from Morica won't be letting us go home. They'll execute us. If this little imp says you can release a demon that can save us, then I'm all for it. What say you, Jango?"

Jango nodded, tears running down his face. "Please, Gar."

63

What was he going to do? "I-I don't know how."

Hiss tugged at him. "Me teach. Master must touch stone. Need Key. Master touch. Hiss teach."

Gar reached out and put his hand against the rock wall. Hiss clambered onto his shoulder and placed a hand on Gar's forehead. Like the time in the meadow, he sensed Hiss inside his mind and winced at the pain that came with it. "Argh! It hurts!" His knees buckled.

"Master no let go stone. Master wish stone open now. Do it."

Through the pain in his head, he envisioned the stone opening. A large seam appeared in the wall and split wide. Pieces of the rock wall tumbled away. A ferocious creature strode out, standing some four or five hands taller than Gar and that many again wide. Huge muscles rippled under the dark-grey skin. Dressed only in a pair of leather breeches, leaving its massive chest exposed, its countenance was of a monstrous beast filled with large fangs and sharp teeth. Eyes, like Hiss's, gleamed black, and hands and feet sported long, sharp claws.

It loosed a bone-shaking shriek.

Gar let go of the wall and slumped to the ground. The pain still kept him in its thrall. He could hear screeching and turned to see Hiss talking with the new demon in their native tongue. When their dialogue ended, the large creature stomped out into the forest, and Hiss came and stroked his face. "Big demon go. Destroy enemy. Master safe."

Soon screams emanated from the forest. They lasted a long time as they differed both in tone and distance. It must have been a significant number of men the monster was hunting down and killing.

What have I done?

***

Night came and, with it, silence. No more could Gar hear the screams of the men of Morica as the demon returned, blood dripping from its jaw and claws, a soft white glow emanating from it. Even the regular sounds of the evening, the chirping of crickets, the hoots of an owl, nothing pervaded the stillness outside the entrance.

The beast sat on the earthen floor in the middle of the cave. Both Jango and Baxus gave room and crouched against the wall. Hiss scuttled from the huge demon to Gar and back again. He would converse in his harsh language with the creature then return to Gar with tidbits of information. "He killed all within hundred paces of cave. None left who saw him. He's slain twenty-two... No, he correct me, twenty-three. He tired, wishes rest. He go out, kill more in morning."

Tension gripped Gar. "More? How many more? Surely they have moved off. Who would want to fight a monster such as him?"

"He says more men out there, outside forest. He not know how many."

Baxus moved to stand near. "Perhaps now is our chance to escape. Under the cover of darkness, we might slip past them and make our way back to Sechland."

Hiss dodged round them and scampered to the entrance. "Hiss check for Master. See how many. Hiss back soon."

He disappeared into the underbrush and Gar returned his attention to Baxus. "We should wait until he comes back."

"Are you nuts? He's a demon just like that—" Baxus nodded towards the large demon "—thing over there. We need to run while the imp is gone and this one is too tired to chase us."

Gar looked at Jango, who was still cowering against the wall, pale and sickly looking. His friend could not travel far in his condition. He then eyed the demon lounging on the ground. It stretched and nestled down like some giant cat. As fearsome as the creature appeared, he did not think it meant them any harm. "No, we're going to get some rest, as well. Jango needs sleep and his wound tended to. I'm not going to go blundering around in the dark without knowing what's out there."

As if on cue, Jango swooned and collapsed to the ground. Gar moved to his friend's side and gave him a gentle shake. "Jango? Can you hear me?"

His friend didn't move, and his breathing was harsh and sporadic. Gar lifted the cloth from Jango's wound. The blood still seeped, the area pink and purple. He ripped a new piece of cloth from the end of his own shirt and pressed it to the wound. He opened Jango's kit and pulled out a blanket to cover him with. "We've got to get some help for him."

Baxus came and stood over them both. "Forget it. He's a goner. It's just you and me. We need to go now."

Bounding into the cave, Hiss rushed straight to Gar. "Master no leave. Many, many men outside. Too many. Thousands. Hiss sneak in camp, listen. They think many men in forest."

Baxus grabbed Gar's arm and hauled him up. "Are you going to listen to this little demon? I say we make a run for it."

Hiss slashed at Baxus' leg. "Leave Master be!"

Baxus howled, and then kicked Hiss aside. The big demon, which had appeared asleep, with lightning speed, jumped up and grabbed the head of Baxus in one hand, lifting him from the ground. It swung back its free hand with its claws extended. Before it could swing through, Gar jumped and grabbed the arm. "No. Don't kill him. Let him go."

The beast dropped Baxus on the dirt and returned to the spot where it had been resting.

Baxus scrambled to his feet and, with eyes bulging, dashed out into the darkness.

Gar returned to Jango's side and put a hand on his friend's forehead. It was hot. "He's fevered. I don't know what to do."

Hiss poked at the wound. "Not good. Die soon. Master must heal."

"I don't know how to heal that. What? Are there some berries or something I can gather that will help? What can I do?"

"Master use magic. Heal friend."

"I-I don't know how to use any magic."

"Hiss help, show how. Master put hand wound, other hand wall."

Gar touched the cold stone with one hand while the other felt the warm, sticky flesh of his friend. "Now what?"

Hiss put a hand to Gar's forehead. "Think heal."

Gar concentrated on the wound and wished it to close. His shoulder hurt as if it were he that was wounded, but he ignored it

66

and kept concentrating. As he watched, the ache in his shoulder abated and the wound closed. "It worked, but he's still unconscious. I think he's fading."

Hiss snarled something at the big demon. The creature knelt next to Jango and put a massive hand over his heart. A pale light passed between the beast's hand and his friend's chest. Jango's chest heaved then returned to normal along with his breathing. The large demon stepped away.

Gar put a hand to his friend's forehead. The fever remained, as did the redness where the wound had been. "He's going to need a couple of days to break this fever." He glanced at the monster already asleep again in the center of the cave then focused on Hiss. "What just happened there?"

"Demon give life force to friend."

He didn't understand what that meant. All that mattered was Jango was alive and getting better. He let go of the wall to pull Jango's blanket tight round him. As he let go, a weakness ran through his body and he dropped to his elbows.

Hiss helped him straighten. "Master weak. Need rest. Hiss keep watch. Master sleep. Friend sleep, couple days."

"I suppose you're right." He finished moving the blanket and stretched out next to Jango. The earth floor was cold. "I could sure use my own kit right now and pull out a cover."

The big demon rose again and picked him up, cradling Gar in his arms. He returned to the same spot once more and laid Gar next to him. Warmth exuded from the massive body. He was being cuddled by a monster. Almost all of his fear of the beast was gone.

"What is your name?"

Hiss scuttled close. "He bad speak common tongue. Trouble saying words. Speak little. He understand though." Hiss spoke in his harsh language at the beast.

The demon, its eyes already closed, re-opened them in slits to examine him. It made a thunderous noise.

"Thunder. I shall call you Thunder."

CHAPTER 12

Morning came, and Gar woke feeling rested. His body sported a few kinks from sleeping on the ground but nothing more difficult than he suffered in the past several days.

He moved over to where Jango still lay asleep. His breathing had slowed and no longer sounded ragged, but when Gar put his hand on Jango's forehead the heat of the fever was still there.

Thunder still lay in the same spot. He cast about for Hiss but saw no sign of him. He stepped to the exit of the cave and peered out. Morning was glinting through the underbrush, the final wisps of fog fading away. "Hiss, are you out here?"

A rustle drew his attention, and, from behind a tree, Hiss scurried over. "Master awake. Good. Master go. Enemy come soon."

He crouched and scanned the surroundings. "I don't see anyone."

"Soon. Come three ways: east, north, west. Master go south."

Gar glanced south. It made no sense. "But that's not the way home."

"Master safe first then home."

He looked back into the cave. "Jango is still sick. He can't walk."

Hiss dodged into the cave. He could hear the screeching and growling of a conversation with Thunder. Hiss reappeared. "Thunder carry. Master go now."

Thunder appeared at the entrance with Jango in his arms, wrapped up in a blanket.

For much of the day, they marched through the woods. Gar groaned when they reached the bank of a wide river. *How are we going to get across?*

A large tree branch floating by gave him an idea. "Thunder, I saw two fallen trees not more than twenty paces back. Can you help me drag them here?"

The demon put Jango down and dashed off into the forest with Gar chasing behind. A loud crashing noise soon was followed by the appearance of the behemoth carrying one tree on his shoulder and dragging the other behind him.

"Alright, then, you carry them. Hiss, find some vines so that we can lash them together."

The imp scampered away, and by the time Gar had instructed Thunder to lay the two trees down, he returned with an armload of the stuff. Gar tied the trees together as best he could and, with Thunder's help, he pushed the makeshift raft into the river. They placed Jango in the middle and, with Thunder paddling at the back and Gar at the front, they crossed quickly, and just in time, as the sun was setting.

On the far side, the shoreline was clear of trees. Once Jango was ashore and being carried again by Thunder, Gar surveyed the land ahead in the gathering dusk. He struggled to recall the map Lieutenant Devron had drawn in the dirt but was unsure of where he was and told Hiss so.

"Me know, Master, me know. We Fermia."

"Fermia? So, how do we get back to Sechland?"

"We west, go Storburg, then north, go Sechland."

Gar scratched his head. "You mean we're two countries away? How did we get so far?"

"Not far, not far. Master see."

He tried to find somewhere to sit. With the tree line several hundred paces behind him and the little light of the stars above, he could only make out endless fields. To his right, the unmistakable glow of a candlelit window drew his attention. "We've walked far enough. I'm tired. I see a homestead over there. I suggest we find out if there's a barn we could hide in while I rest. The couple of times Jango woke up, he mumbled incoherently showing he was still with fever. A night without being jostled would do him wonders. Thunder must be tired from carrying him as well."

Thunder made a grating noise.

Hiss scuttled into the lead. "Master correct. We go."

With a visible goal in sight, Gar's legs felt heavy with exhaustion. They entered the yard and passed the small one-floor home. It looked more like one of the shanties in the Ring than a house. There wasn't a barn, only a large shed and penned area next to it occupied by a small herd of goats. He cursed as a few of them bleated as they passed by. Once they were inside the shed, he expected the noise from the goats to cease, but the animals continued. "Why won't they shut up?"

Thunder lay Jango down on some hay. "Smell."

He stepped near the big demon and sniffed the air. There was definitely a pungent odor about the beast, something he hadn't noticed before through his own sweat and grime.

A groan brought his attention to his friend.

Jango tried to rise, but collapsed back onto the hay. "Water. I could use a drink of water."

Gar checked his canteen. Empty. Each time Jango had awakened during the day, he had done his best to sate his friend's thirst. "I saw a well outside. I'll go get some. It'll only be a moment." He waved toward the demons. "You two stay here. We don't need those goats riled up any more."

As he made for the well, he considered his situation. Anyone who saw him traveling with two demons would assume the worst. Perhaps, when Jango was better, they could simply walk away and leave the monsters behind. He quickly dismissed the idea. *Hiss followed me all the way from Visk to Morica. I'll never be rid of them.*

He reached the well and lowered the bucket by the rope it was attached to. The comforting sound of the splash below told him relief from thirst was on its way. As he pulled the sloshing bucket back up, he froze at the feel of steel against his neck.

"Don't move, or I'll cut ya head clean off!"

Gar let the rope go causing the bucket to make a racket as it caromed down the well walls. He turned slowly to see an old man holding a scythe to his throat.

The man shook the scythe. "Who are ya? Whadya doing on my farm?"

"I-I was just hoping to get a drink of water."

Behind the farmer, the goats once again bleated.

"In the middle of the night? What are ya? A thief? Come ta steal my goats?"

"No, just a traveler. I needed water. I saw the well and didn't want to scare you by knocking on your door after dark."

"Ya know what I think? I think you're some kind of criminal. I don't take kindly ta your sort. I ought ta turn ya in to the authorities."

From the darkness, the massive hand of Thunder reached out and grabbed the scythe from the farmer. Before Gar could react, the monster's second hand slashed down and tore the man in two, blood gushing from his midsection. The sound of ripping flesh and seeing the man's blood spurt made Gar cringe. "No! You didn't have to kill him."

Thunder dropped what remained of the man on the ground. To Gar's surprise, the beast snarled something that sounded like *he danger*. Hiss had told him Thunder had trouble with common tongue and Gar, hearing the garbled words, understood why it never spoke.

"He was just an old man defending his farm." One similar to Pap. "In time, I would have convinced him I was no threat, that I'm a farmer, just like him."

"He too danger, no risk."

There was no point in arguing. The farmer was dead. He returned to the task he set out for and drew the full bucket from the well. Drinking his fill, he filled his canteen and handed it to Thunder. "Give Jango this. I'm going to check out the house."

The demon accepted the container and retreated to the shed. Gar made for the farm home. He knocked on the door and waited. No answer. He knocked again, only harder. Still nothing. Trying the handle, he found it unlocked and peeked in.

Inside, a single candle burned on a small table made from tied branches. He glanced into the two other rooms in the house, a simple kitchen with a chopping block and a bedroom with a small single bed, the mattress stuffed with hay. No one appeared to confront him. The old fellow must have lived alone.

He went back out to the shed where Jango was still drinking from the canteen. "Can you walk?"

"I think so." Jango gripped Gar's arm as he was pulled up. He was a little wobbly at first, but steadied. "Yeah, I can walk. Where to?"

"In the house. There's a bed there. I think a good night's rest for you should shake off that fever."

Jango and the others followed him back to the farmhouse. After some argument over who should sleep in the bed, he helped Jango lie down. Thunder stretched out on the floor, while Hiss bounded about, looking in every nook and cranny.

"Food, Master. There is food here for you."

He hadn't realized how hungry he was as his stomach grumbled. The corner of the kitchen serving as a larder provided a few blocks of goat's cheese and some milk, and he found half a loaf of bread there as well. He carved some of the cheese and brought it and a chunk of the bread to Jango then returned to the table to sit and eat as well. He held out a wedge of cheese to Hiss. "Hungry?"

"Hiss no eat food. Only water."

"You don't eat? What do you do for sustenance?"

"Hiss absorb mana."

"Mana? Isn't that the stuff that warlocks have?"

"Not just warlocks. Everyone have. Some more than others. Warlocks most."

"So is that the same thing for Thunder?"

Hiss glanced at the large demon now stretched out on the floor. "No. Thunder—something else."

He thought about it as he chewed. What had he learned about warlocks? He should have paid more attention in school. There was something about how they were banned from the seven kingdoms. Something about their mana. He just couldn't remember. He wished Darlee was with him. She was the smart one. She would have known.

The dead farmer outside disturbed his thoughts. *At first light, I'll bury the old man. It's the least I can do.*

Finished eating, he considered the two demons resting on the floor. If they were going to continue to accompany him wherever he went, he needed to figure out a way to hide them. He looked into the bedroom. Jango was asleep again. His breathing was steady and relaxed. Gar checked and found his friend's fever subsided. He was going to be okay.

He sorted through the meager clothes hung on some hooks on the wall, but nothing would serve for Thunder. It was then he spotted the extra bedspread folded in a corner. It would have to work. His mother had never shown him a lot of sewing skills, but he could manage a cloak. Combine it with some leggings that would cover Thunder's feet, and the giant demon would appear as a very large man.

Hiss, on the other hand, was a different matter. No amount of clothing was going to alter his appearance enough to fool anyone. He found a big enough rummage sack and emptied it of its contents. It would have to do. The little imp wasn't going to like what he planned, but he could see no other way.

CHAPTER 13

Captain Brusk trudged home as quickly as he could move the troops. He dared not tarry too long at any spot for fear of Morica horsemen. The remaining forces of Sechland split once they crossed the border, each group heading for its respective hometown. Of the thousand men he'd started with, his force had dwindled to seven hundred. *Lunacy. Sheer, utter lunacy. Why didn't we have any scouting reports on the enemy? They must have had some on us. Now I have to go back and explain to the city elders why I lost so many men. And for what? Nothing. A lost kingdom. Morica is sure to counter in some manner or another.*

He stopped the men for a short reprieve. As they sank to the ground to rest, he walked among them, passing on what solace he could. They were a bedraggled lot, the bunch of them. Tired, dirty, unshaven, and, worst of all, defeated.

Following his example was one of his lieutenants. A young, good-looking fellow. Unlike the rest, the man was clean shaven. *It takes strength of personal character to maintain one's appearance in times of war.*

Brusk fell into step beside him. A nasty gash marked the man's shoulder, beside the breast plate. "Devron, rest like the others. I can handle this task."

Devron thumped his chest in salute. "Captain. I'm afraid I failed. My unit broke rank and ran."

"No more so than any of the others. Staying would have led to a slaughter, just like I warned them."

"How is it they were so ready for us? I considered the king's plan foolproof."

"The king is a fool. He rushed into this battle unprepared."

Devron stopped walking. "Captain, you are my superior officer, so I will not debate this with you, but, remember, the king is my cousin on my father's side. I would prefer you not insult him."

Brusk didn't care. "Distant relative or not, we got our arses whipped. You've a military upbringing, Devron. Your father was a captain. Give me *your* knowledgeable opinion on the king's campaign."

"I-I suppose what you say has some merit. Still, how is it they bested us so easily? The battle couldn't have raged more than a hand."

"He rushed to action all because of the death of one boy. He should have ensured no word of his mobilization escaped before doing so. Morica's spies must run deep within our boundaries. The worst is yet to come. Now that we have scattered, Morica will surely march into Sechland and conquer the country."

Devron sank to the ground. "Are things as bad as that?"

"I'm surprised they haven't caught us from behind. I can only assume they're chasing the king and the main force from Sechwisk."

"Is all truly lost?"

He sighed. *The first hard lesson for you, eh, young Devron.* "Not yet. There may still be hope. Rest here for a while. We'll be marching again, soon enough. When we get back to Visk, it won't be long until word from Sechwisk reaches us." He reached into his satchel and pulled out a couple of strips of jerky and tossed one to Devron. "Eat, there's still two hands left in the day. You'll need your strength."

He left the man to chew on the strip and bit down on his own as he continued his rounds. A shadow passed over him and he peered up to see the raven. He pulled his dagger and carved a small piece of the jerky and tossed it. The bird settled on the ground to scoop up the meat. "So, you're back. I thought you'd have stayed in Morica. Lots of fresh meat to pick on there in the battlefield."

The bird made a shrill sound then lifted off and headed in the direction they were going.

"Ya, you're right. We should be moving on." He grimaced at the men. "All right, everyone, get up. It's time we get going. If things go right, I'll have you home by the morrow."

***

75

The sun was sinking below the horizon as Brusk led the men through the city gate. He ordered a hot meal to be prepared for the troops while he attended the city hall. The city elders were gathering as he arrived, among them Merchant Trellus, who had used his station to propel himself as leader and spokesman.

"What news from the war? Have you defeated the Morica scum already?"

Brusk snorted in disgust then took his time to remove his armor and drop it and his helmet on the table. He plopped down in a chair and put his feet up. Spotting an attendant, he motioned him near. "Bring me some wine and something to eat. Snap to it." As he did this, he kept an eye on Trellus, who purpled.

"You have not answered me, Captain Brusk. How goes the battle. Has Sechland won?"

He scowled at the man as the servant arrived with the food and drink. He took a long draught of the wine and let loose a satisfying sigh. After placing his wine goblet on the arm of his chair, he grabbed a cooked pheasant, tore a large piece off, bit into it, and then rose to face the awaiting elders. "You are a fool, Merchant Trellus, to think we could have vanquished the enemy so quickly. Nay, we have not won, but lost. Our forces were decimated on the field and have been scattered like chaff in the wind. In the passage of only one hand, I lost a third of my contingent, and the rest of King Lowry's forces fared no better. In fact, I'm surprised to find you still seated here. I thought I'd be reporting to some regent from Morica demanding our unconditional surrender."

"You forget your place, Captain. You serve this town and the citizens you have sworn to protect."

Brusk pulled his sword and swung a heavy blow into the table before him, sending splinters of wood and the remnants of his meal, flying in all directions. "And you forget that it was your insistence to the king that we go to war, all to save your honor for that dead brat of yours. Now the kingdom of Sechland lies at the mercy of our enemy and there's nothing we can do about it. I wouldn't be surprised if by this time tomorrow, there's an enemy host at our gates."

The color drained from the face of the merchant. "Then you should be rushing to prepare the defenses of this city. Were it within my purview, I would have you removed as captain and put someone in charge who cares about our citizens."

Brusk paused to finish the piece of pheasant in his hand then drained the rest of the wine. He slammed down the cup, wiped his mouth on his sleeve, and belched. "But it's not. Only the royal commander or the king himself can order my replacement, and they both have bigger things to worry about than your soiled sensitivities."

He donned his armor and put his helmet under his arm. "I go now to the barracks to inform the troops of what awaits them. May the gods have mercy on us all."

He kicked his chair out of the way and trudged out of the hall. When he returned to the barracks, most of the troops had left for their homes. Only his senior officers and a scattering of men remained. There was no need for him to ask for silence since the room went quiet on his entry. "I just came back from meeting with the town elders. They wanted to know if we already won the war."

A few groans of complaint were muttered. Like him, those who were seasoned had known the plan had little chance of success. He needed to reaffirm his support for them. He held up his hand and the silence returned. "I told them we might be attacked as early as tomorrow. Personally, I doubt it. If anything, Morica will march on Sechwisk and not march all the way out here to the far end of the kingdom, but I wanted to put a measure of fear into them. I figure, by now, most are hiding under their beds."

A few snickers passed through the crowd, relieving the tension. He let out a loud sigh. "Even still, we do need to make what preparations we can. Tonight, I want everyone to get a good night's sleep. In the morning, we'll begin checking the town's defenses and send out notices to all able-bodied men to report for home militia."

***

Over the next few days, Brusk reviewed each and every aspect of the town's defenses. He notified all the capable male citizens of their obligation to assist in the defense of the walls. When the fighting started, many would run and hide, but others would man the walls.

After a knock, one of the guards on sentry duty at the main gate opened his door and came in. "Captain Brusk, a rider has arrived from Sechwisk."

"Bring him in."

The guard signaled to the rider to enter. The man came in, saluted, and handed Brusk a letter. "The commander expects your immediate readiness. My instructions are to return with your answer as to when you will arrive."

He opened the note and scanned through it. "What is this? This is nonsense! March back? Are they mad?"

"No, sir. The royal commander expected a reprisal attack the next day. It didn't materialize. Instead, a scout from Eagle Ridge arrived to inform them that Morica was under attack from the south. They've hunkered down near Morence, setting up defenses, and have left the northern towns scantly defended."

Brusk visualized the map of the seven kingdoms. "Who attacked? Storburg or Fermia?"

"They do not know for sure. It is said an enemy force hid in the woods. Morica has sent its army south, in pursuit."

"So what does his highness want to do? Attack Morica again?"

"I do not know. I am only told the same as what you have in that letter—that all available forces are to march to Sechwisk immediately. My task is to ride ahead and inform them of your coming and your numbers."

Words failed him. His anger at the continued folly of his king was testing even his limits as a soldier. "We'll march on the morrow, and I'll not be bringing every man this time. Visk must be defended. Tell the commander I bring five hundred, no more. Go, have something to eat before you ride. The difference of one hand will not determine Sechland's fate."

The rider saluted and left with the guard in the direction of the commissary. He stepped out of his office and grabbed the nearest man. "Bring me Lieutenant Devron."

The fellow ran off and Brusk returned to his chair. *I'll leave the wounded and tired here. Forcing them to march would only result in more unneeded deaths.* He buried his face in his hands and yawned deeply. *There are days I hate this job.*

Footsteps warned him of someone coming, and he regained his proper posture.

After knocking, Devron entered and saluted. "You wished to see me, Captain?"

"Yes, Lieutenant, sit." He gestured toward an empty chair.

The young man perched on the front edge of the seat.

Ever the eager one. "I've been ordered to march to Sechwisk with as many men as I can spare. I leave in the morning and am taking five hundred with me. While I am gone, you will be in charge here. That should give you some two hundred plus troops to defend these walls. See to the wounded and hold fast. Do *not* leave this city, no matter what orders arrive. Is that understood?"

"Yes, sir, but don't you think it would be better to leave one of the more senior lieutenants in charge?"

"I need them with me. They know the defenses at Sechwisk. If it's a case of defending the city, they'll be better at it. Besides, that shoulder wound of yours could use a little more time to heal up. I doubt you could swing a sword with that thing."

Devron glanced at his shoulder. "I-I suppose you're right." He rose. "I guess I'll get some rest then so as to be ready to take charge at first light."

"You do that." He stood and gripped Devron's forearm. "You're a good man, Devron—better than most. I'd not want something to happen to you because you can't defend yourself."

A flutter at the window announced the arrival of the raven and it alit on his desk. He reached out to stroke its plumage. "Come for a visit, I see. Here, I got a scrap for ya." He pulled out the stub of a jerky and tossed it on the desk.

Devron rose from his eat. "That bird has become your pet—surprising. He's quite large for a raven."

"Yeah, it's kind of weird, but I'll take all the friends I can get in a time of war. It's best you go get some rest. I'm counting on you."

The man nodded and left the office. Brusk followed him out the door and watched him go. *That's done. The city elders won't argue with the king's cousin. Now to figure who's left alive and tell them the good news we're going back.*

CHAPTER 14

Darlee had taken to sitting in the back of the wagon on the way to school since Gar's leaving. Her father still hadn't said a word about it. He acted as if her brother never existed.

The wagon trundled along, bouncing through the same ruts it had bounced through the day before, and the day before that, for as long as she could remember. She'd memorized some of them to the point where could tell how far along they were with her eyes closed. Concentrating on the ruts helped her pass the time and kept her mind free from what bothered her.

When she recognized a specific series of bumps, she knew they were within sight of the city walls. Craning her neck, she looked toward the gate in hopes of catching a glimpse of any of her friends. It was then she noticed the soldiers out in the training field. *Gar!*

She stood up for a better view. The men were forming ranks and made it difficult to make out the faces. "Father, slow down. I want to see if Gar is out there."

In response, her father snapped his switch to spur the horse faster, and she stumbled against the load of firewood her father brought for the tanning vats.

Her eyes welled with tears. *How can he hate his own son so?* She rubbed at them with her palms and stifled a sniffle. She wouldn't let him see her cry.

When the wagon stopped at the gates, she jumped out like always, but instead of going in, she trotted back toward the field. She raced up and down the lines of soldiers trying to spot Gar among them. The men were all shouldering their kits. *They must be marching again. When did they get back? Last night? Where are they going?* Panicked, she picked up her pace. *I must see him to know he's okay.*

As she turned another corner, a hand grabbed her arm. "Hey, young missy, where do you think you'd be going?"

She spun round to face the man holding her. It was Captain Brusk. She recognized him from the market. "I'm looking for my brother. I want to wish him well."

"Your brother? What's his name?"

"Garlin Murdach."

The captain let go of her arm and stroked his chin. "I'm sorry. He's not here. He might be among the wounded inside. Check with Lieutenant Devron. I think Gar was in his unit. If anybody's going to know what happened to the lad, he would."

"Thank you, Captain." She took off for the barracks in town. It would be just like her brother to be the first one hurt. She hoped he was okay. As she passed through the gates, a couple of her friends called her to join them. "Can't. I've got to go to the barracks. See if Gar is there."

Maurus was among her friends. He chased after her. "I'm coming, too. I want to see if Jango's there as well."

She slowed to let him catch up and they changed to a brisk walk. Maurus told her the men arrived the night before, that the army of Sechland lost the battle, and a lot of men were killed. When they reached the barracks, a guard stopped them and asked what they wanted.

"I'm looking to see if my brother, Garlin Murdach, is here."

"Sorry, no admittance to citizens."

She wasn't going to be stopped. "All right. I'll go back out to the field and tell Captain Brusk you wouldn't let me in. What is your name, so I can inform him?"

"Captain Brusk sent you? Hold on, let me get the lieutenant."

The guard disappeared inside then returned shortly with a younger man bandaged across one shoulder. "Here's Lieutenant Devron. You can take it up with him."

The lieutenant stepped out and smiled. "How can I help you?"

"Excuse me, sir. I'm looking to see if my brother is in there. Captain Brusk said he might be among the injured. He wasn't out on the field."

"I know every man inside. What's his name?"

"Garlin Murdach."

Maurus piped up. "And I'm looking for my friend Jango."

The smile on the lieutenant's face turned to a scowl. "I know both those men. They served in my company. When retreat was sounded, I saw your brother Gar pick up Jango and make for the forest to the south."

Hope blossomed in her. Gar hadn't been killed. "So they may still be alive? Are you searching for them?"

The lieutenant sighed and waved them inside. Once they were seated around a table, he took her hand. "First of all, I don't know whether he survived. The horsemen of Morica may have cut him down. If not, they most likely took him prisoner, which would be a fate of torture. As for Jango, the lad was severely wounded. I doubt he could have lasted more than a day or two."

"But it's possible they could both still be alive? It *is* possible, isn't it?"

"Even if it is, and even if they somehow managed to escape from the Morican troops, they're deserters. They failed to retreat with the rest of Sechland's forces. If they are ever found here in Visk, I'll have no choice but to arrest them. It's too bad. Gar did a commendable job on the battlefield holding his corner before the square collapsed."

In an instant, all of her hopes were dashed. "Then...he can never come home?"

"I'm afraid not."

It was too much. The tears came in a flood. The lieutenant rose and guided her to stand as well then hugged her.

"There, there, don't fret so. You brother is a strong, healthy lad. If anyone can survive, he can. There may still be a way that he can redeem himself. He may earn a pardon from my cousin, the king. Much will depend upon the outcome of this war."

Maurus pulled her away gently, his face drawn, eyes downcast. "Come, Darlee. We're late for school."

She stopped and turned to face the lieutenant. "Don't condemn my brother for wanting to live. He did only what any man might do in the heat of battle—act wrongly in fear of his life."

"I cannot change the rules. Only a king can do that. I will petition my cousin for leniency. I can offer nothing more."

Heading for the school, she took the time to dry her face. It would do no good to show up like a child with tears in her eyes. Lialee and the others would take great joy in her pain. Darlee needed to think of a plan to aid her brother in returning home, but what kind of plan, she had no idea. She didn't know where he was or even if he was still alive. She couldn't even think about going to search for him. Outside of the surrounding farmlands, she hadn't been far at all from home or the town. She wouldn't know where to begin. Even if she found Gar, she couldn't bring him home—they'd arrest him.

Her mind whirled. Why didn't Gar retreat with the rest of the men? What made him run the wrong way? She always knew her brother was not the brightest and was easily swayed. Someone else must have talked him into doing it. Jango? No, the lieutenant said Jango was hurt badly. Besides, if anything, Jango was thicker in the head than Gar.

She would wait until she got home and talked with Pap. Maybe, together, they could figure out what was best to be done.

She glanced at Maurus. His head hung while they walked. The news must have upset him. She nudged him. "Chin up. My brother will do his best to take care of Jango. You know that. They'll come home together, alive and well."

A small smile curled up Maurus' lips. "I hope you're right. I'd hate to lose my two best friends."

"We'll get them back—one way or another."

***

When dinner was over, Darlee went to the shed to meet up with her grandfather. She told him everything she'd learned that morning. "What are we going to do, Pap? Father won't even acknowledge Gar as his son anymore. Who's going to defend him?"

Pap sat for a bit, stroking his chin. "There's no changing him, that much is for sure. It's been several days since that critter cut me up, and I've had a chance to heal some. I'll head out in the morning."

84

"Head out? After Gar? No, Pap, I can't ask you to do it."

Pap snorted. "What? You think I'm too old? There's still a lot of life left in this here body of mine. Besides, in my younger days, I got to see a bit of the seven kingdoms. I can make my way around. Before all this hatred returned. Losing that war to Piaxia is what done them in. They've been squabbling ever since."

Maybe Pap *could* find Gar. If anyone could, it might be him. The job required a good hunter and tracker. Then she would deal with the second issue, getting her brother a royal pardon. "Fine, we'll leave together. While you're going after Gar, I'll go to Sechwisk and make a plea to the king. I think Lieutenant Devron will give me a letter of support. He is, after all, the king's cousin."

Pap stared at her. The silence disturbed her. *He's not going to let me go.* Despite her fears, she held his gaze.

Her grandfather stood. "I see it in you how determined you are. I think it best we get back to the house and pack. It's a long walk to Sechwisk."

CHAPTER 15

Gar stayed at the farmhouse for two days while Jango regained his strength. He used the time to fashion a large cloak with a cowl for Thunder. His mother always did the sewing, so his workmanship was far from decent. Most importantly, though, it did the job of covering the beast. He had never seen them, but he'd heard the men from the Karsargi badlands were dark in color. Hopefully the demon could pass off as a traveler from there.

For Hiss, he adjusted Jango's kit as a carrier. He notched holes in it that the demon might see and breathe. Hiss insisted he would not travel in it, but Gar explained it was the only way to get through populated areas without the creature being seen and causing a panic.

In the end, they settled on travelling off road and Hiss would only be relegated to the pack when urgency required it. In the meantime, Hiss went out each night to scout. Gar was still worried about the troops from Morica finding them.

Like he promised, Gar buried the old farmer. As he laid the tattered body in the grave, it reminded him of his own grandfather. *Is this how you end up when your family is gone?* He hurried to pile on the dirt to end the necessity of having to look at the old man.

He slaughtered two goats and, after curing the meat, packed it up with what cheeses and bread he could find. The rest of the animals he set free—there would be no one to feed them. When scouting the larder, Gar was surprised to find a stash of coins in the bottom of one jar. A large number of coppers and seventeen silver pieces. Compared to what a rich man would carry, they possessed a trifle, but he had never seen that much money in his life. He went to put it back but paused halfway through the motion. *Who would it hurt to keep it? The old man is dead. This money could come in handy on the way home. It could buy food and lodgings along the way.* He pocketed the purse then finished his raiding.

On the third day, they set out at dawn. Hiss skittered in the lead, with Gar and Jango following, and Thunder trailed behind. They walked for a hand of the sun before Gar realized where they were headed. "Stop. We're going the wrong way. You're leading us south. Sechland is to the northwest."

Hiss bounced over. "Yes. South. Safe way. Too many scouts along border. Hiss see. Go safe. Go south, then west."

Jango shrugged. "If he knows a safer way, then I suppose it's best to follow him. It's not like Sechland is at war with Fermia. We're just travelers passing through, as long as we stay away from those Morica men."

"I suppose you're right. All right, Hiss. If you say there are troops to—avoid—on."

They trudged the whole day and didn't turn west until a couple of hands before dusk. When evening fell, they found themselves outside the limits of a country hamlet. Tired, Gar decided they would back off a little and set up camp in a copse they'd passed a short time before.

As Gar entered the thicket, he could hear the voices of people passing near. He spied four men walking and cajoling one another as their odd bursts of laughter warranted out. Their chatter was unimportant to him, but he did hear one mention they were going to the hamlet inn for a few drinks.

When they'd safely passed, he nudged Jango. "Come on. Let's go down to that inn for a bit. There's no better place to hear the news. Maybe we can find out if there's any word about the war between Morica and us." He turned to Hiss and Thunder. "You two stay here. Stay out of sight."

Thunder stretched out on the ground and, in an instant, appeared asleep. Hiss fretted back and forth. "Master stay. Not safe."

"I'll be fine. If we're not back in a couple of hands, come looking for us."

He led the way out of the trees and headed off after the four men.

Jango stayed close. "I hope you know what you're doing."

"Don't worry. It's only a village inn. There won't be any troops around, and if we do get into trouble, Thunder can take care of anyone who threatens us."

"Thunder's asleep. Hiss may be soon. What if they don't wake up?"

He laughed. "Don't let Thunder fool you. I've seen him too many times already to know he never really goes to sleep. He pretends. He'll be there in a flash, if need be."

It made him feel good to know the big demon was on his side. A few days before, the creature had terrified him. Now he regarded the monster as his personal bodyguard. How things changed.

Soon he and Jango arrived at the door to the inn. The sound of boisterous laughter inside bolstered his courage, and Gar led the way in. When they entered, the noise faded as almost every head in the place turned to see him enter. All told, he counted some thirty-odd people in the place. Under the stares of most of them, he made his way to a small table and sat down. Jango followed suit.

A heavyset woman came over. "Ignore the locals. We don't get strangers much in these parts. Where are you lads from?"

Gar fought the initial temptation to tell the truth and say Sechland, but his judgment got the better of him. "Storburg. We're just heading home. Can we get a couple of pints of mead?"

"Sure. Coming right up." The woman retreated behind a counter then returned with two mugs. "That'll be two coppers. Storburg, eh? You're less than a day's journey then, provided there's no trouble at the border."

Gar produced the purse and handed her the coins. "Trouble? What kind of trouble?"

"You've not heard then? I suppose not. The rider passed through here yesterday with the news. Seems Sechland, Morica, and Storburg are fighting. Three days ago, a battle raged between Morica and Sechland. Then Morican forces crossed into Storburg and got into a tussle with some of the boys over there. After that, they crossed the river and entered Fermia. They claim they were chasing the men who attacked them. What a load of rubbish. None of our boys have been called to duty." She turned to the table next where the four men who'd passed their camp sat. "Right, fellahs?"

It was then Gar noticed the men were watching and listening.

The closest one nodded. "Right, Trude. Me and the boys would have been called up for sure. We're on alert now. The higher ups don't want to call us to arms just yet. But you never know. The way I heard the story, them Morican boys were right pissed. Seems whoever killed their men messed them up really bad."

The man was talking about Thunder, but Gar couldn't resist asking, "What do you mean?"

"Hacked them up, they did——into pieces. That's why they're so mad."

An old man sitting at the counter got up and came over, wagging a finger at them. "It's demons, I tell ya, demons. Them's what done the killing. It's like in the old stories. They had a savagery about em, they did. Ta feed their hunger. They live on pain and suffering."

The man at the table chuckled. "Gramps, don't go telling those old tales anymore. Those are for children. These lads are too old for that." He gave Gar a wink. "Aren't you, gents?"

Gar took a long drink from his mead. "I agree."

The man got up and guided the storyteller back to his seat. "See? Save those tales for your grandchildren. I've been down by the demon stone a thousand times. It's just a rock carved up with some writing, that's all."

The old man sat down. "Don't say I didn't warn ya. Ya remember this when they come ta eat ya soul."

The man laughed and returned to his seat. "Don't pay him no mind. He's been saying that for years."

Gar was intrigued about there being another stone somewhere nearby. "So there's a demon stone around here? I remember the tale about how the demons were locked up inside them. I'd like to see it."

The man snorted. "Not you, too? It's just a day's travel down the road. You can't miss it. Right near the Storburg border. Listen, demons are the last thing you need to worry about. It was a hundred years ago when that warlock from Piaxia trapped them all in stone. What was his name?..."

89

One of the others at the table nudged him. "Bron."

"Bron. Yeah, that was it. Thank the gods there are none of the likes of him around anymore. But enough of ancient history. The road's a dangerous place for two young travelers such as you. It's a lucky thing you made it here to Trude's place. I'm sure she's got a nice room to let for the night, where you can sleep safe and sound."

Jango finished his mead and banged down his mug. "No, we're fine. We have a camp set in the trees back up the road a ways."

Gar wanted to tell him to shut up. The look exchanged between the men at the next table worried him. "Perhaps it's time to go. If there might be problems at the border, then it would be best to get there quickly before things get worse."

He pulled Jango up by the elbow, and they went out the door. When they were out of earshot, he punched Jango in the shoulder. "You idiot. Don't go telling people where we camped. Let's hope none of them are thinking about trying to rob us."

They made it back and found Thunder in the same spot as when they left. Hiss was nowhere to be seen. He must have been busy, though. A nice fire glowed in the middle of the camp. Gar called out for him, but to no avail. *The little bugger is out scouting around again. I don't think he sleeps.*

He and Jango laid out their bedrolls near the fire. Not tired yet, he sat and poked a stick into the flames.

Jango was also sitting, with his knees tucked up under his chin. "What do you think, Gar? Are we going to get home, okay? Are the Fermia guards going to arrest us? Or the Storburg ones? This has been a nightmare from the start."

"I don't know. I never paid much attention in class when they discussed the politics of the seven realms. I know Storburg is friends with Sechland and I think Fermia is neutral. The other kingdoms, Braxburrow, Queensland, and Gatway, I haven't the foggiest. Piaxia to the north is friends to none, and neither are the Karsargi in the west. That's about it. I remember the map in school, and there's no way we can get back into Sechland from Fermia without crossing into either Storburg or Morica on the way.

We know Morica's out, so staying south until we hit Storburg seems like the right idea."

"Yeah, I suppose. Still, I can't help but get the feeling your little friend there is leading us the wrong way. I mean, why did we have to go so far south into Fermia before heading west? Seems to me we could have saved a day."

He thought about Hiss. So far, the demon had been faithful, even if it had resulted in the death of Wirbon. No, he'd trust the imp until convinced otherwise. "I'll take my chances following him. For now. Besides, I don't know the countryside around here and, I think, neither do you."

"Well, good night."

Jango lay down and his breathing slowed into the steady rhythm of sleep. Gar toyed with the fire for a little while longer then decided maybe it was time he got some shut-eye. Stretching out on his back, he contemplated all that happened. The fear that Jango expressed about never getting home weighed heavily on his mind. The idea of never seeing his sister again, or Pap, for that matter, disturbed him and kept him awake.

A rustle across the open fire caught his attention as Thunder leapt up and dashed into the darkness of the woods. He sat up and stared into the night. *Where's he off to?* A moment later, he could hear a rustling from behind him. He stood in time to see the four men they followed to the inn enter the campsite.

The one he'd spoken with stepped nearest. "Here you are, young travelers. I see all is well. Me and the lads thought we'd check up on you before calling it a night."

"You mean...you aren't here to rob us?"

He and the other men laughed. "Rob you? Hardly. We're the local guard. I thought you understood when Trude mentioned we hadn't been called up. We're here to protect you. When your friend made mention of where you camped, we thought it best to see you were okay. Seeing that, we'll be on our way."

Thunder charged in from behind the men and killed two of them in an instant by slashing through them with his claws. The third tried to run, but it took the beast one step to catch the man and tear his head off. The one who'd spoken backed up to block

Gar. "By the gods, a demon." He drew his sword. "Stay behind me. I'll defend you."

Gar felt stupefied. *I must stop this.* "No, Thunder, don't kill him!"

The man spun to face Gar, surprise etched across his face, his eyes wide. "You know this monster?"

Thunder closed the gap, and reaching round, tore the man's throat out. In a shower of blood, he collapsed. Gar dropped and tried to stem the flow of blood, but the man's struggles soon ceased. Gar felt the flush of anger mount in him as he rose. "Why'd you kill them? They meant no harm." He pounded on Thunder's chest. "You can't kill everyone. You must stop it. Stop it now!"

Thunder grabbed him and held him tight. The beast's eyes were darting back and forth, scanning the woods. *He still thinks he's protecting me.*

Jango woke during the commotion. "Gar, what's happening?"

More innocent people dead at the hand of Thunder. First the old farmer and now these men. His fury abated, and he wilted. Thunder let him down to sit on the ground.

Another noise announced the return of Hiss. The imp came close and turned Gar's head left and right as he stared. "Master hurt?"

There must have been blood all over him. He wiped at his face. "No, Hiss. I'm fine. Look round you. It's these other men that are dead. Thunder killed them all despite my asking him not to."

Hiss bounded over to Thunder and the two engaged in a conversation in their own language. After some time, Hiss faced Gar once more. "Thunder apologizes. He trouble common tongue. No understand. He see sword—attack. He promise no more kill unless Master say so."

Gar cringed at the sight of the fallen men. "We should leave now before someone comes looking for them."

Hiss spoke to Thunder, who began to pick up the bodies. "Master need rest. Thunder hide bodies. We go first light. Sleep now."

92

Gar's eyelids felt heavy. Hiss was right. He would not be able to walk far without some sleep. He crawled over to his rig and, after finding a cloth to wipe clean off as much of the blood as possible, pulled his blanket over him. He would worry about things in the morning.

CHAPTER 16

Lieutenant Devron walked the walls of Visk, examining the fortifications, but with little attention as his thoughts plagued him. Why was the king so anxious for war? Was Captain Brusk correct in his judgment? To what end must he go in his duties as a soldier?

Brusk was clearly wavering. His insubordination combined with his dedication to duty made strange bedfellows. He found it a dichotomy within the captain. He didn't know whether to take the man's orders seriously or not. That he be the last one, not to leave the city, no matter what orders arrive, was the most confusing. What if his cousin should demand he march? Would he defy the king? In the days since Brusk left, a similar order was suggested by the city elders—one in which he decidedly refused.

The defense of the city was his paramount concern. But what good such a defense if its citizens were to be used as target practice for Morica's horsemen? The confusion of command weighed heavily on him.

His examination brought him to the south wall. He stared out in the distance toward Sechwisk. He wondered whether the girl Darlee completed the traverse there, his letter in her hand, or whether invading marauders had waylaid her on the open road. Such was the plight of many in wartime.

He sighed. He needed to attend to his own evils. He headed for the jail.

Interrogating prisoners was an unsightly business. He entered the building and made his way to where the man was being questioned. As he neared the door, the screams of agony from within assailed him. Stepping in, the smell of burnt flesh accosted his nostrils. The man was strapped to a large metal chair. Several hot iron marks showed on his naked body. A number of his fingernails were torn out, the exposed flesh bruised and blood encrusted.

Devron greeted the interrogator. "Anything?"

"Nothing, Lieutenant. He continues to claim he was only to report our movements."

He approached the man whose head hung limp against his chest. He lifted the man's chin to stare into his eyes. "I can end this suffering if you answer me truthfully. Who killed the lad Wirbon, the son of merchant, Trellus? Was it you?"

The man grimaced and spat blood on the floor. "Not me."

"You have not answered my first question. To date, you have only been subject to superficial wounds that would heal in time. If I cannot get the answer I want, we will be forced to begin to remove parts of your body—fingers, toes, limbs, until you are no more. Do you want that to happen to you?"

The man cried, the tears streaking through the dirt and ashes on his cheeks. "I don't know. I don't know! Our orders were to track movements, nothing else. I don't know who killed him."

The man continued to sob uncontrollably. Devron stood and watched.

After a period of time, the man who was to exact the torture stepped closer. "Lieutenant?"

He took a deep breath. The decision in front of him was a distasteful one, but he needed to know for sure. "The left hand."

The eyes of the prisoner widened and he began to struggle against his bonds. "No! Not my hand! No! Please, I don't know! Not my hand!" His sobbing continued as he struggled in vain.

The torturer lifted a large axe above the man's wrist. The additional smell of urine filled the air as the man lost control of his bladder. The blade crashed down with a resounding thunk as the metal bit all the way through to the table. The man screamed in pain then passed out.

He does not know. "Return him to his cell and tend to his wounds. I will investigate this matter further."

"Yes, Lieutenant."

Outside, he stopped to breathe in the fresh air. Such punishment was an affront to his values, but an evil necessity. Still, he felt unclean. Better to kill a man face-to-face on the battlefield than resort to such atrocities as he just witnessed.

Devron headed for the barracks. He held no doubt the prisoner was not involved in the killing of the merchant's son. There were none left in the city that could have done the deed. It was an unsolved mystery that perplexed him. Knowing the defenses of the merchant's estate, the only remaining possibility was the lad killed by his own father. That did not make any sense. He was stymied.

When he entered the barracks, his second approached. "Lieutenant, you're wanted at the gatehouse. They're holding someone for you there."

He turned about and began the short trek to the city entrance. When he got there, he was greeted by one of the gate guards.

"He's tied up inside. Tried to sneak in with a caravan of farmers but we weeded him out."

He entered the gatehouse to find a bound man sitting on the floor. "Well, well, well, if it isn't my estranged soldier, Baxus. Come for a return visit to jail? Captain Brusk erred in letting you out."

"I got a full pardon. You can't arrest me again."

"Oh, but I can. It's called desertion. You abandoned your position in the line—the first to do so, if I recall. Under military law, I can have you executed on the spot. Where are your compatriots who ran after you?"

"If you mean those two kids, they're probably demon food by now."

The answer so surprised him, he could not respond right away. He scrutinized the man as he weighed what he'd heard. "Demon food?"

"Yeah, demon food. Your boy Gar, there—seems he has a couple not-so-nice friends. Demons. One little one that can scamper all over without being seen, and one big one with claws that can rip a man to shreds in seconds."

"That's impossible. There have been no demons for a hundred years. I don't know what you hope to achieve by such a lie."

"My life for the details. You know the law of the seven realms. No magic. Once the other kingdoms learn someone from Sechland has released demons through magic, they will unite and attack in force."

The temptation to pull his sword and run the man through was tough to resist. Would Baxus stop at nothing in an effort to escape the gallows? "I say you lie, but I will spare you until I can prove it, for if you are telling the truth, then we are all doomed. You will say nothing of this to anyone until then, or I will have no choice but to expedite your execution."

Devron ordered one of the guards to take Baxus to the prison. He then set out for the town hall. There he hoped to find the records necessary to help him sort out the nonsense Baxus spewed.

When he arrived, none of the city elders were present. *Good. I won't need to answer a whole bunch of fool questions.* He chased down a clerk. He didn't want to reveal his true purpose so he decided to skirt round the question. "I want to see the town records about the demon wars. I want to review the defenses used and the strategies of the day."

"Right this way, Lieutenant."

The clerk led him to a back room where many of the town's records were kept. Sitting at a table, he waited as the clerk retrieved a number of tomes, maps, and charts. The drawings depicting the military movements were quite fascinating, and in truth he spent more time than he should have gazing at them. Many hands passed as he studied the various tomes.

Like so many, to him, the demon wars were ancient history. The texts told of how a consortium of warlocks from the seven realms combined their magic and created a rift deep into the bedrock in search of the source of the Key, an energy that multiplied their magical powers many fold. Instead, they opened a gateway into a netherworld and a number of demons escaped onto the surface. The mages were slain by the demons that then rampaged across the countryside, killing many and putting the rest to flight. After the arrival of Bron, a young warlock from Piaxia, the rift was closed and the demons defeated.

Since then, the different kingdoms of the seven realms blamed each other for what occurred, and their peaceful coexistence was shattered. The only thing they agreed upon was the banishment of magic so such a thing could never happen again. When he reviewed the actual treaty, known as the Warlock Pact, it read that if any of the seven should engage in the dark arts, the others would unite and obliterate the offender.

Much of this he knew from childhood tales. What he needed to find was a way to confirm or refute the tale from Baxus. In one of the maps, he found his answer. It showed the location of all the demon stones. There were two in Sechland. One was near the homestead of the young girl who'd visited him.

He took the map and headed for the barracks. Checking the sky, there were only a couple of hands before it would be dark. *I've got enough time. I won't sleep well tonight if I don't find out what I need to know.*

Ordering horses, he took three men with him and rode out to where the map guided. In almost a hundred years, little change had occurred in the way of road markers. He followed the map easily enough. They crossed over some recently planted farmland to the creek and the lowlands lying near it. Bringing his horse to a stop, he alit near the middle of the lea by a jumble of piled rocks. *Could this be it? The breaks in these rocks do look fresh. But where are the markings?* He moved the pieces of rock aside in an effort to find the base of the stone. When he cleared enough, he could see them. Doubtless, this was a demon stone, or what was left of it.

Dusk was settling over the land. He mounted his horse and rode to the top of a nearby hill, where he spotted a farmhouse in the distance. He motioned to his men to follow. "Come. Let us find out whose farm this is."

He rode over and was met by a man, standing on the porch, holding a horse switch.

"Who are you and what do you want?"

"Good farmer, I am Lieutenant Devron. Surely you must recognize the insignia of your home town of Visk?"

"I recognize it. I haven't done anything wrong, so what are you doing here?"

He grimaced at the disrespect. "I only wanted to verify to whom this farm belongs. I take it to be yours. May I have your name?"

"The name's Murdach, and yes, this is my farm. Now be off with you."

"Murdach? I had a soldier in my company named Garlin Murdach. Your son?"

"I have no son."

No son? "Then what of Darlee Murdach? Is she your daughter?"

"You've seen Darlee? Where is she?"

"I would imagine somewhere halfway to Sechwisk by now. She left yesterday morn with my letter in her hand to petition the king on behalf of her brother, Garlin. You were not aware of this?"

The man reddened. "I think you best be going. I told you before, I haven't got a son, and now it sounds like I haven't got a daughter either."

He paused to take stock of the situation. What did the father know of the broken demon stone? Was he aware of the freeing of the creature? These were questions he could not leave unanswered. He nodded to the three guardsmen. "Take him. I will question him back at the prison. The day is soon gone and I would prefer to return to the city."

His troops dismounted and arrested the farmer. The man struggled some but was no match for the soldiers. They tied him up and tossed him across one of the horses.

A woman, most likely the farmer's wife, came out of the house. She came straight to Devron and grabbed his leg.

"No, please, good sir, don't take him. He's all I have left." She began to weep.

He reached down and pried her away. "You will have him back soon. I only intend to question him. There are things I need answered, and I cannot delay in knowing."

He whistled and spurred his mount. "Let's go."

The others fell in behind. He would get to the bottom of this thing before the night was through.

CHAPTER 17

It took the entire day and then some for Gar and the others to reach the border with Storburg because they decided to avoid the road and go cross-country. Although it was already into the second hand of the moon, he could see the border because of the lit watchtowers. Spaced some hundred paces apart on the far side of the Lorne River, they would do little to expose a solitary figure trying to sneak across, but any large group would sure to be spotted.

He stood in the dark some five hundred paces away trying to decide what to do—cross over at the bridge, which was guarded, or make an attempt somewhere further down the way.

Jango nudged him. "Look at all those fires. They can't have those burning all the time, can they?"

"You heard those men last night. Storburg has mobilized. They're going to be guarding the border closely until things sort out."

"So what are we going to do?"

"I'm thinking you and I take our chances and cross at the road. Thunder will have to swim. Hiss can hide in the pack. If we try and sneak across and they catch us, our uniforms won't protect us. They'll think we're spies."

"You think they'll let us cross?"

"Sure. Storburg and Sechland are allies. Why wouldn't they let us cross?"

"I wasn't thinking about them. I was wondering about Fermia's guards. Won't they be around somewhere, too?"

Gar hadn't thought about that. There were sure to be guards on this side of the border as well. Those men also said Fermia was on alert, just not called to arms. "Maybe it's best if we all sneak across after all."

"But what if we get caught trying? Will they still treat us as allies?"

"I don't know, but we have to try."

A tug on his cloak proved to be Hiss. "Master, you forget stone. Free demon there. Get you across."

The demon stone. It *had* slipped his mind. The day-long drudgery through deep grasses and gnarled woods had cleared it from his thoughts. "That man said it was by the road near the border. We'll be seen if we go there."

"Not so close, Master. Not so close. Hiss show."

"Lead the way."

Jango grabbed at his arm. "Another demon, Gar? Are you sure?"

He paused. He wasn't sure of anything. The demons helped, that was for sure. They were also the cause of a lot of his problems. Maybe Jango had a point. "Hold up, Hiss. I'm unsure another one of you is the answer."

Hiss smiled. "Master happy this one. Very happy. Best demon for man. You see. Come. Come."

What is Hiss on about? Intrigued, he wavered for a moment then waved Jango forward. "Come on, let's get it over with. If Hiss says I'll be happy, I'm going to believe him."

They followed Hiss toward the road. Like the imp said, the stone was still some distance from the road, at least three hundred paces, if not farther. Unlike the stone back on his farm Hiss emerged from—and not at all like the rock wall that held Thunder—this one had the appearance of a carved obelisk. Its edges were smooth and a swirling pattern ran through it.

Gar took a deep breath then stepped forward and placed his hands on the stone. "Okay, Hiss, do your stuff."

The imp climbed up and put a hand on Gar's forehead. "Master think open."

Gar concentrated on opening the stone. He grimaced at the expected pain but was surprised to find it to be far less than previous times.

An opening appeared and spread slowly, the stone crumbling in fine pieces as the gap grew. Stepping out from the opening was the very shapely figure of a woman. In fact, excessively so, and her simple pull-over short dress with a belt cinching it at her waist did little to cover her. She was tall, almost his own height. Her hips

101

swayed as she moved and the large, rounded breasts above her slim waist held his attention. She surprised, yet excited him. Like Hiss and Thunder, her skin was dark slate grey and hairless. Also, the same black eyes, but set in a beautiful face. She smiled at Gar, revealing white pointed teeth.

Hiss scrambled to the ground. "See, Master? Master happy?"

The woman sashayed up to Gar. "So what have we here? A handsome young man as my savior? Fate has been kind to send you to my rescue." Playing across his chest, her hand featured the same pointed fingers as her brethren.

Gar let go of the stone. "You—you speak well."

She laughed, a tinkling sound, like chimes in the wind. "Of course I do. What is your name, my hero?"

"Garlin. My friends call me Gar."

"Gar—a good, rugged name. I'm pleased to meet you and…" her gaze fell below his waist, "I can see that you are just as pleased as well."

Gar glanced down. A flush heated in his cheeks as he tried to hide what embarrassed him. "I'm sorry."

"Don't be. If I didn't elicit such a response, I would have thought I'd lost my touch. It pleases me to know you find me sexually attractive." She examined her body and cupped one of her breasts in one hand. "Still, I cannot go around like this. You have something better that I can wear, I hope?"

Gar fumbled with his own cloak and finally pulled it free. "Here, take my cloak for now. I'll make another later."

She took the cloak and donned it then ran a hand over Gar's army-issued shirt. "A military man, I see. You must be a strong one." She leaned forward and stuck out a long, pointed tongue to lick his ear. "I look forward to finding out how strong."

With his cloak covering her, Gar managed to regain a measure of control. "Listen, Hiss says you can get us past the guards down the road there. Can you?"

The demoness nodded toward the small demon. "Hiss, you call him? What a delightful moniker." She knelt and rubbed a hand over Hiss's head. She spoke in the same snarling language Gar heard Hiss use, but hers came out in a softer, soothing way. Hiss replied in his own rasping tone.

She went over to the large demon and placed a hand on its chest. "And this one?"

"I call him Thunder."

Making a fist, she gave a light thump to the beast's torso. "Fitting. Subtlety was never his way."

She returned to stand before Gar. "And what about me? Have you coined an appropriate name?"

He thought about it for a moment. "Silk. You come across that way."

She gave the same tinkling laugh. "Silk. I like it. It will do."

Silk spun and stopped when she was facing the lit watchtowers. "Now, what is it you need me to do?"

"We suspect there are two sets of guards on this roadway—one from Fermia, and on the far side of the bridge, Storburg. We need to get by them without being arrested *and* without Thunder killing them."

She glanced at the large demon. "Too bad, he enjoys it so. Still, I can understand the desire to go unnoticed. The one you call Thunder has a propensity of drawing a crowd, and not exactly the friendly type. The last time I saw him, he was running from a thousand men."

"What difference would it make it if was a thousand, or a hundred thousand? He seems unbeatable."

"Unbeatable, yes, but uncatchable, no. They do not need to kill him to defeat him. Properly bound, he would be of no threat."

Gar wondered how many men it would take to physically subdue the monster. He also wondered how many would die in trying. "I see."

"Now, as to the men ahead. I will go first, and you and the others follow. Stay behind me, as the aura I will release would affect not only them, but you and your skinny little friend."

She shed the cloak. "Be a sweet thing and hold this for me."

Seeing her scantily clad body once more revived the primal urges within him. He held the cloak to cover his predicament. "Will do."

103

Silk started down the road, Gar and the rest some fifteen paces behind. It was not long before they came upon two men seated outside a small guardhouse. The pair rose as Silk neared. The one closest held up a hand and drew his sword. "Stop and name your— by the gods, you're a beauty!"

The sword in the man's hand wavered. He dropped the weapon with a clank on the road and fell to his knees. "Take me— please, please, take me." The other man followed suit, crying out something similar.

Silk paused between them and the men crowded close, grasping at her breasts, her thighs, and anywhere else their hands could find purchase. "Easy now, boys. There's plenty of me to go round."

Gar became angry. *She should not let them touch her so.*

The men then collapsed one by one to the hard surface of the roadway. When both had succumbed, Silk motioned him forward. "Both have passed out. Bring me my cloak so we can continue."

Gar stepped between the fallen men and passed her the cloak. "What happened to them?"

Silk was sheathed in a subtle glow. "I feasted on their will. They surrendered to their carnal desires, at first, which made it easier for me, then the will to stay awake. It's what I do. They will wake come morning with nasty headaches and strange memories of what happened."

"That's the second time I've seen that glow. Thunder had it when he came back from killing a number of men from Morica. Does he feast on will as well?"

"Thunder?" She chuckled. "Thunder feeds on life force. He rips it out of them."

Silk faced the Storburg border. The bridge was perhaps two hundred paces across and, in the light of the towers, they could see a larger guard house and a number of men stationed there. "Now, what? There are too many men over there. I can't subdue them all. I could only weaken them."

"No. Jango and I will cross on our own. Storburg is our ally. Besides, I would not want to see them manhandle you so, like the last ones."

Silk smiled and kissed his cheek. "Is my hero jealous? I promise to make it up to you. Have no worry about me. I can use my powers to insure my own passage, but what about the others?"

"Hiss will hide in Jango's kit. It's only Thunder I worry about. He's so big, he's sure to draw attention. He'll have to swim across somewhere between the towers."

"I'm not so sure of this plan of yours. The ways of men are never so plain. But if you say all will be fine then we shall meet on the other side."

Gar spoke to the behemoth, and Hiss, after some complaining, climbed into the pack after admitting to feeling tired. Thunder disappeared into the night. *Maybe Silk is right and they won't let us pass. No. I have to believe they will. We need their assistance to get the rest of the way home.*

Silk stepped in front of them. "Let me go first. I will pass easily when on my own."

Gar watched her glide toward the outpost on the far side of the bridge. He followed close enough to be able to see her at a distance. She reached the gatehouse and hardly paused as she walked past the guards. In a moment, she had disappeared into the shadows beyond. *Now that's a skill worth having.*

He nodded to Jango. "Let's go."

They strode forward and soon came to the Storburg guard post where a dozen or so men stood round a large oil lamp. An officer stepped before them. "Who are you and where are you going?"

Gar was nervous, but smiled and offered his hand. "Greetings. My friend and I were separated from the troop. We're hoping to make our way home to Sechland. Can you assist us with directions?"

"Separated?" He looked over to the men standing near. "Arrest them."

Gar was encircled by a number of men who grabbed him roughly and dragged him forward. Another group was doing the same to Jango. "What? No. We're Sechlanders. We're your allies. Can't you see our uniforms?"

"All I see is a couple of deserters. Reports are the Sechland army has gathered outside of its capital, Sechwisk. The reason you're not with them is obvious."

"That's not true. We were with the army when it attacked Morence. When the call for retreat sounded, we made the mistake of running south into Fermia."

"So, you admit to your desertion. It'll be the hangman's noose for the both of you."

Gar glanced at all the faces of the Storburg soldiers. He did not like what he saw. They were all set in grim countenances. "You've got it all wrong. We didn't desert. We didn't. We didn't."

The man cuffed him with force, the copper taste of blood surfacing in his mouth.

"Silence. Another word and I'll cut your throat right here."

The sound of a struggle behind him had Gar turning to see a man wrestling the kit from Jango. As he pulled it free, Hiss popped out and slashed the man's face. He landed on the ground and scampered off after Silk.

The officer approached Jango and struck him hard in the head. "What, by the gods, was that?"

Jango collapsed and hung in the arms of the men who held him.

The officer returned to stand before Gar. "You, then. Tell me what manner of creature was in that kit?"

From behind the officer, the large form of Thunder appeared out of the darkness. He pointed over the man's shoulder. "His little brother, and now you've made him angry."

The man turned in time to see Thunder descend on him, and the demon rip his head off in one stroke. The other men all reached for their weapons as Thunder charged through their midst, killing as he went. In close pursuit came Hiss, stabbing at legs and harassing any who were near. The slaughter didn't last long. In a matter of moments, Thunder killed eight of them. Two tried to run but ran straight into Silk who subdued them in her own fashion. Another two escaped into the darkness of the night.

Gar roused Jango. "Come on. We've got to get out of here."

Hiss was busy running from downed man to downed man placing a hand on their heads. "Master, wait. Hiss must feed. Need mana from dead before gone. Hiss use all up help master open last stone."

After he helped Jango to stand, Gar waited for several moments until Hiss finished. Like Thunder and Silk, the imp sported a gentle glow.

Jango fell in step as Gar began walking. "So what now? We can't go back to Fermia. They'll be after us here in Storburg once those two sound the alarm, and it appears we can't go home without getting arrested."

He glanced at Silk who walked beside him, Thunder, who trailed behind, and Hiss who scampered in the lead. "I don't know, Jango. I just don't know."

CHAPTER 18

Brusk surveyed the field. The letter from Lieutenant Devron updating him was scrunched in his hand. His men had been camped outside the walls of Sechwisk for days now and none too happy. *Why are we sitting out here? The king must have lost his mind.*

He turned to his lieutenant. "Put the men through some training paces. I'm going in to see what in blazes is going on."

He'd started toward the main gate when the familiar cry of the raven made him gaze skyward. "Yeah, you can come, ya crazy bird."

The animal became more attached to him as the days passed, to the point where it would perch on his shoulder, a post it now took. He stroked the bird's plumage. "Just don't make a scene when we get in there. I don't need them thinking I'm as crazy as they are." *Listen to who's talking. Me to a stupid raven.*

He marched past the guard at the gate and headed for the palace. At the entrance to the citadel he was halted by the royal guard. "State your business, Captain. The king is indisposed right now. I will deliver your message."

He debated whether to have the man inform the king he was crazy but thought better of it. There was a limit to arrogance even he knew couldn't be crossed. "Where's Purmin? I want to speak with him?"

"I believe the commander is in the map room. If you like, I can take you there."

"Never mind that. I know the way."

The raven took the moment to shriek at the guard. Brusk chuckled. "That's telling him." He stepped past the man. "Outta the way. I'm in a hurry."

He continued through the main hall until he came to the map room. As informed, he found the commander giving orders to a couple of riders. Brusk found a seat and waited until the men were sent on their various deliveries and only the commander and a couple of his lieutenants remained.

"Alright, Captain. I see you waiting there. What do you want?"

Brusk stood. "I'm wondering whether you really have any idea what in the name of the gods is going on here."

The man purpled and stepped over to a spacious map table. "Come over here, Brusk. Tell me what you see."

Brusk approached the table. The map showed the four kingdoms of Sechland, Storburg, Fermia, and Morica. Placed on the board were a large number of pieces representing the armies of all four with most of the pieces in close proximity to one another. "It looks like all four are about to get real stupid and go to war."

He wondered whether his superior officer could get any redder, and it didn't take long to get his answer as the tips of the man's ears crimsoned.

"If it were not for the fact we're about to enter battle and knowing your skill as a captain as a result of your many, many years of service, I would have you removed from duty, but I can't, so let me explain it to you.

"Morica made a mistake when they attacked the Storburg border post right after their battle with us. As a result, Storburg renewed their pledge of allegiance and is prepared to fight at our side. News came a few nights ago of how everyone at another border post between Storburg and Fermia was slaughtered. Fermia is claiming innocence but they have since mobilized as well. Being stuck in the middle as they are, with Morica to the north of them, Storburg to the west, and the three southern kingdoms below them, they want to protect their status as neutrals. That means, when it comes to a fight, it'll be us and Storburg combined against Morica. That's two against one. The odds are in our favor. We've only been waiting until the Storburg troops were ready to go. The king's order to march should come any day now."

Brusk scratched at the stubble on his chin. "The way I see it, it could become six to one—against us."

The raven lifted off from his shoulder, landed on the table, and began to peck at the pieces representing Sechland's forces.

Purmin swiped at the bird, missed, and slapped his hand hard against the table, causing many of the pieces to tumble. "Are you daft, man? Everything is in play for a victory for Sechland."

The raven reseated on Brusk's shoulder. He threw the crumpled note onto the table in front of his senior officer. "Then maybe you'd better be reading this. I just received it this morning. Seems we have a warlock in our midst. Worst of all, the fellow has been releasing demons from the stones. Demons! You know what that means, don't you? The Warlock Pact kicks in. Our country is to be purged of all those wielding magic. For that to happen means only one thing, invasion by all the others."

The man grabbed the paper and scanned its contents. The color in the commander's face, so vivid only a moment before, drained away. "This...this is impossible! No one has trained in the dark arts in Sechland for a century."

"Trained or not, it's happened. My lieutenant has verified it. The demon stone near Visk has been breached. If Morica discovers the same thing about the one near Morence, then the truth will get out."

"The king must be told right away."

"That was my intention, but *his royal highness* does not wish to be disturbed. I figured you'd be the man to do it."

Purmin blanched even further. "No, you do it. I'll get you the audience. Meet me in the throne room in short order."

"As you wish." Brusk retrieved the note from the commander's hand and headed out to wait near the throne room. He chuckled. Purmin was afraid of the king.

When he arrived, he found a number of people waiting outside the doors. *Citizens with their petitions to be heard. A fat lot of good begging the king's favor is going to be now.* He was about to step to the front of the line when he noticed an old man and a young girl resting against the wall. He recognized them and went over. They spotted him coming and rose as he neared. He approached the young lady first. "Darlee Murdach, isn't it?"

"Yes, Captain. My grandfather and I have been waiting a couple of days to present a petition to the king."

Brusk held out his hand. "You better let me see that petition."

"Yes, certainly. Here it is."

Brusk read it quickly then handed it back. "I think waiting in this line is the wrong thing to do."

"Why? Do you think you can get us in to see the king quicker?"

The poor girl. She doesn't know. "Quite the opposite. I want to save you from him and the wrath he'll take out on you."

"I-I don't understand."

"Believe me, it's for the best. Go to my camp—quickly. Tell my lieutenant there to put you in my own tent and not to let anyone near you, understand?" He pulled out a scrap of paper and scratched a quick note. "Here's my authority for you. I haven't time to explain things right now. I've got my own meeting with the king. Do what I say and do it quickly. It may mean your lives."

Behind him, he could hear the double doors to the throne room open and a voice called his name. He glanced quickly then returned his attention to the Murdachs. Darlee's expression was one of despair. "There's no more time. Go."

They scurried off and he spun to find a sentry approaching. "Captain Brusk, your presence is required by his majesty. Do not tarry."

The raven squawked, startling the sentry, who stepped back a pace.

"Don't worry, he doesn't bite. Lead the way."

The man led Brusk past the waiting people, into the throne room. Two other sentries pulled the doors closed behind them.

The king sat on his throne, appearing somewhat disheveled, as if he'd dressed in a hurry. "Come forward, Captain. Commander Purmin informs me you have urgent news that cannot wait. I sincerely hope, for your sake, that is true."

"Yes, Your Majesty, bad news indeed. An investigation into things back at Visk by Lieutenant Devron has revealed a warlock in our midst, who has, of all things, re-released demons into the world. Here is his note attesting to the facts." He handed the note to an attendant, who scurried up to the throne and handed it to the king.

111

Lowry took a moment to peruse the document. Everyone in the hall was silent as he read. Finally, he took a deep breath then folded the note and slipped it inside his pocket. "Thank you, Captain. You may return to your troops. Please be sure as to their readiness. I expect things to escalate soon."

"Begging your pardon, but what about the demons? What about this lad from my town? What about the Warlock Pact?"

"You shouldn't concern yourself with those things. There is no sighting of demons on the loose, no witnesses to the use of magic."

"But the letter...Devron's investigation?"

The king sighed. "My cousin is ever so much the honest soldier, a trait that has its consequences. The letter is merely another example of his zeal to perform. We shall proceed as planned. This audience has ended. Return to your camp."

Dismissed. Brusk controlled the temper flaring in him and held his tongue from blurting out what a fool the king was. It was one thing to criticize the man when in other company, but to do so directly would be going too far, even for him. "Yes, Your Majesty."

He turned to go. The sentries opened the doors, letting him out, and closed them with a thud behind him when he cleared the room. He noted all the expectant faces of the people waiting for an audience. *They're doomed and they don't know it.*

He exited the castle and made straight for his camp. *I hope the girl and her grandfather were smart enough to do what I said. More than likely some scribe wrote down their request for a petition to be heard. I have to get them out of here quick.*

He entered the part of the field where his men were stationed and was met immediately by his lieutenant.

"Captain, two citizens of Visk arrived with your note. I did as was asked. They wait in your tent."

"Good man. Go and get me two saddled horses."

"Captain?"

"Don't ask, just do it. I'll be at my tent."

"Yes, sir."

The man trotted off and he entered the tent to find Darlee and her grandfather pacing. The girl rushed to him.

"Captain Brusk, what's going on? Why shouldn't I have presented my petition?"

"You'd better be sitting down for this one. You're not going to like it."

Darlee sat next to her grandfather and Brusk took her through the details contained in the note from Devron. When he finished, she hung her head, not the reaction he'd expected. "Is there something you know about this? If there is, you'd better give it up."

"Gar did it. He released the demon from the stone in the meadow. He told me. He said it happened while he was sleeping next to the stone. It was like in a dream...but real."

"More like a nightmare, at this point. Unless you want to end up being tortured in the king's jail for what you know, my best advice is go home. I've arranged for two horses to be brought. Travel quickly then return the horses to Lieutenant Devron when you get there. Tell him all you know. He's a fair man."

The lieutenant poked his head in the tent. "Horses are here, sir."

Brusk pulled Darlee up from her seat. "Good. It's time the two of you got going. Get home safe."

Pap stopped and grabbed Brusk's bicep. "Why are you doing this? Why the generosity?"

Brusk looked the old man in the face. "I owe it to you. Two of your sons were lost under my command."

Moisture welled in the corners of the man's eyes.

"I understand. May the gods watch over you."

Brusk escorted them out to the horses, but only when they were mounted and riding north did he relax. *It's not me the gods need to look out for, old man. It's your grandson. When this blasted war is over, he'll be hunted to the ends of the world.*

CHAPTER 19

Gar backtracked to the farm where they'd hidden after their escape from Morica. On the way, Jango grew sullen, demanding to go home. Gar pleaded with his friend to stick with him. As long as they were together, there was hope.

Most of the goats were still in or around the farm. The skills from years of sheep herding at his own farm rekindled, and he gathered the herd. They would provide milk and fresh meat while he pondered what to do next.

They rearranged the small house to accommodate the five of them. At night, Thunder and Hiss would disappear into the nearby forest and return in the morning with kills of rabbit and pheasant. He wouldn't need to kill any more of the goats.

Gar knew little about the preparation of food. His mother had always done it, sometimes Darlee. Thoughts of his sister saddened him. *I miss you, Dar. I hope you're well.*

To his surprise, Silk could cook. "You don't eat meat. Why did you learn?"

She freed that tinkling laugh. "I was the guest of a very wealthy merchant for some time when many of my brethren were caught. The price for my safety was servitude. I never thought I would ever be in need of these skills again."

Hearing that sound always lightened his mood and he found her cooking to be quite good.

On the third day, the clomping of approaching riders had Gar peeking out the window. Four armed men were headed their way.

Jango crouched below the window frame. "What do we do?"

"Stay in the house. I'll go out and talk to them. I don't want Thunder killing anyone else."

"What will you say? What if they ask about the old man?"

"I'll-I'll tell them I'm his grandson here to take over the farm, as the old man has died."

114

He put his hand on the door latch, when Silk stopped him. "Don't go. Send Jango. If they are recruiting soldiers, they'll take you. Your friend could pass for fifteen."

Gar hadn't thought of that. He cursed how slowly his mind worked at times. *If only I had paid more attention in school.* "She's right. You go, Jango. Tell them you're his grandson."

Jango blanched. "Me?"

"Yes, you. You heard Silk. It makes sense."

"Oh, if I have to." Jango paused at the door. "Don't let them take me, Gar. Whatever you—don't let them take me."

"I won't."

Jango stepped out into the yard just as the riders pulled up. The man closest pointed at Jango. "You, there. Where is the old man who owns this farm?"

"He-he died. Just last week. He's buried over there." Jango pointed out the grave.

The man scanned the grounds then focused on him once more. "Who are you then? Is there anyone else here?"

"I'm his grandson. I'm alone here. My family asked me to watch over the farm for a while."

"His grandson? I thought the old hermit had no kin. How old are you, lad?"

"Fif-fifteen, sir."

The man scanned the yard again. "Hmm. You should go home, boy. War has come. A number of militia men were killed near here, possibly by men from Morica. This farm is too close to the border. I cannot protect you at such a distance from town."

Jango bowed. "Yes, sir. Right away, sir."

The man nodded. "Good. See to it." He turned to his comrades. "Let's go."

Gar waited until the riders were out of sight then rushed out into the yard. "Good job, Jango. You fooled them."

Jango was crying. As he went to console his friend, the scent of fresh urine assailed his nostrils. Jango had wet his britches.

Jango broke into more hysterical sobs. "I can't do this anymore, Gar. I want to go home. I don't care what happens to me, if they throw me in jail, or if they hang me. I can't handle this anymore. I'm leaving."

Gar put an arm round the shoulders of his friend. "Don't do it. Don't leave me alone."

"You aren't alone. You have those *creatures* to keep you company. I'm the one who's alone. I'm going before you have a chance to change my mind."

Jango stomped off into the house. Gar followed and watched as his friend loaded his kit with supplies. When his pack was ready, he stopped and held out a hand.

"Good-bye. I wish you luck. If things, by some miracle, go well, I'll send word. I don't know how, but I will."

Gar shook hands. "I wish you well, Jango. I'll miss you. May the gods speed your journey."

Jango glanced round then opened the door. "Well, I'm off then."

Gar followed him out the door and watched his friend walk in the direction of Sechland until he could see him no more.

Hiss came to stand near. "Master friend go?"

"Yes, he's gone."

"Want Thunder bring back?"

He thought about it for a moment—Jango being tracked and captured by the large demon, struggling while being carried back to the farm. He let the thought pass. "No, let him be. If anything, go and make sure he gets into Sechland okay."

"Hiss no Master alone. Hiss stay."

"Send Thunder then. I want my friend safe."

Hiss dodged back into the house. A moment later, Thunder appeared and took off in the same direction as Jango. Hiss returned to Gar's side. "Thunder go. Back friend over border."

"Thank you, Hiss."

Gar spent the rest of the day busy with small tasks. When dusk fell and he went in to eat, the empty seat beside him panged at his emotions. He ate in silence, Hiss and Silk giving him some solitude by stepping outside.

He found a book on horticulture. Though his reading skills were poor, he could manage well enough and took the book into

116

the small bedroom to read. He needed something to occupy his mind.

His eyes had just fluttered closed when a noise at the door caught his attention. "Hiss?"

Silk entered. "Hiss has gone hunting. He won't be back until morning. I wanted to see if I could help ease your sadness at the leaving of your friend."

"He's gone. There's nothing you can do."

"I beg to differ." Silk pulled off her dress and sat on the edge of the single bed.

Gar was entranced by her naked body. Despite his sadness, he could not help the sensations growing in him.

She ran her soft hands over him. "Let's get these clothes off you. I think it's time you learn what manhood is all about."

He helped her shed his clothes and she pushed him back down as she climbed up to sit on him.

"There are other skills I perform much better than cooking."

Gar lay there feeling both a certain amount of excitement as well as trepidation. He was about to experience something usually reserved for his dreams. When she mounted him, a shiver of elation went through him. He grabbed at her hips, to hurry his thrusts.

She pushed his hands away. "Easy, Gar. We have all night."

It was too late, as he felt the contractions in his loins and he climaxed and released into her. A pang of disappointment rushed through him. "I couldn't stop."

She loosed her tinkling laugh. "Don't worry. You're young. You can do it again. But, this time, we'll take things a little slower. I know just what is needed to get you there."

She slid off and began to lick his body with her long, pointed tongue. When she took him in her mouth, he knew she was right. He *would* be able to do it again.

117

CHAPTER 20

Devron sighed as he entered the town hall—again. As of late, the city elders called him to appear two or three times a day. It was becoming impossible to attend to his duties as commander of the troops. How would Brusk have handled it? He pictured the fiery captain telling the city elders what they could do with their meetings in every crude expletive imaginable. He chuckled at the convulsions Trellus would suffer at such a verbal assault.

The door to the meeting chamber stood open before him. He entered to find a full slate of elders present—more than usual. Most times, barely a quorum showed up. "I'm here, gentlemen. What is it this time?"

Merchant Trellus indicated a chair in front of the seated elders. "Sit down, Lieutenant. We have a grave issue to discuss."

He took the seat. "It seems every issue you have is of grave concern. Please don't tell me about some new trivial matter like the last one where some poor beggar came to your back gate looking for a handout and you accused him of being another assassin bent on your demise."

On cue, Trellus purpled. "He may very well have been one, but this issue is definitely tied to the very thing. It has come to our attention that you recently held in your prison, and then released, a dangerous man."

Devron ran through in his mind all of the recent prisoners. None fit the description posed. "I'm afraid you have me at a loss. What man would you be talking about?"

"The farmer Murdach. Did you not detain him?"

Where was this going? He'd questioned the man for a day and felt satisfied he knew nothing of the breach in the demon stone. "Yes. What of it?"

"He is the man who murdered my son. He *was* the assassin."

He shook his head in disbelief. "That's impossible. How did you come to such a conclusion?"

118

Trellus sneered, a cruel smile on his lips. "Is it possible the great Lieutenant Devron failed to understand what he held? The man is a tanner in the market. I have learned how his son vied for the affection of my daughter. Apparently, my son purchased a particular bracelet to give Lialee as a birthday gift. That night, he was murdered. The following day, the tanner's son delivered the very same bracelet to her birthday party. The father killed my boy to get it."

The story sounded incredulous, but he would hear it out. "What makes you assume it was the father who did it?"

"Read the report by your Captain Brusk. My son was stabbed multiple times by a conical pointed weapon. The wounds were unlike any seen by the good captain before. Let me inform you that such a device is common in the tanner's trade, it is called an awl. The pieces all fit. He is the assassin."

As much as Devron could understand the logic of the merchant's claims, he found it hard to believe it to be true. Instead, another possibility popped into his mind. The demon had retrieved the bracelet and killed the boy. The plausibility of that action fit better with all he learned, but he was not ready to frighten the council with news a demon was on the loose. He rose. "I thank you, Merchant Trellus, for this informative meeting. I shall immediately attend to investigating this issue further. If true, it is disappointing to know our country has gone to war over a false claim of foreign agents penetrating your estate. However, I already have my own suspicions on who killed your son. Be sure to understand, whatever my determination, I shall include *that* in my report to my cousin as well."

The color drained from Trellus' face. "At the time it was the *only* plausible answer. I cannot be at fault for a decision by the king."

Devron smiled. "I go now to investigate your claim. I will report back when my findings are complete." He spun and walked out the door.

Once outside, he was disturbed by what he had been told. It was bad enough to learn of the youth Garlin using magic to free

119

the demons. It was even more disturbing to think he'd used the demon to kill Wirbon, the merchant's son.

The day was late. He was tired. He would investigate everything on the morrow. For now, he still had work to do back at the barracks.

***

Darlee and her grandfather followed Captain Brusk's urgings and made great haste to get home. Night had fallen by the time they reached a familiar road in their neighborhood. They passed the main road to the city and started down the lane to their farm. "I'll be glad to sleep in my own bed tonight. I hope there's something warm to eat."

"There's still the matter of your father. I don't think he would have taken too kindly to our leaving like we did. It's best you leave it to me to talk to him. I'll tell him it was all my idea."

She focused on the steady clomp of the horses hooves. Her father—would he forgive her? Somehow she doubted he would. She was lost in thought when Pap grabbed hold of her arm, causing her to bring her horse to stop.

"Shh! Listen."

"What is it, Pap?"

"Horses galloping up ahead. It sounds like their coming our way. Let's move off the track."

They nudged their mounts behind some nearby bushes, and barely in time. Six men on horseback raced by. When they were gone, Darlee and Pap returned to the road and she calculated the route the men fled. "They're headed to town. This late at night, how will they get past the gate?"

She felt a nudge from her grandfather. "Look from whence they came. There's a fire in the distance. We best hurry."

She spurred her horse that whinnied at the urging. It had already been a long ride, and the beast must be tired, but the location where the fire raged was one she knew by heart. It was home.

She dashed into the yard, her horse a couple of strides behind the one ridden by Pap. He was already dismounted and climbing the front porch. The flames had already engulfed most of it.

As she climbed down from her horse and stood staring at the house, she froze at the sight of the flames roiling out of the second floor windows. *It's gone. The house is gone.* Panic set in. Where were her parents? "Mother! Father! Where are you? It's Darlee. Answer me!"

A crack sound of wood splitting turned her attention back to the porch to see Pap crawling free from where the decking collapsed. She ran to help him up and pull him clear of the flames.

Together, they made it back to where she had stood before. He joined her to stare at the fire while he pulled her close with one arm. "It's no good. The fire is too strong. I can't get in, but by the look of your parent's bodies inside, they're dead already."

The tears came and she buried her head in her grandfather's shoulder. "They're gone, Pap. They're gone. My parents are gone. What do I do now?"

He rubbed her back while pulling her tighter. "Shh, now. Your mother and father taught you to be tougher than that. We'll figure something out. That we will. For tonight, we'll camp in the shed. Come morning, I'll search through what remains of the house and see what I can find. If your mother and father were in there, then we'll bury them proper. After we're done, we'll go see that lieutenant about this. This is a matter for the law. They'll find out who those men were, and they'll hang for it."

***

Darlee woke to a clatter and stepped out of the shed to find her grandfather pulling still-smoldering timbers from the collapsed remains of the house. Without a word, she set to work, helping him. It didn't take them long to find the charred remains of her parents. Much of the flesh was burnt away. The smell was nauseating as they gathered up what they could and placed them on wide boards near the family plot where her grandmother was buried and Pap's parents as well. There were also two markers for her uncles who were lost in the war, but her grandfather had once told her the bodies were never recovered from the battle.

Her grandfather began digging the graves while Darlee found different sheets of cloth in the shed and in the barn to cover the bodies with. While her grandfather was still digging, she headed down to the meadow to pick wildflowers to make wreaths for the graves.

When she got there, she remembered the demon stone. She went and examined it. She noted how the stone crumbled away, revealing the cavity in which the demon must have been trapped. How did it live so long in the stone like that? It was a question for another day. She bent to the task of picking the spring flowers and returned to the graves just as her grandfather was finishing.

"Ah, you're here. Help me with the bodies, will you? I don't want to make a mess of things, doing it myself."

Darlee helped him lift the boards they were set on and carefully lower them into the shallow graves. She placed a flower on each and her grandfather set to work covering them over. By the time he was done she fashioned the wreaths and handed one to Pap. "Here. You can place the one on your son. I'll put the one on my mother."

Together they put the wreaths on the mounds and stepped back. The tears flowed again and her grandfather sniffed as well. He hugged her close.

"He wasn't the best of sons, or fathers, for that matter, but your mother loved him all the same. They were Murdachs and together, at peace. The two of them will always be in our hearts."

He left her alone and began to saddle the horses. Dar dried her eyes. "Good-bye, Mother. Good-bye, Father. I know you gave up on Garlin, but he and Pap are the only kin I have left. It's up to me to save what little is left of the family."

She turned to see her grandfather watching her. "I'm ready. Let's go see the lieutenant."

They rode in silence toward the city and the gate. The digging of the graves took so much time, the sun reached its zenith and school must have just let out. She spotted Maurus walking along, and when their eyes met, he waved and jogged over.

"Hi, Dar. How did things go in Sechwisk? Any word on Gar and Jango?"

"Not a thing. I never got a chance to see the king. This war has just got things so mixed up, I don't know what to do. I'm on my way to see Lieutenant Devron now."

"Watch out when you see the lieutenant. Word at school this morning is your father is a suspect in the murder of Wirbon."

She brought the horse to a halt. "Where did you hear that? Lialee, no doubt?"

"Yeah, you guessed it. She says her father has all the evidence to prove it."

She clenched her jaw, determined not to show emotion to Maurus. The last thing she wanted was him reporting back to Lialee how she broke down. "Well, it won't matter. My father is dead. Some men killed him last night."

Maurus went ashen. "Dead? Really? That's horrible. So, with Gar missing, it's just your grandfather, you, and your mom. It's going to be tough managing the farm."

"My mother's dead as well."

"Your...I don't...I mean...look, I'm sorry. I-I gotta go."

Maurus headed toward the city market. *Off to spread the news, I suppose.* Dar kneed her horse to resume its plodding pace toward the barracks.

***

Devron stormed into the town hall, trailed by a company of men from the barracks. Having heard the story from the young Murdach girl, and having ridden out to the farm to confirm it, his anger simmered all the way back. His arrival at the barracks gave him the opportunity to explode. His night guard at the gate had let the six riders pass with signed permissions from the city elders. He learned the men were from the private guard of the merchant Trellus.

He burst into the room to find Trellus and a couple of the city elders sitting together.

"What is the meaning of this intrusion, Lieutenant? We are in a private meeting. Wait outside until we're done."

Devron waved his men forward. "You're under arrest for the murder of the farmer Murdach and his wife." The men grabbed Trellus and hoisted him up.

One of the city elders stood and blocked the way. "You are out of your jurisdiction, Lieutenant. Those men were under orders to carry out the penalty imposed on Mr. Murdoch. After you left the meeting, last night, it was felt you were not going to follow through on your orders to investigate the matter, so a court was held and the farmer found guilty of murder. The sentence was for the man to be executed. It's a disappointment to hear of the death of the wife, but the men claim she attacked them and they had no choice. You know the laws. We acted accordingly."

The men stopped in their act of arresting merchant Trellus and looked to Devron for direction. He tilted his head up at the ceiling and sighed. *These people have no morals. Brusk is right, they deserve no respect.* He returned his attention to the city elder. "You talk to me of laws. I know the laws. Now know this. I've just made a determination that this city is out of control and I am imposing martial law to restore order." He motioned to his men once more. "Clear the room. This council is disbanded."

The old city elder purpled. "You can't do that!"

As angry as he was, he smiled. "Oh, yes I can, and you know it. Now I can't arrest merchant Trellus like I wanted to, but if any of you linger here, I'll arrest the lot of you for civil disobedience. Out!"

As they filed out, Trellus stopped at the door. "You've overstepped your bounds, young lieutenant. When the king hears of this, you'll be sorry you took this path."

"You forget, I'm the one who's the king's cousin. Who is he going to believe, you...or me?"

Trellus snorted. "This isn't the last of it." He stormed out of the room, leaving Devron and his men alone.

His sergeant stepped before him. "What now, Lieutenant?"

"Now," he strode to the elders' table and swept the top clean, knocking an assortment of papers and documents on the floor, "we do as I said. We install military rule until such time as the war is over. I'll deal with my cousin when the time comes. I want you to put together a council of servicemen to take over the duties here. We're going to get things right for a change."

CHAPTER 21

Brusk didn't like it. Something was wrong. The Storburg army had set up camp some leagues away toward their border. What were they waiting for? The longer they lingered, the better the chance for Morica to muster more defenses. His men were growing tired of camping outside the walls. He could hear the grumbling when he strolled among the tents.

What was more, rations were depleting. The delivery of food from within the city walls shrank each day. As he examined the current shipment, he cursed and grabbed the manifest from the clerk in charge of the disbursements. "Let me see that blasted list. I told you the other day, my troops aren't getting enough. You're holding back on me. What are you doing? Selling the excess in the market?"

The man tried to recover the papers, but Brusk shoved him away.

"I'm just doing my job. Take a look. Everything consigned to your troops is here."

He scanned the list. From what he could see of the foodstuffs, the fellow was telling the truth. "What does Commander Purmin want them to do—starve?"

"I don't know what he wants. Today, I've been ordered to cut back all the consignments by twenty percent. Yesterday, it was fifteen. I guess there isn't enough food to go around."

Brusk grabbed the man by the collar and pulled him within a hand of his own face. "And what about the troops within the walls? Are their rations being cut, too?"

The raven on Brusk's shoulder nipped at the clerk's ear, causing the man to crane his head away. "N-no. They're still receiving full rations. It's only the troops from elsewhere in the kingdom who've had their share cut."

His patience gone, he tossed the clerk against the boxes and threw the notes at him. The man scrambled to pick up the documents and beat a hasty retreat.

"Damn that Purmin. I don't care if he is the king's commander. We're going to have a set-to, him and me."

He searched for his lieutenant. He had given the task of retrieving the daily orders to the officer, as Brusk's disgust of the commander made visiting Purmin in the map room intolerable. "Is Purmin still hiding in the castle?"

"Yes sir. He was there just half a hand ago when I left him."

"Fine. I'm off to kick his ass. Take charge of—"

The blast from a horn stopped Brusk from finishing his command. A call to arms. Something was happening. He knew his routine. He dashed to the messenger station. "All lieutenants are to marshal their forces immediately. Have their units lined up on the fields they were assigned. I'm going to find out what's going on."

A second horn blew. Brusk turned in the direction of the trumpeter up on the wall. "What in blazes? Retreat? We haven't even advanced yet. Who are we retreating from?"

A rider, his horse at full stride, approached from the direction of the main gate. The man pulled up in front of Brusk.

"Captain, you are to move all of your troops within the walls immediately. An attack is imminent."

"Attack? From who? Are you alerting the forces from Storburg to come to our aid?"

"That's the problem. Storburg has sided with the enemy. Troops from Morica and Fermia have joined them on the field. They are marching toward us as we speak. They will be here in less than a hand."

"By the gods! We'll be wiped out. There's no way we can withstand the combined might of those armies. How did this happen?"

"I know not. I only have my orders. I must ride to the next camp. Hurry your men." The rider spurred his horse and was gone.

Deep down, he knew. *They've found out about the demons. There's no other answer.*

Brusk rushed to the field where his troops were assembling. His lieutenants were grouped at the front, waiting for him. "Tell all of the men to make haste into the city. We're about to come under attack by the combined forces of Morica, Storburg, and Fermia. May the gods have mercy on us."

Despite what should have been panic setting in, his officers went about their jobs with precision. He had trained them well. His troops, on the other hand, were too green. It was going to be a long day.

From the perch on his shoulder, the raven lifted off, screaming, as it rose into the sky.

***

Brusk was exhausted. He'd lost count of the number of small wounds inflicted on his body, but the most aggravating one was the slash across one of his calves. It made it hard to move. He tied a tourniquet on it, but the wound was deep and blood flowed from under the bandage.

The battle raged for the entire day. It took the enemy forces some time to batter down the gate. When they finally poured in, his boys did a fine job of blocking up the streets and making it impossible for the Morican riders to be effective. Still, their sheer numbers wore down the defenses and the soldiers of Sechland succumbed to the onslaught.

There was no telling how many of his troops were killed, but many more than half, as the enemy forces did not seem interested in taking prisoners. He witnessed when a cadre of his troops throwing down their weapons and raising their hands, only to be cut down by a hail of arrows. *Such a waste of good men.* It saddened him, but educated him as well. He was not going to allow himself to be captured.

With the fall of night, he and two of his lieutenants worked their way through a number of alleys and reached the shattered gate. Guarding it were a dozen or so men from Storburg. Even in the dark, he recognized their bright red-and-gold uniforms.

Behind him, the battle for the castle raged on. The surviving forces of the king had retreated within its walls and were making a last stand. It wouldn't last much longer. *Lowry's done. They'll have his head on a pike by morning.*

128

Using hand signals, he gave instructions to his two lieutenants on how they were going to attack the men at the gate. They moved off to position themselves. *Brave lads. May the gods see them through.*

Sucking up what strength he had left, he charged the guards and slashed through the first man before the fellow could move. The others, seeing his attack, converged on him, as he expected. Timing was everything. His two lieutenants rushed at the same moment and caught the Storburgers from behind. As the enemy soldiers turned to fight, he disemboweled another man who had paused in his rush. *That's evened the odds some, but they still outnumber us almost three to one.*

His lieutenants had survived the battle so far due to their level of skill. These weren't a couple of green recruits pressed into service, but hardened, experience soldiers. They managed to kill three more before one of the Storburgers blew a horn.

Damn! He's called for reinforcements. "Come on, lads. Leave the rest be. We've got to run for it now."

He spun and sprinted toward the tree line some five hundred paces away. The pounding of his men's boots echoed behind him. Once he was within the thicket the enemy wouldn't bother with pursuit. Not in the dark.

A sharp pain in his leg caused him to stumble. *That damned calf wound!* As he struggled to rise again, his men grabbed his arms and hauled him forward. He glanced back toward the gate. No pursuit. They'd been lucky. The Storburgers didn't want to leave the gate unattended. He'd hoped that might be the case, but until it actually happened he hadn't believed it.

They ran a three-man, five-legged race the rest of the way, until the foliage surrounded them.

He found a tree to lean against and, like the others, panted to regain his breath.

One of the men crouched before him. "What now, Captain?"

"You two head back to Visk. Devron needs to be warned. There's no way the town's defenses could hold against such an army. It's been over fifty years since the war against Piaxia, and Visk is no longer the military bastion it used to be. Still, Devron is a smart man. He might be able to negotiate a peaceful surrender and save the town a lot of grief."

"But what about you? Aren't you coming with us?"

"I'm done for. Sechland will become a vassal state, and old soldiers like me are best moved out of the way, if you catch my meaning. No, I've got other plans. I'm going hunting. There's a farm boy out there who's caused all this trouble. I don't know where he is, but I'll find him if it's the last thing I do. And when I do, he'll be sorry I did."

CHAPTER 22

Gar bent to chopping wood for the stove. With his mind occupied, it was too late to hide when he heard the horses approaching. He straightened up to watch the riders near the farmhouse. *It's too late to run. They've seen me. I'll have to bluff my way, like Jango did.*

The riders pulled up in front of him. He recognized the man in the lead as the same one who had come before.

"Who are you? Where is the youth who was here the last time we came?"

Gar struggled to remember exactly what Jango said. "Oh, uh, that was my cousin. He had to go home. I came here to replace him."

The man leaned forward and squinted his eyes, his brows creased together. "You're a big youth. How old are you lad?"

"Um, sixteen." *Darn, I forgot. I should have said fifteen.*

"Only sixteen? You look older than that. Still, old enough. We're at war with Sechland. I'm recruiting every able body I can find. Get your horse and come with us."

"I-I don't have a horse. I thought Fermia was neutral? Why are you at war with Sechland?"

The man's eyes went wide for a moment. He then glanced at the others with him and those men dismounted. "Why do you say, *you are at war,* when it is we? It makes me think you are not a Fermian. What is your name? Who are your family? Where are they located? I would have you answer me, or else."

The three men approached him, and he panicked. He didn't want to be taken. He needed help, but Thunder had yet to return from seeing Jango safely over the border. Only Silk and Hiss were in the house. *Silk. I saw her conquer those men at the border post. She could do it again.* "Silk! Help me!"

Silk stepped out of the house in her simple outfit, a pullover dress cinched with a belt at the waist, which did little to conceal the curves of her body. The men stopped to ogle at her.

131

"My powers can only handle two for total submission. Otherwise they will all still have some will left. The more people whose will I draw from, the less I can draw from each. You must fight."

"Fight?"

"Yes, fight. Otherwise, you will be killed and I will be taken."

Gar was still holding the large axe he used to chop the wood. He hefted it, and the man nearest stopped advancing. The other two were fixated on Silk. She held her hands toward them as she worked her magic.

The man pulled his sword. "So you want to play, do you? All right, I'm game for a little sport."

His assailant swung first and Gar blocked it with the handle of the axe. The Fermian continued to flail away, and he could only block and was unable to counter as the weapon was too slow to maneuver. The leader, dismounted. If he joined the attack, Gar would be finished.

From behind, Hiss pounced on the ankle of the soldier attacking Gar and stabbed with his fingers. The fellow howled in pain and kicked at the imp. It provided the break Gar needed. Taking advantage of the man's distraction he swung through with the axe, the weapon biting deeply into the man's shoulder. Blood showered from the wound, spraying Gar as he pulled the axe free. The leader remounted his horse.

He couldn't let the officer escape. "Stop him. He's getting away."

Hiss scrambled across the gap and attacked the hind leg of the animal. It reared and spilled its rider. Gar followed, and while the man was down, rendered a killing blow to his chest.

He straightened and stumbled a couple of steps backward. The two men in front of Silk lay on the ground, unconscious. The man he first struck had died from his wound.

Gar shook. He'd killed two men. In the battle at Morence he fought before and attacked a number of the enemy with his pike, but couldn't recall if any were killing blows. His job had been more of one of defending the square. The swordsmen and archers were the ones striking to kill.

132

Hiss was running from downed man to downed man, placing a hand on each head. "Master good. Hiss happy."

"We must leave. Someone will surely come looking."

Silk remained standing over the men downed by her magic. "What about these two? You need to finish them."

He stopped to consider the two men. There were smiles on their faces as they slept. "Are you serious?"

"They will report your description and our presence. The entire countryside will be searching for us."

"Then we must go far. We'll take their horses. I cannot kill a sleeping man, even if he would kill me were he awake."

"Then you will be found. And they will kill you, but not until they torture you first. You will be begging to die. And I will be imprisoned, as will Hiss. Is that what you want?"

"I'm prepared to take my chances. I'll not kill them."

She walked past, went to the waiting horses, and stroked the animals. "You are right then. We must leave."

He watched her for a moment then noted Hiss scrambling from forehead to forehead of the men. Once again, the demons sported a soft glow. He had not realized the glow faded until now. He wondered how long it lasted. A day? A couple of days? A week? No more than that.

From the nearby forest, Thunder returned. At first the demon dashed about, growling something at Hiss and Silk. Once the behemoth finished examining the scene, finding the two sleeping men, the other two dead, the rigidity in his posture softened. At least the demon did not attack the two unconscious men. Perhaps Thunder *was* listening to him.

He sighed. "Hiss, tell Thunder to hide the bodies. I'm going to get cleaned up, and then we'll leave."

He went to the well and pulled up the bucket, pouring its contents over him to wash away the blood. Inside the house, he found a change of clothes, packed up what foodstuffs he could, and went back into the yard. Only three horses were there. "Where is the fourth horse?"

Hiss scrambled up to him. "Horse lame. Thunder kill. Put with rest."

Another death, albeit an animal. Where would it end? "Come then. Let's go." Silk was already mounted and waiting. He climbed into the saddle of one of the animals. As Thunder neared, his horse and the riderless one whinnied. He patted the neck of his. "Easy, boy. Nothing's going to happen. He just wants a ride." His horse calmed some, though its ears still twitched. The other was agitated and stamped its feet. Thunder paused a pace away.

Throughout all this time, Silk's animal remained calm. "The animals are spooked by Thunder. Why doesn't yours seem that way?"

"I am using my powers to control it. Bring the other horse close. I can control both for a while. Eventually the animal will get used to Thunder's smell and not be so afraid."

Gar reached down and grabbed the reins of the last horse and guided it to be near Silk. It calmed quickly and Thunder, in a quick graceful motion, jumped on the animals back. Only Hiss remained. "Are you going to ride with me?"

"No, Master. Hiss fast. Hiss run. No lose Hiss."

"Suit yourself. Which direction should we go? We can't go north. Morica and Sechland lie that way. We can't go west. That's where Storburg is. If we head east, we'll eventually come to the coast, but we'll still be in Fermia."

Silk laughed. "You've eliminated all the possibilities but one."

"South it is, then."

He gritted his teeth and kicked the animal forward, the others riding alongside. *Is this how the rest of my days are to be? Forever running? Forever hiding? I've got to figure out what to do.*

CHAPTER 23

They rode long and through the nights, resting when the days were at their brightest. The last thing Gar wanted was to be spotted by Fermian soldiers, so their path wound through much underbrush and trees. No open fields or roads were used to hasten their journey. Combined with the fact the demons were poor riders, barely able to ride faster than a walk, it took the better part of three days to cross over into Gatway. There were no cities near the border, only small villages, and so they made into the country unobserved.

They found a grotto hidden amongst the trees. It would be morning soon. Already, dawn hinted on the horizon. Perhaps it would make a good place to hide for the day. It reminded Gar of the cave where they'd freed Thunder. "There isn't another demon hidden in here, is there?"

Hiss bounded ahead. "Hiss know every demon is. One close, yes, but no demon here." He entered the cave and, after a long moment, emerged. "Safe, go in."

"Fine. We'll camp for here for the day before moving on." It was then he noticed Thunder's ears twitching as the demon's head kept turning from side to side. The big demon exhibited excellent hearing, he knew that from the time when their camp was found by the men from Fermia. He looked over to Silk. "What's bothering Thunder? He's spooked."

"I'll find out." She asked Thunder something but the beast didn't respond. She asked again. He still said nothing, but gave a shake of his head in the negative.

"I don't know what it is. He won't tell me. I don't think he does either, but he knows something's wrong."

They tethered the horses and retired within the cave. As Gar entered, the strong smell of demon accosted his nostrils. "Hiss, I thought you said there were no demons in here?"

"Yes, Master. No demon here. Me know. Hiss know where every demon in stone is. Hiss last one caught."

135

"Then why does it smell like the lot of you combined?"

Silk paused at the entry while Thunder was backing out. "You're right. I smell it, too. *I wonder…*"

A noise akin to a hive full of bees was approaching from outside. Thunder crouched and dashed back into the cave to cower behind Gar. *What could frighten the brute so much?* He soon got his answer as a swarm of tiny flying creatures zipped into the opening and flew all around them. They ignored Gar but landed on the others in bunches. He found it comical to see the three of them slapping at the things and running in circles in an attempt to escape them. Thunder howled and bolted for the outside. Hiss hid behind Gar.

Silk backed into a corner and was swinging madly. "Help me, Gar. They're biting."

Hiss swung a hand at one of the bugs on Silk's leg, leaving a long, bleeding scratch.

"Ouch! Hiss, you clawed me. Take care of yourself."

What a moment before had been comedic, now changed to something serious. He stepped near and helped her swat away the things. As he caught one, he gave it a closer inspection. It resembled a cross between a demon and an insect. Not pretty. He crushed it in his hand and dropped it to the cave floor. He was continuing to kill as many as he could when an idea struck him. "Silk, use your magic to control them."

"I can't. My magic does not work on creatures from the demon world."

The tug on his clothing told him Hiss was climbing his back.

"Master, you control. Hiss help." Hiss clasped a hand to his forehead. "Think them stop, they stop."

Gar studied the swirling mass and concentrated. *Stop. Stop!* Their flight slowed considerably. *All of you—stop now.* Almost as one, they dropped to the ground.

Silk went on the attack and started stomping on them. "Quick, help me kill them all."

He followed suit and soon most of the swarm were crushed. He bent down and picked up a couple of survivors and placed them on a ledge in the cave. "What are these things?"

Silk made to squash them, but he stopped her swing.

"Kill them. These are the mindless ones from the deep. This bunch must have escaped when we did. They feed on our blood."

Indeed, she sported dark-red marks all over her body. "I thought your skin was impervious?"

"Not to living things. Given a chance, they would have drained me until I died."

"Why didn't they bite me?"

"If you were all there was, they would have; they attack any living creature, but when we're not around, they usually attack other insects. Our blood is so much richer to them, though. Would you stop to drink a glass of water, if offered, instead a fine wine? No. Mindless, they are, but instinct tells them what's better to eat."

Hiss climbed down and a quick inspection showed Gar that the imp also suffered a number of bites. Hiss jumped forward and smashed the last two bug creatures. "No more. Safe now."

Gar went to the mouth of the cave and waved for Thunder to come in. "It's all clear." The big demon shook his head. "Come on, you big sissy, they're all dead." Thunder continued to shake his head. "Fine. Stay out here. Keep watch. I'm going to get some rest."

As he turned to reenter the cave, Hiss scampered past.

"Me stay, Thunder, case more mindless return."

"As you wish."

He found Silk dabbing at her bite marks with the edge of her clothing. She had taken it off and was inspecting the small wounds that covered her.

"Look at me, I'm a mess. This will take time to clear up. How alluring can I possibly be with all these marks?"

With each day since the farm he lusted for her more and more. Seeing her naked again, the urge was on him. He felt his manhood swell. "You still look fine to me."

She glanced at him and shook her head. "Now is not the time, Gar. You must rest and be ready to travel again." She slipped her clothes back on, came over, and gave him a kiss. "Later, perhaps, when we are no longer being chased."

He lay down on his mat and frustration welled up in him. *What's wrong? I thought I did okay that other time. She even said so.* He rolled over to lie on his side. It *had* been a long night. Maybe a short nap would help.

One thing he'd discovered. The demons could be hurt, if, at least, by other demons, or even perhaps by humans, but by hand only—no weapons. He closed his eyes and soon succumbed to his weariness.

***

He woke with a start and found Silk standing above him, gently nudging him with her toe. "Time to get up. You've slept long enough."

"Okay, I'm up." He stretched in an attempt to relieve the stiffness from sleeping on the cave floor. He was glad to be awake as his dreams had been about the fight with the little demon bugs, and in it, he couldn't stop them. More like a nightmare. He stood and packed his gear. His mind was full of questions and now might be a good time to ask. There was so much he didn't know. "How come I was able to kill those…things…what did you call them?"

"Mindless ones. They lack any magical enchantments like we have. The ancient ones did not grant them any."

"Ancient ones? What are those?"

"They are our creators."

"You mean—like gods?"

"Yes, I suppose they are something similar. Who knows, they may be the same as your gods, or even be your gods. They rule from within the deep places. They made us."

Gar was never one to put much faith in the gods. There were stories of how man was a creation of theirs. Tales of how they were all knowing, all seeing, and how they were responsible for everything, from the sun in the morning to the stars at night, from the wind in the air to the waters in the sea and the earth on the ground. He'd always found it hard to believe creatures could exist that could do all that. Besides, no one ever saw one. Still, he wasn't about to say they didn't exist. Such heresy was too risky in

138

case they did and punished him for it. Listening to Silk tell of them, it sounded like his gods and hers were indeed one and the same. "Tell me, what is the real story about you and the others? The only thing I know is what they told us as kids to scare us—how, if we didn't behave, a demon would come get us."

She caught his chin with her hand and looked into his eyes. "Believe me when I say we were never created to come get naughty children."

Silk loosed her tinkling laugh. It always put him at ease. He thought about her answer. It only made him have more questions. "So what do you mean—created? Aren't you born like we are?"

She smiled. "Why all these questions? Aren't you happy right now with me?"

"Well, yes, very much so. In fact, I was thinking earlier how I wanted to have you with me forever, but then I got confused. I mean, what about children? A family? And where would we live that people wouldn't be hunting us down all the time?"

Silk frowned and stepped toward the entrance of the cave. "You think too much, Gar. Don't fret about the future. What will come, will come. For now, accept that you have the three of us to guard and protect you. We will make sure you never come to any harm. And every now and then, I will be available to please your inner desires."

A pang of disappointment went through him as he recalled her earlier rebuff. "I would want to enjoy those again right now."

"Not now. We need to keep moving."

Her refusing irked him again and he went to stand by her at the entrance. "It's just that I want to understand you, to know something about you. You're still a mystery to me."

She patted him lightly on the cheek. "A little mystery is a good thing. Enjoy it."

He stepped outside to check the sky. Much of the day had passed. Only a hand or so remained until dusk. Hiss appeared from behind some trees.

"Master ready go? Hiss lead way."

"Yes, Hiss. I'm ready. Let me get my horse."

He saddled the animal and helped Silk and Thunder with theirs. Like Silk predicted, the animals no longer shied from the demons. When they were all mounted, they followed Hiss through the woods.

As he rode, his mind was busy. What kind of magic stopped swords and knives from hurting the demons, yet they were subject to bites from the smallest of creatures? It was too complicated. Maybe his sister would be able to figure out why.

Then there was the question of Silk. Now that he found the time to think, maybe the idea of being with her forever wasn't the wisest. He wanted to have a family and a farm of his own. With Silk, he never could do that. His mind strayed to Lialee. If only she hadn't refused him so. None of this would have happened. He tried to imagine what lying naked with Lialee would have been like. Would she have been like Silk? He would never know.

CHAPTER 24

Brusk stooped to replace the bandage on his leg. As he pulled the old one away, he groaned at the state of the wound. Hacked, red, and angry looking weren't signs of it healing well.

He had made it to Eagle Ridge, the fortification there still in Sechland hands.

Gramby, the lieutenant in charge of the fort, bent to examine the wound. "That doesn't look good. You should have our medic check that out."

"I don't have time to get waylaid by the doctor. He sees this and he'll order me in bed for a week. I've got a mission to accomplish, and nothing's going to hold me up like this minor flesh wound."

Gramby chuckled. "Minor? I'm surprised you can even walk. And what is this mission of yours? When you arrived, you told me Sechwisk City has fallen and King Lowry is probably dead by now. *Who* are you on this mission for?"

Satisfied the new bandage was snug and covering the wound, Brusk rose to test his leg. A bit painful still, but definitely better than what he'd trudged on since the battle. "My own. I know what caused this catastrophe, and I intend to see an end to it."

Gramby put a hand on Brusk's shoulder. "Listen, we fought past battles together. We're kin as far as the army goes. Take me with you. I want to help."

He grabbed the lieutenant's forearm in the traditional military exchange. "You're a good man, Gramby, but this one's personal. I'm going alone. Thanks for the supply kit, the commoner clothes, and the horse. Who knows how many enemy lines I'm going to have to cross? I don't want to put anyone at risk over my own stubbornness. Surrender the fort. There's no need for your men to die defending it. Go home and start a new life."

"Bah! I'd rather die than surrender. If I asked, so would most of the lads here, but they're young and still have their lives to live, so I'd probably do as you say and turn this place over to the bastards."

It would only be a matter of time before the combined forces of Morica, Storburg and Fermia overran the place. His friend would end up a prisoner. "Listen. Take your troops and make for Visk. It's fortified, and I doubt they'll be marching on it anytime soon. I'm off."

Gramby walked him to the gate. "Good luck to you, Brusk. May the gods see you through. I'll take your advice and scuttle this place and march for Visk in the morning."

Brusk nodded. "So be it." He started down the hill to the countryside that awaited him.

Here goes nothing.

***

Brusk crossed the border without incident. There were no patrols. *They must think everyone's back at Sechwisk. There's no one left but fool me to make an incursion onto Morican soil.*

Between him and Morence lay open fields. He reached the last cluster of trees to hide in until the sun went down. He could make out soldiers near the walls walking in pairs round the grounds.

The only sign remaining of the battle was a very large mound of turned earth—a mass grave. *At least they had the courtesy to bury our dead and not leave them for the buzzards. I doubt Lowry would have been that considerate.*

As he sat there, peering through some bushes and chewing on a piece of jerky, he contemplated all that happened. He thought of the thousands who died there, and for what? A tariff on goods? The idiocy of it all burned at him. Moments like these, he wondered if he was on the right side.

No, best not to have those thoughts. I'm a Sechlander, born and bred. Like my father before me and his father before him, a career soldier. Over thirty years I've been doing this job. I'm an old soldier now, and that's how I'll die.

He let his head sag as he thought of his own lost family. His wife and three children had died of disease while he was away on a campaign. He'd returned victorious and received a captaincy for his valor. It had all been for naught. There was no one to share the glory with. Since then, he'd allowed the bitterness within him to grow and his disdain for his superiors with it.

The sound of wings fluttering near gave him enough warning to see the raven come down and land by where he sat. It lightened his mood, and he chuckled. "So, come back, have ya? And where did you run off to when things got a little hot back there? A lot of good you are in a fight, running at the first sign of trouble. I ought to catch you and roast you for dinner."

The bird cocked its head at him, as if wondering whether what he said might occur. Brusk chuckled once more, carved a sliver of the jerky, and tossed it to the bird. "Here ya are, ya crazy thing. Why you want to hang out with a waste of a man such as myself, I'll never know."

The bird made a pleasant chirp and scooped up the fragment of dried meat. Brusk reached out with a finger and brushed the plumage of the creature. Despite everything he now faced, he was glad for the company.

***

In the pitch of night, Brusk knelt on the field where the battle occurred so many days before. He tried to recollect the events as they'd unfolded. *Our squares were set up all round here. The Morican army came from the north. Their cavalry was sweeping behind it, heading west, looking to cut between our lines. Purmin, that idiot, panicked and called retreat. With the horsemen in our midst, some of the men were cut off from running home. Now, the way Devron told it, them fellas lit south.*

He rotated that way. The dark mass of a forest faced him. *So they ran into the trees somewhere about there.* He got up and started walking, his horse trailing behind as he pulled on the reins. He imagined how the men would have run to the closest trees for cover.

This caused him to alter his path only slightly. When he entered the forest, he paused to allow his eyes to adjust. Low-lying brush and other scrub blocked most directions. *If I'm running for my life, I'd take the path of least resistance.*

He resumed walking, still in a southerly direction, with the odd deviation to avoid trees and thick brush. It wasn't too long until he came to a rocky hill sticking up among the trees. He circled to his right and soon found a cave entrance. *This must be the place. In I go.* He pulled a flint from his kit and lit a candle.

It wasn't a very deep cave but high enough so he could stand up with room to spare. A half dozen paces in brought him to the back wall. The ground was littered with shards of stone, and the rock wall was freshly broken in the middle, revealing a smooth area inside. He climbed into it. *No trouble in me fitting in. I'm a big man and the beast is at least five hands taller and three wider. He must be a heck of a thing. Everything in the letter checks out.*

He breathed deep and inhaled a strong odor. It smelled something like burning oil. Not terribly unpleasant, but identifiable should he come across the scent again. *Now I know your stink.*

He exited the cave and blew out the candle.

Okay, which way from here? From this point on, that lad Garlin and the fellow Baxus parted ways. Considering Fermia entered the war then, something tells me they got a good whiff of demon. I guess it only makes sense to head south.

Once his sight readjusted to the gloom of the forest, he started to head that way when he heard noises. Pulling his horse behind some trees and crouching down, he watched two men in the uniform of Morica appear from behind the hill.

"I'm telling you, I saw a light."

"It was probably just a lightning bug. Besides, who would want to come creeping around here? The demon cave is right there. Who knows when a monster of some kind could come rushing out."

"Don't be stupid. The demon's gone. You heard what the lieutenant said. They figured it went south into Fermia and killed those guardsmen they found all torn up."

"Yeah, but I also heard the border patrol in Storburg got attacked. And not just by one demon, but three. You think it's the same one?"

"What, you can't count now? Since when does one demon become three? Besides, there were two attacks in Fermia a week apart. The second one killed a captain. That's what got Fermia so riled up. The guy was pretty important in town."

"Well, maybe the demon went back and forth, you know, killed the four guardsmen, tried to head to Storburg, tried to kill all the sentries, but a couple got away, and so he hightailed it back into Fermia where he ran into that captain."

"Like I said, you are *so* stupid. It's simple math. One—three—three—one. What don't you get? Sheesh! Listen, I'm going in to check. Light a candle for me."

The sparks from a flint soon resulted in a candle glowing in the hand of one of the men. He disappeared into the cave and returned in only a moment. "Nothing. I swear I saw a light." The man blew out the candle.

"Okay, let's go. This place gives me the creeps."

"Yeah, yeah, fine. For once I agree with you. This way."

Brusk focused on the sounds of the two men retreating until he could no longer hear them. A small chuckle escaped his lips. *It sounded to me like the one who kept getting called stupid is the smart one. He figured it right.*

Mounting his horse, he headed south.

CHAPTER 25

Gar and the others rode through the rest of the day and were outside of a small village when they came to a stop. His thoughts had been troubled the entire trip. When it came to the demons, Hiss had obeyed his every word from the very start. Thunder took some time to follow suit, but he figured that was attributable to the fact the big beast didn't speak common tongue well.

Silk, on the other hand, was more free willed. Yes, she would cook now and then and stayed close company, but her rejection earlier in the day he found troubling. He had come to the conclusion his freeing of the demons meant they owed him their fealty, as if he were their king. He was becoming used to it and, in fact, was getting to like it. If only she would treat him like the others did.

He got off his horse and stretched. "I haven't done this much riding ever in my life. I'm as sore as if I'd just finished plowing the entire farm. How much farther are you taking me, Hiss?"

"We here, Master. This is the place. Look. See?"

He focused on where the imp was pointing. In the darkness he could see little, but a vague outline of something sticking up loomed on a small hillock. He stepped closer. "Another demon stone?"

"Yes, Master. Another servant for you."

He should have figured it. Earlier, Hiss had mentioned one was close, but it hadn't registered until then. He wanted to end his situation, not worsen it. "I don't know about this. Why would I want to release another demon? I think I'm going to pass this one by."

Hiss skittered around him. "No, Master, no. You want. She good servant."

Silk stepped next to them. "Who's in this one, Hiss?"

Hiss glanced at her, but didn't answer. She leaned over the imp and grabbed one of his arms. She let fly the rasping tongue of the demons but without the softness she usually applied to it. She gave the small demon a shake while doing it.

After a moment, Hiss responded in their language. Silk let him go and the imp moved to hide behind Gar. Silk put a hand on Gar's elbow and tried to draw him away from the stone. "You're right, Gar. You don't want to release this one. Let's go."

He pulled his arm free. Still upset with her, he wasn't in the mood to have her boss him around. She'd refused him, and Hiss did say this demon was a *she*. Maybe she would want to serve him more. "Why shouldn't I let this one out? What's so different about her?"

He went and put his hand on the stone. It was a tall outcropping of rock on top of the hillock. At his touch, he felt something in his mind. An urge to be satisfied by this new demoness flashed through him. Maybe she would be better than Silk. Maybe, just maybe, Silk didn't want the competition. His desire continued to grow. He had to have her. "Help me, Hiss."

"Yes, Master." Hiss climbed to put a hand on Gar's forehead.

He concentrated on the stone opening.

Silk tried to tug him away. "No, Gar, don't."

He held his ground and continued to concentrate. In a rumble, the stone burst open and the shards of rock fell away. A woman demon, taller than him by a hand, stepped from the opening. She was as beautiful as Silk, leaner and smaller bosomed, though ample still. As the others, she sported all of the tell-tale markings of her kin: slate grey skin, black eyes, and pointed ears, hairless and sharp pointed fingers. Unlike Silk, when freed, this one wore a leather outfit so tight it hid none of her curves.

She looked round at the others and spoke in their language. Hiss, having climbed down, scampered between them. "Master free you." He pointed at Gar. "New Master."

She faced him and smiled. Like Silk, she flashed pointed, teeth but longer. "So you are my savior. I sensed you when you touched the stone, and I know what you want."

His urge was uncontrollable. "Yes, I want you…now…here."

She laughed, like the tinkling laugh of Silk but slightly deeper. "Then, what are we waiting for."

He could resist no longer and began to pull off his clothes. She pulled at them, ripping his shirt in the process. Once he was naked she pushed him to the ground and pulled him on top of her.

"I am here to please new Master."

He didn't care the others were near, that Silk was watching. His passion was unbridled. His hands fondled her everywhere. He didn't want the sex to stop. The lust in him was all consuming. He started to tire but he didn't care. He wanted to continue. They changed positions with him below her.

Suddenly, she was pulled from off him by Silk. "Stop it. You're using your powers on him too much. He's just a human."

The new demon laughed as she pushed free from Silk. "It's what he wants. I'm only looking to satisfy him."

Gar sat up. A weakness overtook him and he didn't have the strength to stand. He didn't want Silk to interfere. "Leave her alone."

Silk pulled him up. "You don't know what you're saying. Hers is the power of lust. She was using it on you. You weren't in control of yourself."

He didn't believe her. He shrugged her away. "You're just jealous, Silk. She wants to please me. It's more than you want to do. I don't care what you say."

The new demoness put an arm round him. "Silk? Is that what you call her? And what of the others?"

He pointed at the small demon. "That one I call Hiss. The big one is Thunder."

She kissed him and rubbed against him, wrapping one leg round his. "And me? What will you call me?"

What would he call her? She was very eager to please. "Pleasure. I will call you Pleasure."

She purred in his ear. "Ooh! I like that. Pleasure is what I'm good at. Shall I please you again?"

Silk placed a hand on his arm. "You must resist."

Yes, I must resist. She's using me against my will. "Perhaps it's better that we don't."

Pleasure laughed. "Now who's using her powers for her own ends?"

She let go and so did Silk. Gar gave his head a shake to clear it. He understood now. Not only did these demons feed on human strengths, they could impart them as well. He recalled Thunder placing a hand on Jango when his friend was near to death. Silk said Thunder fed on life. He must have passed on some life force to Jango at that time. Gar had figured out a while ago that Hiss was feeding him mana for the magic. And now, both Pleasure and Silk were battling over his control with their own skills. He found it impossible to resist their powers. How were they ever beaten all those years ago?

As he got dressed, he kept glancing between Silk and Pleasure. If he had to choose, the idea of being with Pleasure once more still appealed to him. He was about to say yes when Thunder made a noise and disappeared into the surrounding trees. Gar motioned for Hiss to come near. "What? What is it?"

"Thunder hear. Many come."

"Many?" He scanned the area but could see or hear nothing. "How many?"

"Many, many. Master, go. Leave now."

He dashed as best he could to his horse, the weakness still somewhat with him. Pleasure was about to climb up behind him when Silk stopped her.

"Take Thunder's horse. He can run faster than these animals when he wants to. Two of you on one horse will slow us down."

Pleasure hesitated then did as Silk requested. "It makes sense—for now. Pleasing will have to wait."

Once Silk was mounted, he turned to Hiss. "Lead us out of here."

The imp bounded off, and they kicked their horses to follow. Thunder emerged from the trees and ran alongside. In the darkness, it was hard to go fast, but the horses managed well enough. Gar glanced at the moon. They were still headed south.

149

CHAPTER 26

Darlee wasn't in the mood to go home. School was finished, but the only thing awaiting her back at the farm was making do in a converted shed. Her grandfather was busy rebuilding the family home. She helped any way she could, but, as of late, a number of neighboring farmers, having heard of the tragedy, had come to help. She ended up being more in the way than anything.

She decided to spend the afternoon in the market people watching. It was always something she found entertaining. She'd even brought a copper with the intention of treating herself to a pastry.

Stopping at the baker's stall, she complimented the owner how everything he had for sale looked so tasty but with only the one coin she couldn't afford much. The man, who showed the effect of eating too much of his own product, was happy to pick out the largest pastry there and handed it to her for the coin. She thanked him profusely and gave him a kiss on the cheek, knowing it was worth twice the price.

The baker chuckled. "Alright, enough of that. If the missus sees me accepting kisses, I'll be barred from working in the market ever again."

"I'll bet the missus kisses a handsome man like you all the time."

He laughed. "Enough, already. Here, take another pastry, and be off with you before I get into any more trouble."

She gratefully accepted the gift and headed across the market to an area where she could sit down and watch the shoppers come and go. It was always a game with her trying to predict which patrons were wealthy and which were not. Experience taught her not to automatically judge by their clothing, but instead by the way in which they bought things. Some would haggle, even for a long time, but in the end, they always bought.

Once in a rare while, she would spot someone stealing. She didn't think it her place to report the thefts because almost always it was usually some minor thing like a trinket or a piece of fruit. Darlee knew the law and wouldn't be able to forgive herself should someone be judged harshly and lose a hand.

Just about to take a bite of the larger pastry, she spotted someone lurking near the baker's stall. His clothes were ragged and very unkempt, but it didn't hide the truth from her, it was Jango. Just as she rose from her seat, Jango snatched a bread roll from the stall and dashed away. He hadn't gone five steps when he was nabbed by one of the soldiers who patrolled the market.

She needed to intervene. She dashed over just as the soldier was returning the stolen item to the baker, Jango still held firmly in his grip. She latched onto Jango's arm. "There you are. I've been looking everywhere for you. See? I have pastries for both of us."

The soldier reached out and pried her hand off. "I'm sorry, Miss, but this lad's been caught stealing. I'm taking him with me."

She wasn't giving up that easily. She decided to act distressed and sobbed. "You can't take my friend; his family needs him. What will his poor mother do?"

She turned to the baker. "I would gladly pay for what he took but I gave you my only coin. Here are the pastries you gave me. They're still uneaten. I'd be happy to give them back to you, and you can keep the copper. Just let him go." She held out the pastries for the man to take.

The soldier paused and looked to the baker. "Sir?"

The baker, who was frowning, sighed, and then smiled. "Let him go." He pushed the pastries back at her. "Keep them, but keep him away from my stall. Next time, I won't be so lenient."

"Oh, thank you, thank you." She went to kiss his cheek again, but the man held his hands up and fended her off. "No, no more kisses. Now, go. I've work to do."

She grabbed Jango's hand and dragged him away, back to the spot she'd been sitting. "Sit. Talk to me. Where's my brother? Where is Gar?"

Jango slumped heavily on the bench. With his sad expression, she thought he was going to start crying, but he didn't.

"I don't know where he is…somewhere in Fermia, I suppose. I left him there five days ago. I just got into town this morning."

"You left him alone?"

Jango reddened. "He's not alone. He's got his…friends with him."

"Friends? What friends?"

"The…the demons."

"Demons? You mean there's more than one of them? Where did he find the other one?"

"Not just one more—two. He's been letting them out of the stones."

Three demons? What could Gar be possibly thinking? The news deflated her. She sat down beside him. "So what are you doing here, and why are you trying to steal bread rolls?"

Jango sniffed. "I'm hungry. I haven't had anything to eat in three days."

She remembered the pastries and handed him the bigger one. "Here, have this for now. Why don't you just go home and eat?"

Jango took the pastry and shoved it into his mouth, biting off a large piece. "Thanks. I tried. My father called me a deserter and chased me out. I don't know where to go."

As she watched, the tears from Jango finally came. She put an arm round and hugged him. "Things will work out—somehow. Tell me the whole story. Don't miss anything."

She listened carefully as Jango related how he was injured, how Gar saved him, where they ran to, how the other demons were released, and how he finally decided to come home. During the telling, she spotted him eyeing her remaining pastry, so she gave that one to him as well. When he finished both the story and the pastry, she came to a decision. "You have to go see Lieutenant Devron."

Jango paled. "The lieutenant? Are you nuts? He'll throw me in prison, for sure."

"Not if you tell him what you told me. An injured man dragged off is not a deserter. He'll understand. I'll go with you to make certain."

"You'll go with me?"

She stood and helped him to his feet. "All the way."

As they started for the barracks, Darlee spotted Lialee directly ahead. The last thing she wanted to do was cross paths with the girl. She grabbed Jango by the elbow and pushed him to change their direction. "Come on. Let's go this way."

Jango hesitated. "Look, it's Maurus."

Darlee paused as well to follow Jango's line of sight. He was right. There was Maurus, as well, right next to Lialee. She hadn't noticed, at first. *Figures. With my brother gone and Wirbon dead, Maurus is wooing Lialee. I wonder how many days he waited before trying? Ten? Five? Or, right away?*

Her grip on Jango had relaxed and he stepped toward the two, leaving her behind. She had no choice but to chase after him.

Lialee spotted them and sneered, but Maurus' face lit up as he rushed to meet his oncoming friend.

"Jango, you're back! When did you arrive?"

"Just this morning."

Lialee grabbed Maurus' elbow and pulled him back half a step. "Pff! I thought they arrested deserters. How did you get into the city?"

Jango flushed. "I *didn't* desert, and I walked in. No one stopped me."

Lialee glanced up and down him. "No wonder. You look like a street beggar, not a wayward soldier."

Darlee, having caught up, pushed Jango to the side. "Come on. You don't want to waste time talking to them."

"I see you keep good company, the daughter of a murderer."

Darlee stopped and pointed a finger at Lialee. "Your family are the murderers, sending troops to kill my parents. You're the one who should be in jail."

Jango paled. "Is this true? Your parents are dead?"

She wanted to cry, but no way was she going to let Lialee see any tears. "It's true. Her father sent his own personal bodyguards out to our farm, and they killed both my mother and father, then they burned the house down to the ground."

Lialee lifted her chin. "They didn't kill them, they executed them. Your father killed my brother."

Jango's gaze was swiveling back and forth between Lialee and her. "I-I don't know what to believe. If I have to believe one or the other, I'm going to believe Darlee first. Maurus, what really happened?"

Maurus kicked at the dirt and looked down. "I don't know. It's not my place to say…"

Lialee stepped between the two. "Maurus is on my side. You would be smart to be on it as well. This martial law won't last forever, and when it does end, my father will be back in charge. Then we'll see who's right."

Darlee had heard enough. "Come on, Jango. Let's go."

Jango held up. "Now I know to believe you. You're trying to help me, not threaten me. Come on, Maurus. You don't want to hang around with someone like that."

Maurus stayed behind Lialee. "It's nice to see you again, Jango."

"Maurus?"

Darlee pushed Jango in the direction of the barracks once again. "He's not coming. He's picked his side."

Jango stopped resisting and walked with her. From the corner of her eye, she caught his last look back. He was crying again.

Darlee stopped in her tracks when a trumpet blared. She turned toward the sound and watched Lieutenant Devron step up on the town square podium. People began to crowd round, and she joined them, Jango at her side.

"People of Visk, I bring grim tidings. The capital city of Sechland, Sechwisk, has fallen. King Lowry is dead. The city is under the control of the combined armed forces of Morica, Storburg and Fermia. Their envoy has arrived, entreating us to lay down our arms and surrender. I will hold a town hall meeting this evening to announce my decision. Should any citizens wish to leave the city before the armies of our enemies arrive, I would urge you do so at your earliest. May the gods protect us."

He stepped down and headed straight for the barracks. Before chasing after him, she paused to spot Lialee. One glance at the girl's face was all she needed. She was scared stiff. Darlee smiled. *It looks like her father won't be back in charge after all.*

She nudged Jango. "Come on, there's the lieutenant. Let's go."

The lieutenant, flanked by a couple of his men, was walking briskly, and it took a while to chase him down.

"Lieutenant Devron, I need to speak with you."

One of the men stopped and held her back. "The lieutenant has more urgent matters to deal with than whatever problems you may have, young miss."

She struggled in his arms, but to no avail. "But it's about Gar...and the demons."

The lieutenant stopped dead and spun to face her. "What news do you have?" He nodded to the man holding her.

The soldier released her, and she grabbed Jango's hand to pull him forward. "This is Jango. He's just returned from being with Gar since the battle. He has much to tell you."

"I remember you now, Jango. An archer, or, at least, an attempt at being one. You fled the battle, as I recall."

"No, sir. I was carried off, and I was badly wounded. I couldn't have fled if I'd wanted to."

"I see no serious wound on you. Do you take me for a fool?"

"I was healed. Please, let me explain."

The lieutenant studied their faces then nodded to his men once more. "Bring them both."

The one closest grabbed Darlee by the shoulders, the other took hold of Jango. With Lieutenant Devron leading the way, the two of them were hustled off toward the barracks.

This is probably my last chance to save Gar from being put to death.

CHAPTER 27

It took two days of tracking to bring Brusk to where he was. He picked up the footprint of the large demon and followed its trail to the farm. It was difficult, as the many days passed resulted in most of the prints erased by weather or the passing of animals. The multiple sets of tracks in and out at the farm told him what the one soldier speculated was true—they had come there twice.

It saddened him to find the grave. Who had they killed? Some farmer? The boy was cut from the same stock. How could Gar have stooped so low as to kill a kindred farmer?

The hoof prints changed things. He needed to pick up his pace if he wanted to close the gap. He followed the trail as it skirted past a small town. Night was about to fall, and it would be impossible to track in the dark. Tired, the idea of a proper bed for a change seemed like a good one.

His horse must have been of like mind, as it went without prodding in the direction of the hamlet. "I bet a night in a barn with lots of fresh hay and some oats to eat would be good, wouldn't it?" He patted the animal's neck and received a short whinny in return. He chuckled. "I'll take that as a yes."

He cantered into the town square to the stares of a few of the villagers. Spotting an inn, he made for it. As he neared, a young lad ran up to grab his reins.

"Are you staying at the inn tonight?"

He smiled at the boy. "Is it a good inn?"

"It's the best one for a hundred leagues around."

He climbed down from his horse and chuckled. "It's probably the only one for a hundred leagues around."

The boy flashed him a toothy grin. "That still makes it the best."

He reached into his coin purse and tossed the boy a silver. "Alright, you sold me. Make sure my horse gets a good brush down and a bag of oats."

156

The eyes of the lad widened as he stared at the coin in his hand. "A whole silver! You bet. But I'm not big enough to take down the saddle alone. I'll need your help."

He sniffed the air. "Lead the way, lad. I smell some good cooking coming from inside. The sooner we get this horse stabled, the better."

"That's my mother's cooking. She the best cook—"

"I know, I know, for a hundred leagues."

The boy grinned again. "Right this way, then, good sir."

He followed the boy to the stable and pulled off the saddle. The raven flew in and took a perch up in the rafters. The lad chased down a feed bag loaded with oats and Brusk took it to place on the horse. He patted the beast's neck. "I'll see you in the morning." He looked into the rafters at the bird. "And you stay here. I don't need you squawking at everyone and scaring the wits out of them."

The raven gave a small shriek but didn't follow him as he headed for the exit. He left the stable to the happy sound of the boy whistling while brushing the animal down. As he entered the inn, a number of patrons were seated at various tables round the great room. He spotted a table near what must be the door to the kitchen and took a seat.

A plump woman approached him. "What'll ye have?"

"I'll have whatever you got cooking in that kitchen and a mug of your best wine."

"No wine here, just mead. Braised pork shoulder is the meal."

He sighed. A good drink of Riaz red would have been nice. "Mead will do. I'm hungry. Make it a healthy plate of food."

"On its way."

The woman disappeared through the kitchen door and returned in short order with a heaping platter, steaming with a healthy amount of roast pork, potatoes, and carrots. She dropped a large mug next to it. "Three coppers."

He pulled out his coin purse. "How much for a room for the night?"

"Aye, if yer staying the night, it's a silver, but the grub is included. The mead's still a copper, though."

He pulled two silvers from his purse. "Keep the mead coming. It's been a long road."

She scooped up the two coins, and they disappeared quickly into a pocket. "Right, top of the stairs, second room to the right is yours. There's a latrine out back. I ain't got no chamber pots in the rooms."

He nodded at her. "Right. As long as the bed is soft and there's no bugs, I'm happy with that."

"No bugs here. I've got the softest beds for a hundred leagues."

He rolled his eyes. *Now I know where the lad gets it from.* "Your son's already filled me in about this place."

The woman took the seat opposite him. "Name's Trude, by the way. What's a gent like you doing, travelling alone in these times, anyway?"

He paused in his eating to take in the situation. *The last thing I'm going to do is tell you what I'm up to. Best to play dumb.* "Why? Is there a problem round here?"

"Ha! Haven't you heard? There's a war going on."

"Who's fighting?"

"We are, assuming you're Fermian and all, against Sechland. You are Fermian, aren't you?"

He'd thought through what lies he would tell should this situation arise and was able to reply without hesitation. "No, I'm from Queensland. I'm on my way home. Been up north, visiting some kin."

"Where up north? Morica? I got relatives up there too. Where in Morica are they?"

"Not Morica—Piaxia."

The woman scrunched up her face. "In that warlock infested land? I heard they make sacrifices of people up there to get their magical powers from the gods. Your kin warlocks?"

"No, nothing of the sort. Simple farmers and sheep herders."

"It's the simple folk who bear the brunt of those monsters. A pox on them all." She spat on the floor.

Brusk paused to drain his mead. "You know, they had warlocks in the seven kingdoms once, a long time ago. I don't think they were sacrificing anyone back then. That's just a myth."

The woman rose, grabbed his empty mug and went behind a counter to fill it. She plopped the fresh one down. "A bad lot they were, letting all those demons loose on the land. It's a good thing we done away with them. It's been peaceful round here since then, but now we got Sechlanders going round doing that black magic and letting the demons out. I hear tell the demon stone down the road's been opened. Four of the local guardsmen got killed by them monsters. And to think them Sechlanders were just a couple of lads. It makes my heart sick, it does."

He perked up at what the innkeeper said. "Two lads? Are you sure?"

"Sure as I'm standing here. They was in my place, they was. Each enjoyed a couple of mugs of the very same stuff you're drinking. When they left, the local boys decided to go check up on them at their camp, they being so young and all. That was the last I seen of them. News came how their bodies were found, all torn up. I grieved for them boys. I hope they find that pair and give them what's coming to them."

"*That's* something I could drink to." He hoisted the mug and drained it.

The woman smiled and went to get him another. "I knew I liked the look of ya. I've got other customers to tend to. Remember, the name's Trude. Give me a holler when you need more, or if there's something else I can provide that might warm ya a bit more...later." She winked and walked away.

He chuckled. *It's a sad state I've fallen to when portly innkeepers are the best offer I can get.* He took a sip of the new mug and stretched his legs out a bit. A sharp twinge made him wince. He glanced down and spotted a fresh red spot widening in the material of his leggings. *Damn it. The wound re-opened. I'd best get to my room and redress it.*

He rose to head for the stair. Across the way, Trude stole a glance at him then returned to her conversation with a couple of young men. He sighed and began the climb. *Too bad, plump or*

159

not, I could have enjoyed myself for a change, but anyone seeing this wound's going to know I've been fighting, and there goes my cover.

He found the second door to the right and went in. The room was small—only a single bed, a chair, and a table with a washbasin on it. A pitcher sat on the floor beside it. He poured some water in the basin and sat in the chair to pull off his leggings.

The wound was seeping blood and the skin was angry all round. He should have let the doctor put some stitches in it when he was at Eagle Ridge. There was no choice left but to do it himself. He opened his kit and found the standard medical supplies. Tucked in, was the hooked needle, thread and some salve made from the gods knew what. He found a leather strap as well. Placing it in his mouth, between his teeth, he threaded the needle and hovered it above the wound. *It's now or never.*

He stabbed the needle in. The pain was excruciating. Tears flowed from the corners of his eyes. He worked as quickly as he could and sewed five stitches in a haphazard manner to close the wound. He cleaned it as best he could and wrapped a fresh bandage on it.

When he finally took the bit of leather out of his mouth, he felt as weak as a kitten. He eyed the door. *Thank the gods I didn't scream.* There was a dead bar he could drop in place to block the door. He made use of it. *Just in case she gets any bright ideas of her own.*

He climbed into the bed and was pleased to find it soft and clean smelling. It wasn't long before sleep overtook him.

CHAPTER 28

Gar and the demons hadn't gone very far since opening the demon stone that held Pleasure. They found an empty hunting lodge in the woods. If the rules in Gatway were anything like the ones in Sechland, no one would be coming to the lodge anytime soon. Deer hunting was outlawed when the does were either still with fawn or had just given birth, as was often the case in the spring.

Gar wanted to stay put for a while. The lodge comprised an open great room with a large fireplace set in the middle and round the perimeter were a number of storage rooms, a larder, and four small bedrooms.

He searched through the larder. Although it held nothing to eat, it did contain a variety of spices and a fair quantity of salt. *They must have cured the meat here. At least there's something to cook with.*

A closer inspection of the store rooms showed the walls and floors were stained dark. Hooks hung from the ceiling. Thunder peered in, sniffed, and left immediately, grumbling in his language.

Hiss bounded in. "Thunder say was slaughter room."

"Yeah, I kinda figured that. Too bad there's nothing here to slaughter. Some fresh meat would go a long way in satisfying me right now."

"Me go, take Thunder, bring back fresh kill."

Before the imp could scamper away, Gar reached down and grabbed the demon's arm to stop him. "Okay, go, but no deer. Understand?"

Hiss smiled. "Me understand, me tell Thunder, too."

"Good. Take your time. I'm going to get some sleep first."

Hiss dashed out of the room and Gar followed.

Pleasure was leaning against the wall outside the door. "Why do you care whether or not they kill a deer? The meat in such an animal would feed you for a long time. Those two will probably end up bringing you a couple of hares. Hardly a feast for one such as you."

"It's the law. I'm not about to break it, even if this isn't Sechland."

She laughed. The tinkling resonation in it didn't soothe him as Silk's did; it energized him. "You are the master of four powerful demons. You should be setting the laws, not abiding by them. With a command, you could have the nearest small town obliterated, its entire populace bent to your wishes. You should be ruler of this domain, not running from it."

He stopped walking to consider what she'd said. She grinned, her sharp teeth gleaming. She had a point. He was in charge of them. Why shouldn't he take advantage of it?

Pleasure wrapped an arm over his shoulder and brought her mouth close to his ear. "Think of it. The one you call Thunder is unstoppable. With the aid of Hiss, Silk, and myself, you could become king."

King. It seemed absurd, yet not. What would it take to do such a thing? To become king?

Silk approached and pulled him from Pleasure's grasp. "Don't go filling his head with ideas just yet. Gar is probably tired and in need of rest." She led him to one of the bedrooms. "Come, Gar, go to bed for a while. After a good night's sleep, you'll be better able to decide what to do next."

Pleasure said something Silk responded to, but as it was in their harsh language, he didn't understand a word. He did feel very tired. He was worn out from running. All he wanted to do was rest. "Yes, some sleep. That's what I need. Let me get some sleep and I'll feel better."

Silk led him into one of the rooms and guided him to lie down. She unfolded a blanket and draped it over him then sat on the edge of the bed. "Listen, Gar. There's more than one type of lust in the world. The lust for sex is one thing, but the lust for power is another. Pleasure exudes that lust and thrusts it into you. I can't give you the will to fight these lustful urgings all the time. You're going to have to learn to fight it yourself—close your mind to it. It can be done, I know."

"How do you know?"

"Why do you think I was found in the stone? When the warlock Bron caught up with me, I tried to use my powers to have him surrender his will to me. It was impossible. His mind blocked my best attempts. I didn't want to be locked forever in rock, so I resorted to my last option, defeating him with my womanly charms. I hoped he would surrender to my beauty. Even this, he resisted. The next thing that happened was my entombment."

"This Bron. I've heard him mentioned before. What was he like? I heard he was a very powerful warlock."

Silk sighed. "A lot like you, maybe a little older. Tall, though, again, not quite as tall as you, and rugged. He was from a family of sheep herders. He'd lived his entire life in the open fields of his country, Piaxia. And, yes, a very powerful wizard, the most powerful in the land."

"I wonder if he's still alive, and if so, would he come down here to try and trap you again?"

"I doubt it. Unlike us, you people age. He would be well over a hundred years old by now. I don't think any humans live that long. But if he did, there would be none of us who could stand against him." She tucked the blanket round him. "Now get some sleep. I'll wake you in the morning." She kissed him on the cheek and rose.

His eyes grew heavy. "Yes, sleep. I need to sleep."

***

A noise woke him. It was dark in the room and he could see little. Someone was standing by the door. "Silk?"

The shadow rushed forward. "No, it's not Silk. It's me, Pleasure. I've come to resume my pleasing."

He felt groggy, like he hadn't slept at all. "Is it morning?"

"You don't want morning—you want me." She pulled off her outfit and slid under the blanket beside him, running her hands over his body. "It *is* me you want, isn't it? Not Silk? Not that girl back home, the one called Lialee. Yes, I know of her. Hiss told me."

163

Despite his exhaustion, he could feel the lust running through him. "Yes, you—I want you."

She chuckled. "I thought as much. And I want you. Let us enjoy the wanting together."

He realized there would be no rest for him that night.

***

In the final moments before morning, Pleasure left the room. As the sun streamed its early rays through the window, Silk entered and roused him.

"I'm still tired. Let me sleep some more."

Silk scanned the small room. "When did she leave?"

"I don't know, not very long ago."

"Fine—sleep till you're ready. In the meantime, Thunder and Hiss have returned with a brace of rabbits. I'll prep them to eat when you're ready."

She left the room and he rolled over in an attempt to block the sun from his closed eyelids. It was no use. The sound of the demons talking in their own language carried from the great room to where he lay.

Gar tossed off the blanket and pulled on his clothes, which lay discarded on the floor. He stumbled out into the main room rubbing at his eyes. Pleasure was at him in an instant.

"Did Master have a good night last night?" She wrapped her arms round him and licked his ear.

He extricated from her grip with some effort. "Don't you sleep at all?"

"We have no need to. We don't eat food. We only drink water, and little at that. We don't suffer the many frailties of mankind."

"Well, I do, and I can't keep going like this. I'm exhausted, and you're giving me no chance to recover. You have to leave me alone, all of you."

Silk said something to Thunder and the big beast rose from where he lay, stepped up to Gar and put a hand on his chest. A sudden surge of energy coursed through his body, as if he had the strength to lift a horse. Thunder must have imparted some life force into him. He nodded to the demon. "Thank you, Thunder."

The creature nodded and went back to lie on the floor.

Pleasure tried to once again attach herself to him.

"Now that you have energy once more, what do you say we use some?"

He pushed her off. "No. I mean it. I need all of you to let me alone for a while. It's become where I don't know whether I have any control over what's happening anymore. You are using your power to make me do things and think things. So is Silk. Thunder is impossible to control when it comes to killing, and Hiss is constantly leading me who knows where. I want all of you to stop trying to control me."

Silk stepped between him and Pleasure. "So what is it *you* want to do, Gar? I'll abide and so..." she spun to glare for a moment at Pleasure who scowled back at her, "will my fellow demons. Give us your decision."

He sat down. "I want to stay put for a while. I'm saddle sore and unsure. Give me some time to think."

Silk stepped away. "As you wish."

Pleasure smiled. "I'll respect your decision. But I don't think hiding here can happen forever. You'll need to do something."

"I know. But for the next couple of days, at least, I'd like to do nothing."

Pleasure moved to the far side of the room. He thought he sensed something, but he couldn't put a finger on it. Something...was gone. He surmised it was the influence of one or both of the women. *I'll never know when my thoughts are truly my own. What am I going to do? How do I get out of this terrible mess I'm in?*

CHAPTER 29

Devron sat and quietly contemplated the man sitting across from him. The fact the fellow was Morican was a detail he needed to keep in mind. The litany of demands the fellow was iterating was beyond his own expectations.

"…and furthermore, all citizens are to be taxed fifty percent of their wealth and earnings in payment to Morica for damages and losses as a result of the conflict. I am instructed to—"

He'd heard enough. "Hold for a moment. It is sufficient we are prepared to allow the entry of your troops without resistance so you may ascertain on your own there are no warlocks or other delvers into the dark arts within our walls. We are agreed Visk will fall under foreign rule, with a consortium of the other kingdoms to preside until *such* time as they are convinced of our adherence to the Warlock Pact, but *such* a financial demand on our people will result in poverty for all. It would be better if you just finished us off now rather than put the people through *such* hardship. With *such* a ruling, every citizen of Visk will be a beggar in a fortnight."

The man grinned at him. "*Such* are the fortunes of war."

Devron needed time. "I shall consider your proposal." He motioned toward the soldier stationed near the door to approach. "My man will guide you safely to the gate. We shall resume this discussion at a later time."

The negotiator recoiled in his chair. "No. Wait. I'm supposed to take charge here and start collecting the tax immediately. You're to follow my orders, not the other way around."

Devron rose and the guard lifted the Morican emissary from his seat. "I understood completely what was said. A council made up of the other six kingdoms is to be put in place to rule. As I only see a representative of one of those nations here—you—I am obliged to wait until the other five arrive. Those are the terms, are they not? I have read the rules and stipulations of the Warlock Pact quite carefully. Are you suggesting we should deviate from it? It

166

would be interesting to find out what the other nations think of your proposal."

"Well, I suppose you have a point. Until the others arrive, then."

"Until the others arrive."

The man exited and Devron slumped back into his chair. It was clear the emissary had no knowledge of Garlin Murdach or the opening of the demon stone near town. Had that been the case, the terms he would have faced would have been much harsher, and the combined troops of Morica, Storburg, and Fermia would not still be languishing at Sechwisk but instead would be outside the walls of Visk in force.

He was glad of the decision he made to put the young man Jango in a cell. Even though the lad's story had merit, he could not risk it being told to every passerby. He'd promised the girl Darlee that Jango would not be punished but held for his own safety until such time as the situation resolved itself. There was no knowing how long that would be.

Despite her pleas, he made no promises in regards to her brother. There was no conclusive evidence as to Garlin's innocence of any kind. The boy's actions brought about the downfall of the kingdom, regardless of his intent. Justice was required.

A knock on the door drew his attention. "Enter."

The duty officer came in. "Lieutenant, a delegation to see you."

"Who now?"

"It is the former city elder council. They wish an immediate audience. I told them I would ask but made no promises."

He chuckled. "I don't know which one is worse to talk to, the emissary from Morica, or this lot. Very well, show them in, but before you do, take away those chairs before me. I would have them stand."

The soldier laughed, grabbed the four chairs, and left the room. The six men entered with Merchant Trellus in the lead. He looked about and turned for a moment to face the retreating guard.

The fool is looking for the chairs and now realizes they just went out the door.

Trellus returned his focus. "Lieutenant Devron, we are here to determine what plans you have for protecting the citizenry of this city?"

"Ha! Plans? What plans? I intend to turn Visk over to the enemy without conflict. That's my plan."

Trellus purpled. "You can't be serious. They'll loot the city! No one will be safe."

"You mean, they'll loot the rich, like yourself. They will leave the average person alone. This is not a conquest, it's a temporary occupation. Once they have completed what they have come for, they will leave."

"How can you be so sure? You, a simple lieutenant, have nothing to risk. Your meager army wages would afford you little. The wealthy of this city are its backbone. Without our trade, our commerce, there would be nothing. I demand you meet your obligation as a soldier to protect our interests."

"You will make no demands of me, Merchant Trellus. Personally, I hope they strip you to the bone, but I have my doubts they will. Twice already, my men have intercepted your messengers as they have sought to negotiate your own deal with the enemy's emissary camped outside our walls. You have no idea what is going on or what risks I take or do not take. My decision stands. Now, leave, before I have you arrested for interfering with the negotiations."

Trellus raised a finger as if about to begin another protest, and then spun on his heel and headed out the door, the other elders right behind him.

He sighed. Little did Merchant Trellus and the city elders comprehend how much his own life was at risk. As a cousin of King Lowry, he would be granted no leniency. More than likely, he was the closest relative to the throne who yet lived. The other kingdoms would not risk his remaining free. The safest course of action was probably a self-imposed exile.

The idea was abhorrent. How could he abandon his people in their moment of greatest need? But perhaps there was a way in

168

which he could still continue to serve. He called out for the duty officer.

"Yes, Lieutenant."

"Bring me Lieutenant Gramby."

"Right away, sir."

He rose and began to remove his personal belongings from the table. It wasn't long until Gramby appeared at his door.

"You looking for me, Devron?"

Although his senior lieutenant, Gramby insisted Devron retain command since his arrival from Eagle Ridge the day before. News of Captain Brusk heading into Morica on some private mission had been most disturbing. He still hadn't come to a full comprehension of the man, perhaps he never would, but it gave him an idea. "You're in charge now, Gramby. I've decided to surrender command to you. I've got something to do, and staying here is only putting my own life in peril once the enemy armies arrive."

"Not you, too? What are they putting in the drinking water here in Visk? I think I'd better have it tested to determine whether there's something funny with it."

He chuckled. "It's not the water. Maybe I've picked up some of Brusk's bad habits. I only know that, as Lowry's cousin, I don't give my chances much once the occupation force arrives. I'm heading to the stables to make arrangements for my departure. I'd like it if you'd accompany me so I can brief you as best as I can as to the current state of affairs. Who knows, you might come up with some better solutions than I have."

They walked together and met with the stable master. He helped pick out the best horse for what Devron's intentions were and provided advice as to what the saddle bags should contain. Along the way, Gramby listened carefully as Devron detailed all he knew about the demons and those involved—Garlin and Darlee Murdach, their friend Jango, even the theory of how Wirbon, the son of merchant Trellus, had been killed. Gramby asked a few clarifying questions but never once challenged what was said. He had to trust Gramby would do what was right. He was leaving the fate of Visk in the man's hands.

Devron packed his belongings and tied the bundle on the back of the saddle. "It'll be dark soon, and I'd prefer the emissary and his men not notice my leaving. I don't know what I'll encounter when I get there, but if there's a chance they can help, then I have to try."

"It's risky business, this plan of yours. Those warlocks of theirs will read your mind and know the truth of things before you know it. In the meantime, I'll do what I have to do to keep those Morican pigs from running amok in the city. I wish you luck."

They clasped forearms. "And you, Lieutenant." He glanced out of the stable door to see the last of the light fading. "It's time I get going. It's a long ride ahead of me."

Gramby smiled. "Hmm-hmm. Their capital, Lia, is the full length of the country away. Even by horseback, it should take you a fortnight. May the gods be with you."

He climbed into the saddle and spurred the animal toward the city gate. The sky was clear. *At least I won't have to ride in the rain.* At his command, the gate was opened, and he set out at a brisk trot. The emissary's camp was several hundred paces away. Obviously, the man wanted his own privacy and security from those coming and going through the gate. *All the better.*

He picked out those stars he knew would aid in guiding him on his journey and turned the horse north. The border of Piaxia was less than two days away.

CHAPTER 30

Darlee hoisted the small pack and bent to give Pap a kiss on the cheek before heading for the city. "I'm off to school. I'll see you this afternoon when I get back."

Her grandfather looked up from the bowl of oatmeal and smiled. "Don't tarry today, Darlee. I'm going to need your help working on the house. The other farmers have been dropping off the last couple of days as they have their own things to tend to. I'm not sure how many, if any, will show today, and I want to finish getting that roof on. My old bones tell me rain is coming soon."

"Will do. See you then."

She exited the shed that was home and set out on the path toward Visk. The sun was yet to rise but she knew it wouldn't be long until it did. In the meantime, she picked her way along, avoiding the mud-filled ruts that she knew by heart. Her pack was a little heavier than usual. Because they couldn't afford ink and paper, as always she carried her writing board, a piece of hard, flat slate she would scrawl on with chalk. Also in the bag were some dried fruits she intended to give to Jango. She'd visited him the day before, and although they were feeding him, it was simple gruel.

As she continued along, the sun broke over the horizon and bathed the countryside with its morning light. As far as she could see in all directions were the numerous small farms of the people of Visk. The land was dotted with houses set within the obvious perimeter each farm displayed, either through the variance in the way the fields were plowed or the difference in the early growth of the crops from first planting. She tried to identify who was growing what, but the plants were so small, it was tough to tell one from another.

Preoccupied, she was surprised, when she turned onto the last stretch of road heading toward the city, to find the area filled with soldiers setting up camp. The forces that conquered Sechwisk had arrived.

As she passed between the different camps, she recognized the colors of Morica, Fermia, and Storburg. *Storburg. I thought they were our friends.*

Soldiers noticed her and made rude comments as she passed. She did her best to ignore them, but when a couple of the men stepped into the road directly in front of her, she panicked. She focused straight at the ground and tried to walk determinedly through them, but the one closest grabbed her by the shoulders.

"Hey, sweet thing, what's the rush? We just got here."

She brushed away his arms. "Leave me alone."

He moved to block her again. "Now is that a nice way to greet guests. We *are* your guests, right?" Other soldiers were crowding in and the man's comments brought a roar of laughter.

"You're not my guests. Please move out of my way."

"Not your guests? Well, then, you might as well be mine. My tent's over this way." He grabbed her round the waist and lifted her off the ground, tucked under his arm.

She screamed. The men laughed again. *He's taking me!* "Help! Somebody help me!"

"No one's going to help you, little girl. You're mine now."

"No, no, no! You can't do this. Put me down. Let me go!"

"That's not going to happen. You're my early payment on this—"

The man's grasp released and she fell to the ground. She scrambled to her feet and watched as her abductor slumped to his knees then fall over.

Standing behind him was an officer from Morica, holding a sword with the hilt held forward, the end with a touch of blood from the soldier's head. "There'll be none of this nonsense!" He pointed at two men standing near. "You and you, take this man to detention."

The indicated soldiers picked up the fallen man and dragged him away. The officer approached Dar and held out his hand. "Come, child. My name is Commander Padronus. I'll escort you the rest of the way."

She refused to take his hand but instead wrapped her arms round her. "I'll go by myself. Just keep these ruffians away from me."

The officer dropped his extended hand and sighed. "As you wish—on with you, then. They will bother you no more."

She stepped lively toward the main gate, now only some thirty paces away. Once inside, she found a hitching post to lean against. She was shaking. How close had she come to being used by those brutes? Too close. She needed to catch her breath and allow her heart to quit racing. She sat on the ground and rested against the post.

Maurus passed by and spotted her. "Hey, Darlee, what'cha doing?"

She didn't want him to know the truth. She stood up and brushed the dust from her clothing. "Nothing. Just taking a break. It's a long walk from home, since my father's no longer around to give me a ride in."

Maurus scowled, looked down, and kicked at the dirt. "Yeah, that was bad." He focused on her again. "Any word on Gar?"

"No, there've been no reports. Lieutenant Devron said he would notify me the moment he heard anything."

"Ha! Devron! Haven't you heard? He left town last night. He upped and rode off. No one knows where he went, or at least they aren't saying. He left Lieutenant Gramby in charge. Lialee says her father found out and she overheard him telling someone "Good riddance." He's going to approach the new lieutenant in charge today to request martial law be rescinded and civic matters returned to the council."

Anger welled in her at hearing the girl's name. "Lialee? That trollop! Honestly, Maurus, what do you see in that girl? She isn't overly pretty. If anything, she's a bit fat. That's probably from eating the sweets all day her parents spoil her with. She's mean to everyone and looks down her nose at people like you and me. She doesn't have a nice bone in her body."

Maurus reddened. "It's not nice for you to talk that way about Lialee. She's allowing me to court her."

173

Darlee laughed. "Allowing you? Don't you realize how silly that sounds? You need to wake up, Maurus. She's using you, just like she uses everybody."

Maurus reddened further, but instead of retorting he turned away. "I gotta go. I'm going to be late for class."

Darlee chased after him. "I'm coming with you. I still go to school, too, you know."

They arrived at the school together and Darlee noted Lialee standing outside with her two girlfriends. Lialee scowled at her and stepped over to intercept them as they neared.

"Maurus, what are you doing walking with this criminal?"

He hung his head. "Just walking to school."

"She's the wrong kind of person to be walking with. Besides, I waited here to have you come to my house where it'll be safer. My father has his own soldiers guarding the estate. You'd better come with me." She hooked her arm into his and dragged him away.

Maurus held up for a moment. "Bye, Darlee."

"Bye." She pressed her lips tight then sighed heavily. How she hated that girl. *Maurus doesn't know what he's in for.* Shaking her head to clear it, Darlee proceeded into the classroom and sat down. As the other students entered, a lot of whispering surrounded her, but no one spoke with her directly. She accepted the situation. *I really don't feel like talking to anyone anyway.*

Over two thirds of the class was not in attendance. Considering the troops stationed outside the gates, it was surprising there was class at all.

The teacher entered and gave Darlee a curious stare then turned her focus to the entire class. "Students, we will not be following our regular regimen. As you are all probably aware, an invading army has come to Visk to take over the city. We will, instead, be reviewing the articles of the Warlock Pact so you can all understand why this has come to pass."

The Warlock Pact? There are no warlocks in Visk. They must mean Gar because he released those demons. Oh, Gar. Look what you've done.

174

She listened carefully to every word and made notes about every detail. Maybe, just maybe, there might be some clause she could hang her hopes on for getting Gar back safe and sound.

When class ended, she made straight for the jail. She'd promised Pap she wouldn't dally, so she would have to hurry to drop off the dried fruits to Jango.

The guards at the door let her in when she showed a permission notice from Lieutenant Devron. She entered the center hall area and was led up two flights of stairs to the top floor. Each floor was identical, with a number of cells spread lining the outside wall with a center room where a jailer sat. *That's a lot of cells, and I heard there are two levels below ground with the bottom level where they torture prisoners.* She spied Jango sitting in his cell and raced over. The guard unlocked the door and let her in then locked it behind her and went across the room to sit down. She gave Jango a hug. "I can't stay long. How are you doing?"

"I'm okay. Any news?"

She handed him the dried fruit. He looked fit. *He's probably eating better here than he did at home.* "The armies of Morica, Storburg, and Fermia have arrived. They're setting up camp outside the walls."

"Yeah, I know. I could hear them from the window. What about Gar, any word?"

"Nothing. They taught us all about the Warlock Pact today in school. They won't find any warlocks here."

"I don't know. The new lieutenant came by to see me this morning asking a lot of questions about Gar and you."

A cold sensation swept through her. "What kind of questions?"

"He wanted to know stuff. Stuff like what you were like. Who were your friends? Where did you go during the day?"

Why did the new lieutenant want to know those things? Something doesn't sound right. "Listen, Jango. I've got to go. Pap wants me home early. In the meantime, don't say anything, okay?"

Jango nodded. "Okay, not that I told him much anyway."

Darlee rose and called for the jailer to let her out. The man ambled over and unlocked the cell. She started for the stairwell when the sound of many boots tramping up gave her pause. Emerging from below appeared a man in a lieutenant's uniform. *That must be the new Lieutenant Gramby.* He was accompanied by three other officers wearing the colors of the armies outside the walls and a couple of other guardsmen. She recognized Commander Padronus, the officer who'd saved her earlier.

Gramby stopped when he neared her. "And who's this?"

"My name's Darlee Murdach. I came to visit my friend Jango. I have permission from Lieutenant Devron to do so." She waved the letter in front of him.

Gramby took the letter, glanced at it, and put it in his pocket. "You've saved me the trouble, young miss, of having to chase you down." He turned to the other men. "This is the one I was telling you about. Her and the lad in that cell there." He pointed out Jango.

Padronus scowled. "It's sad to see you're the one." He nodded to Gramby. "We'll need to use your facilities here."

"I understand." He nodded toward the two guardsmen. "Take her down to the lowest level then come back for the other one."

The men grabbed her by the forearms. She struggled for an instant. "What's going on?"

"I'm surrendering the two of you to these men for questioning. I've assured them there are no others in town who may be delving into the black arts and they've agreed to limit their investigation for now. I do this for the good of the town. May the gods forgive me."

"No, you can't. I didn't do anything. This isn't right."

Gramby stepped aside. "Do it."

The men proceeded to hustle her down the stairwell to the bottom level. They put her into a cell and locked the door. As they left she stared out into the main room. In the center stood a table with a number of iron rings set in it. She could also make out the various tools of the torturer's trade set out on an adjacent table. *This can't be happening.*

It wasn't long before the two men returned with Jango and placed him in a cell across the room. He was crying and pleading for the men to let him go.

She needed to be brave and so did he. "Don't worry, Jango. Everything will be alright. We're innocent. They'll let us go in time."

"Leave me alone." Jango moved to the back of his cell out of her line of vision. She could hear him continue to sob.

A voice from the cell next startled her. "So they got him, too."

The cells were all stone with doors of iron bars and she couldn't see whoever was talking. "Who's there?"

The man chuckled. "The name's Baxus, and your friend over there was with me at the battle at Morence. He won't survive down here, I know."

"How do you know?"

The man's arm came through the bars of his door so she could see it. Two fingers were cut off. "I know."

She felt a cold chill run through her, and she backed up to a stone bench with some straw on it set against the wall that must serve as the bed. Climbing on, she pulled her knees up to her chin and wrapped her arms around them. She had never been so scared in all her life.

CHAPTER 31

Brusk continued to follow the trail wherever it led. He discovered the cave and all of the squashed things that were some kind of demon bugs, and then the rock outcropping burst open like the others were. He paused to check the opening. This demon was taller than him but the indentations in the rock indicated something else, slimness at the waist and arms and a healthy bosom, a female.

Now he faced a hunting lodge, some hundred paces away, set deep within the woods. Tendrils of smoke emanated from the central chimney. Someone was there and based on the tracks, it could only be Gar and the demons.

He tethered his horse to a nearby tree and checked the wind. Not quite into his face, but enough to prevent his scent from carrying. He was perspiring heavily and was sure he could be smelled a furlong away downwind.

There was nothing he could do about the sweat. He became feverish over the last half a day and his body was wracked with chills. Even his vision was blurring at times. He knew what the problem was. The wound in his leg had festered. More than likely, it would take his life in a day or two. *Now that I've found him, that should be more than enough time to do what I came to do.*

He spotted an open window immediately left of a door and noticed movement inside. Its location was leeward from the wind. It would give him a chance to get a peek inside. The timing was good. Night was falling and anyone looking out from the lit room would unlikely see him in the dark.

A flutter told him the raven was close by. It landed on his shoulder and nipped at his ear. He lifted the animal off and held it before him. "I need you to be quiet now. I don't want anyone hearing me coming."

The bird's head bobbed, as if in recognition. The animal took off and headed toward the lodge.

"Lead the way."

He moved with all the skill he could muster. A start-stop, haphazard approach masked his steps with their inconsistency. He pulled his sword and left the scabbard behind so it wouldn't clang against his body. He even abandoned his shirt for fear an errant sleeve might catch on a branch.

When two steps from the window, he could hear voices. One he recognized as Gar's, the others were both feminine, one deeper than the other. He peeked over the sill and spotted a huge demon sprawled out on the floor, sleeping. *There's that monster from the cave in Morica. By the gods, he's a big one.*

He turned his head to follow the voices and located Gar seated between two women who were both standing nearby. Despite their grey skin and lack of hair he found them both stunningly beautiful. *Two demon vixens. The lad's been busy.*

He estimated the number of paces from the door to his right to where Gar sat. It was three at most once he crossed under the lintel. He checked back to the giant demon to make sure it was still asleep. The beast was gone. *Now where, by the gods, did that thing get to?*

A screech overhead made him glance to his left in time to see the big demon bearing down on him. From out of the night sky the raven flashed down and raked the monster's face. It howled as it swung at Brusk. The bird must have distracted it enough. The huge clawed hand passed over his head and into the side of the building sending a shower of splinters as the wood post shattered. Had it hit him it would have torn his head clean off. He swung his sword at the beast only to watch it bounce off.

Forget fighting this thing, I'd best do what I came to do. Brusk spun to his right and burst through the door. Gar was now standing. He charged, raising his sword to strike a fatal blow. *It's time to make you pay.*

From out of nowhere, a small demon tackled his ankles and he stumbled. He gave the imp a vicious kick that sent it sprawling across the room. He turned to face Gar but he was unable to raise the sword again. The smaller vixen was staring hard at him with her hands extended. It was as if all of his willpower was gone. He slumped to his knees.

The fever took him with a vengeance. His vision blurred and a flush raced through him. His body was giving up. He was about to die. After all he had been through, he had failed. The last thing he saw was the giant demon, with a large bleeding gash above its right eye, charging at him from the open doorway. His eyes closed and he collapsed to the floor.

***

Gar jumped in front of the oncoming Thunder, hands held up. "Stop! Don't hurt him!"

The behemoth, headlong in flight, jumped over Gar, rolled and returned to a standing position in one sweeping motion. Gar marveled at the dexterity the beast displayed. He was also surprised to see the dark blood seeping through a cut on its forehead, the drops steaming as they hit the floor.

Hiss skittered close, returning from being kicked. Gar could see no injury. "Are you okay?"

"Hiss good. Human no hurt."

He pointed toward Thunder's cut. "Can you heal the wound on his head?"

"He demon, no magic heal. Thunder heal using own power."

Gar bent to the prone body of Captain Brusk. He could see no wounds but the man was lathered in sweat. He glanced up at Silk. "Did you do this?"

"I only drained him of will. He collapsed on his own."

Thunder growled something.

Silk knelt next to Gar. "Thunder says he smells bad."

Pleasure laughed. "I'll say. I can smell him from across the room. One has to wonder when he bathed last."

Thunder spoke more in demon tongue. Silk moved toward Brusk's legs. "He says not that kind of smell, a bad smell, like something spoiled. He says the smell is coming from his legs."

Gar moved to join her and discovered the bandage under Brusk's leggings. Silk used her sharp fingers to tear open the leggings to free the bandage. What greeted Gar's sight was an ugly wound, badly stitched, and a variety of colors about it.

180

Silk covered her nose. "It's gangrene. He's dying."

Gar motioned for Hiss to come close. "Help me, Hiss. We must save him."

Pleasure stopped the small demon. "Are you mad? He just tried to kill you."

Gar knew that. But something inside him told him saving Brusk's life was the right thing to do. "I don't care. He's from my hometown. He's an honorable man. He must have his reasons. Maybe he thought killing me would stop all of you. I don't know. All I know is I want to save his life."

Hiss freed himself from Pleasure's grasp. "Hiss can't help, Master. Me no mana left. Me use fight mindless ones, free Pleasure. Hiss no chance renew from other human."

A fluttering caught Gar's attention to see a raven fly through the open window and land next to Brusk. Thunder jumped for it, but the bird eluded him and landed once more beside the unconscious captain.

Gar moved again between Thunder and the captain. "I recognize this bird. It's the captain's pet. Someone tell Thunder to leave it alone."

Silk conveyed the message and her and Thunder spoke for a moment in demon tongue. "Thunder says the bird cut him. It shouldn't be allowed to live."

He wanted to keep the captain's pet alive should the captain revive. "I'll compromise. If the captain dies, Thunder can have the bird, but if he recovers, the bird lives."

Silk and Thunder spoke again and after a few back and forths, she nodded. "He agrees. He thinks the man will be dead soon, so he'll wait."

The captain. What was Gar going to do? He'd heard once the way to save a man from gangrene was to cut his leg off. It sounded horrendous. He doubted he could do it. More than likely, he would only expedite the man's death. If only Hiss still had mana to help him conduct a magical healing like he did with Jango.

To his surprise, the bird hopped onto his arm and tilted its head at him with a sideways stare. It was imploring him to do something. *I've got to heal him.*

181

"Well, I've got to try. Maybe I can do it on my own. You've taught me how."

He reached down and put his hands on the wounded leg of Captain Brusk. He concentrated. *Heal. Heal. Heal.* Nothing was happening. There must be some kind of trick to it. He tried to remember what exactly went through his mind when Hiss helped him before. What steps he was missing.

Then it came to him. Stone. He needed to be touching stone— something about the Key. The Key was in the stone. He recalled a whetting stone in one of the slaughter rooms. He went and got it and put it beside him. He placed a hand on the whetting stone and a hand on Brusk's leg. *Heal.* Nothing yet.

The raven hopped up onto the captain's leg and put one talon onto the hand pressing onto the wound. The bird was trying to help. He took a deep breath and concentrated again. Heal. A sudden surge went through Gar. He felt more energy than any of the times Hiss helped. He watched as vile fluids poured out of the wound. When they stopped, the colors disappeared and the wound closed. It wasn't long until only a ruddy redness and the haphazard stitches were all that remained to show where the wound once was. "It's done."

Silk used her fingers and cut and pulled the stitches free. "He won't need those anymore." She placed a hand on his chest and another on Brusk's forehead. "He's still fevered and his breathing is ragged." A soft white glow emanated from Silk's hands into the captain. "There. I've given him the will to fight the fever. All I can spare. Like Hiss, I'm without until we encounter others." She began another demon conversation with Thunder.

When it ended, Thunder came and put a hand on Brusk's chest. Gar recognized it for what it was—a boost of life energy.

Silk smiled and laughed her tinkling laugh. "Thunder is unhappy because he won't get the bird."

"Tell him there's a whole forest full of them out there. Go and get all the birds he wants."

She told Thunder and the big demon bolted out the door. Hiss picked up the whetting stone and rotated it in his hands as he examined it.

"Master, how you do it?"

"I did what you taught me, Hiss. I healed him. I found the additional power in the stone like the times before."

Hiss shook his head. "Only stone of all work-mountain, bedrock, stone beneath everything—not loose stone. Loose stone no have Key."

"Well, maybe this one did. Does it matter? Captain Brusk is healed."

Hiss returned his attention to the stone. "Maybe matter, maybe no."

With Thunder gone, Gar lifted the captain and took him into one of the bedrooms. He made sure to put extra covers on the man. Hopefully, he would sweat out the fever quickly. The raven hopped up on the prone figure of the captain and let out a small squawk.

"You're welcome."

When he re-entered the main room he felt tired. Perhaps lying down was not a bad idea. He went to the bedroom he claimed as his own and pulled the covers over him. It took a while to fall asleep because through the window he could hear the constant screeches of birds. Thunder must have been busy.

CHAPTER 32

Devron had taken a wrong road and only with the help of directions from a good farmer did he finally arrive at the city of Zon. Even in the dark of night he could make out the walls as eerie orbs of light floated round some three hundred paces out and some thirty hands in the air. No one would be able to approach those walls unnoticed.

The first sight of magic being used unnerved him. To think those wielders of the dark arts could summon such things as the orbs made him wonder to what extent their powers ranged.

As his horse clomped along the road toward the nearest gate he noted the walls were in a state of repair. No, on second thought, they were being replaced. New walls made from field stone were replacing wooden ones, one section at a time.

He thought back to the walls of Visk. Like the early version here in Zon, they were mostly wood with stone towers spaced between each section. He considered them superior to the old walls of Zon, but no match for these new ones. *They are preparing for war.*

The idea of another army invading Sechland from the north while it was besieged by three armies from the south and east deflated him. *If what I suspect is true, then my homeland is truly doomed.*

He reached the gate and was halted by four guardsmen in light brown livery. The one closest stepped before his horse, arms raised in the air. "Halt! What business do you have in Zon, stranger?"

"My good man, my name is Lieutenant Devron of the city of Visk in the realm of Sechland to the south. I seek an audience with whoever is in command here. I am on an urgent mission and need to speak with him immediately. Would you be so kind as to announce me?"

The man laughed. "A Sechlander, eh? I shoulda figured based on the uniform you're wearing. Go home, Sechlander. Lord Kipron is too busy for the likes of you. Besides, at this hour he's probably asleep and chambers aren't open again until two hands past dawn."

"Then perhaps I could employ the use of one of your inns to rest the night and present my petition in the morning. Would you be gracious enough to point out a good one in town?"

The man glanced behind him. "Are you blind? The gates closed for the night. Only those with passes are entitled to come and go."

Behind the man he could see the gates were indeed closed. "I see. Then how would I go about getting one of these passes?"

The man's face turned ugly with a scowl. "Ya don't. Now be off with ya before I have ya arrested."

A perplexing question. As he debated whether to go and camp in the nearby woods for the night or to take up the man's offer of arrest which would guarantee him entry into the city, another man, dressed all in black, and accented by light brown piping on his clothes, emerged from the guardhouse door.

"Bring the lieutenant forward, soldier. I would talk with him. Save your bullying for someone else."

The man sighed and turned to face the newcomer. He was obviously disappointed in not being able to send Devron on his way. "Yes, Master Gaffrey. I was just having a little fun is all." He spun to face Devron once more. "Off the horse, Sechlander. The warlock wants to see you."

A warlock. A lifetime of hearing of these men as great evils created an impression in his mind that for the moment froze him.

"Get down I say!"

He shook free from his reverie and alit next to the guard. "As you please. Take good care of my horse, if you will."

"What do I look like, a stable hand?"

The warlock stepped closer. "Do as he requests. The man is our guest."

"Ugh. Yes sir."

As the warlock continued to near, Devron studied him. Outside of the clothing, he appeared no different than any other man of some forty-five odd years. In fact, he looked...softer. *I must not misjudge him by his appearance. He may be planning on turning me into some foul creature with his magic. We are in dire need of the help of these people.*

The warlock stopped and smiled. "Lieutenant Devron, did you say? My name is Gaffrey. Come. You must be weary from your travels. Do not be fearful of me. I mean you no harm. Perhaps we might share a bottle of Riaz red while you explain the urgency of your mission. Follow me."

As Gaffrey turned and headed toward the gate, Devron hesitated. *They say these warlocks can read one's mind. He addressed the very concerns I was thinking. Was it coincidence or dark magic?*

Gaffrey stopped to face him. "Are you coming?"

He sighed. *I'm here for a reason. There's no going back now.* He started walking. "Right behind you."

They passed through the guard door set in the side of the front gate wall, into a long narrow room with slots that opened into the portico area between what were in fact two sets of gates. *A kill zone. Very nice.* His impression of the defenses of Zon just went up a notch.

They exited through another door on the far side, which emptied, into a courtyard inside the gates. He paused to examine the inner gate. It was sturdier than the outer one. Enemy troops caught in the kill zone would be unable to continue forward and trapped by their own troops pressing from behind. "A masterful gate system. It must protect you well. But from who? Sechland and Morica are your only neighbors to the south and I can attest to the fact my country has no aspirations to venture north."

Gaffrey paused to glance at the gate, his face marred by a scowl. "Things are not always what they appear, Lieutenant. It is not attacks from outside Piaxia that urged this construction, but from within. We recently endured a civil war that saw the original gates demolished. Much of Piaxia operates as individual city states with the central government stationed in Lia. The city states were in conflict."

Devron recalled hearing of the conflict but as it never spilled over into Sechland, he paid it little mind. "So an enemy army smashed through the old gates?"

Gaffrey's countenance changed as he chuckled. "Not an army—a single man."

He was stunned by the statement. "A single man?"

"Yes. The warlock Bron. Unhappy with the lord at that time, he decided to put an end to the man. He attacked and conquered the city with nothing more than a herd of sheep and a powerful wind. It is an inglorious moment we have promised never to be repeated."

Could that be the same Bron who defeated the demons a hundred years before? "This Bron, is he still around? I would like to speak with him."

"No. I heard he died at the battle of Rok, but not before he obliterated the entire combined armies of six city states including Lia's."

His heart sank at the news. The idea a single man could defeat such a force was mind boggling. Such an individual would be just the answer needed for Sechland. Still, if there had been one such warlock in Piaxia, perhaps there might be another.

They continued until they reached the citadel set in the city center set against a small mountain that formed the western edge of the city with the walls running like a horseshoe round it. Likewise, the castle inside was well fortified with its own wall and guarded entry.

Gaffrey led on, entering the castle, leading him into what must be the stateroom. A soldier was lounging in the room and jumped to attention when they entered. Gaffrey went to him. "Go into the kitchen and have someone bring food and wine for us. Then when you're finished, go and get Lord Kipron."

"Lord Kipron?"

"Yes, man. Are you deaf? Lord Kipron, and snap to it."

The soldier was about to go through one door when Gaffrey reminded him to get the food first. The fellow then disappeared through a different door set in the back of the room.

He and Gaffrey sat down, the warlock questioning him on how long Devron had travelled. In less than a hundred beats, a woman entered from the same door with a tray laden with foods and a bottle of wine.

Gaffrey accepted the tray. "Thank you, my dear. Check on us in a while, will you?"

The woman nodded. "Yes, Master Warlock."

Gaffrey poured the wine and settled back into his chair. "Now then, Lieutenant. Tell me about this mission of yours. I sense the urgency in your mind and your desire for our assistance. Despite our proximity, there is still little trading that goes on between Sechland and Piaxia. Let's not forget you and the other nations of the seven kingdoms attacked us some fifty years ago."

"So it's true then, you can read my mind. If so, then you know my intentions are sincere and my desire for your aid desperate."

"Read your mind? No. But I can sense your feelings and pick up thoughts that are on the surface. When all you can think of is an urgent need for help, it comes to me clear as a bell. I heard it all the way from the guard house when you arrived at the gate. I do not possess the skills to bore into your memories. Although I am master warlock here in Zon, sadly, that is beyond my skill."

Devron relaxed some, his shoulders slumped as he sighed. He needed to be straightforward. "It's as simple as this. Demons are once again loose in the seven kingdoms. Their presence has resulted in Sechland coming under attack from the other realms as they believe the freeing of the demons as an act of my country. Unless these demons are stopped, the fate of my people is doomed."

As they partook of the food and wine and the woman from the kitchen returned to replenish things, Devron explained in detail all that occurred. As he finished his tale, the door opened and a man dressed in fine robes entered. He surmised it to be Lord Kipron.

"Gaffrey, what is the urgency at this ungodly hour? Who is this you are seated with?"

"It is an emissary from our Sechland neighbors to the south, Lieutenant Devron."

Devron rose and bowed. "Greetings, my lord. My apologies for disturbing you but my need is great. I have just finished detailing all to your master warlock here."

"Hmm. In all honesty, I appreciate the interruption. I've been in consultations all evening with a host of others demanding my time. I could use the reprieve." Kipron availed himself of the wine on the table and filled a mug. "Gaffrey, what is it he wants of us? Have you checked him out?"

"Indeed. I have. I can tell you there is no deceit in the man. He is in need of the assistance of a warlock who has knowledge of the Key."

The lord spluttered into his wine mug, the burgundy liquid splashing onto the floor. "The Key? None here in Zon contain such skill."

"I am aware, my lord."

Kipron poured a fresh mug. "Perhaps Regent Tarlok might help. It is said he destroyed the walls of Lia in the last great battle of the war. Such skill would require the Key. His only hope would be found there, in the capital."

Devron bowed again. "Then I should make all haste to your capital at once."

Lord Kipron sat down just as the woman from the kitchen arrived with another bottle. "At this time of night? No, you'll stay until morning. In the year since I've been lord here, I've never enjoyed a visitor from Sechland. I would have you spend a little time longer explaining to me all you have told my good friend Gaffrey here and perhaps a few details more, or at least until the wine runs out. We'll give you a good bed for the night and feed you well in the morning. I'll have the captain of the guard assign you a guide for your journey. Highwaymen plague the trade routes as of late. It's a long way to Lia."

Devron joined him at the table. "As you wish, my lord." He poured a fresh mug and started telling the story once more from the top.

CHAPTER 33

Gar was dreaming of sex. Sex with Pleasure. Nonstop sex. It woke him up. As he sat upright, sitting on the edge of the bed, naked, was Pleasure.

She pushed him back down and climbed on top. "Now that you're awake, it's time for the real thing."

She had been in his mind. He knew what Silk said, Pleasure's power was that of lust, and he wanted to fight it, but couldn't. He found it too irresistible. He succumbed to it.

When his manhood waned, Pleasure nestled down beside him and stroked the pointed tips of her fingers over his chest. "I know what's in your mind, Gar. You want this running and hiding to end and I know how you can do it. You just have to want it enough. You have to do what it takes to change things so you won't have to run and hide anymore. You can make it so those who right now seek to destroy you will instead be the ones running and hiding. I can help you do it. Let me help you. Let me show you how instead of being the one who is cursed, you can be the one who is honored."

As he lay there he contemplated what she said. So much of it was true. He was tired of running—tired of hiding. He had at his disposal four powerful demons. No one could stand in his way if he wanted it so. He needed only to wish it. "What is it you would have me do?"

"We must go to the next stone. Hiss knows the way. With the opening of each stone you will gain mastery of all. You will be king!"

"The next stone. Are you sure? Do I want to release another demon? Demons are why I'm in the mess I'm in so far."

"True, but these same demons have saved your life time and again. The trouble is you haven't given them enough pieces to put together your kingdom. You need to go to the next stone."

He sat up. Why shouldn't he? As he already held sway over four, why not five? Or six? Or all of them for that matter. He could conquer all of the seven realms and be the supreme ruler.

Pleasure sat up as well and caressed his head and neck while planting kisses and licks on his ears and throat. "You are the supreme lord. Take what is yours."

He got out of bed and stood up. "I will! I'll take what is mine to have." He helped Pleasure rise. "Rouse the others. Find Hiss. We ride this morning."

"As you command, but first, you must get dressed. A king does not go about naked."

Gar realized she was right. He found his clothes and put them on.

Pleasure slipped into her one piece outfit quickly and headed for the door. "I'll go get the others. What do you wish to do with the one who attacked you last night?"

In his excitement, he forgot about Captain Brusk. "I don't know. Let's go check on him." Finally dressed, he stepped into the main room to see Silk watching him intently. Her gaze swung back and forth from him to Pleasure, and her countenance was marked with a frown. He ignored it and stepped into the bedroom where the captain slept.

Brusk was still asleep. He noted for the first time how grizzled the warrior appeared. The many days of unshaved hair on his face were mostly grey. Lines creased his face in many places. *He looks old.* Gar bent close and felt the man's forehead. The fever was broken. Straightening up, he sighed in relief. "He's better. Perhaps it's best to leave him here. When he gets up and feels fit enough he can return to Sechland."

Pleasure stopped him from leaving the room. "Do not leave him behind. Finish him. Left alone, he will simply track you down and try again, and maybe next time get lucky and complete the job as he will know what to expect."

Gar paused to stare at the prone figure of his once commanding officer. He could not bring himself to commit such an act. The raven was still in the room, perched at the foot of the bed. It made a clucking noise then fluttered to land on Brusk's chest, keeping an eye on Gar the entire time. "No, I won't do that. I didn't save him last night to see his demise today. We'll just have to take him with us until I can reason with him."

***

Brusk woke to a gentle shaking. His eyelids felt heavy and his limbs weak. As he squinted at the morning light, he took survey of his surroundings. He was in a bed in a small room with one window. The farm boy, Garlin Murdach, stood over him, pushing on his shoulder.

"Wake up, Captain. I need you to wake up."

His last memory was of failing to kill the lad and collapsing on the floor. *What happened?* He was confused. *Why am I here in this bed? Why didn't that big beast finish me?*

"Captain. You're awake now. Do you need help to get up?"

He focused on Gar. "Where am I?"

"You're in bed in one of the rooms here at the lodge. You collapsed last night and after I healed you, I put you in this bed to sweat out the fever. It seems to be gone."

Healed? He pulled the covers away and exposed his legs, the material of his clothes cut away from the injured one. He turned his leg to examine the wound. It was gone. Only small marks indicating where the stitching had been was all that remained. "How in the name of the gods did you do that?"

Gar smiled. "Magic. It has its good uses. You're the second person I've healed and saved their life."

He frowned. The idea of being saved by the young man he tried to kill the night before was distasteful to him. It was more disturbing when he thought of how he felt sorry for the lad when they first met. He swung his legs to put his feet on the ground. "I'm feeling good enough to get up on my own."

As he stood, a squawk, followed by a flutter of wings turned his head in time to see the raven coast in to perch on his shoulder. "And how's my little friend today? Did *you* fight off that big demon for me?"

Gar chuckled. "That he did. That bird opened a nasty gash above the left eye of Thunder."

He scowled at the lad. "Thunder? You say it like he's an old friend. Don't you realize the horror you've done? Don't you understand what they are? By the gods! Have you lost your mind?"

Gar frowned and looked down at his feet. "You don't understand. You don't know everything that happened."

"What's there to know—to understand? You've released four demons back into the seven realms. You brought about the destruction of Sechland and the loss of how many other good men killed in trying to defend it. You're just as bad as those creatures."

One of the females appeared in the door. Brusk recognized her as the smaller one, though she was at least his own height.

She glanced at him then stepped up to the lad. "Gar, is what Pleasure says true? You want to go on to the next stone?"

"Yes, Silk. I do. It's the only way for me to stop running. I want to be free to live my life."

"Can't you see it? She's using her powers again and I can't stop her. I've no willpower left to grant you to resist. You've got to fight her control over you; otherwise, you'll never be free."

Gar's face scrunched up. "I-I don't know."

Brusk's attention was drawn to the door as the taller demoness now entered the room. *That must be the one called Pleasure.*

"Everything is set, Gar. It's time to go."

The face of the lad softened, a dreamy expression overtook him. "Yes. I'm ready."

Gar walked out the door, his arms hanging loose at his side. *She has him under some kind of spell. The lad isn't in control of his own mind.*

Pleasure smiled at the one named Silk. "Are you coming with us?"

"Don't play games with me. Yes, I'm coming. I know you're using your powers on Gar again. He's gaining strength. One of these days he'll be able to resist you."

Pleasure laughed. "No man has ever been able to resist."

"One did."

193

The smile disappeared from the face of the taller one. "That was a long time ago and likely never to happen again. From what I understand, he resisted you as well."

"He resisted all of us."

"Well, no matter. He's probably dead by now. I doubt there'll ever be another."

Pleasure left the room and the one named Silk was about to follow her out when Brusk laid a staying hand on her shoulder. *This demon wench seemed to stand up for Gar. Perhaps here might be an ally.* "What sorcery is going on? Does that tall demoness have Gar in her thrall?"

The woman smiled, but with a sadness to it. "Yes. Hers is the power of lust and she has used it to control Gar. I could use my powers and give him the *will* to resist her, for *that* is what I control, but I used them up granting you the *will* to live. Until such time I encounter others where I can draw their will from them to replenish me, I am unable to help him."

"Why does a creature such as you want to help Gar?"

"Because he is young, honest, and naïve. He does not deserve the fate that awaits him. Understand, I am glad he freed me. I would not see him suffer because of that." She stepped to the doorway. "He saved your life, even after you tried to kill him. Shouldn't that tell you enough about the boy?"

He had no answer. Pressing his lips tight, while Silk watched, he gathered up his belongings set on a nearby table. *I'll bide my time for a bit. I need to know for sure before I try again to kill him.* "I'm coming as well."

She nodded. "That was what I expected."

CHAPTER 34

Devron woke with a start. From the small window of the room he was assigned in the citadel he noted the sun was already a full hand in the sky. *I've slept in. Too much wine. Why didn't someone wake me?*

Once he donned his uniform, he stepped into the hallway to find an armed guard outside his door.

"Good morning, Lieutenant Devron. I am to escort you to the throne room upon your awakening. Lord Kipron is waiting."

This is most unusual. Why would they want me to be tardy? I guess I'll find out soon enough. "Lead the way."

After a few turns through some corridors, Devron entered the main hall and was led to a large set of double doors with two guards stationed outside.

The man who accompanied him held up his hand. "Wait here. I'll announce you."

As he fidgeted standing there while the man went inside, he decided to scan the hall. There were a number of tables in it. He figured it must serve as a dining hall for at least several hundred. A quick glance showed the hall almost empty. He thought of the town hall in Visk or in the capital Sechwisk. Both would be filled with people queued to air their complaints and seeking jurisprudence. He turned to face one of the guards near. "Do not the citizens come here to bring their grievances?"

"The warlocks administer law in the streets. The people have no need to pester the lord."

He dwelled on that for a moment—administer law. By the sounds of it the warlocks must be judge and enforcer of the law at the same time. Thinking back how Master Gaffrey could read his thoughts, he came to appreciate what a time saver that must be.

He studied the room in more detail. The ceiling was at least thirty hands high in the middle with a number of skylights letting in the day. There were no windows in the side walls. *This must be in the center of the citadel.*

As he continued to examine the hall he noted there were a group of men at one of the far tables, and they were all looking and pointing at him. It was only then he realized they were in uniform as well. The many colors at the table at first had him thinking otherwise, but on closer inspection he could make out the colors of Fermia, Storburg, and Morica. *By the gods, the enemy is already here.*

The sound of the door to the throne room opening spun him round to see the same guard who brought him, waving him in. "Lord Kipron will see you now."

Glancing back over his shoulder, he followed the man in. Seated on a throne of solid stone, carved right out of the mountain face immediately behind him, was Lord Kipron. Also present was Master Gaffrey, a number of Zon soldiers spread about the room, and three officers from the coalition that conquered Sechland. The last eyed him as he stepped forward. "Good morning, Lord Kipron. I was unaware the people you played host to last night were the invaders of my country. I trust this does not change the arrangements we have made."

Kipron frowned. "A complication has arisen, Lieutenant. These representatives from three other countries tell me you are a wanted criminal and demand I surrender you to them."

He glanced at the three, gave them a nod then returned his focus to the lord. "May I ask, did they inform you of my crime?"

"For that matter, no."

"Then allow me to elucidate. My full name is Devron Sech, cousin to King Lowry Sech, lord and ruler of all Sechland. I have knowledge that my relative, the king, is dead and more than likely everyone else in the royal family in the capital city of Sechwisk. I have committed no crime. These men merely hope to depose of me as perhaps the last remaining person of the royal bloodline. Should you surrender me, there will be no trial, I will only be found dead in a ditch somewhere between here and the border."

Kipron turned to Gaffrey. "Is this the truth?"

Gaffrey nodded. "He does not lie."

Kipron scratched at his head. He fluttered air through his lips making a sound similar to a horse. "This is no good. No good at all." He rose and walked round a table covered in a board that showed his city in relief. "It's times like this I wish I didn't have this blasted job." He shoved a couple of the pieces on the board then knocked them over.

Devron watched the man intently. Clearly, a difficult decision lay before him. Only when the lord peeked at Devron did he have an inkling things might go his way.

Lord Kipron returned to the throne. Sitting with a thud, he sighed deeply. "I've decided to defer this." He faced the men from Storburg, Morica, and Fermia. "Your request for a blockade of the border is denied. Likewise, your request for Lieutenant Devron to be remanded into your custody is also denied."

He then faced Devron. "I'm also going to deny you any official aid in reaching the capital. You're free to go but I won't help you get there. I'm not taking sides in this. Let Queen Tessia deal with it."

"Queen Tessia? But last night you told me that Regent Tarlok might be the one to help me."

"That I did. It is Tarlok who chairs the warlock council, but in Piaxia, it is Tessia who is monarch. It will be up to her whether assistance is given to one side or the other."

Kipron stood once more. "I have rendered my decision. There will be no further discussion. May the gods be with you."

The soldiers present suddenly moved and ushered everyone out of the throne room. As Devron exited, he passed near the Morican representative.

"You may have survived for today, Devron. But mark my words, we'll get you in the end."

Once out in the great hall, Devron paused to watch the three men join up with the others waiting and exit. Master Gaffrey came to stand at his side and nudged him. "I'd bet they'll try to waylay you on the road to Lia. You need a guide to take you cross country."

"You heard Lord Kipron. I'm to be denied one."

"True. But he never said anything about whether or not you could hire one. Do you have any coin?"

He thought about the number of gold, silver, and copper pieces in his purse. He didn't want to reveal how much he carried. "Some. How much will a guide cost?"

"Not much. I have the perfect person in mind. Follow me."

Devron followed the man out of the castle and into the streets of Zon. As they walked, Gaffrey extolled the virtues of the city and its citizens. In hindsight, he considered the conquest of the city by the shepherd warlock Bron as not a defeat, but liberation.

They meandered through a number of lanes until they entered a quiet dead end court of some fifteen houses. The master warlock knocked on the door of one and an attractive woman, blonde, buxom, above average height, and by the look of it, some ten years Devron's senior, answered. She wore clothes more suited for a cross country messenger, than a woman of the city.

"Gaffrey, what brings you by? Is that lord of yours still driving you crazy?"

Gaffrey chuckled. "He's your lord as well, Daphora, whether you like it or not. But in answer to your question, the truth is yes, he's still indecisive as ever. Why Queen Tessia ever gave him the job is beyond me. In the meantime, I want to introduce you to your latest customer, Lieutenant Devron Sech, of Sechland."

Devron took the woman's hand and bowed. "My lady, the pleasure is mine."

She laughed. "Lady? It's been a long time since anyone's called me that. But with such nice manners, from such a handsome young man, I can at least hear what it is you want of me. Come on in."

They stepped in to a main room furnished far better than what the exterior would have implied. There were lavish accouterments everywhere. As he settled onto an intricately embroidered settee, he was most careful not to allow his sword or armor rub against it. "Miss Daphora, Master Gaffrey has informed me you might be able, for a fee, take me cross country to Lia. I am willing to pay, just name your price."

Daphora gave Gaffrey a hard stare. "What have you been telling him? And for that matter, how did you even know I was home? I could have been halfway across Piaxia."

"I make it my business to know when you are in town. As to what I have told him so far—nothing. But I intend to divulge all before the two of you head out. It is important that he know."

"Head out? I just got home yesterday and haven't even had a proper bath yet. Who says I'll even take the job?"

"I do. I have never imposed on you like this before, but this is a matter of too great of importance to be left to fate. You'll do it for me."

Daphora sighed. "Fine. I'll do it. My fee for such a trip will be eight golden..."

"One copper."

Daphora flushed. "One copper! Are you insane? I wouldn't bend over to pick a single copper up if it was lying before me. Why would I do it for one copper? Why not just free?"

"Because there must be a semblance of a contract, regardless of the price, should there be questions."

"Ha! You know I cannot be read by any warlock."

"True." Gaffrey gestured toward Devron. "But the same cannot be said for our good lieutenant here."

"All right, all right, I'll do it. We'll leave first thing tomorrow."

"Today, and as soon as possible."

Daphora jumped up. "You are testing my limits. Wait here while I do something first."

"What is that?"

"Draw a bath!"

She stormed out of the room and Gaffrey chuckled. "Come, let's raid her larder while she cleans up. I haven't had a thing to eat yet and I suspect neither have you. I'll bet we'll be able to find enough provisions to pack while we're at it. She always keeps a healthy store of dried meats and fruits."

From behind the door Daphora left through, came a shriek. "I heard that! Make sure you leave enough for the next time."

Devron got up and followed Gaffrey through another door that led into a kitchen. At the far end was a trap door that led down to a large cellar stuffed with cured meats, cheeses, dried fruits and bottles of wine. He stooped to pick up a large cured ham. "There's

199

enough here to feed a hundred men! What is it that Daphora does for a living?"

"She's a supplier to the highwaymen that plague the countryside. All those things upstairs are part of her compensation. The men often give her goods in trade for what she brings them."

He almost dropped the ham. "By herself? And no harm befalls her?"

"She can more than defend herself. She has all the skills I do. None of the rogues out there would dare cross her. Besides, her talents are invaluable to them. The art of healing alone is priceless. When one or two get nicked up in a fight, they can't exactly come to town to find a warlock to heal them else they'd end up in prison."

"I don't understand. I thought warlocks were supposed to enforce the law. You're the master warlock and yet you condone this and don't arrest her. Why?"

Gaffrey paused from stacking food items, sighed and turned to face Devron. "In Piaxia, it's against the law for women to practice magic. They are called witches. If she was arrested she would be put to death."

"How did she learn to be a witch in the first place?"

"I trained her."

"You did? Why?"

"Magic tends to run in some families. Where a father may be a warlock, so may be the children, and so on. My grandfather was a warlock. It skipped a generation. She's my sister."

Devron was about to say something else but decided he'd heard enough. He set back to work loading up supplies and carrying them upstairs. They sat and made a meal to break fast with. As they were finishing, Daphora entered the room, rubbing at her wet hair with a towel.

"I hope you saved me some."

Gaffrey rose. "There's plenty. I've had my fill. I shall attend to the lieutenant's good horse and make sure it is waiting and ready at the north gate."

When he was gone, Daphora sat down next to Devron. "So what did he tell you?"

"That you're his sister and a witch."

"You know enough then. Just don't cross me." She stared at the plate of food before her. "This stuff has gone cold." She pointed at it and a flame leapt from her fingertip. In a few beats it was over and the food steamed once more.

When she summoned the fire, he held his breath in amazement. The concept of these people commanding fire at will was terrifying. Not until it was over for many beats did he finally allow himself to exhale. *You bet I won't cross you.*

CHAPTER 35

Darlee was startled awake by a loud clang. It took her a moment to gather her senses. When did she fall asleep? Her last recollection was one of being huddled on the bed where it met the corner of the room. Her plan had been to stay awake the entire night, but the gloom in the dungeon level was such that she had no idea as to what time of day it was. For all she could tell, it was still night.

Another clang allowed her to identify the source of the noise. A cell door had slammed closed. A rotund man wearing an oversized apron was standing with one of the guards. He kicked at someone lying on the floor. "This one's dead. Take him out of here before he rots."

The guard picked up the body and tossed it over one shoulder. Darlee could not make out the face of the dead man and her worst fears jumped to mind. "Jango?"

The guard hesitated and looked her way. "You say something?"

She moved to the bars of her door. "I-I thought the man you were carrying was my friend Jango."

The guard freed a hand and tilted the dead man's head so she could see the face. "This one?"

She let loose a sigh of relief. "No, that's not him."

"Humph." The guard exited up the stairs and disappeared from view, his grisly package with him.

A rustling from the cell she knew to be Jango's was followed by his appearance at his door. "Here I am, Darlee."

She smiled. "Thank the gods. I thought that dead man was you."

"It might just as well have been me. I'm a goner for sure."

She needed to be brave, if only for his sake. "Don't talk like that. Once they finish questioning us, we'll be out of here in no time. Just you wait and see."

Laughter erupted from the cell next to her where Baxus was held. "There's no getting out of here unless you're carried out, like the last one."

From out of nowhere, a club banged against her cell door causing her to jump back. The man with the apron stepped in front. "Shut up. All of you. There's to be no talking. Not unless you want to pay for it with a finger."

Darlee returned to the stone bed. She needed to think. *If they question me, what will I tell them? Should I tell them everything I know, or should I hold back what I can to protect Gar?* She stared out at the torture table. *If they torture me, would it matter? Will I tell them whatever they want to hear?*

She wondered about Gar and where he might be now. She hugged her knees, tucked her chin on top and began to rock. "Oh, Gar. I won't be able to do it. I won't be able to."

"What won't you be able to do?"

She drew in a sharp breath and looked up to see Lieutenant Gramby watching her through the bars. "I'm sorry. I didn't see you there."

"You didn't answer my question. What won't you be able to do?"

She released the grip on her legs, put her feet down and lifted her chin. "Stand up to torture."

The lieutenant called one of the guards over to unlock the door. When it was opened, he stepped in and sat down next to her. "If you cooperate, there won't be any need for that."

"Cooperate? You've surrendered me to the enemy, taken me prisoner, thrown me in a dungeon and you want my cooperation? Why would I do that?"

Gramby pressed his lips together and sighed through his nose. "If you care about the people of this town, about your friends, your family, and everyone else, you'll do as I say."

Anger set her lip to quivering. "This town? So far this town has killed my parents, burned down my house, thrown me and my friend in jail and made a fugitive out of my brother. The only one left is my grandfather. I have no reason to care about this town anymore."

The lieutenant reached out, grabbed her wrist and squeezed. "Listen. Before he left, Devron spoke of you as an intelligent lass. I need you to show me that intelligence right now. In a few moments, the men of the alliance that has taken over this city will be down here looking for answers. You're the one who's going to give them what they want to hear. If everything goes well, they'll finish their search of this city in a day or two and be on their way. What they won't accept is any kind of a challenge. Do you understand me?"

He let go of her wrist and she rubbed at it. Maybe playing along might be a way to get out of there. "What is it you want me to say?"

"That your brother is a warlock and was taught by your father." He pointed to the cell Jango was in. "Your friend over there is an acolyte, which is why he stuck with your brother after the battle at Morence. When the townsfolk learned of their treachery, they put your father to death."

"But-but those are all lies. Jango was carried off by my brother because he was wounded. My father knew nothing of magic. Why must I name so many?"

"Because they'll never accept all of this was the result of the actions of one farm boy. They'll tear the city apart searching for a coven of warlocks. If we can convince them that hive was your farm and has been wiped out, they may buy it."

She thought of what they would do to poor Jango, and Pap, what of him? Right now he was trying to rebuild the farmhouse. "If I say all of that, they'll suspect my grandfather as well. It would be his and Jango's death sentence."

"What you say is true, but think, girl, you'll live."

She turned away to contemplate what the lieutenant was telling her. How could she abandon Jango and doom Pap? She needed to convince Gramby to find another way. "It all sounds too far-fetched to believe. What makes you think they'll accept my story as fact?"

"Your admittance is only the corroboration of the details, nothing more. This account is being fabricated as we speak. I have Merchant Trellus and the city elders already weaving this lie, and with gusto, as they half believe it themselves. Nothing is more convincing than a hypocrite who thinks he is telling the truth. I have Baxus there in the next cell ready to play his part and the men who killed your parents testifying your father attempted to use sorcery against them. Except you, all is in place." He nodded toward the table in the middle of the room. "The alternative will not be to your liking."

She once more looked through the bars at the long table and the many blood-stained leather straps connected to it. The man with the apron she surmised to be the torturer as he was busy sharpening an odd shaped blade. The horror of lying on that table gnawed at her. She glanced at Gramby who folded his arms across his chest. *He's waiting for my answer.* She stared out at the table again, but this time she imagined Jango lying there. Her thoughts shifted quickly to it being Pap, and finally, Gar.

She closed her eyes and allowed a calm to settle into her. When she opened them, her decision was made. "I won't do it."

Gramby shook his head, sighed, and stood up. "I thought you were smarter than that." He stepped out of the cell. "Jailer, bring her out."

The man entered and grabbed her by the wrists. She struggled but was no match as he dragged her out to the waiting table. The torturer put down whatever he was sharpening and helped the guard strap her to the table.

Jango rattled the door to his cell. "Darlee, give them what they want. Don't let them torture you!"

If she gave them what they wanted, Jango would be the one on the table right now. He may still be.

Gramby leaned close. "In the end, Miss Murdach, you will still tell them what I want you to tell them."

She stared into the lieutenant's eyes. "How can you do this to me?"

He straightened. "I will do whatever it takes to save this town." He turned to the guard. "Go now. You have your orders."

"Yes, sir." The guard saluted and dashed up the steps.

The torturer finished strapping her arms, legs, and torso into place. The only thing she could move was her head. The sounds of boots scuffing on the stone steps made her lift it to see who was arriving. Padronus entered. He was accompanied by two other officers from the enemy alliance. As they reached the bottom, the commander came to stand at the foot of the table. "I take it she has refused to provide the information we require. It's a shame a pretty little thing like this must suffer."

Gramby nodded. "I agree. If I may, perhaps some leniency could be afforded."

"I agree." The captain nodded to the torturer. "Start with her toes."

She watched as the man with the apron lifted a pair of pliers from a different table. She put her head back and closed her eyes, tears started to flow.

She recognized the cold of the metal as her smallest toe was clamped. The pain that followed brought a scream from her lips.

CHAPTER 36

Devron arrived at the north gate to find his horse and Gaffrey waiting for him.

"May the gods be with you on your journey, Lieutenant. Be careful on the road. The contingent from your adversaries passed through the east gate scarcely a hand ago." He turned to Daphora and gave her a hug. "Take care of him, sister. I fear your journey will not be easy." He whispered something in her ear.

She smiled. "Why brother, you know what a careful girl I am."

She clambered up onto her own horse, and Devron made note of the large bow and two quivers of arrows strapped to the animal she rode. He did not doubt whether she was proficient in the weapon.

He gripped Gaffrey's forearm in a customary military greeting. "Thank you for this. I do not know what I would have done without your assistance." He slung and tied the supply packs across the rump of his horse and mounted. "It's best we be off then while there is still plenty of daylight. I wish you well." He nodded to Daphora. "Lead the way."

She spurred her animal and Devron urged his to match. Together, they exited through the gate and the road ahead. When they passed the cleared grounds that circled the city, he noted the vegetation was cut back from both sides of the road for some fifty paces. At such a distance, no raiders could surprise them before they could defend themselves. "Is the road cleared so well all the way to Lia?"

"This road leads straight north to the twin cities of Jag and Fel, and from there, to Rok. Lia is to the northeast so we will need to take another path when we are no longer in sight from Zon."

He glanced over his shoulder at the receding walls. "Are we are being watched?"

"My brother said there are strange men waiting near the gate. They wear livery of green but it does not match that of Jag."

Moricans. "They are from the realm that neighbors both yours and mine, Morica. It looks like my trip to your capital is to be denied."

As they continued along, he kept glancing back. When he bumped into Daphora, he realized his constant looking back had resulted in his pulling the reins of his horse into the collision.

She shoved his shoulder. "Mind the road! They won't begin their pursuit for at least another quarter league."

He pulled the reins to move his horse a pace apart from hers. "How can you know that?"

She sneered at him. "They will want to make sure we do not see them exit the city where we can take stock of their numbers. If only a handful, then I'll take my chances and fight it out now, but if their numbers are many, we will have no choice but to run. Whatever the decision, it will not be visible from the walls and Lord Kipron will be unaware of their actions. They will not want to incur his displeasure, something that may affect their mission here. Think. Have you no brains in that head of yours?"

What she said made sense—too much of it. Why hadn't he figured that out? "I suppose you're right. The machination of men is not my forte. I left that to my cousin, the king. I am but a simple soldier. Should we not be spurring our animals then? Or leaving the road?"

"If you don't start soon, you're going to be a dead soldier. I'm not interested in going down with you. *Whew.* Why did I ever agree to this insane mission in the first place? No, spurring our horses will only tire the animals, and over the long haul they will catch us. Jag is days away. Leaving the road now would slow us in the underbrush, and if there is one who can track amongst them, we would be at their mercy. We wait until they show themselves. I would rather face them on the open road if their numbers are few and spur my horse only when necessity dictates."

He pressed his lips together, not wishing to respond. Any comment would only prove his ignorance and lower her opinion of him even further. Instead, he concentrated on the approaching countryside. He made note of those points where horses could easily ride and where passage would be difficult.

They continued along in silence, but his quick glances at Daphora told him she was doing the same thing, scouting the area. At least now he felt a modicum of satisfaction he was doing something right for a change.

The faint sound of hooves on the road behind them caused him to turn and scan the road. No longer visible were the walls of Zon or even the open grounds near it. Along the way, imperceptibly, the road had snaked and curved enough to be obscured by trees at a thousand paces. It didn't take long for what he was expecting to see appear—four riders charging at them. "What do we do now?"

A tight smile was on her lips. "We stand here." She loosed the long bow from where it was strapped and pulled an arrow from one of the quivers.

He followed suit, moved his shield from where it rested on his back to his left arm and unsheathed his long sword. "I'm ready."

The riders continued to near and he noted the two in the rear were holding short bows. The ones in the lead were armed as he was. Beside him, he heard the snap of Daphora's longbow as she loosed her first shot. It sailed over the head of the first rider and plunged into the shoulder of the man behind. The man dropped his bow and stopped charging.

The distance between them continued to narrow and the other bowman fired at Devron. Positioning his shield, he managed to deflect the arrow away, but he was unable to parry the sword stroke of the rider closest whose blade crashed against his shield and sent him to the ground.

A flash caught his attention and he spotted the rider closest to Daphora bursting into flame. His horse reared and the burning man fell to the ground, screaming in agony. *By the gods, she set him on fire!*

Scrambling to his feet, he faced the mounted swordsman who unseated him. He ducked under the man's blade and thrust upward with his own, catching the man below his chest plate and piercing him deep. Blood gushed from the wound and the fellow crumpled from the horse, dropping both his sword and shield as he fell.

A stabbing pain high in his thigh was a result from an arrow plunged deep into the muscle. His sword still embedded in the other man, he let go, fell to one knee, and struggled to face the archer. The man was knocking another arrow. He started to pull the shield in front of him when lightning arced over his head, hitting the archer dead center. With the sound of thunder, the blast knocked the man flying from his horse to land flat on his back behind the animal. Smoke curled up from the man's chest where the bolt struck.

Devron freed his weapon and staggered over to stand above the man, sword held to strike should he move. One look into the man's face was enough to tell him the Morican was dead.

He turned to see Daphora putting away her bow. "Did you get them all?"

"No. The one I wounded rode off. I never would have caught him before he made it back to Zon. We must go. He will surely send others."

The use of her magic to kill amazed him. "Can you not blast them all with those fireballs and lightning bolts?"

"No. My magic is half spent. To ensure the attacks are lethal I need to put much into them. I can fire a number of lesser blasts, but those would only wound or stun them and I would still run out."

He cursed the arrow protruding from his leg near his hip. He gave a tug on it but quit as soon as he started, as the pain accompanying it told him what he feared. The arrowhead was barbed. "I've got to get this arrow out."

She gathered the reins to his horse and brought the animal close. "Later. For now, cut away the shaft. The time is now for us to be free from the road. I'm not in the mood to explain how these men are lying dead to the next passerby. Get on your horse."

It took some time, and she had to help him, but he managed to regain the saddle. She led the way into the woods and he followed close behind. At first it seemed to him they were simply crashing through the underbrush, but then he realized that was far from the truth. He noted the way was already beaten, his best guess by the native animals of the woods.

In time, as the sun was descending, they reached a small creek trickling slowly along. At an area where the water pooled, the surrounding ground was clear of brush. Hundreds of footprints showed it to be the favorite watering spot of the local fauna.

Daphora dismounted. "We'll let the horses' water. Come. I saw a small clearing just a few paces away. It'll be a good place to make camp tonight and we can tend to that wound."

They climbed a small knoll to find an open spot among the trees. The ground was stone strewn and he recognized the mound to be a small rock outcropping. He found a protruding rock ledge large enough to lean against and he slumped down to make use of it. He undid the buckles holding his chest plate in place and dropped the armor to the ground beside him. The entire area of his leggings near the arrow was soaked in blood. He had lost a lot. He tried once more to pull the arrow free, but it was no use. The barb was hooked in good.

Daphora knelt beside him. "It looks like we're going to have to cut it free." She pulled a knife from a sheath at her hip. Straightening, she undid her belt and handed it to him. "Here, bite on the leather. This is going to hurt."

He accepted the belt and folded it between his teeth. She was watching him, and when he nodded, she plunged the knife into his leg beside the arrow. He wanted to yell, but instead bit hard into the leather and grasped the ground with his hands. She worked the blade back and forth while pulling on the arrow and, after a few beats, yanked the projectile free. She pulled her knife out and blood streamed from the open wound. Although the pain subsided, he now feared he would die from loss of blood. "Quick, we need to stitch that closed."

She smiled and placed her hands on the wound. "Just relax. Everything will be fine in a moment."

A pale blue glow shimmered where her hands touched his leg, and he watched in amazement as the wound closed and soon disappeared altogether leaving only a red mark where it had been.

She let go. "There. All fixed. You'll need to eat and drink to replace the lost blood. Take those leggings off and, while getting the horses and some water for us, wash them out. I'll make a fire and set up camp."

"Okay." He stood up and was surprised to find no pain. He realized he was still holding the belt. It was damaged from his bite. "Here's your belt back. I'm sorry, I think I ruined it."

He walked back to the pool, took off his boots, and after slating his thirst and filling the water skins, he sat down where it was deep enough to cover his legs and scrubbed at the bloodstains. After doing what he considered a passable job, he got up, grabbed his boots, the reins of the horses, and returned to the knoll.

After tying the animals to a nearby tree and pulling off the packs, he entered the camp area to already find a fire blazing in its middle. He dropped his pack and undid the blanket roll to wrap it round him, as he was feeling cold from soaking in the water.

Daphora grabbed her own pack and began to set up her own bedroll, when she stopped and pulled his blanket from his hands. "Take off those wet leggings and put them on the rocks to dry."

He blushed. "I can't. I'm naked underneath."

She laughed. "Like as if I haven't seen a naked man before. Don't be silly and do as I said. You'll catch your death of a cold. There are some things I can't heal."

He hesitated, but he was feeling chilled by his sopping wet pants. Sighing, he undid his belt and let the leggings drop to the ground being careful to turn away from Daphora as he did so. He stretched the leggings across a rock near the fire and went to get his blanket, when Daphora grabbed his shoulder to spin him.

"Let's see the wound." The area it had been was red. "Good. No scar. The redness will fade in time. And your leg feels fine?"

He nodded. "Yes. No problems when I walk."

She smirked. "That's good. Now let's see if everything else works."

She reached to grab him between the legs. At her touch, his manhood reacted. "Daphora…"

She steered him to her own bedroll and sat him down. "This may be a fool's mission, but at least it's with a good looking one. Your leggings need drying and you'll be cold. Besides, my belt is busted and I have nothing to hold my own up." She dropped her own leggings to the ground. "No sense in us both freezing to death. Besides, you promised not to cross me."

212

She pushed him down the rest of the way and climbed on top. Yes, indeed, he made that promise. This was one he was more than willing to keep.

CHAPTER 37

Brusk studied every aspect of the strange crowd he accompanied. The demoness who went by the name of Silk was the only one who would talk to him. Despite the slate grey skin and no hair, the woman was stunningly beautiful. Every inch his height, if not even a smidgen more. She walked with such sex appeal it took much for him not to want to ravish her. Her large bosom and incredible curves were more than any average man could withstand without feeling primal urgings. It was the simple fact she did talk to him and was his only conduit of information that made him able to resist those urgings. He needed to know all he could find out.

The other succubus, the one they called Pleasure, though as alluring as Silk, with a slimmer, taller figure that still would make the blood of men boil, did nothing more than snarl in his direction. He learned of her skill in the power of lust, but she used none of it on him. With her obvious distaste at his presence, he was able to ignore her charms. No, that use of evil magic was being exerted on his quarry, the lad, Gar. She stayed close to him and the results were obvious. Gar was under her total control.

When dusk came and they paused in their southward rush to rest the animals and take their own respites, he sat with Silk. "Who is in the stone we are rushing to? Is it another temptress like…like Pleasure?"

She sighed. "And me?"

"I didn't say that."

She laughed, and it had a pleasing tinkling sound that put him at ease. "No, but I suspect you thought it. It's possible, but I somehow doubt it. I don't know who's in the stones, only Hiss does and he's not telling. When we went to the stone that released Pleasure, I tried to stop Gar, but I was too late. Even from within the stone she took control of his lust. If I knew sooner I might have been able to avert it and scolded Hiss so. Now he won't say who's in the stone ahead."

He glanced over to the small imp. "The little one—that's Hiss?"

"For now. It's the name Gar gave him. His real name is not pronounceable in your tongue. For that fact, neither is mine, or any of ours."

Brusk paused to finish the food given him by Silk with the exception of one small morsel of meat he put to the side. He was surprised to find how good it tasted. *Gorgeous and a great cook. A winning combination. What a waste in a demon.* He swallowed and drank from his water skin before returning his attention to the demoness. "Just so I understand, you didn't want Pleasure released and don't seem too keen on this next one either. Why? You're *all* demons. I would think you'd want to free each and every one of them."

Rather than say anything, she gathered up his metal plate and went to a nearby stream to rinse it. When she returned and handed it to him, she held on tight as he tried to take it. "First of all, I dislike the use of the name demons. As best as I can put it in common tongue, we are the Children of the Gods. And yes, I would prefer they all be free as I am. Locked in stone for nearly a hundred years is not the curse I would put on any living creature. Someone such as you would instantly die, but for me it was like living in a dream all that time, or a nightmare. The elation I felt at new freedom has instilled a personal promise never to be captured again. And so, I stay with my kind to protect me.

But just like you, there are those among us who are dark in their thoughts—those who would kill first before seeking peace. When we were first released into your world, there were many who wanted nothing more than to be free to live. But there were others who wanted to control your world and as a result, *all* of us were targeted for extinction. I have killed no one but am wanted dead. You are not my enemy, but I am yours."

She let go of the plate. Its sudden release caught him by surprise and he rocked backward. By the time he regained his balance she went to be with Thunder and Hiss. He then noticed Gar was busy at the moment having sex with Pleasure. *In front of all of us. Has the lad no sense of decency?*

215

He turned away to tidy up from dinner. As he stowed the plate in his kit, he realized what Silk said never occurred to him. Why should all demons be evil? Why can't they be like regular people—some good, some bad?

With the plate put away, he returned his focus on the others. Silk put an excellent argument before him and he decided to try and re-evaluate the others. Perhaps she was right and all they wanted was freedom to live. He then caught Pleasure's eye and received a scowl in return. No, not all, that was for sure. The tall demoness was using dark powers to control Gar. That alone was more than enough proof of how dangerous she was, how she needed to be stopped. From reading into what Silk said, the little one, Hiss, was in league with Pleasure. He had to go as well. And the giant, Thunder, was far too frightening for his acceptance anywhere.

He sighed. For that matter, despite all her positives, and all she said, Silk was still a demon in the eyes of humanity. She would never be accepted. There was no other choice. He debated the issue within, gone full circle, and returned to his original position. They all had to be destroyed. The question was—how? He recalled the stories from his youth, how the demons were immune to man-made weapons. Neither arrow nor blade could pierce their hide. His own encounter with Thunder proved that tale. His sword didn't even nick the monster.

The raven fluttered down to perch on his shoulder. "There you are. I was wondering where you'd got to. I saved you a scrap from dinner." He lifted the bird and placed it on a rock to where he'd scraped the morsel. The bird eyed it, and then flew away. He chuckled. "What? You don't like demon cooking? Fine. Go find your own food."

He flicked the scrap of meat into the nearby fire. As it sizzled, he recalled when Gar told him how the raven cut a gash above Thunder's eye. *Now how is it the danged bird can cut that monster when my sword won't?*

It was a puzzle he was having trouble solving. *I can't go and get a bunch of birds to slash them to death. I don't even understand why the one I got now did it. They're just dumb animals.*

His attention was drawn to the movement of the others. They were breaking camp. Silk returned. "Come. We're going now."

"It's evening. Where are we going in the dark?"

"Hiss says the next stone is only two leagues away. Gar, under the urging of Pleasure, has decided not to wait until morning."

Brusk rushed to pack up his kit and mounted his horse. The animal whinnied, obviously unhappy about being ridden again. He patted its neck. "Easy there. It's just a short jaunt. You'll be back to chewing on the grass soon."

Hiss set off, and along with the others, he followed behind. After they had gone a league, Brusk sniffed the air. Its aroma had changed. It was subtle at first, but with each stride of the horse it became stronger. They were nearing the sea.

They broke clear of the woods out onto a barren crag extending out into the waters. Straight ahead, the Great Sea lay in darkness. Combined with the clouded skies above he felt like he was riding into an abyss. He looked to his left and only more darkness lay that way as the forest curled up to the cliff edge. Checking to his right, the rocky hill sloped down to the few lights of a small fishing village next to an inlet. *Maybe I can find some help there.*

On the promontory, there stood a large rock outcropping. Hiss ran straight to it and patted it. "Here they catch him. Here."

Silk was right. It wasn't another demoness. He dismounted and approached the stone. It stood several hands taller than him and was as wide as tall. Brusk knew of the legends how you could hear the heartbeat of the demon within, and he placed an ear against its surface to listen. Despite the cool wind and the night, the stone was warm and the sound of the heartbeat unmistakable.

He faced Gar as he approached. "Are you sure of this? Haven't you freed enough already?"

Gar paused and stared at him, blinking. In the next instant Pleasure was at his side and shoved at Brusk. "He's sure. Step aside, Captain, so our master can free his servant."

217

They had taken away Brusk's weapons back at the lodge. The idea of tackling Gar and trying to break the lad's neck ran through his mind, but the giant demon Thunder stood only a pace away. Now knowing the beast's speed, he would never have the chance. He backed away to stand near Silk.

Gar placed his hands on the stone and closed his eyes. "Open, I command you to open."

Brusk could feel the tension in him as he awaited the opening of the demon stone.

Nothing happened.

Gar turned to the imp. "Help me, Hiss. It's not working."

Hiss started to climb up on Gar. "Master, me no mana. Remember, all gone. Me try." The small demon placed his hand on Gar's forehead and Gar focused his attention once more on the stone.

Still nothing. Brusk wondered whether Gar really had the ability to open the stone or if he was just a conduit for the magic of the demon Hiss. After all, he had never seen Gar open any of the other stones.

Gar took one step back. "It's useless. I can't seem to open it."

Hiss clambered down. "Master do magic with stone at lodge. Maybe do again. Hiss keep." From within the folds of his clothing he produced a small stone and handed it to Gar.

Gar held the stone with one hand and placed the other against the outcropping. Several beats past when Gar stepped away again. "It's not working either. This thing is not opening."

Gar hurled the small stone in his hand at the rock face. It bounced off and tumbled to Brusk's feet. He picked it up and turned it in his hands. He chuckled. It was a whetting stone, scarred from extensive use. *How could there be magic in this?*

Gar sat on the ground. "I give up. I don't have the magic and without help from Hiss I'll never get it open."

Pleasure crouched down and nuzzled against him, rubbing her hands over his body. "Then we shall get Hiss the mana." She pointed down the slope. "See? People. With your command it will only take the night to make sure Hiss is fully charged."

Gar stood and looked where she pointed. "Yes, you're right. Go, Hiss. Regain your mana."

Hiss nodded. "Yes, Master. Me go." He bounded down the hill and Thunder charged after him.

Seeing the big demon go brought a sense of panic in Brusk. "Why is Thunder going?"

Silk hooked his arm and pulled him toward the horses. "Hiss is small, and alone the townsfolk would capture him. He can draw the mana from people while the bodies are still warm. Come. I must hurry. Unlike Hiss, I need them alive to draw their will."

He grabbed her arm to stop her. "No. Don't do it."

She pulled free. "It will matter not whether I am there. In a small town such as below, there is nothing that could stop Thunder."

He started after her. "This is madness!"

She climbed on her horse and watched as he mounted his. "Madness? Perhaps. But I must regain my powers to combat Pleasure and you need to come. Thunder won't kill you because of Gar. You may be able to block him to save at least some."

"Who could I save?"

"The children."

He kicked his horse into a gallop.

CHAPTER 38

Gar shook his head. The cloudiness in his mind reminded him of when he once suffered a bad case of the flu. As he walked down the hill, Pleasure was sprinting ahead of him toward a small fishing village. Silk said he was under Pleasure's spell. Perhaps her grip on him was weakening. He didn't believe her. He wasn't sure if he even did now. He enjoyed being with Pleasure. She ceded to his desires. Despite the obvious demon features, she was still beautiful, and the sex whenever the urge came upon him was fantastic.

He glanced behind him. The demon stone protruded up into the night, a deeper blackness than the clouded sky. Why hadn't he been able to open the stone? He opened all the others.

The question gnawed at him. He thought back to each of the times he did it. The first time, it was when sleeping beside the stone near his home. Hiss projected through the rock what he needed to open it. He hadn't opened it alone.

Home. He missed it. He wondered how his family fared. Was his father still angry with him? Probably. His mother would have forgiven him by now, and Pap, though sure to give him a good scolding, would also relent.

Despite how they bickered as siblings, he knew Darlee would understand and would have stood up for him. She was a good sister. He hoped all was well with her.

He discovered he stopped walking and resumed his pace. The thoughts of home distracted him. He recalled the second stone and how Hiss helped again by placing a hand on his forehead. Like the first time, it hurt terribly. Hiss must have had mana then, but maybe only some of what he needed because when he opened the third stone, it didn't hurt. He remembered then how both Hiss and Thunder went out and slain the enemy troops and returned with pale glows. That was when Baxus fled. He wondered what happened to the man. It was clear to him now the fellow was only concerned for his own well-being. Whatever happened to Baxus, he didn't care.

Jango though, was another story. He missed his friend. When they were together, he still felt a part of Visk was still with him. That feeling was gone now. He hoped Jango made it home safe.

The fourth stone he opened with the help of Hiss once more. He also touched the rock in each instance. Hiss said it was necessary to use the Key. What was the Key? He had no idea. But when he healed Captain Brusk he touched the whetstone and it made the difference then. Why didn't it work this time?

A scream from the village ahead brought his head up with a snap. *What's going on?* He broke into a run to cover the last hundred or so paces to get there. With every few steps he heard more screams of terror.

He stepped into the town to find three slain men lying in the road. A door to his right was burst asunder and he stepped in to discover the carnage there. It was the local inn, a gathering place for the people of the village. Inside were the bodies of at least another half-dozen or so scattered about the room. Moving from one to another was Hiss, placing his hand on the foreheads of the fallen.

"Hiss, what has happened here?"

Hiss stopped to look at him. "Me get mana. Soon me have enough." He scampered over to the next body.

Only the big demon could have done this. "Where's Thunder?"

"Outside somewhere—listen, you find."

He stepped back outside just as the curses of Captain Brusk came from his left. He ran to find the captain on his knees outside of a house. "Let me help you." He reached down and grabbed at the man's arm to help him up, but was shoved away.

"Curse you, Garlin Murdach. Curse you forever. Look what you have wrought." The captain rose and wiped some blood from the side of his face. He pointed into the house. "Go and see your handiwork."

Gar crossed the threshold and went no farther. Dead on the floor were a man and woman and a young child, probably no more than five or six years old. He stepped out right away, and as he did, the captain grabbed him by the shirt and thrust him against the wall.

"I tried to stop Thunder. I tried, and was no match. He tossed me aside as if I was a twig, his claw raking me in the process. I should kill you right now for all you've done, but before I do, I'm hoping you'll do one good thing and stop that monster. Stop him now before he kills every man, woman, and child in this village."

Brusk let go of him and the sound of many shouts told him which way to go. "I'll try." Gar sprinted into the town square to find at least a score of men of all ages armed with knives, axes, and farming tools facing Thunder, Pleasure, and Silk. Both of the demonesses were holding out their hands and men wilted where they stood, unable to properly hold their weapons at ready. Thunder charged and began to rip them apart. From behind him, Hiss bolted into the scene dashing to the fallen to draw their mana.

All four glowed. For a moment, Gar was frozen in place as the horror unfolded. Brusk appeared at his side.

"Stop them!"

The shout spurred him to action, and he dashed between the behemoth and its next victim. "Stop, you have enough."

The big beast dropped his raised arm and stepped behind him. Hiss went to the last fallen man, drew the mana, and joined Thunder. Both Silk and Pleasure lowered their arms.

Gar took a count. Seven more were dead, two wounded. His stomach knotted at the sight. *So much death. I'm to blame for it.*

An old man hefting a hand scythe took a step toward him. "What kind of evil sorcerer are you to bring demons to our village?"

Thunder moved toward the man, but Gar put a staying hand on him. "I'm no sorcerer. I'm just a simple farmer, but I have stopped these demons from killing any more. We will go and leave you to tend to your wounded and bury your dead. Do not follow us, if you value your lives. Go, now."

The men did not move away but brandished their weapons. A screech filled the air and the captain's raven flew above everyone and landed on Brusk's shoulder. The captain stroked the bird. "I've been wondering where you've been. I suppose you saw what just happened."

The bird's arrival provided the impetus to alter the stalemate. The men picked up the two wounded and backed away. When the square was empty, Gar sighed, turned, and headed back toward the hill. Pleasure joined him, wrapping an arm round his waist, and laughed, the tinkling sound putting him at some ease.

"They were foolhardy to challenge us. They had no chance."

He glanced at her as they walked. "How is it your power of lust controlled them? I know Silk drew their will, but there were so many, more than she could control. It must have been yours as well helping in doing that."

"Don't let Silk fool you. True, she can only totally control two men at a time, but she can spread her powers to affect a whole city, if she must. It is not a complete control, just a weakening of their will to resist. The more people, the less the effect. I, on the other hand, draw their lust for life. Combined, for a small group such as that, there were none who could muster the strength to fight. They were there to be slaughtered."

He was still feeling revulsion at all of the needless killings and he frowned. *What am I to do?*

Pleasure licked at his ear. "So, now, my love, let us return to the stone and have Hiss help you open it."

"I-I don't want to."

She stepped in front of him and put both arms round his neck, pulling him into a deep kiss. "Let's not forget why you will. Think of the freedom you will have when none can challenge you. You could come and go anywhere you pleased. And the power you will have. You could make yourself king in these lands. Think of it— King Gar."

Her magic worked through him. It was the first time he actually could recognize it, but he was unable to stop it. He wanted to fight it. He did, didn't he? Or did he? He was confused.

Her hand roamed his body and stopped at his crotch. She took one of his hands and placed it within her outfit, onto one of her large breasts. "And after you've opened the stone, I'll please you once more."

Yes, he wanted that freedom, and if they wouldn't give it to him freely, then he would take it. He was sexually excited again. He would have her and the power. He would open the stone. "Let's do it quickly."

They ascended the hill, the others following behind, and stepped up to the outcropping. Hiss climbed up and placed a hand on his forehead. Gar placed his hands on the stone. "Open for me, now."

He could feel the magic working—another new experience. He sensed how the mana from Hiss flowed into him and expired through the magic. The stone crumbled away.

From the opening emerged a demon featuring six arms, his face grotesque. Gar thought the countenance of Thunder was fearful—this one was loathsome, sporting both fangs and mandibles. The first thing to cross Gar's mind was a demon spider. Its posture was hunched over, but even if the demon stood erect, he would be shorter than Gar, though much wider.

It blinked its black eyes and took in everyone gathered. It faced Pleasure and spoke in their language. They conversed for a moment then it came to stand before Gar. "Kneel."

Gar blinked and looked at Pleasure. "Am I hearing him right?"

The demon put a hand on his shoulder and pushed down. "Kneel!"

He brushed the arm away. "No, you kneel. *I'm* the one in charge."

The monster held its hands out at him. "No more. Kneel."

Anger raced through him. He drew his breath in and held it. He cursed for being weak. He hated his inability to command. He was disgusted at himself. *I should just end my own life now. I hate me.* No, it didn't make sense. It must be the demon's power. He wanted to resist, but it was so hard...so hard. Hatred coursed through him and he grabbed his head. "Stop it. Stop it."

A hand touched his back, and the feeling abated. He dropped his arms and turned to see Silk behind him. She was strengthening his will. He gritted his teeth and faced the new demon once more. "I will not kneel. I will not succumb to you or your magic. You will obey me!"

The beast took a step back and Silk yelled something at it in their tongue. Thunder stepped in, put a hand on its shoulder, and forced it to its knees. Although Gar did not understand their language, the tone it argued with was not one sounding pleased.

Finally, it quit resisting. "Me sorry. Young man like you imprison me. I thought might happen again. I not bear be imprisoned once more."

The tension in Gar fled as he relaxed at the newcomer's capitulation. For a moment, he'd believed the worst, his control of the demons lost.

Captain Brusk came to stand by his left side. "Where will it end, Gar?"

"Huh...what?"

The captain grabbed his bicep. "This madness—another demon released back into the world. Where will it end?"

He shrugged free. "Listen, Captain, right now the only things between me and the torturer's table are these demons. Can you think of any other way? They are my protectors."

Brusk shook his head and chuckled. "You are a fool, lad. A big farm boy fool. They aren't protecting you. They're keeping you. They need you to open them damned stones."

Pleasure stepped between them and wrapped her arm round Gar's waist. "Ignore him. He's jealous because I reserve myself for you. Which reminds me, I promised to please you again."

Gar allowed her to lead him away, the idea of sex once again foremost on his mind. It was Pleasure's magic working in him, but he didn't want to resist. Still, what Brusk had said was troubling. He glanced over his shoulder at the captain one last time. The raven on his shoulder squawked loudly and lifted off, flying north into the night sky.

CHAPTER 39

The early morning sunlight squinted through the trees as Devron fastened the last straps on his horse for the continuation of his journey. A slap across his buttocks made him turn to see Daphora mounting her horse.

"Your britches are dry, I see. Come, the day is wasting. Let us get going." She kicked her animal and set off into the woods.

He clambered aboard his own mount and caught up. He was feeling awkward. They'd spent half the night lovemaking, and when she decided enough was enough, she'd sent him to his own sleeping pallet and fallen asleep. She rose first, just before dawn, and woke him like as if nothing happened.

They rode in silence for some time, and his mind strayed to the events from the day before. He examined his leg through the hole in his clothing to see if everything was still okay. It was magic that woman possessed for him to marvel at.

They exited the woods and rode across an open field of grasses and wildflowers. Riding beside her, he watched her for a while.

She glanced over and saw him. "You're staring. What is it you want?"

"My apologies. I'm just thinking about you."

She resumed looking ahead and chuckled. "About me? Listen, don't get any ideas. Last night was just a bit of fun, nothing more. I live my life on my own terms. Consider it payment for saving your life." She glanced at him and winked. "Of course, I may decide in the days ahead not enough payment has been received."

The idea he might have amorous thoughts about her had not crossed his mind. He needed to refute that. "No, no, no, it's not what I was thinking about. I was wondering about your magic. Just how much can you do? I mean, is there any limit to what your powers are?"

"Of course there are limits. And no, I cannot do anything I want. My magic is limited to controlling things of nature—fire, wind, water, earth, and life. I can't make things appear out of nothing or turn people into toads, though that is a threat I often use against those who displease me. I once made this big ruffian who was bothering me so scared he soiled himself and then ran away."

She laughed and he smiled. There was a wicked humor to this woman. "I see. So, take, for example, your powers over living things. Healing my leg as you did was, in my mind, a miracle. How far can you go? Can you tear my body apart or take over my mind?"

"No." She snickered. "Healing is possible because that is what the body wants to do. I merely assist it. As to taking over your mind, that is an ugly rumor I also use when it suits me. Only mindless creatures, such as insects, can be manipulated by me. In truth, we can only read the surface thoughts of those whose minds are unguarded, which is the vast majority of people. I've had many a merchant hire me to teach them how to block out the mental prying of a warlock. For that, they pay most handsomely."

He thought about what she just said. It implied everyone had magical abilities. He needed to know for sure. "If you can teach that to anyone, can you teach me? Do I have magical powers?"

She studied him for a moment. "Everyone has some mana, but it takes a high level to actually wield it. The blocking is more of a gift I impart because they allow it other than an actual skill I teach. Still, I have run into a few whose mana level was so low, I could not do it. You have a sufficient level, but no more. You could not wield magic."

"How do you know?"

"I know. When I concentrate, I can see your level. It shines round your head like a corona. Yours is too small."

A pang of disappointment ran through him. "Too bad. It would have been wonderful to have the skills you possess."

"I don't just *have* them. I studied for years in order to use my gift. No one, no matter how much mana they have, just ups and creates magic. It's a learned skill. The students need the necessary mana to make that learning possible."

They rode on for a while longer in silence and passed a spot where someone must have set up camp many days before. The charred spot where the campfire had been still marred the ground. "What about the other things, like fire. I watched you heat your food yesterday morn and saw the glowing orbs circling your city on my arrival the night before. How big can you make a fire or, for that matter, the lightning bolt you cast at that poor wretch."

"Fire is the easiest. I expel the mana from my fingertips and ignite it as it goes. Lightning is the same, though it requires more mana. The glowing orbs are still more, as they require a steady stream to maintain themselves."

"And water, wind, and earth?"

She glared at him for a second. "You ask a lot of questions."

"I'm just curious. All of this business of warlocks and witches is new to me."

She sighed. "Very well. Those three are much harder. In each I must manipulate the element to my command. Even so, there is very little I can do." She brought her horse to a halt. "Stop here."

He did as she commanded. "What now?"

"Stay still."

She spread her arms and a fresh, light breeze blew into his face. "Amazing!"

She dropped her arms and took a deep breath. "Enough. Let us continue on our journey." She kicked her animal into a trot.

He caught up to her. "That was impressive. Just how fast can you make the wind blow?"

"That's about it. I dare not try anymore, lest I use up what mana I still have. Before the war, the lords mastered a skill called the Key. It allowed them to magnify their powers many times over. Somewhere in the neighborhood of ten times. From what I've heard, there are none left who possess that knowledge. I could cause ripples in a pond or get a single jug of water to splash in your face. As it is, it will take the rest of the day for it to restore. When pushed, I could get the earth to move enough to open a shallow grave for those who ask *too* many questions."

He chuckled at the threat. She had indulged him so far and perhaps he should be grateful for that. He gazed down at the ground as his shadow passed over it. A shadow now loomed over his homeland. He did not yet have the answers he sought. "Then only one question more. What about stone?"

"Don't be daft. I can barely command a pebble to roll round in my hand. No warlock manipulates stone. Why do you ask?"

"Because, in my homeland, and throughout the seven kingdoms, a warlock entombed the demons in stone. They once more, roam our lands."

She laughed. "So that is your mission? To ask for a warlock to come and entomb them once more? It`s a fool's mission, and I`m a fool for leading you. No warlock possesses such power."

"Bron did."

"The same Bron who devastated my home town of Zon? The same Bron who single-handedly commanded gale winds and storms and an army of sheep?"

He nodded. "I believe so, yes."

"Word is, he died. Too bad. A terrible loss."

"Perhaps there might be another in the kingdom. But I'm confused. He killed your lord and conquered your city, yet you lament his passing. Why?"

For the first time, he saw her frown in sadness. "I was away at the time of that attack, but I wish I had been there. Such power, to see it wielded so. It would have been *glorious*."

CHAPTER 40

There were noises. At first, Darlee didn't recognize them, and then they came into clarity. They were voices, loud and harsh. Someone was yelling. She must have been unconscious. The shouting had roused her.

She tried to open her eyes, but without success. She went to rub them but her arms would not move. She remembered then. They were held down, as were her legs and her entire body, by leather straps.

There was much pain coursing through her. Both feet hurt terribly as did one ankle. Some fingers also felt like they were on fire, but most agonizing of all was the throbbing pain in her head and left eye. Her right did not hurt, but was glued shut. *Am I blind?*

Too weak to strain against the straps, she decided to try and focus on the voices. To hear what was being said.

"You fool! What have you done? Your orders were to get her to confess, not practice your butchery. See what you've done? You've taken out her eye, lopped off an ear, and by the looks of it, broken her ankle. She has more piercings in her than a handmaid's pin cushion. Was this all necessary?"

That's Gramby. I recognize his voice.

"My apologies, Lieutenant, but she wouldn't confess, no matter how hard I tried. I needed to take more drastic measures."

That's the torturer, the man with the apron.

"And?"

"Nothing. She remained unwilling. I would try cutting off an arm or a leg, but I still doubt she'd talk, and it would probably kill her."

"In truth, I'm amazed she yet lives. Where are the men from the other kingdoms?"

"They left when she passed out. I suppose they've gone to report to their superiors."

"Get her off that table then."

230

She felt the straps being unfastened and when her arms were free, she struggled to lift her hands to her face. She rubbed at her left eye and whatever encrusted it broke away and the lid opened. On her knuckle she could see the dry blood that must have been there. She probed lightly at her left eye socket. The eye was gone. The flesh was tender and each touch brought another spasm of pain. She wanted to cry, but no tears would come. She had shed them all.

The last of the straps were undone, and the torturer nudged her. "Alright then, get up."

Trying to rise, she collapsed back to the table. There was no strength left in her. She wanted to tell the man she couldn't, but her mouth would not work. The taste of blood still permeated it, and her lips were glued at the edges. She recalled the number of times she'd bitten her tongue to the point of having nipped off the tip. She tried again. "I-I can't."

The man sighed, grabbed her under the arms, and pulled. She slid off, and when he let go, crumpled to the floor in agony.

Gramby pushed the man out of the way. "You idiot. You broke her ankle. She can't stand on her own." He lifted her. "Open her cell."

The torturer unlocked the door. Gramby ducked in and placed her on the stone bed. "Bring some water and a clean cloth." He brushed some strands of hair from her face. "You're one tough kid, I'll give you that. No grown man could have withstood what you did."

She focused on him, but his face was blurry in the semi-darkness of her cell. She could not tell his expression. "My grandfather?"

"Gone. My men went to your home, but word must have beaten them, as he was nowhere to be found. We're searching the woods for him, but no luck, so far."

The tears finally came. Pap was safe. "You'll never find him. He's at home in the forest."

"Maybe it's all for the best. Without your testimony, his disappearance will do well enough to convince the invaders I spoke the truth."

"But you lied."

"So I did, but only you and I know that. And you know why."

She turned her head toward the cell across the way. "Jango?"

Gramby followed her gaze. "He's still there. He cries more than a newborn babe."

The man returned with the water and washcloth. He helped her struggle into a sitting position, her back against the wall. Gramby pulled a full ladle from the pail and held it before her. "Here, drink."

She leaned forward and drank from the ladle. The water was tepid, but nevertheless slaked her thirst. He proffered a second, which she took with her hands and drank from as if it were a cup. Some strength was returning.

Gramby soaked the cloth and washed her face. Although the pressure of the cleansing hurt, it was refreshing as well. He continued to bathe her round the throat and head, rinsing the cloth every now and then. When he twisted it, the water that squeezed out was red. There must have been a lot of blood.

He continued by washing her arms. As the dirt and blood cleared away she made note of the many cuts, burns, and bruises that riddled them up and down. Three fingernails were missing from her left hand and two fingers in her right were broken. She tried to recall when each injury occurred, but there were so many she couldn't be sure which happened when.

Gramby stopped and grimaced. "There. That's about as good as I can do for now. It's a shame the fool went so far. He should know his trade better, but I guess torturing a woman is a rare thing. Are you in great pain?"

She shook her head. "What do you care? You put me here."

He hung his head for a moment then regained eye contact. "I have children of my own. Four daughters, to be exact. One of them should be about your age. If they lived here in Visk instead of the small village they're in, she would probably be your friend. Do not think for one moment I do not feel for your torment."

Noise from the stairs caught her attention. It was Commander Padronus, and he came straight to the cell door.

"I was told I would find you here. The situation has changed. My men have been ordered elsewhere. Word has come of other demon stones being opened, and it is believed they are somewhere in Fermia, possibly even Gatway. Already there are consortiums of troops scouring the countryside, looking for them. With the addition of our forces, the net can be cast much wider. Rest assured, they will be found."

The lieutenant rose and stepped out into the main room. "When will you be leaving?"

"We march after the fourth hand."

"Then you have accepted our case that the use of magic was not of our doing but of a rogue family and the people of Visk are innocent?"

"I accept nothing of the sort. I am no fool, Lieutenant." He turned to Darlee for a moment, sighed, and shook his head. "The bravery of that girl is more than I can attest for you and the rest of this city. If there is anyone innocent, it's her. Your story has not convinced me. I'll be leaving a company of men to continue the investigation and take command. Do *not* give me a reason to return, for if I must, then I shall burn the city down to the ground."

The commander nodded at Darlee. "Take care, young miss. I apologize for what you've been through." He looked once more at Gramby, snorted, climbed the stairs, and left.

The entire scene was not lost on her. The lieutenant's gamble had failed. All her suffering had been for nothing. She was maimed for life and the enemy troops still remained.

The torturer moved to stand in front of the lieutenant. "What now? Do you still want me to get a confession?"

Gramby glanced her way. "No. Let her go. It's of no use anymore."

He started for the stairs and she called to stop him. "What of Jango?"

From the second step, Gramby faced her. "He can go, too."

A rattling from the cell next to her caused everyone to look. The man, Baxus, was reaching out from the bars. "Lieutenant, I did as you asked. Honor your promise."

Gramby scowled. "It matters not. These are probably the last commands I will ever give. You can go as well."

He raced up the steps and disappeared from sight. Darlee put her feet on the ground, but there was too much pain in the broken ankle to stand.

The jailer unlocked the cell across from her. Jango dashed out and came straight for her. "Darlee, I'm so ashamed. I'm useless."

She smiled. Even that hurt. "Help me up. I can't walk on my own."

The jailer unlocked the cell next and Baxus stepped into view. "I'm impressed. You're tougher than I thought."

Jango reached out and grabbed Baxus by the sleeve. "Help me. I cannot carry her on my own."

He pulled free from Jango's grasp. "If I had the chance, I would kill you both. Stay out of my way." With some shakiness, he walked up the steps and left.

Darlee watched him go, the jailer in the lead, and noted when he put his hand against the wall for support, another finger was missing. His clothes showed many blood stains as well. *I wonder how much they did to him?* She reached for Jango. "Never mind carrying me. Just support the side with my broken ankle and I'll hobble my way out."

Jango stooped to allow her to put her arm round his neck and together they made their way up the stairs. The torturer followed along and gave clearance to the guards allowing her to leave the jail. As she stepped out into the midday sun, she shaded her good eye from the brightness. She was free, but to go where?

Her good leg wobbled and she begged Jango to let her down to the ground. He leaned her against the side of a building. "Wait here. I'll go get help."

Jango left in the direction of the market. She closed her eye and let the warmth of the sun soak into her upturned face. Pain still throbbed everywhere, but breathing in the fresh air was invigorating.

It wasn't long before Jango returned with the tanner in tow. The man frowned and lifted her from the ground. "I'm taking you home."

The smell of the tanning solution in his clothing caused her to wretch, forcing the little water given by Gramby to erupt from her mouth and causing her great discomfort. The man brought her to his shop and loaded her into the back of a wagon. In it were a great many finished hides that made the ride more comfortable than she'd hoped for.

In less than a hand, she recognized the surroundings as those of home. The tanner carried her toward the half-built house. "By the gods, I'd heard what happened here, but seeing it makes me realize what horrors you've gone through. This home is inhabitable. Where will you stay?"

She pointed to the shed. "There. It's all we have, for now."

He opened the door and deposited her on her makeshift bed. He found some water and dried meat and set it by her. "That's all I can find for now. I'll have my wife come by later today to check in on you. Will you be okay until then?"

She nodded. "I'll be fine. I just need to rest."

The man's lips drew tight. "It's a shame. I best be going. Look for my wife in a couple of hands."

The tanner left and she tried to sleep. It wouldn't come. She lay there in her misery, and dwelled on all that happened.

After some time, she heard a noise outside. *It can't be a couple of hands already. Has the tanner's wife come so soon?*

The door opened slowly and then, to her delight, her grandfather peeked in. "Darlee?"

"Pap!"

He rushed in and scooped her into his arms. "Oh, my poor Darlee. What have they done to you?"

She could feel his tears against her cheek. Her own tears came. "I'm home, Pap. That's all that matters. I'm home with you."

CHAPTER 41

With morning, Gar wanted to put as much territory as possible between him and the fishing village. Those who'd died at the hands of Thunder were still fresh in his mind.

Past midday, they stopped at the bank of a shallow river to water the horses and grab a bite to eat. Even though the road led to the spot as a crossing point, the surrounding brush afforded them some cover, and he was glad for it. The last thing he wanted was to be spotted out in the open.

Brusk sat down next to him. "So what are your plans? Where are we headed?"

"West. I'm going to go through Queensland and Braxburrow to avoid Fermia. After that, we'll head north into Storburg and then home from there."

Brusk snorted. "And then what? You're a wanted man, Gar. You, and this company of demons who accompany you. There's no where you can go in the seven kingdoms. You'll be hunted forever."

Gar elected not to respond but continued to eat. It bothered him that what the captain was saying could be true. He'd never wanted any of this. He wanted to live a normal life. Why couldn't everybody leave him be? It wasn't fair. He'd been forced to open the stones. Hiss had taken advantage of him while he slept. Thunder was necessary to save his own life from the troops of Morica. Silk...well, Silk had been his decision, but she never hurt anyone. As for Pleasure, maybe it was his choice, maybe not. The more he thought about it, the more it seemed she influenced him from inside the stone.

He turned to check on the new demon, Dread—the name he gave him seemed most appropriate. Gar dreaded spiders. The presence of that one bothered him. Dread watched him all the time. What was going on in that grotesque head of his? He half considered telling him to go its own way, but the idea of safety in greater numbers held sway in his mind.

236

Where is he? Gar stood to get a better look. Dread was missing. "Hiss, where did Dread go?"

The imp glanced round quickly. "Me no know, Master."

Thunder was lying on the grass, his eyes half-closed. Gar had seen this trick too many times already to not know the giant demon was still alert. "Thunder, where did he go?"

Thunder growled out something in his demon language. Hiss nodded. "He says Dread went downstream, along the bank."

"Come on, help me find him."

Thunder took his time to rise then sprinted away with Hiss chasing behind. It took all of Gar's strength to try and keep up. Even at a full run, they were slowly leaving him behind. A crashing noise behind him had Gar glancing to see the captain in pursuit. At some distance farther, Silk and Pleasure also gave chase.

Ahead of him, he spotted Dread with Thunder and Hiss. The beast's back was toward him and it instead was facing out toward a meadow. As he reached the trio, he could see what Dread could. Spread on the bank was a blanket and a picnic meal. Rolling in the dirt fighting were a man and woman, both half naked and bleeding profusely, both brandishing bloodied knives. They shouted obscenities at each other.

It didn't take long for Gar to realize what must be happening. The demon had chanced upon two lovers and was using his dark power. He grabbed Dread by the shoulder. "Stop it. Stop it now."

The demon, exuding a mild glow, scowled at him and stepped away, but not before the male plunged his blade into the woman's chest. She screamed for a moment then lay lifeless. The male blinked several times. "What have I done?" He pulled the dead woman into his arms and wept.

Gar could watch no more. "I'm headed back to the camp. Thunder, bring Dread, by force, if necessary."

The others arrived and all saw what remained of the lover's tryst. Brusk attacked him, punching Gar across the chin. "This is insanity. Had I my blade, I would have run you through."

Thunder, Dread held in one arm, grabbed the captain with his other and growled out something in his native tongue. Still unable to understand what the big monster said, it didn't take a lot for Gar to figure it out. *I'll sort it out somehow.*

Pleasure put an arm round his waist and rubbed a soft hand on his chin. "Come, I know just how to make you forget that pain."

He walked back toward the camp, head down in thought. *What am I to do? The captain must be made to understand my predicament. As for Dread, he doesn't fit with what I had in mind.*

Before he could take another step, Thunder dropped Dread and Brusk and clamped a hand over Gar's mouth. Looking over the massive fingers, he saw Thunder motion at the camp. Gar peered through the underbrush to spot men in different uniforms milling about. Hiss scampered forward. He and the others crouched behind some cover.

A voice carried to where he stood. "They must be around here somewhere. Search up and down the river until you find them."

The horses. If we don't get them back, we'll never make it.

Hiss reappeared. He climbed up and cupped Gar's ear. "Many, many men. Maybe forty. What Master want we do?"

Forty men? Could Thunder defeat that many with the help of the others? He was not sure. The sound of men thrashing through the underbrush in their direction panicked him. Should they run?

Dread stepped past him, all arms outstretched. What good would hate do?

The voices of the men working their way closer could be heard over the sound of the foliage being brushed aside.

"Watch where you swing that thing."

"Then stay out of my way, you stupid Fermian."

"Who you calling stupid? I'll show you who's stupid."

The sudden clang of swords crossing was followed by shouts for help. Soon, other voices and other weapons joined in. Through it all, Dread stayed transfixed. Gar watched as the small glow faded away. It slowly returned to a level even brighter than before. There must be real hate between those men fighting.

Over time, the noise abated and moved away from them back toward where the camp was. Dread put down his arms and joined them where they hid. When Gar couldn't hear any more fighting, he motioned everyone forward. Thunder beat him to the clearing, and as he stepped out, it was in time to see the behemoth shred apart the last two men standing.

Hiss scurried from fallen man to fallen man, placing his hands on their foreheads. "Master be happy. Dread good."

The imp had a point. Only moments before, Gar had been contemplating leaving Dread behind. Now he could see where the demon could be useful, but would he follow orders?

Brusk walked among the soldiers, checking them. "Dead. All dead. Your victim list keeps piling up. At what point will you be satisfied? When there isn't another living soul in the seven realms?"

"Would you rather it was us lying there?"

"Gladly. If it meant the end of these..." he waved at the demons. "...things as well."

Gar froze. He scanned the bloodied grounds. Soldiers of Fermia and Gatway lay everywhere. What was happening to him? In a few short weeks he'd changed from farm boy to *this*. Starting with the battle at Morence, the amount of killing he witnessed had inured him. He needed to put a stop to it. "I'm not ready to die, but you're right. These needless deaths have to stop."

They were all watching him. Good. He had their attention. "From now on, no one will die. I want no more bloodshed on our hands. Is that understood?"

Silk was the first to agree. He'd expected that, but when he got an assenting nod from Thunder, it surprised him. Dread merely turned away. A dissenter. Predictable as well.

Pleasure came and wrapped her arms round him. "Oh, why do you want to be so stringent? Something like what happened here was unavoidable. Would you rather we surrender?" She nuzzled his neck and licked at his ear. "Then you would lose me."

He gently pushed her off. "No, but we have to try. Promise me you'll try."

She frowned at first, and then smiled at him. "Fine. I'll do as you ask."

Gar turned his attention to Hiss. The little demon was wildly looking about at his compatriots. "Well? What about you?"

"Uh, Master, uh, Hiss never kill, but how me get mana?"

239

The imp was glowing as bright as ever. "You have plenty right now. I can see it on you. I need your consent. Do you agree?"

Hiss glanced once more at Dread's back, his hands wringing away. "Yes, Master, me agree."

"Good. As Dread does not want to consent, he can stay here. It's time we were going. Pack up our gear, and let's go."

He hustled to load what few campfire items were strewn about back into the saddle bags of his horse. As he mounted, he noted Dread climb aboard one of the horses that belonged to the dead troops and move into formation behind the others. "Dread, what are you doing?"

"I come."

"I don't want you to come. I can't trust you."

Pleasure spoke to Dread in their language. Even with the usual lilt to her voice, Gar could tell the exchange was heated.

She smiled at Gar. "I got him to promise me he won't kill anyone. He's one of us, Gar. We can't leave him behind."

Silk moved her horse between them. "That's *not* what he said."

"What did he say?"

"He said he would obey Pleasure, that's all."

Pleasure nudged her horse past Silk to be closer to Gar. "And I'll make sure he obeys you. Let's not argue anymore."

Brusk laughed. "As if this bunch is going to do what you say. The next troop we come across will suffer the same fate."

Gar was losing his patience with the captain. The man challenged everything. "Then we won't run into any troops. From now on, we'll stay in the woods and away from people and roads. We'll travel at night. We'll do whatever it takes to pass through the realms unnoticed until we get home."

"That'll take almost two weeks. We'll have to live off the land. That'll slow you even more."

"I don't care if it takes months. We won't be seen again. But that's not your problem." He reached over Pleasure's horse and pulled Brusk's sword and shield, free of the saddle. He threw them in the direction of the captain. "You're free to go whatever way you wish, just not with us."

240

Brusk retrieved his weaponry from the ground. "It's to your doom you go, lad, as long as that crew is with you."

Gar kicked his horse forward and crossed the river. As he clambered up the bank on the other side, he spied the nearest forest some quarter league away and headed for it. He was going to prove the captain wrong.

CHAPTER 42

Having ridden for eight days, Devron asked the question for the millionth time. "How much farther?"

Daphora nodded to her left. "Two days ride to the east."

They had crossed over an obvious trade road a while back. Easterly, it must lead to Lia. "Why are we still riding north?"

"I'm stopping in to see an old friend who will put us up for the night."

This wasn't her first side trip along the way. The last had been with an unsavory bunch of characters who could only be highwaymen, their camp nowhere near any settlement nor farm. She performed a healing on one of them and then ate, drank, and laughed the night away. Devron couldn't get into the spirit and slept with his dagger in his hand. "Won't we lose more time? The men from the other kingdoms will beat us there."

She snorted. "I told you before. We crossed the river Xia at the only ford between there and the Great Sea. My brother said they left by the east gate. They're going the coastal route, the long way around. We'll still beat them by at least a day, maybe two."

He sighed. Not that he knew any better, but whenever he tried to provide any kind of direction, she ignored him. "So what band of cutthroats are we visiting this time?"

"Just one. Name's Grott. And he's not a cutthroat anymore— went legit during the last war. For a time, he was the lord of Zon. Now he's just a simple shepherd."

"Lord of Zon? Seriously?"

"Yes. He was a proxy for the merchant's league who ran the revolt. Once the war ended, he took up residence in the hills just ahead."

As they topped the next rise, he noted the hills were heavily dotted with white. The herd was vast. "That's a lot of sheep."

To reach a small house by a creek, they needed to pass through the herd, and Devron felt uneasy. It was as if the sheep were watching him, not with the idle curiosity of a dumb animal, but like the guards he encountered at the gate to Zon. The many rams with their large curved horns were the ones most attentive. He leaned toward Daphora while keeping an eye on the biggest ram "They remind me of a tale I heard of how Zon was conquered by a herd of sheep."

She glanced about at the animals then smiled at him. "They should. This is the very herd."

He gulped. "This is the one? But I thought the herd was led by the warlock Bron."

"It was. Grott has taken over as shepherd. They say he and the warlock were very close."

A very large man emerged from the house, scarred and missing half an ear. He held a wooden staff. "Greetings, Daph. Who might ya have with ya?"

She dismounted and gave the big man a kiss on the cheek. "My charge. I'm to escort him to Lia." She turned to face Devron. "Grott, I want you to meet Lieutenant Devron Sech. Devron, this is Grott, the toughest highwayman there ever was, now reduced to a lowly shepherd."

Devron dismounted and held out a hand. "Pleased to meet you."

Daphora elbowed Grott and winked. "Watch out. He's a dandy."

Grott spanked her bottom. "Enough of ya kiddin', lass." He stepped forward and took Devron's forearm, his grip encircling it and squeezing—hard. "Likewise, any friend of Daph's is a friend of mine."

Devron tried to repay the military greeting and grip the man's arm as well, but his forearm was just too thick for his hand to go round. He didn't want to show any weakness and kept his composure, even though his arm was hurting. "Daphora says you would be kind enough to give us lodging for the night."

After checking him over from top to bottom, Grott let go and laughed. "Aye, that I will. A dandy—maybe, but a tough one at that. Come. Let's go see what Hera has cooking inside."

Once Grott turned his back to lead the way in, Devron rubbed at his arm. *Damn, that hurt. The man's a mountain.* He followed him into a comfortable room with a fireplace in the far wall. A half-dozen chairs were scattered about, no two alike. There was a table next to a doorway he surmised led to the kitchen as a robust woman in a flour-dusted apron entered from it.

"Daphora, nice ta see ya, girlie. Who's y'ar friend?"

Devron decided to preempt the introduction, took the woman's hand and bowed. "Lieutenant Devron Sech, my lady, at your service."

She laughed. "My lady? That's the first time I've ever heard that." She gave a playful slap to the back of the head of her husband. "Ya might learn a thing or two from this lad."

Grott gave her a pat on her bottom. "Now dearie, when have I ever been disrespectful? We've got guests here. See what ya can scrounge up ta treat them with." He kissed her on the cheek.

"I think I've got something ta warm their innards. And after that, some of my pastries ta sweeten 'em up."

Grott motioned to the table. "Let's sit a spell and ya can catch me up with what's going on."

They talked into the evening with Hera trying to shove more food into Devron than he would eat in three sittings.

When they finished eating, Grott rubbed a hand across his chin. "Ya realize, Piaxia suffered a civil war only a year ago. A lot of men died back then. I doubt much of an army could be raised today."

"It's not the armies of Piaxia I need. It's a powerful warlock to lock the demons in stone once more. Someone like the one they called Bron. I understand you knew him well. Is there another who can do it?"

"Bron was one of a kind." Grott grabbed some meat scraps from the meal and went and put them on the window sill. "But you never know where help might come from."

The sound of fluttering wings was followed by a large raven coming in from the dark of night and landing on the sill next to Grott. It pecked at the scraps while Grott rubbed a finger across its back. Devron went to stand next to Grott. "That's amazing. My old captain has a pet bird just like that one. It's impossible to tell, as they look so alike, but, I swear, this one is identical."

Grott chuckled. "How do ya know this ain't the same one?"

244

"It can't be. Captain Brusk is hundreds of leagues from here, somewhere in the southern kingdoms."

Grott picked up the bird and the scraps and returned to the table, placing them there. "This bird returned two days ago. He comes and goes as he pleases. He's been with me ever since I met Bron. In truth, I think it was his bird. He used it ta keep an eye on me. When Bron died out there on the battlefield in front of Rok, I was the first to his body. First, except for this ruddy bird. Once I picked up Bron's staff, it flew away, like as if its job was done." He's stopped by a couple of times since then, but never fer long."

Devron turned to examine the wood staff next to the door. "That staff?"

"Aye, that be the one. It's imbued with Bron's magic, it is. I carry it with me always."

Daphora got up and went to it. "May I?"

Grott joined her. "Be my guest."

She hefted the staff. "It just feels like a piece of dried wood. What does it do?"

Grott took it from her and opened the door. "Come. I'll show ya." Devron jumped up to join the pair, and he followed Grott as the man made his way into the midst of a large number of sheep. All of the animals turned his way as he passed them. It was eerie how they crowded in close without a sound. The biggest of all the rams took his place right next to the staff.

Grott pointed at a spot in front of him. "Daph, stand close. I need ta be able ta reach ya."

She did as she was told. "Now what?"

"Do some magic."

"What would you like me to do?"

Devron thought back to his first arrival in Piaxia. "Make one of those floating, glowing orbs like I saw patrolling Zon."

Daphora smiled. "It's one of the first things I learned." She held her hands out, and a globe of light materialized between them. She lifted her arms higher and the orb floated up into the sky. It hovered about fifteen hands above them, shining down enough light to illuminate the area for seven or eight paces in all directions.

Grott put a hand on her shoulder. "Don't lose yar concentration. Now it's my turn."

It started with the ram next to him. The animal glowed gold. Like a wave, it spread through all of the other animals crowded close. To Devron's amazement, the glow flowed into Grott and from there into Daphora, where it changed into a blue corona round her. He didn't know what startled him more, the glows round the sheep, Grott and Daphora or the sudden intensity in brightness of the globe overhead. He looked up at it, and it hurt his eyes, as if he was staring into the sun. Ducking his head and turning away, he rubbed at his eyes for a moment to clear them of the spots he was seeing. When his vision returned, the surrounding countryside was bathed in light, as if it were daytime. It extended at least a couple hundred paces, if not more. "Amazing!"

The illumination waned, and he turned to see that Grott had released his grip on Daphora and the sheep no longer glowed.

"Now ya know. I think Bron only wanted me ta use it. I don't know why, fer sure."

Dervon scouted the nearby ground. *Maybe I don't need to go to Lia.* "Can you try it again? But over here?"

Daphora stepped close. "Why?"

He kneeled to put a coin on a small rock outcrop at his feet. "I want to see if you can encase that coin with stone."

Grott raised his staff and the rest of the herd gathered in. There were thousands of the animals, all quiet. He placed his hand on Daphora's shoulder once more and the process repeated itself. Devron watched as Daphora raised her hands toward the stone. After a few beats, he noticed movement! Edges of the stone crept up and touched the sides of the coin. In time, the entire coin was covered in a thin layer.

After a while, Daphora quit. "I can't continue. I'm spent."

Dervon let his shoulders sag. Bending, he examined the covered coin. "At such a thickness, I don't think any demon is going to stand still long enough for you to trap it. What went wrong?"

Grott was supporting her as he guided her back to the house. "She ain't got the Key, plain and simple. She needs the key ta multiply the power—like Bron did."

A loud screech made him look up to see the raven pass overhead. "What, by the gods? That was some announcement."

Grott paused to watch the bird. "It's heading south. It's telling me something—something I gotta think about." He nodded toward the door. "Come on. I've got some good mead in the cellar. We'll have a drink and talk it over."

He followed them back in. *I guess I'm still going to have to go to Lia.*

CHAPTER 43

They set out early. Daphora wanted to arrive before dusk. "There's a lot fewer questions at the gate that way."

They stayed to the road to hasten their travel and, with little more than a hand to go before evening, the walls of Lia came into view.

Well, they were walls, if Devron could call them that. Much of the south one was nothing more than a huge jumble of cut stones lying in a haphazard line from the western limit of the city to the water's edge of what he was told by Daphora was the river Piax. A section was cleared and a wooden gateway spanned the opening. "What happened here? An earthquake? Or was this more of Bron's doing?"

Daphora laughed. "The wall was destroyed by a monster wave created by none other than the new queen's husband, or so I'm told. I'm thinking my friend Grott may have had a hand to play in this after what he showed us yesterday. The stories told of the battle are always a little different with each person telling it. When you spend as much time in as many taverns as I do, you hear all kinds of tales as to what happened. It takes some of my skills to discern how much is the truth and how much is the vivid imagination of the one who is relating the story."

They crossed the open field and reached the makeshift gate guarded by a half-a-dozen soldiers and another man dressed all in black with purple piping. *He reminds me of Master Gaffrey, though older. No doubt one of the warlocks serving here.*

Devron recalled his first encounter with a gate guard back at Zon and hoped this one would fare much better. Following Daphora's example, he dismounted before covering the final paces between him and the men waiting.

"Who are you and what's your business, soldier?"

"Greetings, I am an emissary from Sechland. My name is Lieutenant Devron Sech, and I'm here to petition your queen. May I have your leave to enter?"

The warlock stepped close and met his stare for a moment. "I sense no deception in what you say…" he frowned at Daphora, "but I cannot read your friend here. Why is that?"

She nodded. "My brother is Master Gaffrey of Zon. He taught me how to guard my mind."

The man stroked his chin. "Gaffrey, you say. A good man. We shared a pint or two at the last winter solstice warlock gathering. Now that you say it, I can see the family resemblance. Still, the man should not be teaching such things to a woman."

The warlock returned his gaze back to Devron. "An emissary of Sechland, you say? Come, then. The court will be closing soon, so if you wish to present your petition today, you must hurry. I'll show you the way. Check your weapons with the guard here, as none can approach the violet throne so armed."

"As you wish." He surrendered his sword, dagger, and shield, and Daphora relinquished her daggers, her bow and quivers still strapped to her horse. He chuckled at how many weapons she hid on her body. At the final count, she laid five small blades in the hands of the man taking them.

The warlock scowled. "Are you sure there aren't any more?"

She held her arms out wide and spread her legs, a wicked smile on her lips. "Would you like to check?"

The man blanched and took a step backward. "Uh, no. I trust you. Come, we must hurry."

He led them through an area of new and destroyed houses, many in the process of being rebuilt. When they reached the open plaza beyond it was easy to recognize the palace and the citadel walls that encircled it. The building was some seven stories high, and there were a number of parapets protruding from it on all sides as the building tapered upward.

When they reached the guarded portico entry, the warlock passed without stopping. "They're with me."

They crossed the courtyard and arrived at the castle doors, where more guards were in attendance. Again, they hardly paused. *This warlock is definitely held in high regard. There's no doubt about the many levels of security to gain access. Is the threat of attack real? I wonder.*

When they reached a set of massive doors, another set of armed men guarded it. The warlock waved for the doors to be opened. The soldiers stepped aside and they entered the throne room. Seated on the throne was a young, beautiful woman with long, brown, curly locks. Standing beside her was a tall, handsome young man dressed in the clothing of a warlock. *This Queen Tessia can't be more than twenty.*

The first warlock motioned for Devron and Daphora to stay where they were. "My liege, Lieutenant Devron Sech, an emissary from the southern kingdom of Sechland, seeks an audience with you."

She glanced at Devron. Her face sank, and then she returned her attention to the warlock. "Warlock Prattrow, please accommodate the emissary for the time being. Word has already arrived of the conflict in his country and I do not have the strength to deal with it right now. I do not feel well and must retire for the night. I will be happy to hear his request in the morning."

Devron didn't want to be dismissed so easily, and he took a few steps closer. "Your Majesty, I have travelled far and through much peril to get here. I implore you hear me out before you go."

His movement caused soldiers in the room to move toward him, brandishing the halberds they carried.

The young man next to the queen stepped down from the throne. "Hold." He turned back toward the queen. "Tessia, if I may, I will speak with this man while you rest."

She smiled weakly. "I suppose that will be fine."

She got up slowly and Devron noted she was most pregnant. The young man dashed up the stairs to offer his arm. She clutched it until a handmaiden appeared from behind the throne and took over. After she was led away, the guardsmen encircling him stepped back to allow the young man to approach.

"Welcome, Lieutenant. My name is Tarlok, regent to the queen. I would be happy to listen to what you have to say. Accompany me, if you will, to where we might relax and you and your entourage can grab a bite to eat. I don't want it to be said the hospitality of Piaxia is lacking."

Daphora chuckled. "An entourage. The first time I've ever been called that."

Tarlok offered his arm. "My apologies, my lady. I meant no discourtesy. Come, sit with me and tell me what brings the two of you to our court."

She accepted his arm. "Lead the way."

He led them into an antechamber immediately to one side of the throne room. Once there, he told a waiting attendant to fetch food and wine. As they were about to sit, a very tall man, more Devron's own age, entered. His uniform indicated the rank of commander. *Is everyone in charge here so young?*

"Glad to meet you, Lieutenant. My name is Savan. I thought I'd join this little chat just to make sure the regent behaves. I wouldn't want him giving away any secrets to our southern neighbor. After all, one can never know what your true motives are in coming here."

The man took Devron's forearm in a military greeting. The fellow was large, though not as thick as Grott, and he was able to return the grip. *This one mistrusts me.*

Savan went over and mussed Tarlok's hair. "Right, little brother?"

Tarlok pushed him away. "Sit down, Savan, and be polite. These people are our guests."

"Certainly. Allow me first to greet the pretty damsel." Savan stepped close and bowed to Daphora.

The attendant returned with the wine, and Savan grabbed the bottle. "Riaz red. Brother, you brought out the good stuff." He took a long swallow. "Ah, tasty." He held it toward Devron. "Try some? Or is drinking from the same bottle as your long-time enemy something you cannot stomach?"

He's testing me. Devron took the bottle and made sure to take a larger swallow than Savan did. He smacked his lips when finished. "Not bad. My preference is for the stouter wines of my homeland. More punch to them. But I can understand a Piaxian fear of strong drink."

Savan gripped the bottle and pulled, but Devron held firm. The commander glared at him. Their eyes locked in a battle of wills.

Daphora broke the staring contest by wrenching the bottle free. "What's it take for a woman to get a drink around here?" She tilted it back and drained the last of it.

Savan burst out laughing. "Well done. Come, sit by me, and we'll let these two talk." He turned to his brother. "You won't need your magic on this one, little brother. He's a man of honor. I can tell. Make sure to get more than one more bottle of wine though. I intend to get roaring drunk tonight."

The attendant didn't need telling as he dashed off. Tarlok smiled and waved toward two chairs. "Shall we?"

Devron nodded and took the closest seat. He waited until everyone was seated then focused on the regent. "You announce yourself as regent, yet the queen still sits on the throne. I am at a loss on how you may assist me."

"It is her choice to grant me all the powers of regent to rule Piaxia together. I can make any decision a king could, including a declaration of war, but in such major matters, I prefer to discuss things with her first. Before coming to that, let us first begin with you and your mission."

"If you have already received reports about the war back home, then you must know how it now fares and the threat to my people. The other kingdoms of the seven realms intend to reduce it to nothing, all as of a result from the actions of one individual. If I can reverse that person's actions, I may yet save my country from annihilation."

Tarlok leaned forward. "Educate me. Tell me everything."

Devron told the entire story. It comforted him the regent listened closely and asked questions when he was unclear. Every now and then, Tarlok would glance at Savan, and more than once Devron caught them exchanging nods.

On the third such exchange, he paused. "There are representatives from the other realms on their way here to press their own agenda, but they shouldn't arrive for another day or two.

It seems to me like as if you have heard this all before. As I came straight away, I'm wondering how."

The regent looked over at the commander one more time and then sighed. "They were here two days ago. We promised them not to intervene."

Devron sat back, shaken. Two days ago? He glanced at Daphora who shrugged and shook her head. "We came cross-country in an effort to get here first. My guide here claims we should have beaten them by at least a day, more likely two."

"They arrived by boat. They took passage at the first chance they could while you toiled over land. A ship neither rests nor sleeps."

It was hard to resist standing, as the frustration built inside him. "And you made a decision without hearing my side of the story?"

"We had no idea of your coming. *That* they did not divulge to us."

Now anger at the situation made him snort. "No wonder. They sent four men to assassinate us on the road. They probably figured us for dead."

Savan jumped up. "*That* they did not divulge to us either. To take such an action within the boundaries of our country is unacceptable." He looked to the regent. "Little brother, is what he says true?"

Daphora now stood. "It's true. We had to defend ourselves. It was only my knowledge of the woods that allowed us to escape unharmed."

The regent remained still and continued to stare at Devron. "Think of what happened, Lieutenant. I wish to verify it for myself."

Daphora moved between them. "It's true, I tell you. I am a citizen of Zon, of Piaxia. You should accept my word."

Tarlok glanced at her. "I cannot read your mind. You are blocked to me." He returned his gaze to Devron.

Devron didn't know what to do. Daphora's secret was at risk. What was it she'd told him? Something about only surface thoughts could be read. He needed to think of something else. Try as he might, the images of her use of magic continued to pop in his mind. It was no use. He could control his own movements with great dexterity, but to dictate how his mind harbored memories was beyond his control. He stood and waited for the regent to finish.

Tarlok rose as well. "What he claims is true. They were set upon by four men who still wore the uniforms of their homelands."

Savan kicked at the nearest chair. "The bastards! I knew I didn't care for their sort when they were here." He came to stand in front of Devron. "I figured you to be a warrior of honor. How did you fend off four men?"

Before he could answer, Tarlok interceded and pulled Savan back. "Let's just say they did, and leave it at that." He nodded in Daphora's direction, his lips pressed tight.

Thank the gods. He's not going to tell. "So what are you going to do about my request?"

Savan clapped his brother on the shoulder. "There may yet be time to intercept them before they cross the border. We should send riders."

Tarlok shed his brother's grip. "I must consult with my wife, the queen. This situation is most stressful. She is due any day, and I am concerned about worrying her with this. Prepare a detail of riders. Make sure a warlock is among them. Send Prattrow. He is most capable. I shall return within the hand."

Both men exited the room leaving Devron and Daphora alone. He sat down and motioned for her to do the same. "It appears your secret is safe. It would have been insufferable if my thoughts would have led to your death."

"Until such time as I actually leave this city, I will never be sure."

They chatted for a bit, speculating as to what answer the regent would return with. The attendant arrived first with a platter of roast pheasant and the two of them decided to dig in while waiting. Just as they were finishing, the door opened and the regent returned, followed by Queen Tessia and her handmaidens.

Devron rose and bowed.

She came straight for him. "My husband has informed me of all the details, and I have given my Commander of Arms permission to intercept the representatives of the other realms, if he can. As to providing warlocks to recapture the demons, I am unsure what can be done. My husband says it might be possible, and he will ride out tomorrow to elicit help from Grott, whose skills may come in handy."

"Your Majesty, my sincere thanks. It is my hope your assistance will make the difference. If it is within my power, I will insure Sechland is a friend to Piaxia forevermore." He faced Tarlok. "As to Grott, he left this morning to head for Zon, taking his entire flock with him. You should have no trouble catching up with him on the road."

The queen went to Daphora, who bowed as well. "While you are here, I would appreciate a woman healer's hands on me for a change. Although capable, my husband is constantly fretting over my well-being, and I loathe approaching the other warlocks here. Will you attend to me?"

Daphora smiled. "With pleasure, my queen."

The women left, and as they did, Savan re-entered. "It's done. There's no catching them along the coast so we've sent the riders to Zon in hopes of heading them off there." He wrapped his arm across the shoulders of Devron. "Now that business is out of the way, I say it's time we found a good tavern where the ale is hearty and the wenches heartier." He guided Devron toward the door. "Luckily, I know *just* the place."

***

Devron woke to the sound of the door to his assigned suite banging closed and bells in the distance. Sitting up quickly was probably a bad idea as his head hurt from the night of drinking. He rubbed his eyes and made note of the two young ladies snuggled together, sleeping naked in the bed next to him. He vaguely recalled Commander Savan arranging the two to accompany him.

He found his britches lying on the floor and shrugged into them, hopping toward the bedroom door and the sound of someone

255

in the main room beyond. Opening it, he discovered Daphora pulling off her boots. "Oh, it's you."

She stopped what she was doing to glare at him. "Who did you think it was—an assassin from Morica? We're *in* the palace."

He glanced back into the bedroom where the two young women were still sleeping. Thinking it discreet, he pulled the door closed behind him.

Daphora finished removing her boots and was busy shedding some outer clothing. "I'm exhausted. Is that the bedroom?"

He glanced round. If he recalled correctly, there were another two bedrooms to the suite. "I think there's a couple more down the hall there." The morning sun peeked into the room and he squinted against the light. He could still hear the bells. "What's with all the noise?"

"I helped the queen deliver a baby girl. Where do you think I've been all night? Out partying like you? No sooner did we get to her quarters when her water broke. They've started the celebration." She made for the door behind him. "This one's closest. Besides, you're up already."

He moved to block her way. "Perhaps it's best if you used one of the others."

She glanced at him, and then pushed past. "Why? Are you hiding something?" She opened the door and spotted the two girls who woke at her intrusion. A wicked smile crossed her lips. She gave him a kiss on the cheek. "Why, Devron, you shouldn't have. How did you know I've been craving a woman after spending the night with the queen and all her handmaidens? The softer touch of a female is just what I need. And look, you got me two!"

She stepped into the room. "I'll see you later." She closed the door.

He tapped on the door. "My uniform!"

It opened and she tossed his clothing at him then shut it again.

He picked everything up off the floor and proceeded to get dressed. From behind the door he could hear women's laughter. By the time he finished dressing, it changed to soft moaning. Headache or not, he decided it best to leave. Daphora never ceased to amaze him.

After chasing down something to eat, he headed off to find Savan. An attendant informed him where the commander could be found at the barracks. Stepping into the building, he was surprised to see it busy so early in the morning. Savan spotted him as he entered.

"Ah, Lieutenant. Up and about, I see. Come, tell me what provisions you and your guide need for your return journey. I'm just organizing mine."

"Yours? Are you coming with us?"

"Not just me. I'm bringing two thousand men. Something tells me the border is going to need defending, whether we catch those men or not."

CHAPTER 44

It had been fifteen or sixteen days since Darlee's release from the prison. She wasn't sure. True to his word, the tanner's wife came daily to check on her and bring her something to eat. She would arrive with sweets and home-cooked meals, but Darlee had little appetite. By the second day home, the fever had set in.

On this morning, Darlee woke to find her grandfather sleeping in a chair next to her bed. *He looks so haggard. How many nights has he slept there beside me rather than his own bed?*

She still felt the flush of the fever, but her mind was less clouded. Maybe she was getting better. For once, she felt hungry. On the table, behind where Pap now slept, she could make out a loaf of bread and some goat cheese.

She took her time and sat up, careful not to make noise in doing so. A short spell of wooziness passed through her, but once it had gone, she felt better. She shifted to bring her legs around off the edge of the bed. When they came free of the blankets, she gazed at her broken ankle. Pap had immobilized it with a splint and the swelling had finally subsided, leaving the area round it purpled and blotchy. It itched, but outside of a mild ache she was pleased her body was free of the pain. The cuts and burns that adorned her were all scabbed and healing. In a few of them, she could see the stitches the tanner's wife had sewn sticking through.

Leaning against the wall, near the head of her bed, was a crutch her grandfather had carved from a single piece of wood. She wondered how long he had searched the forest to find the exact piece. She grabbed it, and after pushing herself up from the bed, she propped it under her arm to steady her balance. *So far, so good. Now to move round Pap without waking him.*

Darlee went slowly, careful not to scrape the base of the crutch against the floor. It took time, but she managed the maneuver well enough to reach the table without a sound. She smiled at her achievement and reached for the bread. It was dry.

Hunger wasn't going to let her stop. *All I need is a little water to wash it down.*

She picked up the water ewer to find it empty. *Is there no helping my luck?* From where she stood she could see out the window to the well in the middle of the yard. *I've gone this far. Let's see if I can make it out there.*

Opening the door was the tricky part. At about halfway open, it always squeaked. She lifted the lever and pulled it to just shy of the squeak mark. Squeezing her way through, she made it without nudging the door.

Once outside, she stopped to take in the early morning sun. The fresh air strengthened her, and the flush Darlee felt on waking abated even further. *Despite everything, I'm still alive. I'm not done yet.*

The crutch in one hand and the ewer in the other, she made her way to the well. It took twenty-seven steps to get there—she counted every one of them. Leaning the crutch against the well and placing the ewer on the lip, she lifted the bucket and lowered it into the opening. As it dropped out of sight, she slowed how quickly she let the line go. The last thing she needed was a splash when it hit the water.

Her gaze shifted to scanning the forest line. A couple hundred paces away, something caught her eye. There was movement behind the first line of trees. She stopped lowering the bucket to concentrate. Maybe it was a deer. If so, waking Pap might be a good idea. Trapping one of those would give them plenty to eat, and the hide would come in handy as retribution to the tanner.

Darlee saw the movement again. Stepping toward her from the tree line was the imp demon Gar freed! She crouched behind the well. Glancing at the shed, the idea to shout and wake Pap weighed in her mind. It would rouse him, but it would also alert the demon to her presence. Maybe it would go away.

From her crouched position, she continued to watch the creature skitter in all directions. What happened next took her breath away. Emerging from the woods was a monstrous demon. She was shocked at how large the beast was. Her mind was made up. She needed to get Pap's help.

As she let go of the rope, the pail plunged the remaining distance and the sound of the splash echoed up from the well. She lunged for her crutch while trying to keep an eye on the demons, and instead of grabbing it, she knocked it to the ground. She dropped down to pick it up and glanced at the forest one more time. No doubt, they had seen her. Even worse, there were more emerging from the woods, and these were on horseback.

As she righted and placed the crutch under her arm, she measured the distance back to the shed, recalling the twenty-seven steps it took to get to where she was. *Can I make it? I've got to try.*

She set off, focused on the door. The thunder of hooves pounded in her direction. A voice called her name. *It's me they want.* "Pap! Help me! The demons have returned!"

Another nine steps and she would be back inside. The horses sounded real close. A shadow loomed over her and she dared to look up. With the sun behind the rider, the only thing she glimpsed was a man jumping down from a horse, reaching for her. She tried to dive for the door, but an arm scooped her round the waist from behind and pulled her into his grip.

She flailed with all her might. "Let me go!"

"Darlee, stop. It's me. It's Gar."

His grip weakened and she faced him. It really was her brother. "Gar, where have you been? I've been so worried about you. When Jango came back alone I feared the worst." She wrapped her arms around his waist and hugged with all her might. "Don't ever leave again. Pap and I need you."

He stroked her hair. "I'm here, Darlee, but what's happened here? Where's Father and Mother? What happened to the house?" He pushed her off and looked her up and down. "And what's happened to you?"

"Oh, Gar, it's horrible. Men from the city came and killed our parents and burned down the house. Pap and I weren't home at the time."

The creak from the shed door opening wide told her Pap was awake. She turned to see him brandishing a pitchfork in the doorway.

"Gar, what is the meaning of this? Why are all of these demons on our land?"

She glanced past her brother and took count. No longer just the one small one from the meadow, there were now five demons nearby. Three were on horseback, and two of those were female. Despite their dark grey appearances, the two women were stunning. The other male, though, was frightening, with his six arms and mandibles. He stared at her and she shrank behind Gar. "Why did you bring them here?"

Gar faced the creatures. "They're my companions. They have kept me safe from harm. You have no need to fear them."

Pap approached. "Well, get them off our farm. We don't need any more trouble. Because of them, they killed your folks and they damned near killed your sister."

To her surprise, Gar trotted away. Darlee picked up her crutch and tried her best to follow. "Gar. Where are you going?"

He stopped at the small graveyard where the still visible graves for their parents were. By the time she managed to catch up, he had sunk to his knees beside the markers. She heard him sniff and saw him wipe his hand across his eyes. Her own welled. She put a hand on his shoulder. "Pap and I felt it best we bury them here, near the house."

"He always hated me, I don't know why. I should be happy he's gone. Nevertheless, they didn't deserve this. They were my parents. It isn't right."

She knelt to hug him. "They were my parents, too. But they're gone, Gar. You can't bring them back. We only have each other now, each other and Pap."

He hugged her for a while. When he released his embrace, he gently touched her broken ankle. They did this to you?"

Placing a hand over his, she gripped his fingers. "It's healing. I'm going to be okay."

Gar pulled his hand free and went to reached for the patch over her eye. She leaned away.

"Stop, Darlee. I want to see."

"All right." It took a great deal of will not to move as he pulled the cloth back to reveal her empty eye socket. His fingers, ever so gently, touched the rim. When he pulled his hand back, his fingers were shaking.

"They did *that* to you as well." He turned to the demons. "Hiss, come here. We must heal Darlee."

The demon scampered over. "Sorry, Master, the eye gone. You cannot heal what not there."

Gar moved his hands back to her ankle. "Her leg then. Let me at least heal that."

"Hiss mana fade, Master. Hiss have no more."

"I'll do it myself. Give me the stone."

The demon her brother called Hiss fumbled through his pocket and produced a small rock, scarred and worn. *It's just a whetting stone. What good will that do?*

Her brother snatched it from the hand of the imp and held it in one hand while he held her leg in the other. "Now, let the power of this stone heal."

Would it really heal her? She watched her leg, but nothing happened.

Gar tossed the stone in fury at Hiss. "Why isn't it working?"

Hiss picked it up. "Me give, but stone no help. Magic is skill. Mana make work. Master has mana, not skill. Hiss teach skill already. Master must use skill and own mana. Stone in ground is Key, make skill many times more powerful. This one not in ground. No Key. Try, Master. Use skill like Hiss teach. You do magic."

Gar placed both hands on her leg. She could see his brows knit in concentration. She felt a tingling in her leg. The purple blotches faded. In a few beats, they were gone; so were the itching and the mild ache.

Gar sat back, pulled a dagger from his belt, and cut free the splint Pap made. "It worked. Your ankle is healed. You won't need that crutch anymore."

She flexed her leg and ankle. Gar stood and offered her a hand. She took it and rose to stand on both feet. There was no pain. Her ankle was normal. "It's amazing."

Her brother smiled. "Not everything about magic is evil." His smile faded. "But I still cannot replace the eye you lost. Who were these people that did this to you? And who were the ones who killed Mother and Father?"

She thought of Lieutenant Gramby and the torturer. Although she'd never agreed with Gramby's plan, she understood why he did it. What were Gar's plans? Would he go after them? For that matter, was it his intention to go after Merchant Trellus as well? He was watching her in a way that frightened her. His hard stare bored into her forehead. She reset the patch. "I still have one good eye. I'm still alive. It's all that matters."

"It's *not* all that matters!" Gar stood and pulled the pitchfork from Pap's hands, a flush coloring his cheeks.

Pap yanked the pitchfork back. "Why? Don't you think you've caused enough trouble?"

Gar made for his horse. He swung a hand toward all the demons. "Come, it's time we leave here before anyone sees us and causes my family any more grief. We have much to do. Perhaps it is time you all renewed your healthy glows."

The six-armed demon smiled, baring its mandibles wide, and Darlee chilled at the sight of it. "What are you going to do, Gar?"

"I'll make them pay, Darlee. I have something to do first, but, tonight, I'll make them all pay." He mounted his horse and rode back the way he came, the others following. One of the women demons paused to look back at Darlee with a sad frown. She gave a slow shake of her head, and then rode off to catch up with the others.

An arm across her shoulders told her that her grandfather moved to stand with her. "What are *we* going to do, Pap?"

"Nothing, child. He's a different man now. His decisions are his own."

263

CHAPTER 45

Brusk watched Gar and the demons retreat into the woods. It had been a difficult task, what with that big demon Thunder being able to see, smell, and hear, better than any man, but he'd managed to track them without getting spotted. Most of the time, he stayed downwind where the scent of the demons was easy to follow.

He did lose them one time, but then, out of the blue, the raven returned and led him straight to where they were camped.

Now that he knew where they were, it was time to do something about it. He stole back to where he'd left his horse and kicked the animal into a gallop toward Visk. He hoped that Devron had managed to keep things together in his absence and kept the troops ready because he would need each and every one of them if he was going to capture all those demons.

As he neared the main gate, he could make out the men posted there were in a different-colored livery than his own troops. *Something ain't right here. That's the green color of Morica. Why are they guarding the gate? Has the city fallen?* The raven flew above the walls. As he followed the bird's flight, he noted no men were stationed up there.

He needed to make a snap decision. Turn away now or face whatever came. As he mulled the options, his horse continued on until the decision was made for him. It didn't take long for a dozen men to surround him and grab the reins of his horse. Two bows were trained on him and he held his hands up in surrender. "Easy now, boys, I'm just trying to come home."

The man holding the reins of his horse pointed to the ground. "Get down and surrender your weapons. Visk is under the control of the alliance. The military here has been disbanded."

He did as he was told. "The alliance? All I see is men from Morica. Are there other troops inside to keep an eye on you?"

He never saw which one hit him, as the blow to the back of his head sent him reeling to the ground. A couple of the others put a few boots to him then backed off.

The man holding the reins passed them to another man then crouched to grab Brusk by the collar. "You'll listen and obey what we say, dog. Is that understood?"

"Perfectly." He struggled to his feet and dusted himself off. "Now, if you gentlemen will be so kind as to let me pass, there's a pub in there calling my name."

They parted to let him by, but before he could take another step, one kicked him in the ass. Together, the men from Morica burst out laughing. He smiled at them in return. *That's another thing they owe me for.*

Still early, he expected the inn he had in mind to be empty. It was a favorite haunt of soldiers and he knew if he waited, his men would show, sooner or later. With the raven once again on his shoulder, he stepped into the gloom to find it was not. A number of the men under his command were seated at one table, two sound asleep. The one closest to the door spotted him and jumped to salute.

"Captain Brusk!"

He motioned for the man to sit back down. "At ease. I'm just a citizen like you, right now, but I could use a little information about what's been happening here in my absence. Where's Lieutenant Devron? Can one of you chase him down for me?"

The man who saluted, snorted. "Devron's gone. He left town the day the enemy troops arrived. Ran like the wind, he did."

Surprising. He figured the soldier bred in the man would have kept him put. "Then who was in charge?"

"Lieutenant Gramby."

"Fine, I'll talk to Gramby. Where's he at?"

The man pointed toward the corner of the room. "There."

Brusk spotted a man sleeping on a bench behind one of the tables. He went over and shook the lieutenant. "Gramby, wake up. It's Brusk. I'm back. I need to talk to you."

Gramby woke and struggled into a sitting position. "Brusk? Is it…is it really you?"

The stench of alcohol was strong on the man. His clothes were disheveled and stained. He reeked of perspiration. How many days had the man spent in this corner? "Look alive, man. I need a report.

Shake off whatever funk you're in and act the officer I know you to be."

Gramby rubbed his face with his hands. "I'm sorry, Captain. I've failed you. I let them have the city without a fight."

"Then it's time to be prepared to take it back. How many men do they have stationed here? I didn't see many on my way. There were none on the walls, just a guard at the gate."

"They posted a company, no more."

This was good news. "A company? You have triple that in troops here. What's stopped you?"

"They took all of our weapons. Everything is locked up in the armory. What would you have us do, fight with kitchen knives?"

"If what I suspect is about to happen, we won't have to fight at all. We just need to be ready to act when the time comes." He told Gramby about Gar, the demons, and the attack he expected that evening. When he finished, his lieutenant started to shake.

"That means, he'll come for me as well. I was the one who ordered the torture of his sister."

He listened as Gramby told of the attempted ruse.

"Then we must be prepared to capture the demons once they've finished off the troops from Morica. We'll need nets, plenty of them, and rope and chains to tie the demons when we catch them."

"I'll take care of it."

Gramby started to rise but he caught the man by the arm. "Before you go, what of Devron? Did he really desert us?"

A weak smile played across Gramby's lips. "No. He's gone to Piaxia to ask for help. It was my hope he would be back by now. I guess his mission failed."

The raven screamed and startled the lieutenant so he fell backward in his chair. Brusk chuckled. "It appears my friend here disagrees with you."

Gramby pointed at the raven, and then snatched his hand back when it pecked at him. "It's just a bird. How would it know?"

Brusk stroked the animal. "I don't know if it does. But there's one thing I can tell you about it. So far, it's never let me down. Maybe Devron *is* on his way with an army of Piaxia at his side.

Who knows, for sure. If that happens, all the better. In the meantime, we must be ready to retake the city. Go. Make the preparations. Pass the word to all of the officers to gather their troops and meet here at one hand before sundown."

Gramby rose. "I'm on my way."

"Oh, and one more thing. Clean yourself up. An officer must command respect."

His lieutenant nodded and slipped out the door. Brusk instructed the other four soldiers to scatter and pass the word, and, while they were at it, secure any weapons they could find.

He left the inn and headed for his own simple home. Unless the troops from Morica were very thorough in their search, he doubted they would find the cache of weapons he hid in the floorboards. The sword and armor was ceremonial from when granted his captaincy, but it would have to do. From there, he needed to visit the blacksmiths. There was much he needed them to do before the day was over.

CHAPTER 46

As he and the others continued north, Gar contemplated what the rest of the day had in store for him. Leaving Pap and his sister behind was a difficult decision he had already questioned a hundred times. Was he doing the right thing? It would take the skills of all of the demons to achieve what he hoped to do. It was key they all were imbued with enough mana left to make it work. If not, they would need to gain some, somewhere along the way.

Another thought occurred to him. He had already made mana of his own, and plenty of it. It wasn't more mana he got from Hiss, it was know-how. Hiss passed the knowledge on and Gar's mind retained it. He wondered just how much mana he emanated. Did he have what it took to lock the demons back into the stone? No, he'd needed the Key to release them. He would need the Key to bind them as well. What were the odds he could find some bedrock to touch at the same time as when he wanted to trap one? Probably not likely.

How had Bron done it then? When he thought of the different stones he released demons from, only the one holding Dread stood on bedrock. Obviously, Bron had possessed much greater skill than him.

He recalled each of the stone openings and how the pain he suffered lessened each time. In the later ones, Hiss glowed with his absorption of mana from those Thunder killed. Maybe Hiss was supplying some mana after all, making it easier for him. That only made sense.

The idea of binding the demons once more was not what he was concerned with. He needed them now. There was justice to be had, and he couldn't acquire it alone. It was why he was following Hiss once more, north of Visk to somewhere near the border with Piaxia. Ever since they neared home, Hiss was urging him to go there. Gar wanted to make sure he had the necessary support to do what needed to be done. Gar was sure Pleasure was using her skill to push his lust for vengeance, but he didn't care.

Silk came to ride by his side. "Gar, are you sure about this? There are already enough of us so we can set out on our own and make a new place where we won't be bothered."

"Where, Silk? Where would that be? Certainly, not anywhere within the seven kingdoms. They are hunting us as we speak."

"You're speculating. They may be content to leave us be if we're no trouble to them."

"No, it's not speculation. I know."

She reached over to pull on his arm, and the two horses came to stop. "How do you know?"

He pulled his arm free and kicked his mount back into a trot. "From Darlee, the commander of the forces from Morica spoke of such a plan in her presence."

Silk got hers to keep pace. "I was there, right beside you. She made no such statement."

He halted the horses once more and stared deep into Silk's black eyes. "It was in her mind. It was there along with a host of other things I needed to know. I could see the thoughts as clearly as if they were my own. Everything was there. I could recall every detail of how Commander Padronus was leaving behind a single company to rule Visk while he was taking the rest of his troops to search for us throughout the seven kingdoms. I could see the moment she learned that it was the men of Merchant Trellus who killed my parents. It was if I were lying with her on that table when Lieutenant Gramby ordered her torture. I even felt the memory of the terrible suffering she went through. It was horrific, Silk, simply horrific. No young girl should ever have to endure such evil."

He nudged his horse into a canter and Silk stayed alongside once more.

"So you can read minds like Hiss, now."

"Apparently so. In fact, I think I just figured out that I always had the power to do all of the things that Hiss has helped me with—the mind reading, the healing, using the Key, and, yes, opening the stones. I just never had the know-how to use it. Hiss has taught me that, whether he wanted to or not."

She went silent and he glanced her way. She met his eyes for a brief moment, and then turned away. When he concentrated, her

269

thoughts came to him as well. Her mind was filled with one thought, pity for him. She feared he had lost his humanity.

Gar focused on tracking the imp as it scampered in the lead. He couldn't let what Silk thought deter him from his plan. Not now. Not ever.

They came to a thick stand of trees and shrubs, a jungle. It was too dense for the horses to pass; they needed to go on foot. Hiss squirted his way through and Thunder was next, tearing through the thick vegetation, leaving a path wide enough for Gar and the rest to follow.

In less than a quarter hand, Hiss came scampering back from between a number of small trees. "Me find, me find. Me knew it was here. Come, Master. Come see."

Thunder attacked the copse of trees with the ferocity Gar was now accustomed to seeing. As the low growth fell away, he could make out the unmistakable rock surface with its hieroglyph markings.

He approached the demon stone determined in his convictions. With the stone buried in a tight copse of trees that grew round it, he instructed Thunder to tear away the surrounding vegetation so he could stand next to it with ease.

"Come, Hiss. It's time to release another of your brethren. Tonight, we will make those in Visk pay for what they have done to my family. Show me once more how to access the Key."

The imp clambered up and placed a hand on Gar's forehead. He placed his hands on the stone. *Without the additional mana from Hiss, this is going to hurt again, but I don't care.* He concentrated on opening the stone. It was large, bigger even than the one that had held Dread. He closed his eyes to focus on his thoughts. The skill to unlock the Key flowed easily in his mind. He recognized it well enough to believe he would not need the help from the small demon anymore. The stone shook and crumbled away. As expected, his head ached from the act and he crumpled to his knees as the demon stepped forth.

It was as tall as Thunder, though not so massive. Rather, it sported a sleek figure, almost serpentine in appearance. Even the shape of its skull flared like the hood of a snake. It glared at him kneeling there then took in the others gathered around.

From the beast resonated a deep, rumbling laugh. "I am free at last. Free. Free to exact vengeance against those that imprisoned me."

Pleasure was the first to approach the new demon, stroking its chest while conversing in her native tongue. Gar could do no more than sit on his heels and listen as he waited for the worst of the pain to pass. When she finished, the new demon reached and cupped Gar's chin in his hand.

"So you are the one who has served our people so well. I am told there is a debt to be paid. Our goals, for now, are the same. Allow me to show you the gift I bring to make those who oppose us quiver in their boots."

Gar could sense the creature exact its skill on him, and he tried to bend away from the demon's touch. Within him was a sense of terror and dread at what was to come. He knew what he was succumbing to. It was fear.

The sensation passed quickly. Struggling against the pain in his head, Gar stood to face the new demon. The dullness of the creature's skin told him enough. It retained no mana with which to continue its power. He needed to assert his authority while he could. "As fear is your skill, I shall call you Doom, for that is what I want for others."

Doom sneered at him. "No one names me. I am not your creation. That was a task of the gods. I will abide by this titling for the meantime, but when all is done, this game will end."

"Come, then. There is much to do, and I am anxious to do it. When it's over, I don't care what happens next. I'll consider the debt you speak of to be paid."

CHAPTER 47

The journey took longer than Devron would have liked. His second entry into Zon was much easier than the first. Of course, it didn't hurt that the Commander of Piaxia and a two thousand strong troop marched at his side. There was even the same smug guard on duty who had harassed him so that night. When Devron made eye contact with the man, the fellow blanched and hurried his steps to make sure none barred their path.

It was not yet dusk, so the gates were still open. Barely had he crossed through the portico when he, Commander Savan, and Daphora were greeted by Master Gaffrey.

"I see your journey was safe. Word reached us earlier of your pending arrival. Come. A meal has been prepared in the main hall. We can dine, and then, after that, discuss the situation."

The commander was the first to greet the master warlock. "I, too, received word from your rider. The men from the other six kingdoms. Where are you holding them?"

"There were too many to put under guard in the castle. We were forced to use the dungeons."

"Hmm. A foul mood they'll be in then. No matter. They brought it on themselves." Savan took a deep breath. "Now, did I hear you say there was hot food ready? What are we doing standing out here near the stables? Quick, man, show us the way."

They marched to the castle and its great hall. Along the way, Daphora chatted in private with her brother, too muted for Devron to hear, but every now and then he noted the pair stealing glances in his direction. He only hoped she wasn't too revealing of all that had occurred. Savan had been kind enough to provide him with, among other supplies, a tent. Despite being camped among two thousand men, Daphora had decided it was more than enough privacy and made good use of both it and him on the way back.

Upon entering the hall, Savan went straight to the head table and greeted Lord Kipron. Already present in the room were men dressed in the purple livery of Lia. Devron guessed they must have been the troop sent to capture the men who ordered his death. Scanning the group, he spotted the warlock Prattrow among them, confirming his suspicions.

When they were seated, Gaffrey occupied the chair across from him. "News has not been good out of Visk and Sechwisk. After you left, I urged Lord Kipron to send spies. It appears the cities are now fully under the control of forces from Morica. The militaries have been disbanded, their armories seized. I have every suspicion to believe Morica intends to absorb all of Sechland. Dark days are ahead for your country, Lieutenant."

It took all his will not to bang the table with his fist and upset everyone's plate. He calmed down. "What news of the demons? Have they managed to capture them? Their capture would free the other kingdoms of the Warlock Pact. True, they may be allies right now, but I suspect more than one country might take exception to Morica being the only one to gain as a result of it."

"No news of that. Their Commander Padronus of Morica is a wily one. He has the forces of the other kingdoms scouring the countryside looking for the creatures while his own set up shop in Sechland's cities. *His* main force remains parked outside the gates of Sechwisk."

He decided to concentrate on the food put before him. The others at the table speculated at what may or may not happen, but his heart was not in to rejoining the conversation. If the demons were never caught, what were his options? Commander Savan was here in force, but would he dare to cross the border and engulf his country in a war? Unlikely.

The commander's brother, Regent Tarlok, was even more cryptic. He spoke of getting help from the big fellow, Grott, but Devron knew that, even with the big man's help, a warlock without this Key they talk about would not be able to wield enough magic.

Perhaps he had gone the wrong way for help. Storburg was much farther from Visk, but at least they had a history of being allies to Sechland. Perhaps it might not yet be too late to plead his case to their king.

The meal finished, Lord Kipron was the first to rise. "I think it is time we address the problem at hand. Send for the prisoners, we can discuss the matter in the throne room. Commander Savan, Lieutenant Devron, Master Gaffrey, please join me there, along with whoever has information to present."

Devron rose, along with Daphora, and followed the lord. Lord Kipron took the throne with Commander Savan stationed next to the lord. A number of soldiers took up positions round the room, along with Master Gaffrey. Three other warlocks were present as well.

The prisoners were brought in, were shackled together, and were made to sit on the floor, surrounded by a half-a-dozen guardsmen.

When everyone was settled and the room quieted, Lord Kipron nodded toward Master Gaffrey.

"Men of Morica, Storburg, and Fermia, you came before this court some time ago begging our permission to travel to our capital city, Lia, in hopes of persuading our queen to side with you in your struggle with Sechland. Lord Kipron granted you that permission. This was a very generous gesture on his part, as you were a significant group of armed men traversing our countryside. We trusted you would travel our kingdom in peace, make your plea, and go. You betrayed that trust when you sent some of your party to kill another guest of the kingdom, Lieutenant Devron Sech, from Sechland, and his Piaxian guide, within the borders of our country. This was an act we could not tolerate. Your apprehension and holding was necessary until the arrival of Commander Savan who has been vested the authority by the queen to deal with this matter. You have been interrogated and the facts have been confirmed. Before a decision is rendered, do you have anything else to say? Who is your spokesman?"

A lieutenant dressed in the livery of Morica stood. "It's all a lie. We came in good faith, and you set upon us without provocation."

Gaffrey sighed, made eye contact with Lord Kipron, and then faced the standing man. "Lieutenant, surely you must know of the gift we warlocks possess in dealing with matters such as these. Even now, I can sense you are lying to this court. Have you no shame?"

A sneer formed on the man's face, and he spat on the floor. "Warlocks. It is you who are the bane to our world. Your dark magic has been banned from the seven realms, but here, it remains a blight not yet eradicated. May the gods forever curse you and all your kind."

Before Gaffrey could answer, Commander Savan stepped between him and the prisoners. "I have arrived at my decision. You, Lieutenant, and all of your men are to be set free. You will leave the way you came, but without weapons. It was our hope the hatreds of ages past would have been forgotten by now, but it appears is not to be the case. Should any of the seven realms be willing to accept us as we are and forge new bonds, we will be open to them. Until such time, our borders will be closed. Be gone from this place."

Guardsmen rushed the prisoners and unlocked the shackles that held them. When the last was set free, the soldiers brusquely ushered them toward the door.

The lieutenant from Morica stopped at the entrance to face Savan once more. "What if Sechland accepts you? What if the cousin of the king there..." he pointed at Devron "...should offer you such a treaty. Will you accept?"

"We will accept."

The spokesman laughed. "You understand what such acceptance would mean? It would mean war."

"If that is your decision, Piaxia stands ready. Do you?"

The man's eyes widened. He turned and left with the others. It was with a resounding boom that the doors closed.

Devron put his head down into his hands. What was he to do? If he did as Savan suggested, he would plunge the region into a war with Sechland in the middle. The people would suffer. If he did nothing, no war would ravage his homeland, but it would be his homeland no more.

CHAPTER 48

Gar nudged his horse onto the road. He recognized the stretch. The countless time he'd trod this section on his way to and from school was etched in his mind. *The gate is less than a half-league away*. He glanced at the sun. Not more than a half a hand remained before nightfall.

The demons gathered near him. "We must reach the gate before dark. They will surely close it then, making our entry that much more difficult. They will not be able to make out who you are until we are close enough. Make sure all of you are ready."

Doom alit from the back of the horse he shared with Pleasure and stretched. "I was never comfortable riding on those beasts. For the rest of the way, I'll run with the one you call Thunder. It will urge my anger higher to make all those in my path suffer when I get there."

"Not all. It is only the men of Morica who must pay—them, Lieutenant Gramby, and those who work for Merchant Trellus. No others. Is that understood?"

Doom ignored him. Gar moved closer and placed a hand on the demon's shoulder. "I said…is that understood?"

A scowl, followed by a nod, was all he got.

"Good. Then let's get going. As strong as I think Thunder is, I think it would still take him much time to break through the gate if it's closed."

He kicked his horse into a canter, and the rest followed.

They cleared the last of the trees, and he slowed them to a walk for the last few hundred paces. He didn't want to alarm the guards at the gate by having them see a group charging in. It was his hope the dusk in the setting sun would mask the slate-grey complexions of the demons.

When they were no more than thirty paces away, one of the guards was watching them as they approached. It was more the sudden jerking motion of the man backward than his stare that informed Gar they were spotted. "Go!" Gar kicked his horse into a gallop.

The soldier ran for the gate. "Demons!"

Even with his horse charging, the speed of Thunder still surprised him. The large demon was past him and at the man before he could escape through the opening. Other soldiers were trying to close the doors as Thunder crashed into them, throwing men away as Gar and the others rushed through.

He brought his horse to a halt in the open area behind the gate. "None of you need for me to tell you what to do. Let's get this ugly business over with."

Pleasure, Silk, and Dread dismounted and spread their arms. Soldiers poured out of the barracks and charged them but, when they neared, they slackened. Some fought each other. Doom stepped toward those closest and laughed. The men cringed to the ground. He wrested a sword from the nearest and swung freely. Heads rolled and blood spurted from the decapitated bodies.

Gar looked into the eyes of the ones who still remained on the field. They were all fear stricken. None of them moved. They all continued to cringe and watch as Doom walked among them, dealing death and gaining glow. Dread joined in the slaughter, using the talons of his six arms to slash repeatedly at the soldiers. Despite their numbers, the combined magic of the demons froze them where they were.

He glanced over their heads to see others at the entrance to the barracks backing up. More were pouring out with bows and fired arrows at him and the demons. Gar fell off his horse in an effort to avoid them, and when he straightened, he found Thunder standing above him, blocking any more from reaching him. When a couple of the arrows bounced off Thunder, the behemoth charged toward the archers.

The archers panicked, and too many tried to squeeze back into the barracks at one time. As a result, Thunder plowed into the ones still outside, while others were trying to close the door against the few remaining who wanted back in.

The door slammed shut and even from where he stood, Gar could hear the sound of it being barricaded from the inside. He surveyed the area round him. Between those at the gate and what lay on the ground, he guessed at least forty of the troops from Morica were slain. The number remaining in the barracks and wherever some may be scattered throughout the city were too few to pose a threat. He did not want to spend too much time trying to breach the barracks. "Come. A more important task awaits. Follow me."

Hiss, sporting a healthy glow, scampered to his side.

"Where, Master? Where we go?"

Gar remounted his horse. "To the home of Merchant Trellus."

"Me know place."

He thought back to that first night when Hiss gave him the bracelet. He shuddered at the continuous circumstances that had brought him to where he was now. "Yes, Hiss. I know you do. Lead the way."

The imp scampered away, and Gar kicked his horse to follow. Dread, Pleasure, and Silk followed on horseback, while Thunder and Doom strode alongside.

The streets were empty. Word of their arrival must have spread like the wind and every citizen of Visk had probably locked their doors. Passing one street, Gar caught a glimpse of a number of men running parallel to them a block away. One wore bright armor. It did not matter. He was focused on what lay ahead.

When they reached the estate, the wood and wrought-iron gate was closed. He spotted archers in the small towers to either side. In the courtyard behind, more men could be seen dashing left and right.

Doom laughed. "They think a mere gate can stop us? Silk, focus on one of them. Get that gate opened."

Astride the horse next to Gar, Silk reached out and put a hand on his arm. "Stop this, Gar. There's no need. What's to be gained? Vengeance will not bring your parents back. Don't give them another reason to hunt you."

His fists clenched as he weighed her words. Nothing *would* bring his parents back. He knew that. But, as to being hunted to the end of his days, it was no longer something he feared. He expected the end to come soon enough. "Do it, Silk. Do it now."

She sighed and dismounted. As she walked toward the gate, a host of arrows rained down on her and bounced harmlessly to the ground. Gar followed her line of sight to locate the man she concentrated on, some ten paces behind the gate. For a moment, the man held still, and then, on shaky legs, he walked toward her.

The others must have been watching as well, and together, they advanced to wait outside the portal. When the man was almost at the gate, Gar could hear someone screaming at him to get away. The fellow's head turned for a moment, as if seeking out where the voice came from, then he continued on and reached for something Gar couldn't see. More than likely, whatever it was that locked the gate into place.

More screams from men inside, pleading with the man to stop. It was too late, the left door of the gate swung open. The demons poured in.

The first to die was the poor man in Silk's thrall. It wasn't much longer before all of the others defending the estate met a similar demise. Gar dismounted and went into the courtyard.

The front doors to the manor were also locked from the inside. It didn't take Thunder long to break them down. Once inside, a handful more of defenders sought to stop the advance of the demons. Doom and Dread made quick work of them.

Hiss bolted in and disappeared down a hall, only to reappear shortly. "This way, Master. Me find merchant."

Gar followed the small demon to a room near the back of the manor. Once more, Thunder hammered the door open, and Gar stepped in.

The merchant was cowering behind a chair. His head swiveled left and right then his sight settled on Gar. "If it's gold you want, I can give it to you."

The man tossed a large sack to the floor at Gar's feet. It clanked heavy with the sound of many coins. A few of them spilled out of the bag. Gold. He guessed there were hundreds of the coins. It was more wealth than he could imagine. He kicked the bag aside. "I cannot be bought. No amount of gold can buy my family back."

Trellus collapsed to the floor and crawled to Gar's feet. "Please, spare me. What more can I do to have you let me live?"

In his mind, the answer was "nothing," but as he held his weapon aloft to strike the killing blow, he couldn't do it.

As he paused, midstrike, Doom interceded and swung his sword, severing the man's head from his body. Blood gushed forth, soiling Gar's boots and leggings.

The demon sneered. "His plea for mercy sickened even me. I now understand why you wanted this done. I have finished what you could not."

Gar locked eyes with the demon for a moment then turned away. His unwillingness to kill the man must have been apparent. There was no point in arguing. The deed was done. "Let's go."

As they retreated down the hall toward the front door, a noise from a room to his right sent Thunder bursting into it. He didn't want anyone else to die. "Thunder, wait!"

Following the behemoth into the room, he recognized it as the dining room where he'd attended the birthday lunch. Hiding under the massive table was Lialee, and she wasn't alone. Next to her was his friend Maurus. Thunder reached for him, and Gar felt a pang of disappointment. "Don't kill him."

Maurus was shaking. "Gar, what's going on? Why are you doing this?"

What could he say? Wasn't it all obvious? He could not accept Maurus was ignorant of the facts. "You know why."

Pleasure pulled Lialee from under the table and laughed. "So *this* is the young female you pined over. I fail to see why. Still, if she is what you want, you may have her." She thrust Lialee in his direction. "Go to him. Give him your love."

The fear on Lialee's face disappeared, replaced by a smile. She licked her lips. "Gar, I've been waiting for you. Why have you stayed away so long? I've been yearning for you. I want you to take me."

She undressed and Gar could feel his own libido rising. He glanced at Pleasure to see her arms outstretched. *She's using her gift.*

Lialee continued to strip until entirely naked. "Come on, Gar. I want you to be the first. Let's have sex. I can't wait any longer." She reached for his belt and started to undo it.

His desire to do it was strong although he was disappointed in Lialee's naked body. Compared to Pleasure's, her breasts were small, and she sported a bit of a paunch at her waistline. Her skin, although creamy in color, lacked any tone showing in the muscles beneath. She was about to pull his leggings down when he reached out and grabbed her arms, preventing her. "Stop it, Pleasure. I don't want it this way. In truth, I don't think I'll ever want it. Let her be."

Pleasure's arms dropped and Lialee slumped to the floor, sobbing. Gar, still holding her arms, shook her. "Get dressed and go before anything else happens."

She glared at him, gathered her clothing, and dashed out the door. Gar nodded toward Maurus. "Let him go as well. We were friends. I owe him that much."

Thunder released Maurus, who bolted after Lialee.

Pleasure sidled up to him and kissed his neck while wrapping an arm and a leg round him. "A wise choice. What would sex with such a pitiful thing as that girl be compared to what you have with me?"

He pushed free of her. "I wish to leave this place. It sickens me."

He stepped out into the hall and paused to gaze round at the opulence of the home. He recalled the house that had once been his and how much he'd detested the poor state of it. Still, it had been his home, and now it was gone. Anger roiled in him once more and with it he wished that fire would consume this mansion, as it had consumed his family's home.

To his surprise, flame erupted from the palms of his hands. He stared at them for a moment then realized he'd uncovered another magic. He concentrated and turned his palms outward toward the walls. The flames shot out and splashed against the walls, igniting them.

The fire spread quickly. Gar could feel the heat. The flames in his palms went out. *This is a skill Hiss did not teach me. I wonder what others there are?*

He stepped back out into the courtyard. Night had fallen and the stars were out. It wasn't long until the flames burst through the roof of the manor making the stars hard to see. Gar watched for a while longer. It was time to go. He'd seen and done enough.

CHAPTER 49

For Brusk, the day unfolded as he expected. By the time Gar and his demon friends arrived at the gate, he had gathered almost two hundred men at the inn. Only a handful bore weapons, but that mattered not. It was what else they carried that he hoped would be sufficient. Nets, ropes, and chains of various sizes and lengths were gathered from everywhere they could get their hands on them.

Now, they were waiting outside the gate of the burning home of Merchant Trellus. He watched the demon's conquest of the defenders and mused as to why the men who guarded the manor still carried their weapons when everyone else in Visk was stripped of them. No doubt, Trellus bought off the men from Morica.

The demons were in the estate courtyard. All was in readiness. Everything was dependent on speed. He and his men needed to trap them all before the demons could wield the powers they possessed. There was a new one with them Brusk had not seen before. He wondered what skill that demon wielded. Back at the gate, the new one had exhibited a more evil lust for pain and murder than all the others.

It was big, as well, but still not as large as Thunder. He hefted the strongest of the chains and wondered if it would be able to hold the demon. *I guess I'm going to find out.*

As the demons stepped through the gate, he set his plan into action. "Now!"

From everywhere, his men charged toward the fiends, dragging open nets and tossing rope loops. He had designated the majority of his men to the capture of Thunder. If the behemoth remained free, capturing the rest would only be temporary.

Along with his main group, Brusk raced toward the large demon. Four men in the lead threw a net on top of the beast. It was disappointing to see the ease with which the demon ripped the net to shreds, but regardless, the act of tearing the net apart took a few precious beats, giving him and his men the chance to wrap two fetters across the behemoth.

"Quickly now, wrap the chain." He took a moment to glance at how the rest of his men fared. Capturing the two women was progressing well, but the new demon and the one called Dread were still free. He returned his focus to Thunder. More chains were being thrown over the monster, and the men were struggling to hold the thing down. Its struggles could result in several men being thrown from their feet and losing the grip on the chain they held. He needed to secure those lines, or all would be lost.

"Spike those chains into the ground. Make haste, now." Men with metalworkers' hammers pounded at large metal spikes brought for just that purpose. They were desperate to get a ring of spikes round the demon so the men could anchor their lines. The ringing of the hammers competed with the roar of the monster as it fought the fetters. It was a race, and his men needed to win it. Their task was no easy one, as the paving stones of the street prevented a quick penetration by the spikes.

Despair crept into his mind. Glancing once more, he spotted the other demons spreading their arms to enact their evil magic. He shook off the sensation as best he could. He needed to rally the men. "Remember, do not fall victim to what you feel. It's only their spells. They cannot hurt you. Fight it and keep at it."

He hoped there were enough of them that the demon's magic would be spread too thin to be effective. He had seen its effect in the fishing village and watched how well it worked against a single company of men, both at the river that day, and again, at the gate. There were three times as many with him now. *May the gods be with us, that's enough.*

Curses to his right brought his attention to a number of men trying to hammer spikes in. "What's the problem?"

One of the men holding a hammer motioned him over. "Bedrock, Captain. It's right below the paving stones in this spot. There's nothing we can sink the spikes into."

He dashed to the man and looked down. Sure enough, a number of the paving stones were cast aside, and the rock glistened in the firelight from the burning mansion. *Curse the luck.* "Join the others in holding the chains." He faced the few men waiting. Bring the manacles now. We'll have to try and get them on the thing as it is."

Four men carrying a huge set of shackles rushed forward. It had taken the entire day to craft them. The question was, could they get them on the thrashing monster?

He took one more peek at the other demons. Things weren't going so well. Many of the men nearest them had succumbed to the spells and were either running or cowering. There were still a few struggling on. His only hope was to bind Thunder quickly so his group could aid the rest.

He decided to join the men with the fetters. If, at the very least, they could get them on the creature's ankles, there would still be a chance.

As he and the others got close, he stepped past the bodies of several of his men. Some were dead, others maimed so badly they couldn't move. As well, he had to duck or jump over the many chains being held from various sides. As the demon continued to thrash, the chains bounced round, reminding him of his youth and skipping rope. He took the fetters. "Go for his legs and grab hold. I'll leap in and lock on the shackle."

The men did as he asked. He jumped over a chain and dived for an ankle. Holding the shackle before him, he managed to close it onto the leg and drive the locking pin home. "That's one. Pull the other leg close. We're almost there."

Two men nodded, but before they could do as he asked, their bodies went flying as Thunder swept them away with one blow. The other two with him reached for the free leg, and in the same instant, with one hand, Thunder tore the head of a man clean off. The other man rolled on the ground, and Thunder lifted his foot and stomped down in a sickening crush. It was up to Brusk.

He yanked at the fetter, hoping to upend the demon. Thunder staggered but stayed erect. The other leg came close as the monster tried to maintain its balance. It was all the chance Brusk needed. He wrapped the second ankle with the fetters and engaged the locking pin.

A sense of disorientation passed through him as he was hoisted up in the air. He soon was staring eye to eye with Thunder, one of its huge claws poised to strike at him. The beast snarled and glanced at Gar. He then tossed Brusk aside some seven or eight paces away.

He landed heavily on his back and it took the wind out of him. *He could have killed me and didn't. He must really obey Gar.*

He rolled his head to see what was happening. The many chains had finally pulled the behemoth down. Dozens of men were pouncing on him, trying to lock on the manacles. They might actually subdue the giant.

Across the way, things with the other demons weren't so good. Many of his men had fled and the rest lay dead. The females were in the process of being freed by their counterparts. The new demon was laying waste to any men nearby.

Surprisingly, in the gap between those struggling with Thunder and the other demons, Garlin Murdach stood unmolested.

Gar stepped over to where the paving stones were removed and put a hand down on the exposed bedrock. "It ends here, Doom." He held a hand toward the new demon.

The lad is changing sides. What was Gar trying to do? The demon he called Doom tried to step toward Gar, but stopped midstride. Rock formed round the foot of the creature. *He's trying to encase him back in stone.*

Doom screamed in rage and shouted in his harsh language. The demon Dread raced over and clubbed Gar in the head, knocking him down.

Brusk struggled up and charged at the six-armed monster. He knew his sword was no good but pulled it anyway. *At the very least, I can keep the thing busy.*

A roar to his right surprised Brusk, glancing to see the behemoth Thunder break free from the men on top of him. Though his legs were still shackled, he still made good speed to beat Brusk to where Gar was. With one swipe of its clawed hand, it sent Dread reeling backward. Dark blood streamed from the gash opened in one arm and sputtered on the stones where it hit.

By then, his men recovered and yanked on the chains holding Thunder once more. The behemoth staggered backward. His men took advantage of Thunder's loss of balance and clamped the manacles on the beast.

Brusk made for Gar, but arrived at the same time as the demoness Pleasure. She clawed at him, but he ducked below it. He went to strike her with his sword, but a terrible chill filled him. Never before had he felt such fear.

Doom came to stand before him. "Such is my power that I can make even the most stout of heart tremble in fear. Your interference has come to an end."

He cringed at the impending blow from the sword, but Doom turned to face eight of his men rushing toward him. The demon aimed his spell at the onrush and most stopped, while a few still staggered forward. Doom decapitated the closest, the head falling in front of Brusk, a man he knew well. It sorrowed him to think of the man's wife and three children, now alone.

Doom called to the other demons. Dread, sporting a severe cut in his shoulder and looking like his top right arm was broken, gathered up the fallen Gar and made for the horses.

Pleasure and Silk stood near, with arms open. His men stopped altogether and the demons backed away, mounted their own horses, and rode off. Only after they were gone for several beats did Brusk find the will to stand straight and take stock of the situation.

To his right, his men finished trussing up Thunder in every chain at their disposal. Brusk could hardly make out the demon's arms and legs through the mass of metal.

All over the street, the dead and the wounded lay. Perhaps some seventy-odd men were strewn on the ground, many with savage wounds from Doom's sword. Others lay broken, their limbs twisted unnaturally. Still standing were only forty or so men. That meant at least a hundred ran. How many actually died he had yet to count.

He considered the way the demons fled. *They're headed for the gate, that's for sure. There's no chasing after them tonight.*

He grabbed hold of two men standing idly, stunned looks on their faces. "Check for survivors among the fallen. Commandeer some wagons and get them to the inn. Gramby's there with every available doctor in the town."

Gramby. He'd left the man behind on purpose. The man was still fearful for his life so he ordered him to set up a recovery station at the inn. The fellow would have been no good in the fight.

He glanced up, but with the night sky, even despite the fire raging at the merchant's manor, there was no sign of the raven. *Where has that blasted bird gotten to now?*

He sighed and went to face Thunder. "Why did you attack Dread? You're going to tell me what's going on."

Thunder shook his head.

"No, I suppose you can't. But you understand well enough. I'll keep my questions to yes and no answers, but not right now. I've other things to attend to."

He nodded toward the group of men holding the chains. "Drag him to the prison and put him in the strongest cell. We'll figure out what to do later."

As they hauled Thunder away, he sent the rest to aid in putting out the fire. Because of the high wall and surrounding street, it was unlikely it would spread to any of the other houses. Merchant Trellus, after all, deserved what was coming to him. Still, he didn't want the other citizens of Visk to see his indifference.

He turned and walked to the spot where Doom had been held. Sure enough, sprouting from between the paving stones was a solid ring of rock in the shape of a foot. Pieces were hacked away. What little rock formed round the demon's foot had not been enough to hold him for long. Whatever magic Gar possessed wasn't enough to do the job right.

Brusk grabbed one end of a litter and made for the inn. When he got there, he tried not to show his disappointment in the fifty-odd men who were, in his mind, hiding. *They would have been the difference, I just know it.*

It was time to make them useful. "All right, listen up. I need every able-bodied man to come with me to retake the barracks. There can't be more than a couple of dozen men from Morica

288

there. We'll need a ram for the door, and then we'll take back our town. Who's with me?"

Gramby came over and put a hand on Brusk's shoulder. "There's no need. Word came half-a-hand ago. Once the demons headed into the city, the men in the barracks bolted. There's not a foreign soldier left in the city. I sent a squad to remove all the bodies and hold the barracks for the time being."

"I should have expected they'd run. I guess I'll head over there and take a look see. You've got things in hand here. I'll be back later."

Gramby nodded and returned to helping the wounded men. Brusk knew Gramby was experienced in field dressing wounds. It was best to let him do his job.

As he strolled toward the gate, the air, with a wind picking up, started to cool. Unlike the usual northwesterly winds from the mountains, this one blew from the south. *It's a foul omen coming in, it is. I hope those men have that fire out before this wind grows too strong.*

He arrived at the barracks to find things exactly as Gramby had described. The dead were stacked like cordwood on three wagons. He stopped the nearest man. "Why haven't you taken them away to be buried?"

"We will, Captain, as soon as we can locate teams of horses to draw the wagons."

"Just take four horses from the stables. They'll learn how to draw a wagon together soon enough."

"We can't. The stables are empty. The men from Morica took all the horses. We have men going to a couple of the private stables right now in order to borrow some."

No horses meant no cavalry. Some armed force he commanded. He walked to the open gate and stepped out past the city walls. A lone man guarded the entry. They exchanged salutes. "Did you happen to see which way the demons went?"

"No, Captain. They were long gone before we got here."

It had been too much to have hoped for an answer. "Any sign of which way the men from Morica fled?"

"Straight south, Captain. Down the road to Sechwisk."

"Hmm. Straight for the main force they have posted there along with the troops from Storburg and Fermia."

"One more thing, Captain. Another man left shortly after them, headed north."

Brusk faced that way. "To Piaxia, I assume. It appears our northern neighbor is keeping an eye on things as well."

The man nodded. "Afraid you might be right, Captain. What you think we should do?"

He clapped an arm across the man's shoulders. "First off, let's get inside and close this gate."

CHAPTER 50

Gar's head hurt where Dread had hit him above the temple. As he opened his eyes, he couldn't see much at all. He was sitting against a tree. It took him a moment to realize it was still night out and they were deep within a forest somewhere, with little light filtering down through the canopy.

There were voices in the dark and he recognized it as the guttural talk of the demons. He could just make out their forms several paces away. He decided to try and stand and leaned against the trunk to help him stand. He probed his throbbing head to find a sizable lump on his temple. *Maybe I can heal it.*

He concentrated, using the skill he'd learned from Hiss. As he took measured breaths, he touched the swelling, but after several beats with no perceptible change in the lump, he came to the conclusion he could only heal others.

It was time for him to find out what was going on. His eyes becoming more accustomed to the dark, he tentatively stepped toward the demons. Each step was difficult as he had trouble maintaining his balance. Dread must have hit him really hard.

He had no trouble mistaking which one was the first to notice him. Doom moved quickly to grab Gar by the arm and drag him forward.

"You're awake. Good. You had your vengeance, and then you tried to trap me back into the stone. It's time to change the relationship. You will do *our* bidding now."

He shrugged free. "I think not. Do what you want. I don't care anymore. I'm not going to help you do anything."

Doom chuckled. "I think you will." He grabbed Gar once more and shoved him into the many-armed grip of Dread. "Bring him along. We've got somewhere to go to convince him."

Dread tied his hands and held the rest of the rope like a leash then put him on a horse. Gar couldn't help but notice how the demon favored one arm, refusing to use it for anything. In the darkness it was hard to tell, but it was different than the rest, dislocated or something. What had happened? After staring for a moment more, he noticed the large gash in the shoulder above. *Only Thunder could have done that. It must have happened after I was unconscious. Why would Thunder attack him? Would it be because Dread attacked me?*

The big demon wasn't with them. He recalled Thunder fighting off a host of men with chains and ropes. Had they been successful in capturing the behemoth?

With a hint of dawn on the horizon, Doom ordered everyone to follow him. They rode in silence, working their way through the trees. When they finally reached an area of open land, Gar pulled up next to Silk. "Where's Thunder?"

She scowled. "The humans have him."

"Well, shouldn't you be trying to set him free?"

"No. It would result in the rest of us being caught. Besides, Doom has never put up with his insubordination."

A sharp tug on the rope tied round his hands almost knocked him out of the saddle. It took a tense moment to regain his balance. By then, Silk had moved away.

Dread pulled beside him. "No talking, or I tie you behind my horse instead of letting you ride."

He frowned at the demon but nodded. The idea of being dragged across the countryside was more than enough to get him to shut up. He was left to try and sort out things on his own.

What did Silk mean when she said Doom *never* put up with Thunder's insubordination? The statement implied it happened before. It certainly hadn't happened since he'd released Doom from the stone. Did Silk and the others submit to Doom as their leader? He certainly was acting that way. In a fair fight, he doubted whether Doom and Dread together would stand a chance against Thunder.

Glancing once more at the limp arm Dread cradled with his others, he surmised Thunder must have attacked the six-armed demon after it struck Gar in the temple. *Thunder is on my side. It's the only thing that makes sense.*

He took in the two demonesses. Silk rode a little apart from the rest. Perhaps she didn't really want to be with the group but had no other choice. He should have listened to her when she told him not to open the other stones. Why hadn't he listened to her?

Pleasure rode next to Doom. Something told him here was a position she was used to having, like a second in command—or a partner. Of course. From the start, Pleasure had used her power to control him, and he'd accepted it. *I'm a fool. A big, stupid fool.*

He studied Doom. Disappointment at being unable to encase the demon in stone stung at him. Alone, he just didn't have enough mana and magic to reverse what he had done. He'd hoped to be able to trap the demons. Now his only relief was in what he expected was a certain death.

A fluttering above made him scan the skies in time to see the large black bird he hoped to be Captain Brusk's pass overhead. It screamed down at them and the others all followed his example and looked up.

He thought about the captain. More than once, Brusk had tried to convince Gar of the mistakes he was making. The man had even tried to kill him. He wondered if everything might have been better if the man succeeded. Dread and Doom would still be bound in their stone prisons, and the others might have been caught by now.

The images he'd pulled from his sister resurfaced in his mind. Whether the captain succeeded or not in killing him would not have stopped the brutal murder of his parents, nor, for that matter, the maiming of Darlee. That was one debt still unpaid, but Gar no longer felt the desire to find Lieutenant Gramby and exact revenge from the man. There were more urgent matters than punishing a soldier for doing what he'd likely considered his duty.

Their slow pace had bothered him on the journey home. Whenever, at his urging, they rode fast, the demons had great difficulty staying in the saddle. They weren't the best riders. He studied the rope knotted round his wrists. If only he could free himself, he might be able to make a run for it

The knot was too tight, and his fingers could not reach it. *Perhaps I can burn them off.* He recalled the fire he summoned the night before. The flame erupted once more between his hands. He cupped his fingers and managed to direct the magical fire toward the rope. It burst into flames. The fire he summoned did him no harm, but the burning rope seared his skin like any flame would. He clenched his teeth not to scream out in pain.

The rope burned to the point where the pressure he exerted broke the remaining strands. In a shower of flaming threads, the pieces flew off in all directions attracting the attention of the others. Grabbing the reins, Gar kicked his horse into action. The beast took off in a gallop. As he raced away, he glanced back to check the pursuit. The demons were slow to it. Riding a horse at a full gallop was a lot harder than simply sitting astride an animal walking or in a slow trot. Clearly, they were unaccustomed to it and it showed.

He felt the all-too-familiar tugs at his mind. The siren call of Pleasure to consume him with lust for her combined with Dread's imbuing him with hatred for running away. He needed to close his mind to them. *Concentrate. Concentrate. I can beat them. I know it. I just have to concentrate.*

The demon thoughts peeled away and he was elated at having succeeded, but then the horse beneath him stumbled and fell to the ground and he crashed headfirst into the turf. Although a little woozy, he scrambled to stand and tried his hardest to get the animal to rise from the ground, but the horse refused to move. When he looked back at the approaching demons, he saw Doom with one hand reaching forward. *He must have used his fear skill on the poor beast.*

Doom dropped his hand when he reached Gar. "It was foolish of you to think you could run. Now I must have Dread be more forceful in how he restrains you."

"Don't think for a moment that I won't get away, regardless of what you do. It's just a matter of time."

From behind him, Hiss scampered up to the tall demon. "Master, they there."

He scowled at the imp. "So *he's* Master now. Is this where your true loyalties lie? I should have figured that out when you were so insistent on opening his stone."

Hiss moved to hide behind the legs of Doom's horse. "Doom always Master. Hiss want Gar be friend. Be one us. Be demon. Serve Master then Master good you."

Silk snickered. "He'll never be one of us. All you have to do is look at him. It's the same reason we can never be one of them, no matter how hard we try—no matter how hard *I* tried. There is no home for us here, not unless we make our own." She hung her head and turned away.

Dread grabbed Gar and retied his hands, this time behind his back. The rope chafed against the burns, making it painful. Gar's horse got up and Dread hoisted him onto the animal. The idea of fleeing was something he could no longer consider.

They moved through another patch of forest, and Gar thought he recognized it. When they cleared the trees, he knew why. They were back at his family home.

Dread and Pleasure raced ahead, and, by the time Gar reached the shed, they had dragged out Darlee and Pap.

Doom nodded toward Dread. "Bind them and bring them."

His grandfather submitted to the bonds, but his sister struggled.

"I'm not afraid of you. You must be weak to have to tie up a girl like me. Someone will come along and beat you. I know it."

The demon moved his horse closer. "You will fear me. I promise you that. Now, be quiet or you will see just how fearful you can be." He held out a hand toward her.

She crumpled to the ground, and Gar struggled to get off the horse, falling hard on his shoulder in the process. He managed to walk on his knees and place himself between his sister and Doom. "You've had your fun. Let her be. She's just a little girl."

Doom pulled his hand away. "Come, then. She can ride with you. We have a two-day journey ahead of us, and time is wasting."

After helping Gar and Darlee mount, Dread put Pap on the horse with Silk. Hiss led the way east. Gar did not know where they were going, but they were headed straight for Morica.

CHAPTER 51

Captain Brusk spent the morning taking inventory and sending out notices for a town meeting to be held in the square that evening. The people of Visk needed to know what lay ahead in the coming days. His office in the barracks lay in total disarray created by the enemy troops, and it would take him more than the time he wanted to spend restoring some kind of order to the room. Papers were strewn everywhere.

He was about to head over to the jail, when a soldier knocked on his door.

"Captain, there's a young man here to see you. He says his name is Jango, and he served in the battle at Morence."

Morence. What a fiasco that had been. Where had this soldier been since then? "Bring him in."

A skinny lad who didn't even look like he reached the necessary age of ascension was escorted in by two soldiers who plopped him onto a chair. He couldn't recall this youth, but then they'd pressed a lot of men into service those days, and based on the clothes the lad wore, it was easy to guess he'd lived in the Ring. More than a few of them hadn't returned to the service since the enemy had disbanded the army in Visk. It was one of the many issues he intended to address over the next couple of days. "Soldier Jango, have you come to return to active duty?"

"Um…well…yes, I suppose, but first I need to tell you something."

No salute. No proper form of address either. He sighed. At any other time, he would have the lad taught a lesson, but he needed every able-bodied man, no matter how scrawny. "Spill it, then. My time is precious right now."

"It's like this. I went to visit my friend Darlee Murdach this morning, and when I got there, I was just in time to see her, her grandfather, and her brother, Gar, being tied up and taken away by the demons."

This *was* news. "Did you see which way they went?"

"Due east. I even overheard one of the demons say it was a two-day ride."

"That would take them into Morica. I wonder why?" A thought occurred to him. When he was straightening the furniture, he'd come across a map amongst some documents of Lieutenant Devron's. At the time, he'd tossed it back on the floor. He rose and started digging through the papers.

"Sir?"

"Don't just sit there. Help me find a map amongst this mess."

The lad jumped out of his seat and started searching at the far side of the room. "What's on the map?"

"The location of all the demon stones in the seven kingdoms."

Jango's eyes went wide then he returned to hunting. For a while, the only noise was the rustle of papers as they worked through everything lying on the floor.

Jango jumped up, document in hand, and ran to the desk. "I've found it!"

He joined the lad. "Spread it out, boy. Let's see what there is."

They spread the map until it draped over the edges of the desk. Brusk checked the scale markings and, using his finger, traced a line due east from the closest demon stone by figuring that was the Murdach farm. When he got to where he estimated was a two day ride, his fears were realized. In close proximity to where his finger rested was another demon stone, a word marked under it—Brute. "This doesn't look good. I wonder what kind of demon that one is?"

"Why not ask Thunder? I'll bet he knows."

He was caught by surprise by the lad. "How do you know the demon we caught last night is named Thunder?"

"I was there when Gar released him from the stone. The demon saved my life...twice."

The lad knows more than I thought. I'm going to need to find out everything. "That won't do any good. I was with the beast for weeks. He never spoke a word of common tongue."

Jango shook his head. "Don't let him fool you. He understands every word. From what Hiss said, he just doesn't like to use common tongue—something about trouble with the pronunciation."

He packed up the map and headed for the door. "Come with me. We're going to pay the big demon a visit."

They crossed the grounds and went into the jail to find Thunder imprisoned in the largest cell, lying on the floor, still wrapped in the chains from the night before. His men were probably afraid it could, given enough time, break out of the cell. "The thing's asleep. Hey, Thunder, wake up! I want to talk to you!"

Thunder never moved. Jango nudged Brusk. "Just talk. He's listening. He always pretends he's asleep, but Gar thinks he never does."

Perhaps the lad was right. He'd told the truth, so far. He focused on the behemoth. "I need to know what kind of demon this Brute is. I also want to know what the plans are of this demon now in charge, this Doom. He's headed toward where Brute's demon stone is. What can you tell me?"

Still, nothing. If the demon was awake, he was ignoring him. Brusk sighed and turned to Jango. "It looks like there's going to be no help here. You'd think with Gar being taken prisoner and all, the beast would take some interest."

The sound of the chains moving returned Brusk's attention to the cell, and he stumbled backward when he discovered Thunder standing right next to the bars separating them. How had the beast managed to move so fast while wrapped in chains?

Jango, who'd jumped just as far as he had, nudged him again. "I think you got his attention now."

That was fairly obvious. But what had keyed the reaction? It could only be his mentioning of Gar being taken prisoner. "So you want to help Gar?"

Thunder nodded.

"Then what can you tell me about Doom? What are his plans?"

"Doom bad." The beast spoke with a snarl, making it hard to distinguish the words.

298

The answer could have more than one meaning. "Are you saying Doom is bad and that he has bad intentions?"

Thunder nodded once more.

He suspected as much, but having it confirmed made his mind set as to what needed to be done. Doom was likely going to force Gar to release as many demons as possible. "And what about this Brute. What can you tell me about it?"

"Brute dull."

What was the beast on about? He nudged Jango. "Dull? What do you think he means by that? Is he saying the beast is stupid?"

"No. I think he means Brute has no magical skills. Haven't you noticed when the demons use their powers, they glow?"

In fact, he had. He returned his focus to Thunder. "Is that correct? Brute has no magic?"

Thunder nodded again. "Brute big."

"Big? How big? Bigger than you?"

Thunder nodded. "Much bigger. Obey Doom."

That was not the news he wanted to hear. It had taken a hundred men to capture Thunder. How many would it take to chain this one up? There was no choice. He clapped a hand on Jango's shoulder. "Find Lieutenant Gramby. Tell him he's in charge once again. The demons may have half a day on me, but I've ridden with them before, and they go slowly. I hope to be able to catch them before they make it to the demon stone."

He faced Thunder once more. "I'll try and bring Gar back." It seemed stupid, but he wanted the beast to know. "Wish me luck."

"Go alone, you die. Me go. Me help."

The thought of the big demon fighting at his side was intriguing, but only for a heartbeat. He dared not let the behemoth free. "Sorry, but how can I trust you? No sooner would I let you free than you would join them, and I'd be dead."

"Me prove." Thunder shook and all the chains wrapped round him fell to the floor. Brusk shivered. The manacles holding the beast's wrists were broken and numerous links in the chains fell free, bent open. How long had it taken the beast to silently bend the links? All night? Or just a hand? The fetters on the behemoth's ankles were still in place. Thunder bent and grabbed hold of them,

299

his muscles bulging. In a screech of grinding metal, the demon tore the connecting links apart. He grabbed hold of the cell bars and pulled. The stone floor and ceiling shattered at the points the bars were set in. In the billowing cloud of dust, Thunder stepped up to Brusk. "Me ready. Me help. Me promise."

Brusk released the breath he was holding. "I guess so." Jango was mesmerized. He gave the lad a shake. "Go deliver that message to Gramby. Tell him everything. Hopefully, I'll be back in four days or less."

Jango dashed off. Brusk found a set of jailer's keys and unlocked the remaining brackets from Thunder's ankles and wrists. "I guess you won't want these on anymore, unless you find them fashionable."

A low, deep chuckle, more like a growl than Brusk would have liked, emanated from Thunder. *At least he has a sense of humor.*

CHAPTER 52

Walking through the city market of Zon, Devron made note of how, instead of soldiers on duty to guard against thieves and problems, a pair of warlocks wandered round, chatting with the people. On this day, Master Gaffrey was one of the ones present. Devron fell in step with the warlock. "I see even someone of your station has to share in the simple duties. Back home, Captain Brusk would do the same, even though he was the senior officer in town. I always wondered at why he just didn't assign someone to do it, but watching how you interact with the populace, I have come to appreciate what he did."

Gaffrey chuckled. "Something tells me I would like this Captain Brusk of yours. Yes, there is no better way to get a feel for the mood in the city than here, in the market square. Lord Kipron relies heavily on my reports. Of course, having the ability to read people's surface thoughts doesn't hurt, and it's a great deterrent for crime as well."

"I wanted to thank you for all you've done for me. I doubt without your intervention I would have any chance at making a petition to your queen, let alone still be alive today. I've also wanted to thank Daphora for all she did, as well, but I have yet to see her since our return to Zon."

Gaffrey paused to meet Devron's gaze. "She's busy packing for another trip. She told me she wants to get out of town while there's a possibility of war. She figures it's better to watch this one from a safe distance."

"Where's she headed?"

"I don't know for sure. She never really tells me anything. I have to rely on my own informants. My guess is to one of those highwaymen camps she's so fond of."

It disappointed him she would run and hide when her people needed her. He'd better go and see Daphora before she left, but he wasn't sure he could condone her actions. As he contemplated what to do, a soldier came jogging up to them.

"Commander Savan requires the presence of both of you in the throne room."

Gaffrey nodded. As the soldier turned to lead the way, the master warlock held a finger to his lips. "We will speak of this later. For now, let's see what is going on."

They made their way into the castle where Commander Savan and his brother stood by a large map table showing Piaxia and all the countries bordering it. Savan greeted him with a big smile. Devron was learning not to trust the big man's grin. It usually meant trouble.

"Lieutenant, news has come from Visk. It appears your people have retaken the town and expulsed the foreign soldiers...albeit with a little help."

He was glad to hear the news but sensed something still unsaid. "From your tone, I take it there was much bloodshed and the town is in ruins?"

"On the contrary, the town is intact. There were some losses, yes, but far fewer than a hundred and none killed at the hands of enemy soldiers."

"You have me confused. How were men killed, then?"

Savan's countenance hardened. "Demons. They attacked the town and killed most of the men from Morica. The forces of Visk, under the command of a Captain Brusk, fought the demons and managed to capture one but suffered the losses I mentioned in doing so. Both the demons and the remaining forces from Morica have fled, and the city is now firmly in the hands of troops loyal to it."

Brusk is back. If anyone knows how to handle things, it's him. "Then the news is good. The fact they have captured a demon must show the other kingdoms Sechland's true intentions."

"Not so good. You need to take in the bigger picture. The soldiers who escaped will tell of how they, and only they, were set upon by the demons. The interpretation will be that Sechland is in league with the creatures. Once the word spreads, it's only a matter of time before Visk is set upon by the combined forces of the other realms. There will be no mercy given."

Regent Tarlok pointed toward the board. Devron noted the placement of enemy forces. There were more than he expected. "Take a look at your situation now. Troops have arrived from Queensland, Braxburrow, and Gatway. It will only be a matter of time before they march north. My brother informs me you have yet to make a declaration of your intentions regarding a treaty with us. The time for waffling is over, Lieutenant. If Piaxia is to become involved in this conflict, we need your commitment, as king, now."

King. The concept remained foreign to him. There was little doubt in his mind his cousin was dead, but Tarlok's statement implied much more, that all of the royal family was slain. The issue of whether he could avoid a battle on Sechland ground was now moot. "What is it you want me to do?"

Tarlok grabbed a document from a nearby table. "Sign this. It holds the terms of a treaty between Piaxia and Sechland."

Devron took hold of the parchments and quickly leafed through them. "There's a lot to read here. It will take me a long time to study it."

The regent held a hand toward Devron's head. "If you will allow me, I can make it quick."

He took a deep breath, nodded, and closed his eyes. Tarlok placed his hand on Devron's forehead. After a moment, the details of the document flooded into his mind. Requirements for the establishment of a merchant's league, as well as a brotherhood of warlocks, trade regulations, and border agreements, travel rules and currency details were among a host of particulars crammed on the pages. Most important of all were the defense clauses where Piaxia would come to the aid of Sechland when threatened and Sechland would protect Piaxia's border.

He felt the fingers draw away and looked into the eyes of the young man. "I will sign it."

They sat down at the table and signed two copies of the document. When it was done and a copy was rolled into a protective container and given to him, he stood to join Commander Savan at the map table. "Now that we are allies, just how do you intend to defeat the combined forces of the other kingdoms? You came here with only two thousand men. I don't know how many troops are stationed here in Zon, but it can't be more than a few thousand. From the figures your scouts have accounted for on this board, you'll be outnumbered almost four to one."

Outside, a horn blared. Savan smiled. "Just in time. Come. Let's take a look."

He followed the big man several flights up a stairwell that led to a balcony facing north. From there, he could make out the road he and Daphora had taken on their route to the Piaxian capital. In the distance, the road was dark with oncoming soldiers. "Troops...from where?"

"From the twin cities of Jag and Fel. I sent a rider there when we departed Lia. I can't tell at this distance, but at least another several thousand for sure. Come, let's go to the gate and meet them." The commander headed for the stairs.

Devron turned to head back down, but his peripheral vision caught something white in the east. The countryside was covered by a massive herd of sheep. "Grott."

Savan returned to stand by him. "Yes, he arrived with my brother, last night. I dare tell there were more than a few people in the city who feared Bron was back and wondered if they were about to come under attack. Lord Kipron spent half the night trying to assuage their concerns. Bron is dead. I saw it myself. Too bad. With him, we wouldn't need hardly any of these troops at all." He clapped Devron across the back. "Now, let me introduce you to the commander of the men arriving. I think you'll like him. Then, we can discuss strategy. We'll need your insight into the terrain round Visk."

He followed Savan out of the castle and they headed for the north gate of the city. "Tell me, why has Piaxia committed to this conflict? You could just as easily stay out of it. You risk many men in the coming battle."

"Like you, Devron, I am a young man. My brother and the queen, younger still. Since the last time Piaxia warred with the seven kingdoms, there has been little to no contact between our people and a long border has needed defending. Increased trade would lead to greater prosperity, and a friendly neighbor makes it less of a military commitment here when we still face Karsargi

304

raiders from over the mountains to the west. At least, that is how my brother sees it. This is his, and the queen's, vision for the future. I'm just the guy who has to get us there. Don't think now; think fifty years, or a hundred…or a thousand."

It made sense. Having a friendly neighbor for a thousand years sounded good for Sechland, too.

CHAPTER 53

Darlee drowsed as the horse plodded along. The group was stretched out some. Doom and Pleasure were many paces ahead. The poor beast Dread rode upon trailed a number of paces behind.

She was dead tired. The demons had only stopped for short periods throughout the night, pushing on whenever they felt the animals were rested enough. The horse below her labored, a sheen of sweat caking its body. She feared the animal might die underneath her.

The sun was low in the sky. She calculated not more than a hand until dusk. Their long shadows led the way. She would stare ahead and realize she hadn't been cognitive of what she was looking at; such was her state of mind. She couldn't see a way out of their predicament. Like her, both Gar and Pap had their hands still tied. The only time the ropes were loosed was when they were given an opportunity to relieve themselves.

She'd figured out where they were headed. There was no other reason for the demons to keep them alive. Somewhere in front of them was another demon stone.

The horse stumbled, jarring her in her seat and knocking her against her brother riding behind her, causing him to slip in the saddle. "Hang on." He had continued to worsen over the last two days. The spot at his temple was purpled and a sizable lump still remained.

Gar righted himself. "Ugh. My wrists and my head are killing me. I need to rest."

"I doubt they're going to let us do that. We're prisoners. They'll continue to treat us as such until they don't need us anymore. When that time comes, they'll probably kill us."

"Then we need to get away."

Her brother's response was unrealistic. "And just how do you expect to do that? They've got us tied up. Think, Gar. The only reason we're still alive is they need you to open the stones. Pap and

I are the insurance you do it. When there are no more stones to open, we are of no value."

"Then I won't open the stones."

"Then what? Sometimes I wonder why you are so thickheaded. If you don't open the stones, they'll kill us all the quicker. Is there anything you can do with your magic that can stop them?"

Gar pressed his lips tight then turned his gaze away. It was as bad as she'd expected. There was no way out.

She glanced over to her grandfather to see how he was faring. Pap was glaring right at her, his head held high.

"Have no fear, child. We must put our faith in the gods."

Silk, riding with Pap, moved her horse closer. "The gods…the gods will not rescue you. They are not your gods, they are ours. I tried to warn your brother. He did not listen to me. His anger in revenging you and your family has led to this. Now look at what has happened. I have lost my faith in him."

Darlee studied the demoness—the woman was not happy. Why not? They were in control. Would Silk help them? "What do you want then? Do you also want to see us dead?"

"Dead? No. I would prefer to find somewhere I can be free. Free from the darkness that accompanies death. Free from the bigotry that prevents me from being accepted." She glanced to Pleasure, riding ahead. "Free from the crude lusts of mankind."

Gar flushed. "You *know* I was in Pleasure's thrall. It did not stop you when we were alone at the old man's farm."

"At the time, I felt pity for you. As to Pleasure, you made little effort to resist. It was easy enough for you to do so yesterday morning when you tried to escape. I saw it all. You have it within you, Gar, to block their—our—magic."

"Yesterday was the first time I was ever able to do it. I am still learning to control the magic within me." Gar slumped. "But you're right. I did not resist. It was too enjoyable. I'm a fool. I know it."

Darlee didn't know what she wanted to do more, hug her brother or kick him in the rear. At the moment, she could do neither. "Then maybe you have learned your lesson."

Pap smiled. "That's what life is…a continuous flow of lessons. It's how we grow. You're a new man now, Gar. How you apply what you learn from the lessons is what makes you."

Silk met Darlee's gaze. "You love your brother. That much I can see. Whether what you say is true is yet to be seen. My experience has taught me otherwise. Men usually choose what pleases them."

"You're right. I do love Gar, but I have known him for much longer than you. I have faith in the nature that lies within him. If you want the bloodshed to end, then help us."

"You expect too much of me." Silk guided her horse to create a gap between them.

Resigned to only her brother's company once more, Darlee gazed ahead at the way Doom and Pleasure were leading. She was startled at the sudden appearance of Hiss as the imp scampered in and around the horses.

"It just ahead. Me saw it. Soon reach."

In the distance, she could make out a small hillock with a few trees scattered near it. *That must be where we are going.*

They covered the distance in a quarter hand, and Darlee noted the irregularity of the rocky hillock standing alone in the level field. It must be the demon stone. She glanced at Hiss once more to take stock of his size. *When I compare it to the stone back home in the meadow, this one is massive. How large must the demon be that requires so much rock to hold it?*

Doom dismounted and rubbed his hands across the face of the rock. "Soon, my friend, you will be with us once more."

It was the sound of the horse collapsing to the ground that made Darlee look behind her to see Dread arrive. His mount lay panting on the ground. She wondered if it would recover. "You need to give that animal a lot of water if you want it to live another day."

The monster scowled at her, his mandibles moving in a frightening manner. He strode over to the horse. Darlee was expecting him to help her and Gar down, but instead he simply knocked them both off. Because her hands were still tied, she landed hard. From her position on the ground, she saw Gar hit next to her and a moment later, Pap landed some few paces away.

She struggled to a kneeling position, and then Dread grabbed her by the hair and hoisted her up the rest of the way. Though it hurt, she held her tongue and didn't cry out. Her brother, though, jumped up and banged into Dread.

"Let her down."

Dread let go, and she fell to her knees once more. Gar stood next to her, a defiant gaze in his face as he glared at the demon.

Doom approached them. "The time has come, Gar, for you to work your magic. Open the stone."

"No."

Doom smiled. "No? I think so." He looked to Dread and nodded toward Pap. "Maim the old one."

It was as she feared. They were going to use Pap and her to force Gar to their will.

Pap squared toward Dread. "Go ahead. I've lived my life. You'll save me the grief." Her grandfather looked at her brother. "Do what's right, Gar."

Gar nodded and the muscles in his jaw flexed as if he was gritting his teeth hard.

The demon raised a hand, the spikes of his fingers splayed open for what would surely be a painful strike, when Doom held up a hand and Dread backed off.

Doom approached and picked Darlee up, holding her by the nape of her neck. "I guess the threat against your grandfather isn't enough, but will your resolution hold up when I do the same to your sister?"

It was time to fight back. She kicked at Doom in an attempt to free herself.

She felt the burning as Doom's claws raked across her shoulder. Gar charged at them but was intercepted by Dread and knocked to the ground. Doom dropped her and went to Gar, taking her brother's chin in his hand.

"She still lives, but for how much longer is up to you. Now open the stone."

Gar struggled back to his feet. "You must promise me you will never hurt my sister ever again."

The thought Gar was about to succumb and do their bidding panicked her. "Don't do it, Gar. There's nothing they can do to me that I haven't already faced on the torture table."

"No, I won't let you suffer again." Gar staggered over to the stone. "Hiss, come, give me your mana."

The small demon scurried over and climbed to Gar's shoulder placing a hand on her brother's forehead. "Me ready."

His hands still tied, Gar held them up toward Doom. "I need my hands free."

The demon sliced through the ropes with his sword and Gar placed his palms on the rock face.

Darlee climbed to her feet, stumbling over to try and stop Gar, but Pleasure grabbed her and tossed her back to the ground. She landed facing the way they'd come. Squinting into the setting sun, she made out the form of a man and several horses racing toward her. Running alongside was the big demon she'd seen at the farm the first time Gar returned. She'd wondered what had happened to it. Wherever it had been, it was another demon, and that just made things worse.

She could see no way out of their predicament. The prevailing sense of her own coming demise and of her grandfather made her surrender in her mind. She looked back once more at her brother in a final, desperate hope he would do the right thing.

It was too late. The stone was opening. Chunks of rock the size of bushel baskets fell away. From the aperture stepped the largest of all the demons. It stood as tall as the one now approaching, but sported a massive torso like that of a horse, with two arms, four thick legs, and a large, curved tail. It reminded her of classroom drawings of the scorpions that lived in Karsargi lands, even down to a giant stinger at the end of the tail.

She turned again as the thunder from the hooves of the approaching horses neared. The big demon was running right at her, and astride the lead horse was Captain Brusk. What was going on? Why was the captain with the demon? All eyes were still on the monster emerging from the stone. It was making the most

310

horrific noise. No one else had apparently yet caught on to those approaching.

In an instant, the big demon was beside her, sending both Pleasure and Dread flying with well-placed blows. Captain Brusk leapt from his horse and cut her bonds then handed her the dagger.

"Quick, free your grandfather and get on a horse."

She didn't need to be told twice. She dashed to Pap and cut his bonds. As she did, she could see the big demon fighting with the one just freed. Doom was screaming in his harsh language, and both Dread and Pleasure were headed toward the melee. She pushed her grandfather toward the waiting horses. "Come on. We've got to go now."

Pap shrugged free. "Not without Gar."

Dread held her brother by the arm and clubbed him over the head. He was unconscious. Captain Brusk was headed straight for them. Doom held out a hand and the captain stumbled and fell to the ground. The demon was using his magic to control him. Her grandfather ran toward Gar and she stood there like an idiot. *I've got to help.*

She chase after her grandfather. After a few steps, a great sense of fear compressed her chest. *I'm running to my death. I've got to stop and hide.* She fell to the ground and tucked her knees to her chin. *Someone help me. I'm doomed!*

Deep down, she knew she needed to fight it, but the fear overwhelmed her. She watched as her grandfather also succumbed, his face to the ground. *I've got to get up. I can do it. I must do it.*

Like the lifting of some weight from her shoulders, the fear vanished and she stood. Somehow she found the will to resist. She went to help Pap stand. Together, they took the next few steps to Captain Brusk's side. "Hurry, now's our chance to get Gar."

Pap pushed her aside. "We've got to free him from that demon first." He charged and tackled Dread, forcing the demon to release his grip on her brother.

The captain grabbed her arm. "Get the horses. I'll get Gar."

She hesitated for a heartbeat then took off to do as she was told. By the time she grabbed the reins, Captain Brusk was headed her way with Gar slung over his shoulder. She helped him load her brother onto the back of one of the horses. She went to the next horse to mount it. "Come on, Pap. We're going." He wasn't with them. "Pap?"

The demons were still fighting. The scorpion one was swinging wildly, his tail flashing at the darting form of the big demon. Lying on the ground a short distance away was her grandfather, his chest torn open.

Her hands went to her mouth. She started for him, but Captain Brusk grabbed her arm.

"There's no time for that. He's done for."

She struggled to try and free herself, but the captain held firm.

"He may still be alive."

The captain threw her on the back of the animal and jumped on the one next. "With that wound, he won't be for long. Be thankful for the chance he's given you to escape."

He pulled the reins of both horses she and her brother rode, and he kicked his horse into motion, leading them along. She looked back in the fading sunlight to see a large black bird land on her grandfather. The idea of the bird pecking at Pap's dying body sickened her, so she turned away. It was hard to focus as her one eye brimmed with tears.

CHAPTER 54

The sun would soon be rising. As Devron rode his horse through the city of Zon, he made note of how quiet it was. Outside of the rare person hauling their wares toward the city market in an effort to be ready when the first customers arrived, the streets were deserted. *The people know Piaxia marches to war this day. For many, they fear the worst, another attack on their city. They are hiding in their houses until the troops are gone in hopes what is out of sight is out of mind.*

He needed to hurry. Commander Savan wanted to set out within the first hand. It left Devron little time to do what he set out for if he was going to accompany the commander south.

He arrived at the cozy, little lane where Master Gaffrey had led him once before. Lights were out at all of the homes, save one. The gate to the yard was open and a single horse hitched to a laden wagon stamped and tossed its head, breath steaming in the early morning air. *It looks like I got here just in time. A few more moments and she would have been gone, timing her exit with the morning opening of the gates.*

He alit from his horse and made his way to the side entry where a door stood open. He was about to knock when Daphora exited with an armload of things.

"Ah, I've caught you in time."

She stopped for a moment, and then brushed past him to deposit what she carried into the cart. "So you've caught me. It's not for long. I intend to be on my way shortly. What do you want?"

He had practiced a number of different things he intended to say, but all of them were caught in his throat. "I, uh, just wanted to come by and say thank you."

She never stopped packing the goods. "Fine. You've said it. You're welcome. Now leave me alone. I've got things to do."

She finished stowing the load and started for the door once more. Why was she being so abrupt? As she tried to pass, he grabbed her arm. "Daphora, I want to—"

313

She whirled in his grip and a bolt of lightning erupted from her fingers. It crashed into his chest plate and sent him sprawling to the ground.

"I told you, leave me alone."

Every bone in his body ached, as he struggled to stand. "What was that for? You could have killed me."

She glared, a small ball of fire filling one of her hands. "If I wanted to kill you, you'd be dead right now. Go talk to my brother. Maybe, together, the two of you can find some other calamity to happen to me over and above the one you've already caused. Now go!"

"Okay, I'm going." He brushed himself off and mounted his horse, at a loss for words once more. "Daphora...take care of yourself."

"What do you think I'm doing? I'm trying to get out of here."

A noise from the gate surprised him, and he discovered half-a-dozen armed men standing there. Two bows were drawn on him and Daphora. One soldier bore the insignia of a captain. He stepped forward. "I am here to take into custody the one known as Daphora on charges of witchcraft."

Devron took a step toward the men, his hand on his sword hilt. "This is insanity. This woman saved my life."

The captain held out a hand, indicating he should stop. "Do not involve yourself, Lieutenant. This is a Piaxian matter. As I understand it, you should be with the troops at dawn, headed south. You should make your way to where they are marshaling. I would not wish to harm you for interfering."

He couldn't leave Daphora. "I can't let them take you."

Her shoulders slumped. "Go. There's no sense in your dying on my account. I'll be fine."

He edged past the men, still unsure of what to do. As he cleared them, he hesitated. *I can draw down on them from behind. It may be enough.*

Daphora made eye contact and shook her head. She must have reasoned out his intentions.

"Just go now."

He let go of the hilt. Mounting his horse, he paused. "I shall speak to Commander Savan. Perhaps he can intervene." He turned his steed and made for the south gate.

As he neared the castle, the sun peeked over the horizon. Dawn was upon him. It would not be long now until the trumpets sounded and the army moved out. Perhaps there was yet time. He dismounted and dashed into the castle, stopping the first man he saw. "Master Gaffrey—where can I find him?"

The man pointed toward the main hall. "He passed in that direction not more than a few beats ago."

He thanked the man and quick stepped his way into the room to find the warlock seated, breaking his fast.

Gaffrey frowned when Devron neared. "Lieutenant, I would have thought you were outside, ready for the march."

He took the seat near the warlock. "In a moment, but I would speak to you about Daphora before I go. I went to thank her, and she nearly killed me with a bolt of lightning. She said you would know why. Soldiers arrived and arrested her. What's going on?"

The warlock leaned back in his chair and sighed. "She's angry with me, and you as well. Knowledge of her skills by the queen and the regent has led to this."

Devron recalled that moment when Regent Tarlok discovered the truth. "But the queen and the regent gave every impression they were going to keep it a secret. Why should they betray that trust?"

"Apparently, one of the queen's handmaidens figured it out the night of the royal birth and spoke of it to her lover, a soldier under Commander Savan. By the time they arrived here in Zon, the rumor had spread throughout the camp, and she feared sooner or later there was going to be a reconciling over it."

"I imagine the queen will ensure she is protected, won't she?"

Gaffrey shook his head. "It's one thing for the royal family to forgive her transgression; it's quite another for the entire population of Piaxia to do so. Despite the fact there is a female as monarch, this is still a male-dominated society. There will be factions who will want her dealt with."

This was not what he expected to hear. Had his actions endangered the woman? "What will happen to her?"

"There are many possibilities—imprisonment or even being put to death. I cannot say for sure. I have spoken with Lord Kipron, but he has not decided." Gaffrey put a hand on Devron's shoulder. "You care for her."

Devron bowed his head. Until this moment, he hadn't realized how much that was true. "She is an amazing woman. She saved my life. I owe her everything." He stood up. "I've got to go. If you see her, tell her I'm sorry for what has happened."

"May the gods be with you, Devron, and may they be with all of us in this coming trial."

He hurried back out to his waiting horse and made straightaway for the gate. As he rode, the horn sounded for the march to begin. *I'm late.*

It took him a little while longer to exit the gate and race to the front of the column where Commander Savan and his officers were. He made note of the several war machines in the column. Catapults, ballistae, and more accompanied them. Near the front stood a contingent of men dressed in black. Warlocks. Having seen what they could do, he knew such men in numbers could turn the tide of any battle. The fifteen or so might not be the kind of numbers that could make that difference.

As he pulled alongside Savan, the commander gave him another one of those disarming smiles he was coming to dread.

"Ah, Lieutenant. I'm glad you could make it. After all, it is *your* country we are off to liberate. I wouldn't think it that much of a priority you be at the marshaling point on time."

"My apologies, Commander. There was a matter I needed to attend to before leaving."

Savan inspected him up and down and smirked. "What was her name?"

It bothered him when Savan was flippant. "If you must know, it was Daphora, Master Gaffrey's sister."

"Yes, the woman who guided you through the kingdom. How is the witch?"

The small amount of anger in him dissipated, to be replaced by a sense of shock. "She has been arrested. Does everyone in the kingdom know?"

"Sadly, yes. You have no idea what troubles she has caused me. When we were still a day from Zon, my men wanted to lynch her then and there. The fact you, an outlander, were busy having sex with the woman every night did nothing to abate their appetite for justice. It took much for me to maintain decorum among the troops and keep you ignorant of what was going on. Obviously, you have found out as well."

"It seems silly to me you would have warlocks in your kingdom, but not allow witches."

"This from a man whose kingdom outlawed magic altogether. I would think you would have a deeper comprehension of the political dimensions of the problem."

"Still, I think—"

Savan reached over and grabbed his arm. "Think no more about it. What we face in the coming days makes concern for a single witch trivial in comparison. Focus on the task ahead. I have twenty scouts leading us in pairs by half a hand. They will be rotating back with reports throughout the day. I expect your mind to be focused on what they have to say so I can take counsel from you on how we should proceed. If your mind is muddled with this woman, then you are of no use to me."

Savan let go of his arm, the smile gone from the commander's face.

He's right. The concerns of a kingdom heavily outweigh those of a woman. I must remember my duty to the citizens of Sechland, and of Visk, in particular. Whatever happens to her will be beyond my purview. He glanced back. *Still, I cannot forget her.*

He studied the land before him. Before the day was over, they would be across the border and into his home country. There was much to do, and he needed to be ready.

CHAPTER 55

Brusk settled down near the campfire, exhausted. Since the rescue, he'd ridden all night and the entire following day, only stopping to water the horses and give them a breather.

Stretched out on the ground next to him was Gar. The lad had floated in and out of consciousness throughout the trip. Brusk managed to force water down Gar's throat, but when the lad tried to eat anything, he retched until he was dry.

Darlee placed a hand on Gar's forehead. "We need to get him to a doctor. I'm afraid of how sick he is."

Brusk sighed. It was a difficult decision. At one time, he'd tried to kill Gar but failed. Now, with Gar's health failing, the dilemma of whether he should try and save the lad gnawed at him. "I'm afraid his skull might be cracked. If that's the case, the swelling's going to continue until it kills him. I've seen it before."

"Then we have to figure out how to reduce the swelling." She grabbed the water skin and slowly poured it onto Gar's temple.

Brusk pulled the bottle away from her. "We're going to need that water for drinking. Besides, I ain't no field doctor, but I've seen what they've done in cases like this. They cut into the skull to release the pressure. Half the time, it killed the man right out. But every now and then, one of them would recover."

"That sounds barbaric! There must be another way."

"There isn't. Now, I wasn't saying we should be poking a hole in his head. First of all, I wouldn't know where or how to do it. I say, let's just let him be, and hope for the best."

Darlee got up and went to get the horses. "Help me get Gar back into the saddle. I've already lost my grandfather yesterday. I'll not lose my brother today. He's all I have left."

He pulled the reins away from her and grabbed her by the shoulders. "Sit down. We aren't going anywhere. These animals are plumb wore out. You wouldn't make it a league without one of them collapsing and you maybe getting killed in the fall. Where in the world did you think you were going, anyway?"

"North, to Piaxia. They've got warlocks there who can heal people, just like Gar did for my leg."

Brusk recalled how Gar had saved his life, removing the gangrene from his leg and healing the wound. He had to admit there was something to warlocks having that ability. He'd seen more than his fair share of men die from wounds that could have been healed by magic. He smiled. "That's a fair idea, but the problem is, Piaxia's a good two and a half days ride north and another day's ride to get to the closest city of Zon. We're less than a day away from Visk. If Gar's in need of medical attention right away then, I think, his chances are better us getting him somewhere nearby than somewhere that would take three times as long to get to. Besides, it's another country and one, in years past, we haven't been too friendly with. We don't even know if they'd be willing to help him."

Her shoulders slumped. "I suppose that makes sense."

He let go of her, no longer fearing she'd try to ride away. "All right, then. We'll make for Visk at first light. Now what say we get some sleep?"

She lay down on the blanket next to Gar. "I *am* tired."

"Good. I'll wake you before dawn." He settled against the fallen log and watched the flames for a while.

He glanced to see how the little girl was doing and noted she was already fast asleep. *For a girl that size, missing an eye and most of one ear, she's got a lot of spunk. I gotta hand it to her.*

His own eyes felt heavy. It was time he got some rest as well. He closed them and leaned back, listening to the night. *It's peaceful. Probably the last one I'll ever know.*

The crack of sticks breaking under someone's tread snapped Brusk alert. It could just be some animal, but he couldn't be sure. He doubted it was the demons. From what Darlee had told him, their horses were already spent. They also kept to a slower pace. He doubted they would catch up before they got home.

They were coming, though. It's why he'd agreed to let the boy live. To the demons, Gar was a valuable commodity. Very valuable. Without him, they wouldn't be able to open any more of the stones. They would come because they had to. It was his hope that when they did, he could capture them all.

That might prove to be a more difficult task than he'd originally imagined. Thunder had proven that already. The chains they'd made to hold the behemoth and the cell they put the demon in weren't up to the task.

The sound of another footstep made Brusk jump to his feet. He pulled his sword and made ready. If it was bandits come to rob them, they'd find out how difficult that would be.

Thunder slipped between two trees and fell into the campsite. The demon was a mess. Several gashes raged across the behemoth's body, most notably a deep wound in the beast's left shoulder. It crawled to where Gar lay. "Hurt?"

"Yeah. His head took a real hard knock or two. I'm hoping his skull isn't cracked, but he's showing all the symptoms. All we can do is hope and wait."

Thunder placed a hand on Gar's head. Brusk watched a light glow pass from the demon's hand into Gar. *That must be the life force he shared with me. How is it such a creature of destruction as this one has the ability to share the power of life?*

Darlee woke. "Will that help?"

"I don't know. Maybe. The body and mind fight against the injury. It just might give Gar the strength necessary to win."

Thunder stretched out, his breathing shallower. Brusk noticed the gingerly way in which the demon settled. "He must really be hurting. That giant demon, Brute, is probably more than a match for him."

Darlee took her blanket and covered the resting giant. "Maybe this will help him."

Her concern for the monster was not something he expected. "Now you'll have no blanket for the night. He's a demon. His blood boils. He doesn't need a blanket to keep warm."

"Well, we've got to do something. He saved me and Gar. I owe him for that."

Brusk chuckled. "Oh, and I was no help."

She was stroking the giant. "Of course you were. But you aren't injured. He is. It's our obligation to help him. It seems to me

320

not all of these demons are evil. It's just a perception we carry. Perhaps Silk is like Thunder, here. She may be caught between, not knowing what side to take. At least, I got that impression. She just needs to know someone is on her side. Did you ever wonder where we found the will to resist Doom yesterday? I have my suspicions."

The thought of Silk as a possible ally irked him. It bothered him that it did. He shouldn't care. They were all demons. But there was something in what the girl Darlee said that bounced round in his thoughts. Not *all* of the demons are evil. He recalled how Silk had cooked for him and, when the others avoided him, talked to him as well. She'd treated him kindly. "We're going to have to worry about Silk at another time. Right now, we have enough problems of our own. We need to get home and we need to get Gar tended to."

"What about Thunder here? Is there anything we can do for him?"

"It's possible. Let me try." He pulled out a dagger and cut the blanket to make a large bandage to cover the deep wound in Thunder's shoulder. It should, at the very least, slow, or maybe even stop, the loss of blood. When he finished, Thunder nodded and lay back down. "There. That's the best I can do for now. Sorry, lass, there's no blanket left for you. I suggest you get as close to the fire as possible."

She started to move, but Thunder reached out and pulled her close to him. She didn't struggle, she just accepted it. "You're right. He is warm. I'll stay with him for the night."

As she lay there, she stroked Thunder's arm. The low rumble coming from the beast surprised Brusk. *By the gods, he's purring.*

He made his way back to his spot against the log. *By late tomorrow afternoon, we'll be home. May the gods give me the wisdom on what to do then.*

He closed his eyes and let sleep take him.

***

It was still dark when something woke him. He scanned the campsite and noted the fire was all but out. Only a few embers glowed in the pit. He stood, careful not to make too much noise. As he did, he thought he heard something scampering away. He checked on Darlee. She still slept in the arms of Thunder. The big demon was awake, the small light from the fire glowing in his eyes. "Hiss?"

Thunder nodded.

So, the little bugger's found us. He must be alone, or Thunder would have done something. I'm guessing the other demons are still far enough away I don't need to panic yet, but it might be wise to get a move on.

He began saddling the horses. They whinnied some, unhappy with the early-morning start. By the time he had them ready, Darlee woke. She moved to her brother, a hand on his forehead.

"The swelling is down some. Should we try and wake him?"

He nodded. "It's time we go. Assuming the demons travelled all night, I figure we have several hands before they catch up to us."

She shook her brother. "Gar. Wake up. We've got to go."

Gar opened his eyes. Brusk was glad for that. He didn't want to tie the lad to the horse as he did the day before. "Welcome back to the living. Do ya think you can stand?"

Gar sat up on one elbow. "Where are we?"

"Less than a day's ride east of Visk. We got demons on our trail, so if ya don't mind, we need to move."

Gar clambered to his feet. He wobbled some, but managed to get astride his horse. Brusk put a hand on the animal's neck. "We're going to ride hard. If you feel you're going to fall, slow to a lope. I'll know why."

Gar nodded. "My head hurts bad, but I think I can do it."

Brusk helped Darlee onto her horse then climbed aboard his own. "Good. We're on our way then."

He led the way just as the first tendrils of morning light creased the sky. Thunder jogged alongside. Brusk made note of a jar in the demon's gait that wasn't there before.

***

They made good time, and it was only midafternoon when they reached the city gate. It took a tense moment to calm his men down as Thunder entered with them.

He learned Gramby still operated the inn as the infirmary, so he sent the others there to get checked out while he headed for the barracks. He found the lieutenant inside, going over some lists with his duty officer. "I'm back. What's been happening in my absence?"

Gramby greeted him with a military wrist grip. "The news isn't good. I sent riders toward Sechwisk to check on the enemy. They're on their way. My guess is they'll be at the gates the day after tomorrow. I've drafted every able-bodied man I could find. We've got almost two thousand prepared to defend the walls, but almost all have no fighting skills. I doubt we could hold more than a few hands."

Brusk smiled. "You say the day after tomorrow? The timing is close. I figure we'll be having visitors of a different kind as well, though I suspect they will arrive sooner than that. Those demons are coming back, and, this time, they've got one we won't be able to tackle like we did Thunder. We'll have to make some other plans. In the meantime, we've got some things to do."

CHAPTER 56

Despite the pain associated with the prying fingers, Gar sat still as the woman checked the lump on his head. She was only a midwife, there to help where she could, but neither of the two doctors was prepared to look at him.

"Tsk. It's a bad knock you've taken, young man. I daresay, it's probably addled your brains some, but the good news is, I can't find any fracture. You should be right sooner or later. Just don't go bumping it again."

He nodded. Even that caused some discomfort. "Thank you, miss. I'll try not to."

She checked the lump on his head, glanced over his shoulder, shuddered, and then left. Thunder sat in the corner behind him, eyes closed. Not even the midwife would attend to Thunder's wounds. The occasional hiss would sound when a fresh drop of blood seeped from the wound in the beast's shoulder to hit the floor. *I've got to try and stop his bleeding.*

He stood up with the intent to get a fresh bandage for Thunder when one of the four men guarding him stood in the way.

"Where do you think you're going?"

"To take care of my friend."

He brushed past the man and went to the central table, which the doctors used as a work station. The soldier followed, watching his every move.

He grabbed the largest bandage he could find and retreated to where Thunder was. As he did, he noted the number of men lying round with severe wounds. Angry stares accompanied him wherever he passed. *Most of these were caused by Thunder. It's no wonder none will help him, or me, for that matter. How they all hate me so.*

He'd never placed a bandage on a wound before, but he'd paid enough attention to the midwife to have an idea on how to do it. He untied the shredded blanket Brusk had put on Thunder. The behemoth let out a low growl. Dried blood matted the blanket to the open flesh, and it required some work to pull it free. He did his best to tie on the new bandage, but it was a sloppy job.

Thunder nodded. "Water."

Gar made for the inn's bar and retrieved a pitcher of water. He passed another man who lay limp with both doctors at his side.

One doctor was prying the lids open, peering into the man's eyes. "This one's done for."

The other doctor nodded. "I concur. Let's get his family to take him home before he passes."

Gar stopped. "Maybe I can help."

The doctor who had made the prognosis, an elderly man, turned to face him. "Don't you think you've helped enough? This man lies dying because of you and that demon back there."

Gar knelt and put the water pitcher aside. "That may be true, but since you are giving up on him, then how much more can it hurt to let me try and help?"

The second doctor, younger than the first, put a hand on his colleague's arm. "If there's something he can do, let him try."

Gar put his hands on the man. The wound was terrible. The man must have suffered much before lapsing into unconsciousness. He concentrated on the wound. As he applied his magic to heal it, his own body felt the terrible pain associated with its infliction. Not unexpected because it was part of the process, but, in this case, the pain was so severe, he struggled not to double over. As well, the ache in his head was exploding. It took everything in his willpower to keep his hands on the man and continue to concentrate.

After many beats, the pain from the healing started to abate and the wound before him closed up. The ache in his head, however, increased. Only when he was sure the man was fully healed did he finally let go, collapsing backward to the floor. He could not have been lying on the ground for more than a beat when Thunder was by his side, lifting him. He pointed to the unconscious man. "Thunder, give him some."

Thunder reached out and laid a hand on the man's chest. A quick glow passed between them. The man's eyes opened.

"Where am I?"

Thunder carried Gar back to the spot they had been occupying in the corner of the room. As he lay down, he noted the aura round Thunder was almost gone. Thunder went to put a hand on Gar's chest, but he blocked it. "No, you need the life force to feed and heal yourself. I'll be fine."

Thunder nodded and retreated to the corner.

The younger doctor came over. "I don't know what you did, but it's a miracle. That man should have been dead within the next hand and now he's up and around. For that, at least, I thank you." He went to Thunder. "Let me properly dress that wound."

Thunder obliged by lifting his arms up and out and the doctor rearranged the bandage. "There. That should stop the bleeding."

Gar sat up and offered his hand to the man. "Thank you."

The doctor hesitated, and then took it. "I have others who need tending to. Can you help them as well?"

Gar shook his head, the act sending it throbbing even more. "Not right now. I need time for my mana to rebuild."

The doctor nodded and walked away. Gar glanced at the four guards. *I'm a prisoner, nothing more.* He lay back down. He was going to try and get some sleep.

***

Darlee walked among the timbers of the unfinished house. There was still too much to do before it could ever be considered home again. With Pap gone, that was never going to happen. She paused to stroke the stone fireplace, one of the few things that survived the fire. The support posts on either side of it were charred but still solid.

She examined the one on the left, just to be sure. Yes, the notches were still there. She placed a finger into one of the notches and stood against the post, her head banging into her finger. Moving it a little higher she was able to touch the timber with her forehead. She stepped back to examine where her finger rested in relation to the notch. The difference was the width of one finger. She had grown some since then. Her mother would have got the kitchen knife and cut a new notch. It always made her proud.

There was no mother there to make the cut. No father to complain how she would be eating more. No knife even to cut with.

She sniffed back a sob and moved her hand higher, to the last one that marked Gar's height. The fire had burned away the edges making it more of a sooty depression than a recognizable notch. Still, she knew what it was, and that Gar would measure several fingers higher since then.

Looking in the yard, she could see Jango pacing. The captain had given him permission to accompany her, provided he got her back safely. Brusk had offered her a place to live within his own simple home in the city. It would be dusk in a moment. The sun was falling behind the distant hills. She knew Jango would urge her to leave, but she wasn't finished yet.

She made for the shed. "I'll just be a little while longer. I want to grab a couple of things."

"Okay, but please hurry. The captain's going to have my hide, as it is."

She went inside and stumbled. Already there was too much gloom for her to see anything clearly. She took in everything in the small space—the two beds, the wood stove, and the open shelving where a handful of preserves still waited. That was it. In truth, nothing to take. She just wanted to grab the memory of it one last time. How it looked, how it felt. It was difficult to not cry.

She'd half turned to go when she spotted the cane in the corner by the door. She'd missed it when walking in. Picking it up, she hugged it close. It was the last thing her grandfather had made for her. *Pap, oh Pap, why did you have to die? I miss you terribly. No matter what happens in the days to come, I fear Gar will never be free. From here on in, I'll be alone. What will I do?*

A light breeze rustled past, caressing her cheek. The sensation caused her to start. It reminded her of the soft touch of her grandfather's kiss there. The breeze nudged the door. She followed it out into the yard. It whirled round her once then was gone.

She went to the horses and the waiting Jango. "Come on. Something tells me we've got to go."

She climbed her horse and took in the homestead one last time. She knew she would never be back.

***

As they made camp, Devron figured out how deep they were into Sechland. "My best guess is we should reach Visk by two or three hands after midday tomorrow."

Commander Savan stretched out in front of the fire. "Thank the gods. I've got to get out more often. Too many days spent behind a desk has turned me soft. From riding that horse, my rear end is killing me. I can't imagine what I'd be like if I'd had to walk like the troops."

Devron shook his head. The commander had only ridden his horse a short way. The man spent most of the time moving from one unit to another to march with the men. He cajoled them, sang raunchy songs, and put everyone at ease, even to the point of pulling pranks on his senior officers to the delight of everyone. All in all, Savan probably spent more energy on the trip than the average man could withstand. "If you like, you could have one of the wagons converted to a nice padded carriage. It would mean leaving one of the war machines behind."

Savan chuckled. "Now, wouldn't that be a sight to see. I can just imagine myself all comfy, with lots of soft pillows and a roof over my head to keep the sun off. In a year, I'd probably die from obesity. Sit down, Lieutenant. I need you to tell me more about the defenses of Visk."

He sat cross-legged across from the commander. "Visk? Why? We go to the aid of Visk, not its conquest."

Once more, Savan's smile disappeared. "I need to prepare for all contingencies. What if when we arrive the city is in the hands of our enemy? Am I to just walk away?"

This was another test. He knew it. Savan was seeing how far he was prepared to go in revealing his country's defenses. He'd already detailed as much as he could of the defenses of Sechwisk. The capital city was known by all to be under the control of the other kingdoms, but there was no information to indicate his hometown had fallen. "You need not worry about Visk. With Captain Brusk back in control, the only way that city will have fallen is if it has been burned to the ground. If that's the case, you'll be able to walk right in."

Savan smiled once more. "You're starting to catch on. You may make a fine commander someday."

"A fine commander. Sadly, that day will never come. Other duties await me, should we win out."

Savan nodded. "Ah, yes, I had forgotten. The role of king is your next stop. Too bad. Although my brother is only regent, the burden of ruling wears on him. I can see it. Whereas, for me, the military life is what I'm accustomed to. Like you, I had a soldier's upbringing. My father is commander in the northwest city of Rok, my hometown. It's what I've known since birth. If the queen were to abdicate and surrender the throne to me, I would refuse."

Devron let his shoulders slump. What Savan said struck home. A military life was all he had ever wanted as well. The whole reason he relocated to Visk was to avoid the machinations of court and the palace. Did he have what it took to be king? Did he even want to be? He sighed. "It is not a duty I would have chosen. It is one thrust upon me. I cannot examine it as a matter of choice. It is a matter of duty. Should I fail to claim my hereditary rights, even without this war, the kingdom would fall as those who would carve it up to create their own fiefdoms would have no one to stop them. Were you in my position, you would do no less. From how you describe it, your brother has also assumed the responsibility thrust onto him."

Savan kicked a stray stick into the fire. "I suppose you're right. Still, I'm glad I'm not you."

Talking to Tarlok might be a good idea on how *he* faced the challenge. "Where is your brother? I did not see him at camp tonight, nor the big fellow, Grott."

"They turned southeast at midday. He sent a message that a raven arrived and they've decided to follow it. Don't ask me why. He didn't say. I've learned not to question my brother. Everything he does has a reason."

Devron recalled the night at Grott's when the large, black bird appeared and how it left screaming into the night. His host had reacted most strangely after that. Perhaps there *was* something more about the bird than met the eye. "If he doesn't come, how are we to capture the demons?"

"Right now, I've got more than enough to worry about fighting off the combined armies of six countries. He'll show up. He always does." Savan rose and stretched. "I've got to check in with my officers and make sure we're set for the night. Get some rest. Tomorrow is going to be a busy day."

Before Savan could walk away, a rider arrived and dismounted before him. "Commander, I've returned from monitoring the enemy forces. They're making good time."

"How good? When, in your estimation, will they arrive at the gates to Visk?"

"By midday tomorrow."

"Midday? That's at least two hands before we get there." He faced Devron. "It looks like a short night tonight. I'll order reveille a hand earlier, but even with a quick march, I'm not convinced we can get there before they do."

Savan strode off, leaving Devron with his own thoughts. He stared into the fire. The one question he'd never voiced was whether the people would accept him as king. Would they lay the blame for the war at the feet of the Sech family? Would there be some other unknown in the kingdom who had other plans as to who should rule? If his ascension was rejected, the army he led would not be coming as saviors, but conquerors. *It will be hard to sleep tonight.*

CHAPTER 57

It would be dawn soon and Brusk was surprised the demons had yet to attack. *The buggers must have gotten here long ago. What's keeping them from charging in?*

He decided to take a walk along the parapets where a man was stationed atop the wall every twenty-five paces. He sent Gramby one way while he went the other. With almost half a league of wall surrounding the city, he needed to rotate everyone throughout the night to keep sharp eyes at all the posts. He nodded and exchanged short pleasantries with each as he passed, asking them in turn as to whether they've seen anything. The replies were all negative.

Halfway around, Lieutenant Gramby met up with him on the wall.

"Captain, it might be nothing, but a man a couple hundred paces back reported hearing some noises."

"Noises? What kind of noises?"

"He said it sounded like scratching."

Brusk had his suspicions. "Show me the man."

They jogged until Gramby stopped in front of one soldier. "This man here. Tell the captain your report."

The man saluted. "Well, Captain, it was like this. A couple of hands ago, I thought I heard a noise, but when I checked it out, I couldn't see a thing. I thought maybe a rat, the way it made that scurrying sound. Sometimes they get up here on the wall. I decided to pay it no mind. Then, just a little while ago, I heard it again. I looked high and low for the bugger, but he wasn't here. Then I heard it on the outside of the wall. I leaned over and looked down, but I couldn't see anything. Whatever it was, it was gone."

A few paces away, a lantern burned, and Brusk grabbed it. "Show me the exact spot where you think it was on the wall."

The soldier took two steps to his right and pointed. "Right here, Captain."

Brusk held the lantern over the wall. Sure enough, numerous nicks marred the wood. Two sets. "As I figured. That sneaky little imp Hiss has been in and out. More than likely, he's scouted the whole town."

He returned the lantern to its place. "Come on, Gramby. We need to get ready. My guess is they'll be attacking any moment. We need to move Garlin Murdach. No doubt Hiss knows where he's at. They'll make straight for him. If we lose Gar, all our plans will be for naught, as they'll run."

As they headed down the nearest stairs, he pointed toward the inn. "Go get Gar and bring him to where we planned. I'm headed to the gate. I'm betting they'll use the front door."

Gramby nodded and sped off. As Brusk dashed through the city, dawn broke. *At least we won't be having to fight the demons in the dark. That would have been a big advantage for them. The tall demon Doom may be in charge, but he's no military mind.*

As he approached the gate, a horn sounded. He could see the trumpeter atop one of the gate towers doing the blowing. It was as he guessed; they were coming for the front gate. He dashed up the stairs to see. Charging across the plain toward the gate was the four legged monster Gar had released last. It carried a giant mace. *Where, by the gods, did it get that thing from?* Only on closer examination could he tell the weapon was crude, made from tree saplings and a large stone.

Behind it rode the others. He leaned over the parapet to see the team of men stationed behind the gate. A number of support posts were erected to support the gate from behind. He hoped they would be enough. "Brace for impact!"

His first plan of defense was to keep the demons outside long enough until the enemy troops from the other kingdoms arrived. They reinforced the doors as best they could, and he distributed every pike in the armory, not to use as weapons, but to poke and prod the demons back from wherever they tried to breach the defenses. Hopefully, they would succeed and let Morica and all those others deal with the demons. He glanced to the south. There was still no sign of them.

Brute hit the gate with his mace and it shuddered as if by a direct hit from a catapult. Shards of wood blasted everywhere, but the gate held. The beast continued flailing at it, but its blows lacked the power of its original hit carrying the full weight of its charge. From slits in the stone towers to either side, his men shoved poles at the creature in an attempt to keep it off balance.

What came next was also what he expected. A sense of fear. He wanted to fight it but his will to do so lagged. He spotted Silk and Doom, their arms outstretched, focusing their magic at the defenders. It wasn't as all-encompassing as the night when they took Gar, but now Brusk understood how to fight it. He had stationed most of his men in the immediate area to dissipate the magic—to wear out the powers of the demons through numbers. His troops were all feeling the effects, and when he looked down, he noted many collapsed to the ground, but some still struggled on.

He needed to break the demons' concentration. It took all he could muster to turn and yell into the courtyard with its three waiting catapults. "Fifteen paces onto the road!"

The operator calibrated the first machine and let fly. The heavy stone arced over the wall and landed with a thud some three paces short of the demons. Close enough to startle the horses but not to break the concentration of the riders. He needed more distance. "Eighteen paces!"

The second shot sailed the right distance, but wide right. Brusk shook his head. The stone must have been off balance. "Again!"

The third shot was true and if not for the animal Doom was on, it would have hit him square in the chest. The poor creature took the brunt of the hit and crumpled under the demon. Doom fell and the feeling of fear disappeared. Brusk knew no weapon could cut the demons, but it might be possible to break their bones. When the tall demon stood up, his question was answered. *What cursed magic is it that makes these things invulnerable to man-made weapons?*

Still, the distraction did what he wanted. His men on the ground were rallying some, though the drain of will was still being applied by Silk.

Brute was continuing to smash away at the gate. Bit by bit, the timbers disintegrated, the metal framing bent and broken. The men in the yard behind were reloading all three catapults. He didn't

333

want to waste any more shots at Doom. It wouldn't be long until Brute broke through, and he wanted the machines at the ready.

The doors of the gate could no longer withstand the attack by the monster demon and burst apart. As Brute forced his way through the opening, Brusk commanded the first catapult to fire. At such close range, they couldn't miss. The stone hit the demon, knocking him backward, out of the opening. The monster roared. His men dashed to the opening and dropped several logs into the gap, blocking it.

Brute got up and charged again, but before he could clear the new logs, the second catapult fired, catching the monster once more. It rolled away and was slow to get up. His men finished filling the gap with more cut logs. Only a loose pile, but it would still take the demons time to clear it. Sooner or later, though, his men would run out of wood. Where was that enemy army?

While Brute assailed the logs, Dread tried to scale the wall on the other side of the tower Brusk occupied. As the demon neared the top, a dozen men with pikes stabbed down at him, knocking his grip free. The six-armed demon tried a couple more times, but each time he was repelled by the soldiers on the wall.

Screams from below brought Brusk's attention back to the gate. Brute changed strategy and simply pushed at the pile of wood. The whole thing was moving. The logs near the top rolled away as the small mountain of firewood spread apart. The gate was about to be breached again. He tapped the trumpeter. "Sound retreat." He took one last glance to the south. *That just might be a cloud of dust in the distance. Not a moment too soon.*

The notes blasted from the horn and his men scrambled away. Brusk had barely made it down the stairs when Brute thrust the last of the wood out of the way and entered the city with a roar. A few men who were foolish enough to try and keep the wood piled could not escape the long reach of the monster's scorpion tail. The thrusts of the stinger impaled the men right through.

He made haste to run down the street, a number of his men just ahead of him. When he felt far enough away, he turned to look back. The other demons charged into the city. He hoped they would recognize him despite the distance that separated them. His first plan had failed. Plan two involved leading the demons in a merry chase throughout the city. To make it work, he needed Gar. *Where in blazes are Gramby and that lad?*

***

Despite the headaches, Gar had managed a second healing that early morning. The man he helped was not as bad as the first, but would likely have died in time. As he rested again, Lieutenant Gramby came into the inn, and, after a quick chat with the doctors, came for him.

"Come along now, Gar. The captain needs you."

The lieutenant stood off from him several steps. His focus was more on Thunder than on him. No words were spoken, but it was easy to see Gramby feared the big demon. Gar toyed with the idea for only the briefest moment of setting Thunder after the man. After all, this was the fellow who had put his sister in the hands of the torturer.

His desire for revenge passed. With all the death that had happened, seeing anyone else hurt was the furthest thing from his mind. He only wanted to help.

He stood up and took one step toward the lieutenant, who backed away. Gar paused and took a deep breath, made eye contact with Gramby, and extended a hand. The gesture may have been all for naught as a result of all the horrors he'd committed, but he had to try. "I forgive you."

The lieutenant hesitated, and then took his forearm in a military greeting. "We both have our demons. Mine are on the inside."

It was a small thing. But it gave Gar a great feeling of relief. "Let's go, then. I'm ready to help the captain in any way I can."

He, Gramby, and Thunder went outside and walked toward the gate. As they neared, the sounds of men shouting and the angry roars of Brute filled the air. They made it to the street facing the gate to see Brute attacking the men of Visk and the other demons exerting their magic. Across the open area, down the street, on the far side, he could see Captain Brusk, his armor glinting in the morning sun. The demons were between them.

Gramby grabbed his arm. "Damn. We've come out on the wrong side. Quick, before the demons see you, get out of sight." He shoved Gar back the way they'd come.

It was too late. Doom had spotted them and shouted in his language at the other demons while pointing in Gar's direction. It was easy enough to figure out what Doom was saying, as the demons started for him. He had been briefed on Brusk's plan. "We've got to run."

After only two steps, Thunder picked him up. Even while carrying him, Thunder quickly outdistanced Gramby. The demons were in hot pursuit and on horseback, Dread in the lead. Gramby glanced over his shoulder, smiled, pulled his sword, and turned to face the demons. As Dread charged at him, Gramby cut the horse from under the demon, sending it sprawling. The others slowed until Brute caught up and, with a quick strike of his tail, killed the lieutenant. Even in the lieutenant's death, Gar could still see the smile on Gramby's face.

Thunder turned a corner and the demons were no longer in sight. He needed to get where Captain Brusk was. This was his hometown. He knew every street and back alley. Thunder's pace was slowed by having to carry Gar, but was still faster than a man could run. The demons on horseback, on the other hand, would soon catch up. He had no idea what pace Brute could maintain afoot. He directed Thunder to run to his left.

Doom and Brute came into sight, answering his question. The big monster could run as fast as Thunder. Perhaps faster. *I guess having four legs helps.* He nudged Thunder and pointed. "Go that way."

Thunder entered a narrow alley. Gar tapped him on the shoulder. "Put me down."

Once afoot, he went farther in. "It gets tight, so stay close. There's no way they'll be able to ride the horses through, and I doubt Brute could fit at all."

He could hear the footsteps of the demons to the entrance of the alley but could not see them as the passage had turned twice

336

already. He and Thunder arrived at the narrowest spot he remembered, although it had been some time since his play with his friends brought him through the alley. Seeing it now, it was even tighter than he recalled. He slipped through without problem, but, for Thunder, it was a difficult task. Even turned sideways, the demon's chest wedged in the opening. "Come on, Thunder. You can do it. Squeeze through."

Thunder let loose a roar and ripped through the gap. Both his back and chest ribboned with many cuts and scrapes. Apparently whatever magic protected the demons from weapons provided no effect when it came to houses.

Through the aperture, Gar made out the monstrous form of Brute, caught as Thunder had been, but farther back in the alley. It roared and began to smash at the walls in an attempt to widen the opening. "That will take a little while. Let's go."

They dashed down the street and turned another corner. The captain was just ahead. When he made it to Brusk's side, the captain looked past him first.

"Where's Gramby?"

Gar shook his head. "Dead. We came out on the wrong side of the demons, and he fought to stall them while I made my escape." The captain's face fell at the news. "Just so you know, we made peace, he and I. I believe he died with his honor intact."

"He was a good man. He made a mistake, but he believed he was doing right. I don't begrudge him any. I'll miss him."

A clatter of noise erupted from behind them. Brute must have broken through. Gar knew what he was supposed to do from here. The captain had coached him the night before. "I'm ready. You had better go."

Brusk nodded. "Right. Let's get to it. My men will be waiting. Make sure the demons all follow you in."

The captain and the few men standing nearby cleared the street. Gar waited until Brute and the other demons came into sight. It didn't take long. When Doom pointed in his direction, he started running.

He retraced the steps from the night when vengeance had burned in him. It took him straight to the gate of the home of

Merchant Trellus. Before he entered the estate, he spotted many loaded wagons off to the sides of the entrance. Once he'd stepped through, men slammed the gates shut. Compared to the ones that served the city, these were inferior. It was unlikely they would hold out the demons for more than a moment. Holding them out was not the plan.

He, Thunder, and the men who manned the gate raced to the back of the compound where men waited with two ladders set against the wall. As they started to climb, the one Thunder was on broke. A crash told Gar the front gates were breached. Gar reached down a hand toward Thunder. "They're coming. Hurry. You need to get over the wall."

Gar stood on one of a number of blankets spread across the top of the wall to protect against the embedded glass shards. The men who manned the gate scrambled up. Only Thunder remained below. The demon shook his head and smashed the remaining ladder. He turned as Brute came into view, followed by Doom, Dread, Pleasure, and Silk. Thunder charged them. Before Gar could see what happened, the men yanked him down another ladder on the far side of the wall. The roars of the demons filled the air. He worried for Thunder's life.

He made his way round the walled estate. When he returned to the front, he found the gate blocked by the loaded wagons and a makeshift wall attached to them facing the estate. This blockade wouldn't hold long either. He found Captain Brusk.

The captain nodded. "Good job, Gar. I think they're all in there. I don't know whether they'll be able to scale those walls, but looking at the size of that demon Brute, I don't think they'll bother. I'm surprised they haven't started attacking yet. What are they up to?"

"Thunder's still in there. He's keeping them busy, for now."

A horn sounded from the wall, and they both turned. "What is it?"

"The forces from the other kingdoms have arrived. I have men trying to repair the front gate. They may be finished by now, they may not."

He considered Brusk's plan. "What difference does that make? We need them to fight the demons."

The captain nodded. "True. But the timing was off. I want them to fight each other outside the walls, not in the city. It's going to take some time for the enemy forces to properly marshal out there. We have to hold the demons in here until then. After that, the final stage of my plan goes into effect."

Gar sighed. "I know. I have to lead them out there."

CHAPTER 58

As Devron neared the tree line, the open grounds surrounding Visk came into full view. Arrayed east of the city was a sea of soldiers. The banners fluttering in the wind depicted the colors of the other six kingdoms. It was only a guess on his part, but he estimated the force was some fifteen thousand strong.

Commander Savan reined his horse next to Devron. "We're in time. It looks like they've yet to organize themselves for the fight. While they're busy trying to align their machines toward the city, we can strike at them from the side. They won't be expecting an attack from the north."

He thought about the limited number of men at Savan's command. "That advantage will only last for half a hand at most. They outnumber us almost three to one."

"Hmm. I think it's closer to two to one. Let's say five to two. If we strike quick and hard, we can get the numbers a lot closer. With the chain of command going six ways, one has to wonder as to their ability to counter." He smiled. "Remember, those men out there have never encountered warlocks before. It'll be interesting to see how many run when the first few bolts of lightning and flame balls come crashing into them."

He recalled how Daphora had said she was half spent of her magic after firing only one of each when they were attacked on the road. The limited number of warlocks with them would run out of magic soon enough. After that, it would come down to hand-to-hand combat. "I hope you're right. Otherwise, my reign as king here in Sechland is going to be a real short one."

Savan laughed. "Then I'll try to make sure otherwise." The commander turned to his officers, who were waiting patiently just behind them, and barked out his orders. The soldiers scattered, each off to perform his duty.

The war machines were brought up and readied. Though the men worked silently, the wagons and machines still creaked as they moved. With every noise, Devron expected the enemy forces to hear them and alter their positioning to the new threat. Time seemed to crawl. He checked his armor several times, tightening the straps.

Everything was finally in place. Savan gave the command. A volley of loose stone and ballista bolts lofted into the air toward the enemy. Right behind it, a line of pike men and soldiers, followed by the warlocks and archers, raced onto the field.

The loose stone scattered in the air, pelting down on the unwary men. The pieces were large and sharp enough to kill a man hit in the head, maim him elsewhere. The bolts were aimed at the enemy cavalry. As they rained down, they would plunge right through men and horses alike.

The distance between the front line and the defenders was narrowing quickly. It was time. He kicked his horse into a gallop along with Commander Savan and the rest of his horse soldiers. He could see the enemy troops trying desperately to reorganize and face the oncoming charge.

It was then the warlocks acted. Bolts of lightning and fireballs erupted from their hands over the heads of the front line into the enemy. Men burst into flames or were struck down by the lightning blasts. As Savan predicted, their front line broke as many ran.

He caught up to the warlocks and archers, and the charging frontline parted to allow the riders to stream through. Without a defensive line set, he and the others were able to penetrate easily. Riding through the midst of the enemy, he swung down where he could and continued on toward the set goal, the enemy war machines. Using ropes, they overturned them all, many breaking apart in the process.

Behind him, the now reformed front line of Piaxian soldiers and pike men crashed into the disarrayed enemy forces. Arrows and magical attacks made confusion reign as the battle raged. He and the horse soldiers regrouped to begin another charge through the enemy forces. He figured this would be the last time they would have the full advantage of an unhindered attack. He would need to make as many strikes count as possible. As the battlefield would continue to mix, the final stages would be all hand to hand. *May the gods be with us.*

***

The noises from inside Merchant Trellus' estate changed. No longer could the roars of Thunder and Brute be heard amongst the screaming voices of Doom and the other demons. Instead, the rhythmic pounding on the barricade began. It could only mean one thing. Thunder had fallen. Sadness swept through Gar as he waited on horseback for the demons to emerge.

Behind him, horns were blaring from the tower. He did not know what they meant. They were not any of the simple ones he'd learned from his short time in the army. From beyond the walls, the sounds of combat relived in his mind that time where he had to fight for his life in the battle at Morence. It was after that fight when he freed Thunder and the big demon had become his guardian ever since. It had saved him, Baxus, and Jango from the enemy troops.

Jango. What ever happened to his friend? Did he make it back to Visk okay? Was he a prisoner in the jail, or was he back home with his family? Since his return yesterday, Gar had never asked. It was a failing on his part, one that embarrassed him. He'd never inquired because he feared the answer—perhaps his friend had not made it, but lay dead somewhere. It would be another life lost as a result of his actions.

Captain Brusk, who had gone to investigate when the horns started blowing, returned to his side. "You've got some extra company when the time comes, Gar. It seems Lieutenant Devron was successful after all. He's out there right now with an army from Piaxia, in a fight with the other kingdoms. I spotted his armor leading a cavalry charge into their midst. There's a full-fledged battle going on out there. I've given word to my officers to support the Piaxians in any way they can. When those demons bust loose, won't the enemy be surprised when the demons chase you out the gate."

He met the captain's gaze. "Before this happens, I need to know something. I had a friend who escaped with me back in Morica. His name is Jango. By chance, have you heard anything of

342

him? My fear is he died. It would haunt me forever, but I must know."

"Then you'll be happy to know your friend is fine. I've even pardoned him for desertion. Heck, I had to. If I had every man jailed who's deserted since this war began, I'd have half of Visk in chains. I have Jango guarding your sister. I can't take a chance on her getting nabbed again and used as leverage against you."

Some of the weight of all that happened lifted from him. Jango was okay. "Thank you. It's good to know I saved at least one life."

Brusk rubbed at his chin. "I guess you did, at that. It's still a long way for you to even the table though."

That was true. He accepted it. He owed it to Brusk to try—to the captain, to his friends, to the people of Visk, to his sister, most of all. He was going to do everything he could to make things right.

The makeshift barricade could hold Brute no more. The monster demon burst through and killed the couple of men who'd stayed too long trying to maintain the blockade.

Doom stepped out and their eyes locked. "How many people do you want to die here, Gar? We'll tear down the city and kill everyone in it before we give up. Save your people and surrender."

"I believe you, Doom. That's why I'm leaving the city. If you want to catch me, it will have to be out there. Leave these people be and come get me outside."

He kicked his horse and directed the animal toward the gate. He glanced back to see the demons in pursuit once more.

Gar focused on where he was going. The streets were empty. The clomp of his horse's hooves on the paving stones echoed against the buildings as the din from beyond the walls tried to drown it out. *I only hope Doom doesn't stop to figure out what all the noise is. He may never leave the city.*

The men at the gate had been briefed and, when Gar reached it, they opened their makeshift one so he could exit. He remembered what had happened to the two men at the barricade. "Run. They're right behind me."

As he passed through the gate, the men scattered. Hopefully, none of the demons would pause for them. The grounds outside the

343

wall were filled with a cacophony of war, pain, and death. Men were struggling everywhere with other men. He could make out no front line. All of the combatants on the field were so thoroughly mixed together, it made no difference which way he rode. *Away from the wall then. I'll try and get as far from Visk as possible.*

His horse banged its way past the men flailing away at each other. The animal's pace slowed and reared after someone crashed into its side. He managed to keep his seat and urged his mount forward. The horse walked now, neighing loudly at the flashing steel round it.

Behind him, the shouts of men bemoaning the demons reached his ears. It was followed by the roar of Brute and cries of men dying. The demons were now engaged in the battle. He'd managed to do what Captain Brusk hoped for. Around him, many of the men ran.

An errant blade swing clipped his horse behind its front right leg. The animal crumpled and Gar was thrown to the ground. Dazed, he stood and regained his bearings. *East. I need to run east.* As he focused on his direction, he noted three men and a sea of white outside the battle area. He did not recognize two of them, but the one in the middle, even from the distance, looked like Pap. *That can't be. Darlee said he died saving me.*

A man swung a sword at him, and he managed to dodge the blade. Before the soldier could try again, another man attacked. Gar had been given a sword, but failed to pull it from its scabbard. Doing so took a moment, and a sudden pain in his right shoulder spun him to find another man holding a pike, blood on the tip. He'd been stabbed.

He ducked under the next thrust of the weapon and skewered the man through the chest with his sword. Gar was unable to pull it free before the man fell, twisting the blade from his grip. He didn't care. He turned about to continue his escape. Although he only traveled a few steps, the three men were closer now. The sea of white was a huge herd of sheep, and there was a gold glow about them. The one man was definitely his grandfather. "Pap! I'm coming, Pap. I'm coming."

Behind him, the roar of Brute sounded right in his ear. He glanced back and saw the monster a few paces away. The other demons were mere steps behind it.

He tried to run and stumbled straight into the waiting sword of another man. The blade entered his chest and his lung burned in pain. The soldier's grim smile faded quickly as he looked over Gar's shoulder. In the next instant, the man's head was torn off by Brute's club.

Gar fell to his knees. The world spun. His sight blurred. He reached out with one hand, the other trying to stem the blood pumping from the wound. "Pap." He crumpled to the ground and rolled onto his side. He could still see his grandfather, and a blue light emanating from his hands. Beside him, the ground erupted. From beneath the soil, spears of rock thrust up and attached themselves to Brute. The demon cried out and struggled, but the rock formed round his leg too quickly for the demon to escape. He watched as Brute swung down with his mace, shattering one stone arm grasping at him, but others were quick to replace it and grab the demon's arm. The stone flowed like water up the legs and torso of the demon. It raced up Brute's body to his head. The monster tilted his head back and let out a roar cut short by the enveloping rock. The demon was trapped in stone once again.

Gar closed his eyes and darkness took him.

***

Brusk rallied his men and waited by the gate. Together, they carried a number of nets and chains, things none of the men out in the battleground would have. When he saw the men from the other kingdoms break and run and then watched as the monster demon Brute was entombed in rock, he knew it was time. "Let's go."

They dashed out onto the field and made their way toward the remaining demons. The troops from Piaxia were trying to fight the demons, but, as expected, their weapons were ineffective. *What I'd give for whatever magic it is that protects them like that.*

As he neared Doom, they made eye contact, and the demon held out a hand at him and his men. The sense of fear made his

345

knees buckle. Many of the men with him collapsed to the ground. He hadn't brought enough with him to weaken the spell. From his knees, he watched as Doom, Dread, and Pleasure urged their horses to head south. *They're getting away. I've got to stop them.*

As he struggled to rise, the sense of fear disappeared. Standing, he glanced round to see Silk with her hands raised toward him. His men were rising as well. He nodded toward her and resumed chasing Doom and the others.

It was a good thing the demons were such lousy riders. With the horses only walking, Brusk covered the gap between them quickly. Doom saw him coming and extended both hands toward him. Brusk felt nothing but extreme confidence in what he was about to do.

He leapt and knocked the tall demon from the saddle. Weapons would be of no use, so he punched Doom's jaw as hard as he could. Doom crumpled. *So, that magic don't work when it's only hand-to-hand, no weapons. What Gar told me was right.* With satisfaction, he tied the demon up and turned to see his men having made short work of both Dread and Pleasure.

Three of his men pounced on Silk. He dashed over and pulled them off her. "Not this one. She's on our side."

CHAPTER 59

From the city central tower, Darlee watched. She witnessed the attack by the demons at the gate. She watched as they chased Gar through the streets. She held her breath when they pursued her brother into the walled estate of Merchant Trellus. She panicked when he led the demons into the throes of the raging battle outside the walls. She cried out in despair when the enemy troops struck him down.

Darlee made for the stairs. She had to go to him, to see if he still yet lived. Before she made the first step down, Jango grabbed her by the arm.

"Where do you think you're going? Captain Brusk told me to keep you safe, here in the town hall."

"I've got to go to Gar. He needs my help."

"You can't go out there. They'll kill you just as they—"

Jango clamped his mouth shut. She knew what he was about to say, but she wasn't prepared to believe it just yet. Jango was right about one thing, though. She would have no chance making her way through the battlefield. If one of the soldiers from the other kingdoms did not get her, the demons surely would.

As she thought about the demons, it occurred to her Thunder was nowhere to be seen since they'd entered the gate at the home of Merchant Trellus. If she couldn't get to Gar, maybe the big demon could. "Come on, Jango. We've got to find out what happened to Thunder."

He nodded, and they raced down the steps. The several blocks they ran were deserted. Everyone was either on the wall or in their homes. When they arrived at the manor, she was surprised to see Lialee near the gate.

"What do you want here? It's bad enough I was forced to let Captain Brusk use it. Despite the damage, this is my home and I won't have anyone else enter. Do you hear me?"

She didn't have time for any delay. With two hands, she shoved Lialee. "Out of the way."

The girl tumbled to the ground. "You'll pay for this. I'll have you arrested."

Darlee ignored her and marched round the manor until she came to the rear court. Lying on the ground with a number of wounds seeping blood that spitted and hissed when the drops hit the paving stones, lay Thunder. He wasn't moving.

She dropped to her knees and cradled the massive head in her lap. "Thunder, you've got to get up. You have to save my brother."

His eyes opened. "Weak. No walk. Me fail Master."

If you can't walk, we'll have to carry you." She nudged Jango. "Come on, help me get him up."

Jango grabbed one of Thunder's arms while she took the other. They managed to get him to a sitting position, but they lacked the strength to lift him from the ground. She needed help. She glanced round, but there was no one to be seen.

A soft neighing caught her attention. To her left was the manor stable. She left Jango hanging on and dashed in. She was in luck. Inside was a beautiful white horse that must have been Lialee's. She'd heard how the girl got it for her birthday. Next to it she located a small cart. She found what she needed and hitched the horse to the dray. She led the animal out to the yard and positioned the dray in front of the downed demon. "All we have to do is get him into the cart. The horse will do the rest."

Even with the cart right there, they couldn't do it. Then Lialee reappeared with Maurus in tow.

"There they are, and stealing my horse, too. You're my witness. They're criminals."

Maurus sighed, came over, and grabbed hold of the same arm Darlee was tugging on. "Let me help."

She smiled and gave him a quick kiss on the cheek. "Thanks."

Together, the three of them managed to get Thunder into the cart. Darlee jumped up to take the driver's seat on the buckboard and Jango jumped in beside her.

"What now?"

She shook the reins to get the horse moving. "Now we take him to Gar."

"How? The fight is still raging out there?"

She pulled back on the reins to stop the cart. "No, it isn't. It must have ended. Listen."

He tilted his head toward the wall. There was still some noise, but the sounds of battle, the clashing of steel, the thuds of artillery, the twang of bows, all had ceased. His eyes went wide. "You're right. Let's go."

She urged the horse on once again, and they passed out of the estate with Lialee cursing them in their wake. The trip to the gate passed in silence. She didn't know what they'd find out there, but she was prepared to face it, whatever it might be. Gar needed her.

The makeshift gate was open and unattended. As they exited the city, the field came into full view. On the ground everywhere lay men, dead or dying. To the south, the remnants of the armies of the other kingdoms were in full retreat. To the north, the jubilant forces of Piaxia celebrating their victory. To the far east, a large herd of sheep held sway, following three men walking toward the center of the battlefield. In the middle of all the spent mayhem were the demons, or at least, most of them, trussed up in chains and nets. In their midst was a large rock formation. She could only figure the monstrous demon Brute was inside. She couldn't see Gar from where she was but knew it was in that vicinity she saw him fall.

She flicked the reins and guided the horse as best as she could through the carnage. A couple of men, lying wounded, reached for the cart, pleading for help. Halfway to her goal stood Captain Brusk. She managed to get near him before the way was too blocked by the fallen to continue. "Captain, come help."

Brusk stared at her. "What help do you need? Look around you. Too many have died this day. Too many."

She jumped down from the wagon and went round the back. Thunder was trying to climb out, and she braced him as best she could, underneath one of his arms. As the demon crumpled to his knees, Brusk noticed and took over the task.

She surrendered the job of helping Thunder to the captain. "What happened? Why did the fighting stop?"

"I saw it all, and still I don't believe it. When the demons entered the field, the enemy troops broke and ran. With the forces

349

of the other kingdoms in retreat, Sechland was safe from one adversary, but still faced another in Doom and the rest. What happened next amazed me. From across the field, a gold glow enveloped a man and the sheep that were with him. The ground round the demons split apart and solid rock sprang up to capture Brute where he stood. It was incredible."

Where Captain Brusk pointed, she spotted the three approaching men. A shock went through her on seeing who it was. She broke into a run. "Pap! You're alive!"

He opened his arms and took her into a warm embrace, a large staff he held bracing against her back. "Hello, child."

Tears welled in her eyes, and she squeezed them shut while taking in his comfort. "I can't believe it's you. I saw you fall." She looked into his face and spotted a glint in his eyes. It wasn't tears, but something else. "Pap?"

He released his hug and held her at arm's length. "It's me, Darlee. Me and more."

She glanced at the other two men. One was dressed in black with purple piping on his sleeves and leggings. He wore a warm and pleasant smile. The other was a big brute of a man with an earring in one ear, and, like her, half of the other ear torn off. A large raven was perched on his shoulder. A wicked scar ran across his face but he smiled as well. "What do you mean?"

Pap smiled and also glanced at the two men. "No, not them. They're friends, but not what I'm talking about. I'm sharing this body with another spirit. A great man. It is he who has stopped the demons. Who has saved my life. He talks to me inside my head."

She shook her head. "I don't understand."

The young man in black took her hands. "It is the spirit of Bron, the mighty warlock who defeated these demons long ago. We thought him lost at the battle of Rok almost two years past. We were wrong. His body failed, but his spirit was still alive, locked in the raven you see next to him. The bird travelled far and wide in search of a new host, but not anyone would do. It had to be a man with the power of a warlock lord, one who could use the Key. No other could hold him."

"But...but Pap isn't a warlock. He's just my grandfather."

"The fact he never learned to use his skills does not mean he did not have the power. Such things tend to run in families. I have the skill to read the mana level of another. I see it in you. I know it is in your brother."

The mention of her brother made her turn to look for him. "Gar. We've got to find him. He fell somewhere near here." She spotted Captain Brusk and Thunder kneeling on the ground. Next to them, lying prone, with his back to her, was her brother. "Gar!"

Captain Brusk held up a hand. "It's too late. Your brother is gone."

"No!" How could it be? After all that happened, after all she fought for; she could not accept her brother's demise. She rushed over, pushed Brusk out of the way, and grabbed her brother. "Gar, it's me. Don't die!" Tears rolled down her face, but her brother's head rolled lifeless when she moved him.

She turned to Thunder. "Can't you do anything? You have the magic. Give him life."

The big demon bowed his head. "Empty. Use all. Fail Master."

She jumped up to grab the shirt of her grandfather. "How about you? If the warlock Bron is in there, can he save Gar?"

Pap stared up at the sky for a moment, his lips pursed. She could only guess the discussion going on in her grandfather's mind.

He shook his head. "No. He's my grandson. I have to try." He smiled at her and moved past to kneel on the grass next to Gar and put a hand on his head. "He's still warm. I could heal his wounds while there is yet some of life's heat, but I cannot give the energy of life. If his spirit was still close, it may return, but another spirit's life must be given in exchange."

He reached out and took hold of one of Thunder's massive hands. "I'm old. Take mine and pass the energy on. Bron will have to search for another vessel to hold him." To the big, scarred man, he handed the staff. "Grott, I must ask you to keep this for me a while longer."

Grott accepted the staff, his head hanging. "I just got ya back. Is there no other way?"

351

Pap shook his head. "He needs the spark from a lord warlock. None other would be enough."

Darlee understood what Pap was suggesting. She didn't know what to do. How could she allow the sacrifice of her grandfather to save her brother? "Pap, I want you both. There must be something else that can be done."

"No, child, there isn't." Pap stood and took the raven from Grott's shoulder. The bird accepted its new perch without complaint. He knelt again and signaled for the man in black to kneel close. "Tarlok, I'll need your assistance. You'll have to finish the healing when I'm gone. Timing is everything." He nodded toward Thunder. "Ready?"

Thunder nodded in return, placed a hand on Gar's chest and another on Pap's.

Pap sighed. "Now, then." He placed his hands on Gar, alongside those of Tarlok. A blue shimmer surrounded him. Some of the blue light spread into Gar, some of it into the raven on his shoulder.

At the same time a soft white light glowed between the hand of Thunder and her grandfather's chest. Almost immediately, another soft light appeared between Thunder's other hand and Gar.

Darlee knelt, transfixed by what was happening. Her gaze moved to each of the faces of those involved. Gar's wounds closed, the white light from Thunder ceased, and the blue light from Pap faded away. A scream from the raven surprised her, forcing her to watch the bird lift into the sky. When her gaze came back down to Pap, his eyes were closed and he lay collapsed backward on the ground.

A last light trace of blue from Tarlok disappeared. "It is done."

Gar's chest heaved, and he gasped loudly. His eyes bolted open and he sat up right away. "Pap, no!"

He was alive. She jumped into his arms, crying. "Gar. He did it. He saved you. Pap is gone, but he saved you."

Gar sobbed. "He shouldn't have. I wasn't worth saving."

CHAPTER 60

"You're right. You weren't worth saving. Now I have to figure out what to do with you."

Gar looked up to see Brusk standing over him, a set of shackles in his hands. He stood and offered his wrists. "You're correct, Captain. I shall submit to you and whatever punishment you deem necessary."

Behind him, a deep growl filled the air. He turned to place a hand on the shoulder of his demon guardian. "No, Thunder. We must obey the law. If the law says I have committed a crime, then I must be held accountable for it."

Brusk attached the shackles. "Ya realize, it's probably the death penalty for you. I'll be lucky if the town council doesn't call for you to be torn limb from limb. You killed one of their own in Merchant Trellus and these demons accounted for quite a number of my men at the same time."

A young man, dressed in black, stepped up to the captain. "Perhaps I could take him. Just now, as he lay unconscious, I had the opportunity to read the man's thoughts. There is no evil in Garlin Murdach, only misled youth. He is a lord warlock who knows how to use the Key. This is a skill important to my people. When the next acolyte comes to the Brotherhood who has such power, there will be no one to teach him. Give him to me, and I will make sure he troubles you no more."

Brusk shook his head. "Not likely. I appreciate all you and your fellow Piaxians have done today, but I'm not the law."

Before Brusk could lead him away, Darlee jumped up and interposed herself. "While you were gone, Lieutenant Devron instituted martial law and dismissed the town council. You could do the same thing and keep the decision to yourself. You know Gar did what he could to help these last couple of days. Because of Merchant Trellus, those city elders won't give him a chance. Show some leniency, I beg of you."

Brusk stroked his chin and chuckled. "Devron did that, did he? I guess my charming personality must have rubbed off on him a little. I suppose I could do it, at that. I never did care for Trellus, either, but I have to think about my men and their families. They'll be wanting justice, too. To grant Gar any kind of pardon would require an edict from someone like the king and I just don't rank that high."

"But I do." Behind Brusk, Lieutenant Devron dismounted his horse and came to stand beside the captain.

Brusk shook his head. "I hate to tell ya, but as a lieutenant, you don't even outrank me. How do you figure to command the city elders what to do?"

"As the only surviving member of the Sech family, *I* am king. I expect to be crowned at the first opportunity. Giving relief of penalty to anyone will be my purview, and if I so decree it, then that will be the law. I have already been forced to act in a royal capacity by signing a treaty with Piaxia. You did not think they committed an army to our assistance out of the good of their hearts?"

Brusk put a hand on Gar's shoulder. "But Murdach here? Why would you pardon him? His actions started this blasted war."

Gar watched, as Devron paced for a moment. He had no idea what was going on in the lieutenant's mind. *Why me? What have I done to deserve a pardon? He should let Brusk have his way and put me out of my misery.*

Devron moved to stand before the young man dressed in black. "Why I should, indeed. I've come to the conclusion my cousin, King Lowry, had every intention of going to war. If not for the demons, he would have simply found another reason. In times of trial, such as war, people make difficult choices and expose themselves to danger when other, safer options are available."

He paced back to his horse and withdrew a bound sheaf of papers. "Here is the treaty I have signed. In it are terms for many things, all of which involve a certain level of cooperation if we are to be friends. It is in such a spirit of cooperation I am prepared to consider such a request from Tarlok, the regent of Piaxia. I would, of course, hope he would extend the same courtesy to me, should the opportunity arise."

The regent from Piaxia smiled and reached out to take Devron's hand. "I think such an opportunity is waiting for me back at Zon. A dual banishment then? Are we agreed?"

Devron shook Tarlok's hand. "Agreed."

Gar had no idea what just happened. The only thing he understood was he was going to be banished to Piaxia. "What of Thunder? Can he come with me?"

Tarlok studied the huge demon still sitting on the ground. "He is under your control?"

Gar shook his head. "No. But I believe he will listen to me and do what is right. I have faith in him."

Brusk undid the shackles. "Then I guess I won't be needing these on you anymore. But understand this—if I ever find you in Sechland again, I'll have your head. Is that understood?"

He nodded. "Understood."

Brusk pointed to the other demons. "What about them?"

Tarlok tapped his own chest. "I'll take them. Their powers will have no effect on my warlocks. They have the ability to lock the demons out of their minds. Your own prisons would succumb to their magic."

The captain grabbed Silk by the wrist. "Not this one, though. She proved herself more than once to be on our side. If she will, I'd rather she stayed with me."

Silk laughed with the tinkling sound that always put Gar at ease. She hooked her arm into the captain's. "Why, Captain, I do believe you've finally taken a fancy to me. Are you sure you can handle it?" She gave him a long kiss.

Brusk turned bright red and coughed. "I-I suppose. I'll try."

Everyone laughed and Gar smiled. He was happy for her. He then realized something. "Wait a moment. What about Hiss?"

Brusk nodded. "I haven't seen the imp all day. He must have slipped away, the little bugger. I guess I've got some hunting to do."

"He won't hang around here. Without any other demons, he'll stay on the run and out of sight until he finds one. My guess is he'll head for Karsargi lands. Perhaps the regent Tarlok will let Thunder and I go track him down. I think it's my duty to capture him."

Tarlok shook his head. "Not at this time. You're going to have to stay my...guest for a while, until I'm sure you can be trusted."

Darlee hooked her arm into his. "I'm going with you."

He held her by the shoulders, crouching to bring his head level with hers. "No, you stay here with Captain Brusk. You have your own life to live. Don't let it be one taking care of me. Find someone to love. Get married. Have a family. That's what would make me truly happy."

He hugged her and she cried in his arms. When she finally stopped, he kissed her on the forehead and turned back to everyone. "I'm ready."

EPILOGUE

Darlee found it weird to have a pseudo-mother in the demon Silk, but the woman doted on her constantly, as if she was the demon's own daughter. One thing for sure, she never lacked for confidence when it came to doing anything. Silk made sure of it.

As a father figure, Captain Brusk was somewhat standoffish, but with Silk being so maternal, Darlee was content. She learned how the captain had lost his wife and children and guessed how hard it must be for him to have strange women in the house. Whenever he got too moody, Silk made sure it didn't last.

News from the war was good. Along with a few fresh recruits from Visk, the Piaxian army managed to recapture Sechwisk. It was only a matter of time until the border was restored and the enemy troops all driven out. Word was Storburg was already seeking a treaty and Fermia was trying to restore their neutral position. The most southern kingdoms of Braxburrow, Queensland, and Gatway were still on Morica's side, but with both Storburg and Fermia bowing out, they had no means to send men over land, only by sea.

She received a letter from Gar. He was confined within the castle until Regent Tarlok returned. A master warlock, by the name of Gaffrey, was teaching him some of the skills he didn't know, and he was excited about it. One of the things he was hoping to master was the ability to talk to another lord warlock wherever he might be, through the stone of the earth. Apparently, in their cities, the old lords of Piaxia all had stone thrones so they could talk to each other whenever they wanted. Maybe, someday, he could talk to her that way.

His handwriting was deplorable. He never had been good at school. It was full of errors and spelling mistakes. Still, she treasured every word and kept his letter close to her at all times.

A knock at the door broke Darlee from her reverie. In a race to beat Silk, the two of them arrived at it together. When Silk opened the door, a beautiful, buxom blonde woman Darlee figured was somewhere in her midthirties was at the door. She was wearing clothes that might better have suited a cross-country rider, but at a second glance, the cut of the clothes was more feminine than expected, with the woman filling them well.

"Is this the home of Captain Brusk?"

Silk nodded. "Yes, you must be the lady I was told was coming. Please, come in."

The woman stepped in and looked around. "Hmm, too much of a man's touch in the décor, but I can change that." She eyed Silk up and down. "Except, of course, a furnishing such as you."

Darlee noted Silk also was appraising the stranger and giggled. This new woman was very attractive, but compared to Silk's beauty, there was no comparison. Her stepmother had no challengers.

The woman finally turned to stare at her. "And you must be Darlee. You're the reason I'm here."

Darlee was surprised. She had no idea who this woman was. "Who are you and what do you want of me?"

The woman sat down on the floor and motioned Darlee to do the same. "My name is Daphora. King Devron sent me. I'm to be your private tutor."

Her curiosity was piqued. "A tutor from the king? What is it I'm going to be learning?"

Daphora held her hand out, and a ball of flame appeared in it. "Magic!"

She smiled. *I think I'm going to like this.*

OTHER NOVELS by MICHAEL DRAKICH

GRAVE IS THE DAY

In October of 1957, more than Sputnik fell to Earth...

Set against the back drop of the Space Race and the Cold War, both the United States and the Soviet Union have a new issue to deal with, aliens from outer space. Both the Braannoo and the Muurgu are at war with each other and Earth becomes the newest battleground in their struggle. Spanning time from the launch of Sputnik to the near future, the interplay of historical events from a new light make you ask the question, could this all be true? The capture of aliens near small town USA unites three players from different quarters, Commander Kraanox of the Braannoo, First Lieutenant Wayne Bucknell as his captor and seven year old Justin Spencer, the first to make alien contact.

Grave Is The Day is a superb read! This story is a must read for all the science fiction, extraterrestrial lovers on Earth. Grave Is The Day has earned my rating of 5 stars! --Ramsey's Reviews

I have read books that meld fantasy with historical events before, but never one that takes such minute details and blends them so thoroughly. This is a great read and an exceptional rewrite of history for all ages. – Bitten By Books

He created each character with amazing attention to detail and development. I thoroughly enjoyed this book and found myself identifying with more than one of the delightful characters. --Paranormal Romance Guild - Beth Price

THE BROTHERHOOD OF PIAXIA

Years have passed since the overthrow of the monarchy by the Brotherhood of Warlocks and they rule Piaxia in peaceful accord. But now forces are at work to disrupt this rule from outside the Brotherhood as well as within! In the border town of Rok, a young warlock acolyte, Tarlok and his older brother, Savan, captain of the guard, become embroiled in the machinations of dominance. While in the capital city, Tessia, the daughter of Piaxia's most influential merchant, begins a journey of survival. Follow the three as their paths intertwine, with members of the Brotherhood in pursuit and the powerful merchant's guild manipulating the populace for their own ends.

Great, well-rounded characters? Magic running rampant? A lost princess? Yes, this book has it all. – tHe crooked WorD

If you love fantasy that mixes magic, lost royalty, sacrifices, heroes, and strong characters, I would suggest The Brotherhood of Piaxia. – Captivated Reading

The Brotherhood of Piaxia is what it wants to be - a real entertaining fantasy story. It comes along with more characters than you normally get but a lot less then you meet in a famous series you can watch at HBO. It has definitely more magic than a famous fantasy trilogy you could see in cinemas. There is less blood and gore than in a book with a title how to serve a drink. It is also a book which does not drown in romance. For me is a book which you like to read when you want to have a well dosed mix of well-known books. Or in simple words The Brotherhood of Piaxia is like the espresso you enjoy after a good meal. – Edi's Book Lighthouse

LEST THE DEW RUST THEM

Terrorism in America has a new game…decapitations!

Homeland Security Director Robert Grimmson faces the task of catching five men in New York City. They call themselves the Sword Masters with a single minded plan of terror through decapitations.

Barely has the task begun when a new arrival at JFK is a man importing thousands of swords! Alexander Suten-Mdjai is a trainer in the deadly art of swordsmanship and Robert cannot help but believe there is a connection between him and the Sword Masters.

As he goes about the task, each step in his search is made more difficult through the interference of politicians, the media and his own government.

Robert's examination constantly draws him back to Alexander who regales him with a tale of swordsmanship from his lineage featuring events of mankind's bloody past and often oddly having a connection to the case before him.

With the clock ticking as New York collapses into a deep panic, he must catch the Sword Masters before it is too late!

This one of the best suspense thrillers I have read in a long time. – Voracious Reader

This book was really, really good. It was action packed from beginning to end. I could hardly wait to finish and see what would happen. – The Book Worm

This entire book was nothing but entertaining. I have never read a crime-type book that I liked and this book was so good that it's going on my favorite's shelf. – Angels In The Underworld

THE INFINITE WITHIN

Going into outer space calls to Astronaut Brooke Jones like the sirens of old, and when the chance to be part of the first manned mission to Mars arises, she is ecstatic. But little does she know the fate that awaits her on the surface of the red planet or the results of her encounter when she gets back to Earth.

This book is very entertaining. It will grab hold of you, and keep poking at you to finish it. I would recommend this story to science fiction readers that enjoy something a little different. This will not give you the highs of the shoot-em-up in outer space. It takes place place on earth, for the most part. It could be a real story and has enough elements be good fiction. I look forward to reading more by this author. – Charles Kravetz – Keeping Dreams

I loved the uniqueness of the story and the high-caliber action scenes. The adventure and the sense of awe kept me reading late into wee hours. – Laurie Jenkins – Laurie's Thoughts and Reviews

Wow. First off I'll start by saying the book was amazing. In the beginning I was a little iffy about the whole deal then the book got better, and better, and obviously better. I was surprised at the level of detail in the storytelling – Ezekiel Carsella – Books N Tech

I AM

Genius, wealthy and life regenerated, Adam Spenceworth is living the dream aboard his custom spaceship run by Mum, his first designed AI, protected by Gort, his first robot, and occupied by Eve, his sexbot. With each regeneration he returns to start over as a twenty-five-year-old man ready to enjoy the pleasures of his success. What could go wrong? Except, maybe, planetary wars, territorial space battles, alien invasions, and the disturbing fact that each regeneration is taking exponentially longer than the one before bringing him into one galactic crisis after another.

Michael Drakich's I Am is a brilliant space opera about one man's journey through eons of time in a futuristic world where worlds and galaxies collide in wat, join in peace, and may only survive through Artificial Intelligence that almost believes it is alive.
Diane @ Tome Tender Book Blog – Top 500 Amazon Reviewer

One of the top five independent author'd kooks of all time.
Lilyn @ sciFiandScary, Reviewing Both Independent and Traditionally Published Works

Everything I love about science fiction was in this book. The aliens, the robots, the advanced technology, and the humor make this book an enjoyable and engaging read from start to finish.
Tori@ Tori Lex, Judging Books Beyond The Cover

Overall, the story meets all my criteria for an excellent science fiction. It's epic scale, rich world, plausible futures, and focus on the people (both organic and not) make this one for the bookshelves, definitely worthy of reading over and over again. I'd highly recommend this to folks who love science fiction, hard, epic, space opera and otherwise.
Patricia @ Pure Textuality, Book Reviews, News & Everything In Between

ASSASSINS OF RIAZ

In Riaz, the profession of assassin is an honored one. Hired throughout the other eight realms, their use of powerful magic to complete assignments makes them a valuable commodity. When a regional trade negotiation is scheduled in their capital city of Lymos, the demand for the skills of the assassins is sure to change the dynamic of the meetings. Caught in the maelstrom of political intrigue is young Kero, the ward of the assassin lord. He's joined by Darlee, a girl from Sechland with her own magical powers, and Prince Brumaine of Morica, as each of them struggle to navigate the affair in their own way. Will old animosities prevail, or can new alliances alter the path toward all out war?

Michael Drakich writes for all ages and brings a tale to life that will entice any reader who looks for engaging storytelling, characters to admire or detest and a richly detailed plot that unfolds with mind-boggling energy! Easy to read, hard to put down, highly recommended reading that never lets up, page after page!
Diane @ Tome Tender Book Blog – Top 500 Amazon Reviewer

One of the things I liked about the story is that it feels bigger than it is. Feels like part of a greater story, even though it wraps up nicely in one volume. I got the impression of a greater world, an important aspect in any epic fantasy.
Trish @ Pure Textuality Book Reviews, News & Everything In Between

REQUIEM FOR A GENOCIDE

JAK037 is a warbot.

Built for the sole purpose of killing the enemies of Dalrea, he has survived longer than any other and is the last of his generation still in operation. Being the last JAK model, he is simply referred to as Jak, no unit number necessary. When word comes of a treaty with their nemesis, Carthia, Jak holds out hope his final days will be ones without war. It is with disappointment he learns the treaty is so a new front can be opened against a race of settlers from another world.

Humans.

In the coming conflict, can Jak and his comrades of aged warbots survive against an enemy with superior technology? In a mission to wipe out the settlers, will it succeed? Or will Jak's days finally be numbered. With the aid of a human child, a seven-year-old girl named Hannah, Jak hopes to end the war and save his people from what he believes is a looming disaster. It's a race where not only humans but Carthians, Dalreans, robotic laws, and his own failing body all conspire to stop him.

"Requiem for a Genocide", by Michael Drakich, is a completely compelling science fiction novel that fans of classic sci-fi and new sci-fi will love. I can't remember when I've enjoyed a robot-themed novel this much, and I highly recommend it for sci-fi fans everywhere. It has the kind of universal appeal that underpins a good sci-fi movie. - READER VIEWS GOLD MEDAL AWARD FOR SCIENCE FICTION

This heartwarming sci-fi action drama is like the love child of I, Robot and The Iron Giant. In a way, it comes across as a political parable with an appeal that comes from the touching relationship between a child and a thinking machine. It's a plain and simple story, but one that Michael Drakich has explored dramatically to deliver a strong plotline and compelling characters. Jak may be a machine, but he is oozing with humanity so it is not difficult to identify with him. It has a nice structure to it, with a fast-paced writing style that gives enough details without boring you. Requiem for a Genocide is fiction that feels realistic because it has something to say. It is a story that will win the hearts of both young readers and adults. - READERS FAVORITE

The first-"person" narrative gives us a chance to see into JAK's mind, and what I loved most about the book was his intelligent and down-to-earth philosophical musing about things like war, ethics, free will, and life in general. 5 STARS - Angie Boyter, Amazon Vine Voice ranked in the top 1000 of Amazon's ranked reviewers.